OUT OF THE BLACK

BY EVAN CURRIE

Odyssey One series
Into the Black
Heart of Matter
Homeworld
Out of the Black

Warrior's Wings series
On Silver Wings
Valkyrie Rising
Valkyrie Burning
The Valhalla Call
De Opresso Liber (forthcoming)

Other works
SEAL Team 13
Steam Legion
Thermals

OUT OF THE BLACK

odyssey one

(Book 4)

EVAN CURRIE

47NORTH

Published by 47North, Seattle

www.apub.com

Amazon, the Amazon logo, and 47North are trademarks of Amazon.com, Inc., or its affiliates.

ISBN-13: 9781477817872
ISBN-10: 1477817875

Cover design by Cyanotype Book Architects

Library of Congress Control Number: 2014934825

Printed in the United States of America

This, the fourth book in the Odyssey series, is dedicated to the readers who made the continuation of this story possible. Without your enthusiasm and support, this series would never had reached the heights it's arrived at nor would we clearly only be beginning our climb. Thank you for joining me on this voyage, and I sincerely hope you remain with me as we move further out into the black.

▼

PROLOGUE

Manhattan Borough, New York—D-Fall Plus Five Minutes

▲

▶ *IT IS TIME.*

The voice was a whisper on the wind, lost in the sound of buildings crumbling, dust and dirt falling back to the Earth, and the wailing of people and alarms. The city was a living thing, but it had been wounded deeply and it was bellowing its pain and rage. Within that a whisper had no chance of being heard.

The day had begun largely as a normal day, despite the announcement of a heightened level of military awareness worldwide. The normality had been shattered when thin burning trails had descended from above, tracking across the sky in an eerie silence that caused millions to not even notice until it was far too late. Those that did see often froze, eyes locked on the blazing trails as they pointed and shouted.

One had struck the edge of the city, a building exploding into dust and debris, and another slammed into the tallest skyscraper of the skyline. Everyone heard it when that monument to freedom from terror came raining down on the streets below. Amid the screaming that began then, some were still calm as they watched the skies, and they saw more and more fiery streaks rain down, bursting through the clouds, heading for their city.

Then they saw something else explode out of the clouds, and for many the nature of their world changed in a second.

It was a silhouette recognized across the world, fires blazing from gaping holes in the steel blue hull as the NACS *Odyssey* somehow leveled out over the Eastern seaboard and opened fire at fifteen thousand feet.

Every shot was like the hammer of the gods across the sky, blowing out the glass in dozens of skyscrapers and smaller buildings as the big ship rumbled past. Each thunderclap of destruction, however, was punctuated by a second explosion in the sky as one of the incoming trails of destructive flame exploded in turn.

The *Odyssey* had not been built to fly in atmosphere, however, and her enemies had held the high ground. Flaming trails of destruction rained down from above the iconic ship and slammed into her hull, making the flagship of the Confederacy shudder with each blow. The *Odyssey* listed to port, slowly heeling over, and with another flurry of hits from above, it dipped down and plunged into Long Island Sound.

That had been the beginning.

Strike Fighters filled the skies shortly after, throwing everything they had at the fire from the sky. It was an impressive show, but they were outnumbered and some of the falling objects inevitably struck the ground and delivered hammer blows of destruction to the living city.

For many that was when the nightmare changed from shocking to surreal, because true horrors rose from the craters, and New York became a battleground unlike any ever seen on Earth.

Amid the fighting, as the National Guard rumbled into the city to back up the local police, few noticed that the *Odyssey* had broken up on impact with the water and was now spread across much of the area. Some pieces had bounced, smashing into the waterfront properties and causing immense destruction themselves, while others had slowed and sunk deep below the surface of the sound.

The two immense drums of the *Odyssey*'s habitation sections had broken free and skipped along the water as they spun. One went south, crashing through Queens as it skipped off Eastchester Bay, and the other spiraled west. It splashed down just north of Roosevelt Island on its last bounce before it blew through a block of office buildings and came to rest in Central Park itself.

Wake up.

Again the whisper was lost in the midst of the chaos, dust and debris rolling over the city like the wall of a massive desert haboob engulfing everything in its path. The city was reeling from one shock after another, but it was a city that had some experience with emergencies, and it was waking slowly but surely to the events.

On the west side of Central Park, the *Odyssey*'s forward and command habitat came to rest, rocking gently on an uneven surface of fallen trees and crushed automobiles. The wails of sirens and aftershocks of impacts punctuated the local silence that descended as those who survived witnessing the crash stared in shock at the punctured, scarred, and crushed cylinder that had once controlled the greatest vessel ever built by human hands.

Inside the module, nothing moved.

▶▶▶

▶ *Now! Wake up, now!*

Eric Stanton Weston gasped, sucking in air as he awoke from a nightmare of being trapped in his ship after it had explosively decompressed. He flailed around momentarily, but was unable to move an inch, and he quickly realized why.

He was strapped firmly into the command console, which was now apparently attached to the ceiling. He hung there for a long moment, upside down and deeply confused, as he tried to take in what had happened and what was, in fact, happening.

Where? Eric couldn't think straight. He felt like he'd just been beaten into the ground by a particularly heavy battle tank, or maybe had just plowed his fighter into some poor bastard's field.

He blinked, looking around as memories returned to him, and realized just how close that last thought really was.

"Oh my lord, I hurt," he mumbled, licking his lips and spitting out a piece of his helmet face shield. *Shatterproof my ass.*

Slowly he reached up and began picking pieces of the glass shield from his face. Then he detached the helmet and let it drop to the ceiling below him.

Realization was sinking in slowly, fractured memories of what led him to his current predicament filtering with agonizing ponderousness. He had a headache that felt like someone was pounding on his skull with a pickax from the inside, and he couldn't quite manage to blink the blurred vision away.

Eric was no doctor, to say the least, but he knew the signs of a concussion. He likely needed medical help in the worst way, but considering the fact that he hadn't really expected to wake up at all, he couldn't say that he was feeling all that bad.

This is going to suck. Yup, no doubt about it.

He couldn't stay where he was, that was clear, and he had no idea where he'd managed to land . . . crash . . . so he couldn't count on help.

Besides, the world likely has enough on its plate just now. I'll have to take care of myself.

Eric looked up, or down he supposed, and barely could make out the ceiling of the bridge a few feet below his head. *Yeah, definitely going to suck.*

He took a breath, closed his eyes, and then slapped the quick release on his straps.

Eric fell ten feet, twisting as best he could, and hit the ceiling shoulder first in a clumsy roll that sent a sickening stab of pain through his bones and skull. He skidded to a stop, curled around the extruded housing of the now dead lights, and just lay there until the pain began to subside.

I've felt better after being shot, he thought grimly to himself as he actually sobbed quietly, praying for the headache to subside.

Eric didn't know how long he'd been laying there, but after a time the pain again dropped to manageable levels and he got to his knees and pulled himself over to the door. It was sealed shut, of course, and with no power he had to do things the hard way.

What else is new?

Eric got painfully to his feet, having to reach up to open the panel that was normally only four feet off the ground, and he got hold of the manual level for the door. A hard yank opened it enough for him to wedge his hands in and pry it open, not a lot, but enough to work with. Eric slipped out of the bridge and into the corridor beyond, where he had to pause to get his bearings.

Wait, do I go left or right to get to the closest armory locker?

He blinked, trying to clear the double vision from his eyes while he was wrapping his mind around that. Normally it wouldn't be a problem: Step out the door, walk right around the curve of the habitat, and he'd get to a security room.

At the moment, however, standing on the ceiling of the corridor with double vision and a splitting headache, Eric couldn't remember what direction right *was* without making a signing gesture with his right hand to confirm it.

He finally worked out that he had to go left, and that was when he realized that he had a bigger problem.

Oh shit. The drum isn't rotating. I'm in Earth gravity and that means this whole damn thing is more of an amusement park ride than habitat section.

He sighed, looking over the situation, and slowly shook his head. *This is going to suck.*

He got down onto his hands and knees and turned around, slowly lowering himself down the curving corridor until he began to slide. Eric quickly latched on to the frame of a door to stop himself, feet kicking around until he found another purchase, and then he began to ease himself down.

He had made it about a quarter of the way down when he lost his grip, slid off the ledge he was balancing on, and pitched into the black of the unlit corridor, swearing at the top of his lungs the whole way down.

▶▶▶

▶ Lyssa Myriano was having the mother of all bad days.

It had started with a fight that led to a breakup with her boyfriend, and now the whole damned solar system had apparently decided it was time to pay a visit to the Big Apple.

Just fucking peachy.

"Get down!" the NYPD patrol officer snarled as a dozen people came screaming in her direction.

They scattered as she pumped the old Remington shotgun she'd pulled from the truck of her cruiser. The twelve-gauge slugs were old school, but they still put down damn near anything short of straight-up MilSpec armor, and so she'd never felt the need to change over to the high-powered stuff.

Now she was regretting that decision.

The shotgun roared six times as she pumped and fired as fast as she could, emptying the weapon into the oncoming horror that the crowds were running from. The creatures looked like something out of a movie, only maybe a little less realistic, lumbering on insect-like bodies that appeared to weigh as much as a large truck.

Or small tank.

Lyssa swore some more as she tossed her twelve-gauge and drew her service pistol. That was a little more high tech, a ten-millimeter armor piercer designed to turn civilian-level body armor to Swiss cheese. She fired as she fell back, really just trying to delay one of the invaders so people could clear the area.

All she was really doing was attracting its attention to her.

Great. Just what I needed to top off my friggin' day.

She glanced around and changed direction as she started to run, leading the thing into the park and away from the crowds. The ten-millimeter autoloader reloaded easily, her hands moving on muscle memory as she ran for her life. The park was large enough that the things on her tail would have room to move without knocking over buildings or, hopefully, people, but it also meant that she was about to be a nice wide-open target.

That was about the time that a sizzling sound made her throw herself to the left as a beam scorched the grass ahead of her. Lyssa rolled to her feet, stared for a split second, and started running again.

Great! Ray guns too!

She tapped the ear set she was wearing. "Central, this is Kilo One Nine calling in a Code . . . Central, what the fuck is the code for alien invasion anyway?"

▶ ▶ ▶

▼

NATIONAL GUARD COMMAND POST, *INTREPID* SEA, AIR, & SPACE MUSEUM

▲

▶ "SIR! WE'VE GOT reports across the entire city, those things are everywhere!"

Brigadier Potts growled. "Tell me something I don't know."

The over-excited lieutenant had the decency to look abashed at his outburst, which did unfortunately little for Potts' mood. He had alien invaders all over the city and the fact that he'd actually had twenty-four hours' notice pissed him off even more.

They'd had time to set up an emergency command post, using the old *Intrepid* aircraft carrier that had been parked on the coast of Manhattan Island for over a century. It seemed like a decent enough place to set up, given that they needed a central location that could be defended. It was an old hulk, nearly two centuries old, but it had been kept up and they had room to spare.

As far as military armor went, the *Intrepid* was an antique, but what an antique.

"Sir!"

"What is it, Sergeant?" Potts glanced to where his Command Master Sergeant had appeared.

"Final reports from spotters, sir."

"And?"

"One hundred eighty-three targets, in city."

The general grimaced, but nodded. "Thank you, Sergeant."

"Yes sir. Sir?"

"What is it?"

"We've got field reports from the crash sites splashed by the *Odyssey*," Command Master Sergeant Rigand told him. "Looks like they saved us at least a hundred other bogeys before they went down."

"And probably tore up more of the damned city than the friggin' aliens have in the process," Potts snarled, and then forcibly relaxed. "Any signs of survivors from the ship, Sergeant?"

"No sir, but I put in a note on the boards and got a reply from CONCOM. Word is that they abandoned ship before the *Odyssey* hit the sky, sir."

"Abandoned ship? Someone was running those guns."

"Yes sir. Captain Weston went down with her."

Potts sighed, shaking his head. "Damn shame. He was a good man in the war. I fought under more than one sky he made friendly."

"Yes sir."

"Alright, we don't have time to worry about what we've lost. From what intel says about these things, if we slip off the ball, we'll lose everything. If we can't clear them out of the city, I'm authorized to call in a tactical hit. Let's not make that my only option, right, Sergeant?"

The Command Master Sergeant paled slightly, but nodded fervently. He'd seen a lot of shit in his time in uniform, but he'd never seen an American officer . . . or a Confederate one . . . call in a nuclear strike on any city, let alone one on the home continent, and he wasn't about to see it happen now.

"We'll wipe those fuckers out, sir. Guaranteed."

"See that you do, Sergeant. To the last," Potts said simply. "To the very last."

▼

NACS *ODYSSEY,* COMMAND HABITAT

▲

► ERIC OPENED HIS eyes in the dark and licked his lips as he lay against the floor of the inner section of the habitat.

Well, at least I'm not walking on the ceiling anymore.

The last thing he wanted to do was to move even a quarter of an inch. But as pleasant as lying there in the dark sounded at the moment, Eric sucked it up and rolled over to his knees. Getting to his feet this time was easier, but still sucked. He paused and leaned against the wall, willing the habitat to stop rotating around him while trying to ignore the sheer irony of that thought.

Should be a security station just over here somewhere . . .

He felt himself along the wall, making his way back up the curve of the habitat. The security locker wasn't hard to find. It was the double reinforced door with a lockout that wasn't working because the power was out. Eric popped the door access panel and confirmed quickly that it was indeed dead as the proverbial doornail.

He pulled his suit power and wired it into the door long enough to get the computer to reboot so he could put in the code. It only took him three times to hit the right numbers, which Eric figured wasn't bad given that he was seeing triple at the moment.

Have to remember to hit the middle one.

The door hissed open and he lurched in, trying to walk at an angle without stumbling like he was drunk.

It was all worthwhile, however, when his hands touched something familiar.

Hello, beautiful.

▼

CENTRAL PARK

▲

▶ *I SHOULD HAVE stayed on the street! At least there was decent cover there.*

Her service piece was long since empty and Lyssa didn't even have a single dropped target to her name, but she sure as shit had a few pissed off ones. She chalked those up in the win column, since if they were chasing her they weren't chasing anyone else, but it was a weak claim of victory.

She was winded, tired, and her strength was flagging, but she kept pumping her legs and ran toward Central Park West. Luckily, she supposed, she had one hell of a path to follow. The big ass cylinder that fell out of the sky had wiped out a few acres of trees, giving her room to run with some cover when she needed it.

She broke out of said cover, however, and into the street, somewhat to her surprise. The area was strewn with rubble, a few shattered cars, and almost completely gridlocked, but there was something very good to see as well. Lyssa bolted with one last burst of speed and ducked behind the NYPD SWAT vehicle, collapsing to her knees under cover as a familiar figure grinned down at her.

"You're late, Myriano."

"Oh, shut the fuck up, Paul. You try getting those bastards to chase you all the way across the damned park!"

Lyssa got her breathing under control as she accepted a police issue assault rifle and checked the mag.

"They're not fast," John told her from where he was standing over her.

"With firepower like that, they can afford to take their damned time," she griped. "Almost fried me three times across the park, and I'm not even sure they were aiming at me. Where the fuck is the National Guard?"

"Whole city is in gridlock," John told her with a shrug. "They have to check every car before they run their tanks over them."

"Run their . . . are you *shitting* me?" Lyssa asked, wide-eyed.

"Would take a *lot* longer to move all the cars, trust me."

Lyssa scowled, but couldn't say much against that. With the streets gridlocked as far as she could see, the big lumbering insect things certainly had the mobility advantage. Nothing quite like being able to walk *over* cars, or stomp them into the ground, she supposed. The Guard would have a harder time with their tanks, especially since she was well aware that they still used some antiquated chassis to supplement their forces.

Of course, I'm here with a friggin' M-4C in my hand, so who am I to talk about someone else using outdated gear?

Less than a handful of NYPD officers, all SWAT certified, were issued MilSpec weapons. Modern military battlefield gear was *far* too destructive to deploy in a city under normal circumstances and, honestly, MilSpec urban warfare gear hadn't changed a ton over a hundred years. It got more sophisticated in terms of optics, communications, and computational capacities, but a bullet was a bullet, and most police forces still used calibers comparable to what their great grand-parents packed.

It was just cost effective.

"Here it comes! Hold your fire until we've got them in the kill box!" John called, resting his rifle on the armored surface of the SWAT APC.

Lyssa scrambled to her feet, taking up position beside him as she too looked through the optics of her M-4C rifle. The enemy wasn't exactly trying to sneak up on them—the insects were actually shoving trees out of their way as they approached—so drawing a good sight picture was far from difficult. She just hoped that they were packing enough fire-power to do the job.

"Steady! Aim!" John called as the first of the alien beasties stepped out onto Central Park West. "FIRE!"

The air was rent with the staccato bursts of automatic fire, fifteen cops opening up with everything they had.

▼

NATIONAL GUARD COMMAND POST, *INTREPID* SEA, AIR, & SPACE MUSEUM

▲

▶ "WE'VE GOT REPORTS of fighting all through the city, sir. Most of it involving civilians or police at this point."

"Why are my squads not in position yet, Lieutenant?" Potts growled.

"The city is gridlocked, sir. Opening a path through that mess is taking time."

The general growled, but it was more of a frustrated sound than anything else. He knew how hard it was to move military vehicles through a city at the best of times, and what was going on in New York was far from those. The aliens had slammed into the city in their initial penetration, taking some buildings down and generally causing no end of panic, and now he had millions of empty, or hopefully empty, cars out there blocking every street and alley in the whole damned city.

His men were cutting through it. They had orders to do so without regard for the property, but it was taking time. Even with cowcatchers mounted on the tank chassis, there was a definite limit to how fast you could clear a road.

"More pressing, sir," Lieutenant Sky told him, "we're already detecting troubling signs on our seismic systems."

"You know the orders on those. Flood the subway system with men, flush them out," Potts ordered. "Do it delicately if you can, but do it."

"Yes sir. I have men moving through the tunnels faster than above ground. Anything down there is a top priority."

Potts grunted, but at least that was some encouraging news. He wished he could move more of his units through the tunnels but, aside from the fact that they were still evacuating people through them, there was just no way his armored units would make it cleanly through the stations they'd need to emerge from.

The enemy were diggers, however, according to intel from the *Odyssey,* and now he was seeing that playing out on his tactical map. They had a bit of bad luck there this time, however, since there wasn't a square inch of the entire *planet* that wasn't covered by seismic scanners, and Potts knew for a fact that the DOD had access to every single one of them.

Hell, even China tied their seismic data into the worldwide network. Predicting quakes that could shake down your city was a bit more important than political bullshit, and for the first time he was pleased as all fuck that the eggheads had butted their heads into his security bailiwick. Sharing data with the enemy made it difficult to maintain OPSEC, true, but now the only enemy on his scopes was decidedly unlike the Block and their allies.

Potts heard another air defense barrage open fire, and he looked up reflexively. The ground to air missiles had been designed to eliminate ballistic missiles launched from China and were launched from a Leviathan Class submersible sitting somewhere off the coast. He tracked the missiles with his eyes, looking ahead of their course, and spotted the target.

Eight incoming tracks, that he could see, heading for the city. Either New York or Jersey, he supposed.

The tracks of the defensive missiles intersected with their targets as he watched, flashes of light erupting in the sky. When it was over, only three enemy tracks continued on their course.

Definitely heading for New York.

"Tell the SAM division that I buy the drinks if they splash all three of those fuckers before they get in under our defense."

"Yes sir!"

This job is getting uglier and uglier. If the bastards wanted a fight, I sure wish they would have picked a different battlefield.

▶▶▶

▼

CENTRAL PARK WEST

▲

▶ "THEY'RE JUST WALKING through everything we've got!"

Lyssa grimaced, but couldn't say anything to contradict her superior. Their guns were pretty much just annoying the enemy beasts, or whatever they were, and that was being optimistic about the whole deal.

"Don't we have anything heavier?" she demanded.

"I think we have a light fifty in the truck."

Lyssa snorted, tossing her M-4C aside. "Why the hell didn't you break it out in the first place?"

"It's a damn sniper rifle, Lyssa! Those things are right on top of us!"

She wrenched open the back of the SWAT truck, scrambling inside as she looked around. Like many of her peers, Lyssa Myriano was a veteran of the Block War. She'd spent a sizeable chunk of her life in the Marines and handling big guns was second nature.

The fifty was an older FN model Hecate IV, a semiautomatic anti-matériel rifle. No one had been able to explain what the NYPD was supposed to use it for. She had never seen the use of the damn thing before. It fired bullets that went *through* buildings, fer Christ's sake, but just then Lyssa was happy as hell just to pull the big gun off the rack.

"Grab me a box of ammo, John," she growled, lugging the big gun outside. "And I need a spotter!"

"A what?" John asked, bewildered as he grabbed a box of fifty-caliber ammo.

"Got you covered."

They both turned, surprised by a SWAT officer grabbing a scope from the van and following them. Lyssa just nodded to him as she unfolded the bipod and dropped the rifle on the hood of the truck, ignoring the creepy sizzling sound the enemy weapons made as they tore through the city.

"Can you handle that thing?" the SWAT man asked her, nodding to the big rifle.

"In my sleep. Can you handle that thing?" she countered, nodding to the short spotter's scope with a smirk on her lips.

"Watch me," he responded dryly, dropping the scope on its tripod and resting it on the roof of the truck before resting his eye against the scope. "Target, twelve o'clock. Range, one hundred fifty meters."

"Got it. See anything that looks vital?"

"On that? Your guess is as good as mine."

Lyssa sighed. "Understood. Taking the shot. Red nodule, joint of the forward leg at the . . . shoulder? Whatever."

"Roger that."

She let out her breath, dropping the crosshairs onto the center mass, looking for a spot that wouldn't slam off on one of the distended legs. She got her sight picture and squeezed the trigger down, trying not to flinch in anticipation of the recoil. The rifle roared, slamming into her shoulder and hammering her back about six inches, scratching the holy hell out of the black paint of the truck.

"Hit," the SWAT man called. "High and to the right. Adjust your windage and zero the rifle down two notches."

"Any reaction?" Lyssa asked as she twisted a knob on the scope, eyes flicking to a flag in the distance.

"It looks pissed."

She looked over the scope, and found that it did, indeed, look pissed. The alien was twisting and turning in place, tearing up the ground like a madman. She slowly grinned. "That's not pissed, soldier. That's pain."

"Roger that. Hit him again?"

"Damn right." She put her eyes to the scope, adjusting her aim. "Taking the shot."

"Roger."

The rifle roared and kicked again, slamming back into her shoulder.

"Hit."

She re-acquired her sight picture as quickly as she could, dropping the crosshairs on the target again. "Taking the shot."

"Roger."

The rifle roared a third time, and she winced this time as she felt a bruise forming on her shoulder. The rifle wasn't gentle on a big man, and her hundred and thirty pounds was feeling every pound of the weapon's recoil.

"Hit! Dropped!"

She looked over the scope and saw that the report was right. The alien had gone down after the third round. "Is that a kill?"

"I think so," the SWAT officer confirmed. "It's not moving. I think you got it."

"Good. Next," she growled, shifting her weapon over. "Lead walker, heading this way."

"Confirmed," he told her, looking through the scope. "Range . . . one hundred meters."

"Roger." She didn't bother changing her scope settings.

At a hundred meters, a target that big was basically point blank range for the Hecate. She dropped the crosshairs on the target, judging the shot by eye for a moment when she spotted a heat shimmer appear on the target's mandible.

"Hit the dirt!" she called, dropping behind the truck as a familiar crackle of burning energy filled the air.

Men and women dove for the ground, hugging behind cover at her order, but not all of them were fast enough. A beam swept the street, burning two cops to a cinder before connecting with the SWAT APC a few feet away from where she'd ducked behind the truck. The armor of the APC stood up to the beam for a whole three seconds before an eruption tore through the vehicle and blew it over onto its side.

Lyssa grimaced and turned away.

There had been men and women sheltering behind the APC, now crushed underneath it.

"Holy shit," John whispered.

"We need heavy fire support," Lyssa swallowed. "Contact the Guard. Tell them we can't hold this ground."

John stared at her, clearly shocked into incomprehension, but the SWAT man nodded and tapped his earpiece.

Lyssa risked a glance over the hood of the truck, eyes on the things now beginning to move out of the park and into the street. She reached down and pulled the Hecate back up into place. "John . . . you may want to leave."

"What?"

"John," she told her superior, licking her lips, "when I open up on this bastard, the others are going to triangulate and rain all hell down on this position. You might not want to be here when that happens."

"What about you?" he demanded.

"Someone has to hold the ground until the Guard gets here," she said tersely. "Now get the hell out of here and try and help with the evacuation!"

She shoved him away, then turned back to the rifle and pulled the partial mag. She slapped a full one in its place, then dropped a round in the pipe manually. She was going to want every round she could drop on target if she was right about this. The SWAT man settled in beside her and she shook her head. "No point in a spotter this time, buddy. You may as well get the hell out of here."

He glanced at her. "You going to rock that thing?"

She didn't look back at him as she settled her eyes down over the scope. Instead, she just hummed "I love rock and roll" as she got her sight picture settled.

"Time for you to leave, bud," she said, her nerves fading away.

"Alex."

"What's that?"

"The name is Alex," he told her, picking up his gear. "I would take that from you and make the stand myself, but honestly I figure I'll get my chance today."

"Call me Lyssa, Alex. Semper fi," she said simply. "You've got about twenty seconds. Start running."

"Marines. Figures," Alex chuckled, picking up a go bag from the truck. "Alright, I'm out. You empty that mag and make for the buildings. I'll cover you."

"Roger that," she said. "Get out of here."

He went.

She gave him the full twenty count, even though they'd wasted a few seconds talking, then settled in on the closest of the alien beasties and winked at it through the scope.

"My, aren't you a strapping big bastard?" she whispered, finger curling around the trigger. "Meet Hecate, Goddess of the Crossroads."

The big rifle roared and she rode the kick back without lifting her eyes this time, firing the next round as soon as the scope settled roughly on target. The Hecate IV incorporated the latest methods of recoil compensation available, but it still kicked like the south end of a northbound mule. Lyssa ignored it though, putting a third round into her target a little under two seconds after the first, and then moving on to another invader. She figured that she'd be lucky to be sore in the morning.

She put three more in the next target and moved on, not even looking to see if her first two had gone down. She didn't have time to be making confirmations, and number three got his fair share of her attention in the next couple seconds.

Good thing they're so damned big. Hardly have to aim.

Of course, as she thought that, she realized that it was also because they were a *lot* closer than she'd thought. She had two rounds left in the gun, having fired nine of her ten plus one, and she was trying to decide who got the honors when a now familiar crackle of sizzling energy lifted the hair on the back of her spine.

Lyssa threw herself aside, abandoning the Hecate as a beam swept the SWAT truck and literally cut what was left of the unarmored vehicle in half. She hit the ground rolling and made it back to her feet as scraps of the black vehicle began to rain down around her.

Run girl, run!

She didn't know if they'd finally just spotted her, or if maybe they were using motion tracking systems, but as she started pumping her legs the air filled with that ugly sizzling sound. All around her she could hear loud cracks, almost like gunshots. Lyssa didn't turn around to see what it was. She stayed on target as she bolted for the closest alley, where she could see gunfire erupting from multiple sources.

Running toward gunfire was not a natural response, even for a cop or a Marine, but she just tucked in as low as she could go and kept running. A beam scorched the asphalt in front of her, sweeping toward her from the side, and she had to throw herself clear. Lyssa hit the ground hard, but alive, and rolled behind a chunk of cement that had either been thrown up by the enemy weapons or by the big chunk of spaceship resting only a few dozen meters away. She didn't know which, but she curled behind it for cover and started praying as she heard that sizzling sound again.

The cement was popping and cracking under the heat of the blast, and all she could think of really, was whether it was radioactive or not, oddly enough. She had just about made up her mind to make a break for it, forlorn hope that it was, when an explosion tore through the air above her and she looked up in both shock and awe.

She wasn't the only one. She heard the weapon blast falter. The eerie thudding of the alien beasties' heavy shod feet stopped as they too looked up.

About halfway up the curve of the *Odyssey*'s habitat cylinder, almost a hundred feet off the roadway, a hole had been blown clear out of the hull. As the smoke slowly blew clear, Lyssa spotted a figure stepping out into the open. She watched as he paused, seemed to look down at her and then out at the park beyond, and vanished for a moment.

Lyssa didn't know what to think, but before she could do much of that anyway the figure reappeared, this time with a large object resting on his shoulder.

"Oh shit," she muttered just before the figure triggered the MLARS—Multiple Launch Advanced Rocket System—sending twenty MilSpec Hi-Ex rockets into the park.

▶▶▶

▶Eric flipped the MLARS forward as it launched, not bothering to see what he'd hit. The weapon was fire and forget. Either he'd nailed his targets or he hadn't. There wasn't much more he could do. He dropped the disposable launcher, letting it tumble clear of the impromptu door he'd blown in his ship's hull with a breaching charge, and picked up the Priminae GWIZ as he keyed into the local military channels.

"Strykers, Strykers, have fire mission request. Central Park West. Will laze targets," he called. "I say again, fire mission. Central Park West. Will laze."

"Who is this? There are no assets reporting from CPW. Identify yourself."

"Captain Eric Stanton Weston. Commanding, North American Confederacy Starship *Odyssey*," he said, before taking a deep breath. "Make that formerly commanding."

There was a long pause on the network before the voice came back. "Confirm Ident. Handshake sent."

Eric responded to the security check with the countersign as he finished preparing his kit, knowing that it would only take a few seconds.

"Identity confirmed . . . Captain Weston, you have a fire mission?"

"Roger that. Request air support at my location. Will laze targets."

"Wilco. Air support inbound."

"Hoo-rah," Eric said, keying several pocket drones online and tossing them out of the ship. The tiny flyers buzzed off, flitting through the air above Central Park West as they each painted the targets he'd assigned them. "Targets lazed. Light them up."

"Find cover, Captain. Hell is coming."

"No, son," Eric said in the clear, his voice booming over his armored suit's speakers as well as the radio, "hell is already here."

CHAPTER ONE

Two Hundred Meters below 1600 Pennsylvania Avenue, Washington, D.C.

▶ "WE HAVE CONFIRMED landings in major cities across the planet, Mr. President."

"Washington?" the man at the head of the table asked tightly.

"No sir. Air defense here is some of the tightest in the world. We've been able to take them out before they got within thirty thousand feet. So far."

President Mitchell Conner nodded tiredly, waving for the general to continue.

"New York, however, has over a hundred confirmed landings. Los Angeles is nearly five hundred. Beijing we think has almost a thousand. Near as we can determine the aliens are specifically targeting population centers. The bigger it is, the more they land."

Conner scowled. "How does New York only rank a hundred then?"

"It doesn't," the general said. "New York ranked over three hundred by our tally, maybe more."

"Air defenses get lucky?"

"No sir, Mr. President. The *Odyssey* went down over the city," the General said, before adding, "and she went down shooting."

Conner sighed, running his hands through his hair. They came back wet and stinking of sweat.

"Warrior to the end," he said finally. "Alright. What are our assets on the ground?"

"In country, sir? Not good. Most of our units are overseas. We have two carrier task forces on recall now, but we can't risk lightening our presence *anywhere* they might land. Close counts with these things."

That was one thing that Conner wasn't going to cross any of his people on. He'd read the reports as clear as anyone. He knew what happened if they missed any of these things. One part of the report stuck in his mind though.

"You say they're targeting based on population?"

"Yes sir."

"China? India?"

China and India were the powerhouses of the Block, literally the backbone that held the whole political beast together. While they both had extensive air defenses, they'd never been as effective as Confederate systems. Those two nations also accounted for over half the population of the entire planet between them. Well over half.

"Approximately 80 percent of confirmed planetary landings are in those two nations, sir."

"Shit." The President cursed, automatically wincing as he realized that his uncharacteristic choice of words had, of course, been recorded for posterity.

"That about covers it, sir."

"I want the Block ambassador in here in fifteen minutes."

"Sir, this is a secure facility . . . " A man in a black suit stepped forward, almost out of nowhere, and made his presence known.

"Fifteen minutes."

The general looked into the eyes of his Commander in Chief for a long moment, then over at the Secret Service Agent in Charge who had objected. There were few people in the Administration who could stare down the President. Fewer still make their point stick. The AIC for the Service was one of those few.

Not this time, however. The man nodded after about thirty seconds. "Yes Mr. President."

▶▶▶

▶ The secure bunker under the White House was one of the most heavily defended places on the planet. Just getting to the scanners that were the first line of defense required an invite. Without the invite, you risked getting dead just thinking in that direction.

For obvious reasons the Block ambassador had never gotten an invite and, honestly, never expected one. The few times he'd seen the scanners he had made certain to carefully think in another direction entirely. Block intel didn't know what was past those scanners, at least not that he could access at his level, but they did know what the United States Secret Service procedures were for anyone attempting to violate the area.

So now Shi Wan Jung found himself not only being escorted up to the scanners, but actually bypassing them through an express system that he *didn't* know about. He was in the elevator and on his way down almost before he realized that he hadn't even been scanned.

Not that he was hiding anything, mind you, but it still seemed just a little off.

"Don't get any ideas."

"Pardon me?" he asked the man in black beside him, genuinely confused.

"I said, don't get any ideas," the man said again. "You're carrying a wallet, three credit cards, four hundred eighty dollars in cash, and your business cards. You have a GPS transponder in your belt, and another implanted in your lower intestine. The one in your belt has recording capability. That won't work down here. Neither of them will, actually."

Shi blinked, eyeing the man carefully before he spoke. "You missed my pen."

"This pen?" the man asked, holding up the object in question.

Shi's hand went to his jacket pocket, but it was only instinctive. He knew his own pen well enough to recognize that it wasn't a fake he was looking at.

The Secret Service man squeezed it lightly and a four-inch blade popped out the top. He turned it over, nodding appreciatively. "Cute neurotoxin. Lethal?"

"Paralysis," Shi corrected, somewhat annoyed.

It wasn't that they'd taken the pen. Mind you, he'd expected that. He just didn't like the fact that they'd lifted it without his knowing. That hurt his sense of professionalism.

"Nice. I'll return it when you leave."

"Keep it," Shi snorted. "I'll draw another from the armory."

"Thanks, but the GPS and microbug make it a security issue." The agent smirked.

Shi sighed. "Then destroy it. I will not take it back to my embassy after you've tampered with it."

"As you like. We're here," the agent said, nodding as the doors slid open.

Shi stepped out of the elevator and into the holy grail of Block intelligence, eyes flitting around as he tried to remember everything he was seeing. Opportunities like this just did not come along every day.

This one had taken the beginning of the end of the world, after all.

"This way, sir." The agent gestured. "The President is waiting to speak with you."

▶▶▶

▶President Conner eyed the other man as he took a seat across from him. They were sitting in a perfect replica of the Oval Office, right down to the tri-D "windows" that showed a real-time view of the outside of the actual office. It was mostly built as a place to broadcast from in case of emergency, giving people a sense of security that their President was calm and on the job in his office where he was supposed to be.

It was a not-so-subtle bit of propaganda and population control that was part of a system that Conner had disliked his entire life, even once he'd become part of it. Now, though, it served as a slightly more subtle bit of posturing as it reminded his guest of exactly who he was speaking with. Not really necessary, Conner supposed, but every little edge counted, and the subliminal ones were often the ones you weren't prepared for.

Jung made a show of settling in, looking relaxed and just a little disinterested. It was classic political posturing, and it was something that the President just didn't have time for.

"The Reagan Task Force is in the South China Sea," he said, getting an instant sharp look from his guest, "and the Clinton is in the Persian Gulf. They have enough firepower to flatten three countries apiece, and they are within operational strike range of every major Block population center on the planet."

"Now see here," Shi stiffened, all pretense of disinterest gone. "You cannot threaten us! And to do so at a time like this is *insanity . . .* "

Conner slid a tablet across the desk hard enough that it flew off and Shi had to catch it, interrupting his tirade.

"That tablet contains the secure frequencies, passcodes, and daily countersigns needed to request taskings from either group," he told the shocked man. "You have a problem in your countries. Deal with it. We'll help if you let us, but if you don't I *will* send them in with orders to turn every population center with an alien presence to *glass.*"

Conner stood up. "And don't get any ideas about taking out the task groups. For one, you're right, we can't afford this nonsense right now and, more importantly, both groups are escorted by six Apache Class nuclear submarines. You won't get them, but they will launch if they have to."

"*President* Conner," Shi rose to his feet, face etched in stone, "this is not how these affairs are handled."

"We are facing genocide, Mr. Shi," Conner said. "The systematic and total obliteration of all life on this world and in this system. The old ways of doing things are obsolete. Adapt or die. Now I have things to oversee and you, sir, have a message to deliver. May I arrange transport?"

Shi was more than slightly incensed, but he didn't say anything for a moment as he considered the tablet in his hands.

"Yes," he ground out finally. "Thank you."

"Not at all, Mr. Ambassador. The least I could do," Conner said, gesturing to the door. "Will your embassy be fine, or should I arrange a suborbital back to Bejing?"

"The embassy will be acceptable."

"Excellent. I wasn't certain we could guarantee your safe passage, though I would have provided all possible escorts if that were necessary," Conner said, escorting Shi out of the office and down the hall. "I am sorry for how abrupt I've been, but it is a trying time."

Shi nodded slowly. That he was willing to admit to. "Yes. Yes, it is that."

"The admirals in charge of the Reagan and Clinton task groups have been advised that your superiors may be calling on them. I've made it very clear that they are to offer all possible cooperation," Conner said as they reached the elevator. "So please, tell your superiors not to hesitate. Now is not the time to be proud. We can be proud when we've defeated our common enemy."

Shi swallowed hard, but nodded slowly. "I will inform them."

"Good." Conner smiled, seeing him onto the elevator. "It was a pleasure as always, Mr. Ambassador. Have a safe drive back to the embassy."

"Thank you, Mr. President."

The doors closed. Conner turned around and headed for the war room.

"See that nothing happens to him between here and the embassy," he told the AIC beside him.

"Yes sir."

"Now, I believe that we have some real work to do."

▶▶▶

▶Shi was more than slightly bedeviled by the sheer abrupt nature of the meeting he'd just endured. Yes, endured was the right word for it. The President of the Confederacy had effectively just handed control of two of their largest and most lethal blue-water task groups over to the Block. It was a stunning development, but one that underscored just how serious the NAC was apparently taking the situation.

Though, he supposed, if anything would force this kind of reaction, it would be an alien invasion.

In fact, that was about the *only* scenario he could imagine that would trigger this sort of response from the Confederacy Administration. Anything less than the risk of total annihilation would be handled "in house" as it were.

He looked out at the city as the car drove back to the embassy building, noting how deserted the streets were. He'd seen news out of New York, and knew that they'd been caught more flatfooted there. Streets were backed up with vehicles, forcing the military to physically push their way through using battle tanks, of all ludicrous things.

Tanks had been obsolete for almost a century, yet he was well aware that the Confederacy maintained a massive store of the combat vehicles well beyond anything they could conceivably need. Mostly it was a welfare program for arms manufacturers, building vehicles that even the military didn't have any idea what to do with, but he supposed it may just have paid off.

It would be a stroke of luck on par with winning those absolutely farcical Powerball jackpots, but I suppose that if you keep anything around long enough, you will eventually find a use for it.

His own nation wasn't any better. Shi could admit that to himself. It was a common way to repay political support, after all. Tanks, oil leases, various contracts of all sorts . . . those were the bargaining chips used to secure political support and funding. Legalized bribery by whatever name you called it.

Washington had better warning than New York, he could tell. Or, more accurately, better defenses to buy time for evacuations. The streets were empty, but he could see the men in armor on the rooftops, the Close Air Protection flights passing overhead, and sometimes, as his car moved through the street, he could see the motion of heavy armor down other streets from his position.

It all felt rather familiar to Shi. He had grown up in Beijing and lived in the city during the last year of the War when Confederate air raids were raining explosives down on their heads almost unopposed.

The silent car slid to a halt outside the Block embassy, and he quickly got out and hurried inside. He didn't believe that he was in any danger at the moment, but the intelligence he was holding had unnerved him. There had been a time when having something even a fraction as sensitive would easily have resulted in a lethal sanction from any one of a number of sources, not all of them Confederate or Block in origin.

Once inside, Shi relaxed marginally and made his way to the secure room, ironically passing through more security and invasive scanning techniques than he had in the White House.

He settled behind the desk that sat in the small secure room, wrapped in a Faraday cage and several layers of absorbent materials to prevent vibration induction systems, and turned on the computer that linked directly to a laser uplink on the roof.

Let us hope that the enemy hasn't begun to eliminate orbital assets as of yet, intentionally at least.

Several satellites and key orbital assets had been taken out of play just as incidental damage resulting from the battle in orbit, and most consumer-level electronics were still down from the massive electromagnetic pulse that had resulted from the destruction of *Liberty,* but much of the Block (and, he presumed, the Confederation) assets were still intact as of his last check.

The laser link was successful and he found himself linked directly with the Home Committee for Security of the State.

"Shi," he said, modulating his tone carefully. "Ambassador. Washington."

The system parsed his phrase, checking his voice for tremors that might indicate coercion and, of course, against the database that held all his biometric data. It took just over two minutes, but he suspected that most of that time involved getting hold of someone of sufficient rank to take his contact.

The screen cleared quickly, however, and he found himself looking at his direct supervisor.

It is late in Beijing. Good, the government is taking the situation seriously. They've called in all available people, I hope.

"What is it Ambassador Shi? Things are . . . busy here."

"I have little time. However, this is important. I just came from a meeting with the Confederate President . . . it was held in the secure bunker," Shi said, delivering the last line with just a hint of satisfaction as he saw his supervisor's eyes widen.

"We will require a full debrief . . . "

Shi waved the man off. "Yes, yes, that is the least of things. The Confederacy . . . they are frightened."

With those words, Shi settled in for a long conversation.

▶▶▶

▼

WAR ROOM BENEATH 1600 PENNSYLVANIA AVENUE

▲

▶ THE PRESIDENT'S ARRIVAL in the large command and control center went largely unremarked, something that only went to underscore just how focused people were on the situation at the moment. He wasn't about to complain about the lack of pomp and ceremony, however, and so he just walked around to the place reserved for the Commander in Chief and took his seat.

"Talk to me, General."

"We're still tracking landings, sir, with an eye to seismographic readings worldwide. Total confirmed count is now over three thousand, sir."

"My lord." Conner closed his eyes. "God save us."

"Let's not rely on the almighty just yet, sir," General Caern said. "All the landings have been in major population centers. That's bad for casualties, but it's even worse for the enemy."

Conner scowled. "How could it be worse for the enemy?"

"We can easily strike at every major population center on the planet, Mr. President," Caern answered. "Especially if the choice is do or die. We'll kill a lot of our own, yes, but we'll kill them too. If I were planning a genocidal strike on a planet using a weapon system such as these Drasin, I'd be landing my assets in Antarctica, the Sahara desert, any out of the way, impossible to get to place I could find. I sure as hell would not land them in New York City, Mr. President."

"You think they're planning something?" Conner asked, confused.

"No, sir. I think they're specifically *not* planning."

"I don't follow."

"Captain Weston's reports on these things indicates an almost . . . schizophrenic personality," Caern said. "One personality is a planner, picking targets, using strategy even . . . the other, however, is bestial. Sir, I think that the beast is in charge right now. They're striking at population centers just because they don't like them, not out of any kind of strategy."

"The people?"

"Perhaps," the General conceded, "or maybe they're targeting based on power usage, heat, or any number of other signatures from a major city. The point is, they're not thinking big picture. They're acting like a wounded animal, sir. See the thing that hurt them and rip its heart out. If they were planning, we'd be in a lot more trouble."

"We're in plenty as it stands," Conner said sourly.

"Yes sir, we are. However the problem isn't with the aliens on the ground. We can take them, Mr. President," Caern said confidently. "It's the goddamn battle fleet holding our high orbitals that we can't take. As long as they're up there, we may as well just roll over and die."

"That's *not* going to happen," Conner growled, slamming his hands down on the table.

"Didn't say it was, sir. Just said that we need to take those fuckers out," Caern said bluntly. "Otherwise, sooner or later, we're going to run out of bullets down here, and I can't promise that they'll run out of troops first."

Conner scowled, but nodded curtly, looking over to the Air Force general in charge of SPACECOM. "Thoughts?"

General McCullen sighed, shaking his head. "We've got nothing right now, Mr. President. We're half blind. We think that the *Enterprise* transitioned out of the system almost two days ago, but we can't confirm. Certainly the Priminae ships went to FTL sometime before that, but we can't confirm anything beyond that. We have no more military assets in Sol space, sir."

"Ground to orbit missiles."

McCullen shook his head. "Nothing but nukes and light conventional payloads. Every report we have on the alien armor clearly indicates that those will be of no value."

"What about high-velocity missiles?" the President asked, thinking about the weapon systems the *Odyssey* employed.

"Can't launch those inside Earth's atmosphere. Besides the fact that they'd ablate away from friction, we'd destroy the launch site with the shockwave alone."

"Lasers?"

"We wouldn't even heat up their hulls at this range," the general said.

"The *Odyssey* engaged them from *light seconds* away!"

"The *Odyssey* didn't have to fire through atmosphere, sir."

The President wasn't stupid enough to suggest pulse weapons. He was well aware of what the use of antimatter inside an atmosphere would do. He closed his eyes. "What about the new transition cannons?"

"Those . . . " McCullen hesitated. "I don't know, sir. We've never tried to transition this deep in a gravity well, or through atmosphere. They may be feasible, but we certainly don't have a targeting zero for firing from Earth's surface and, more importantly, we don't have any of the tachyon waveguides or their munitions."

"Then *build* some. Find an egghead to tell you if you can fire them, build some, and do your *jobs!*" Conner growled. "We will *not* go quietly into the night, gentlemen! This is not where the human race ends! Are you listening to me?"

"Yes sir."

"Good. Now go get me some answers. Find me something we can use."

▶▶▶

▶ Earth was a blue-white ball in the black of space, hanging in an eternal dance around the blazing yellow of the Sun. From anywhere in cislunar space, the Earth was the epitome of a peaceful icon.

That is, under all normal conditions.

Even during the worst human wars, all was serene from space.

Serenity, however, had now left the system.

Drasin ships literally surrounded the planet, some firing on random targets, others launching on the planet with regular ferocity. The alien ships evoked a visceral reaction from any human eyes that saw them, a deep burning urge to fight or to flee that couldn't . . . wouldn't be denied.

To human eyes they were the most viscerally terrifying things that ever existed, or ever *could* exist. There was no serenity where the Drasin passed, no life in their wake, and no hope for anything caught in their path.

In Drasin eyes, they were purity and humanity was the abomination.

Two species, literally born to hate and fear one another. One could even say that they had been *designed* to do so.

▼

CHAPTER TWO

Angels Twenty Over NYC

▲

► "STRYKER LEAD, NEW priority tasking."

"Roger command. Standing by."

The F/A-66 Mach Fighter curled slowly on its orbit of the city below, turning easily as Commander Miriam Benoit checked her instruments and waited for targeting information. Her squad had been deployed to provide CAP for the Guard in the city, but there hadn't been a lot to do so far with the Guard mostly caught in *traffic,* of all the damned stupid things.

A tasking, any tasking, was just what she'd been praying for since the first impact shook the city below.

"Stand by, Commander, we are relaying targeting data now."

"Roger that."

Her instruments went active almost instantly, targeting data feeding into the fighter from the ground below. She looked it over briefly, noting its location, and whistled.

"Central Park? We're going to launch on Central Park? Damn, this is fucked up," she said before keying back into the command channel. "Roger command. Have paint on the screen. Stryker Five, follow me in."

"Right behind you, Lead."

Two Mach Fighters peeled off from the squadron, angling down and picking up speed as they lined up for their run. The city grew ahead of them as they dove in, leveling out at Angels Ten as their computers began to calculate the release point.

"Stryker Lead. Weapons free."

"Stryker Five. Weapons free."

The computers took over then as the two Mach Fighters broke mach one at ten thousand feet over the city, calculating the changes in speed and position against the target data coming in from below. The red icons blinked to yellow, then quickly over to green as the computer released the guided munitions.

"Bombs away," Miriam called, pulling up and around in case she had to line up for a second run. "Strike inbound."

▼

CENTRAL PARK WEST

▲

► "STRIKE INBOUND."

Eric felt like throwing up, a spectacularly bad idea while wearing powered armor (or any full face breather, frankly), but managed to hold that off. He clipped his chute pack to the back of his armor and jumped, letting the pack do a minimal slowing of his descent as he dropped behind the NYPD cop who was still sprawled on the ground.

He pushed her further down, covering her with his own armored body, much to the woman's ire.

"Incoming!" he called, loud enough to be heard for quite some range, and was gratified when she instantly stopped fighting.

The hundred-pound guided bomb units, or GBUs, tracked the lasers down all the way and slammed into the Drasin soldier drones with a rumble that could be felt right through the ground. As close as they were, Eric was more concerned with the effects of overpressure on the cop beneath him than he was of shrapnel, but there were quite a few obstructions between them and the worst of the blast to bleed off the power of the explosion.

As the sense of destruction began to settle, Eric looked up and around and made a decision.

"Time to go, lady," he said, hooking one arm around her waist as he gave his chute its orders and was pulled up and away from the ground in a hurry. He kept the angle low, not wanting to draw fire, and skimmed the ground until they reached an alley to drop into. He let her go as he landed, nodding to a man in SWAT uniform who was covering them with his submachine gun.

"That's not going to cut it in this fight, son," he told the younger man. "Get yourself something with a punch, or get yourself out of the battlefield."

"Who the fuck are you?" the man demanded.

"Weston," Eric said, leaning out slightly so he could survey the situation.

"Eric Weston?" the woman asked from where she was crouched, leaning against the wall.

Eric snorted. "Heard of me, I suppose?"

"Yeah. You're the crazy bastard who flew that ship into my city," she scowled.

"Guilty," he admitted, "though I wasn't exactly in full positive control of the *Odyssey* when she dug in."

"No shit," the woman scoffed, shaking her head. "Name's Lyssa. Thanks for the save."

"No problem," Eric said, looking over what he could see of the park. "Just hold on a sec."

He swapped over to a private comm. "Nice hit, Strykers. Targets eliminated."

He lifted his Priminae GWIZ to his shoulder and stroked the trigger once. The crack of the weapon discharging shook the air with enough force to rattle teeth. The diamond round lashed out and slammed into the single Drasin that was still twitching, blowing its superheated blood across the park to cool.

"What the hell is that?" Lyssa screamed at him, though he suspected it was more because she couldn't hear herself properly than anything else.

"Priminae GWIZ," he said, raising the volume on his speaker. "Gravity gun. Was presented to me by an admiral I know back on Ranquil."

The GWIZ was a strange looking beast, lacking many of the features that a Terran would equate with a weapon. It didn't have a barrel; instead there was a set of five free-floating "rail points" that flexed as needed to direct the gravity warp that propelled the projectile. These were mounted along a long rail that included a hand grip, power pack, and other bits and bobs of interior mechanics.

All in all it was the most lethal nonthreatening-looking device he'd ever held, a fact that normally amused him to no end, but for the moment he honestly couldn't remember why. He'd picked it rather than a standard-issue assault rifle because of the fact that the GWIZ could accommodate almost any ammunition he chose to load it with. Right now he was firing diamond rounds, but in a pinch he could toss in practically anything and the gun would launch it without issue.

Lyssa was working her jaw and had a finger in her ear as she tried to get full hearing back. "What?"

Eric chuckled, turning away. "You guys have to get clear. I'm going to spot for the Strykers until the Guard gets here."

"Oh, like hell I'm going anywhere," Lyssa snarled. "This is *my* city, leatherneck. You don't get to tell me what to do."

Eric glanced at her sharply, noting the nickname she'd pinned him with. He hadn't heard that particular appellation for a long time. It wasn't something in common use outside the Corps any longer. He evaluated her for a moment while his computer connected to the military networks and ran facial recognition.

Well, well, well. Melyssa Sirenne Myriano, lieutenant in the Corps. Communications specialist. Her service record flitted by, but he mostly ignored it once he'd determined that she had no significant red flags. He could use a good comm link, actually, and someone who knew the city for that matter, but without some decent equipment she wasn't much more than a meat target.

Eric looked her over. "Alright then, Lieutenant. You want to hang around, that's fine with me. We'll have to get you some proper kit, however."

Lyssa snorted, holding up her empty hands. "Twist my arm."

He turned back to the others in the alley, speaking to them all, but looking at the big man in SWAT gear. "Get these people out of here. Stay near the waterfront and head down toward the Lincoln Tunnel. The Guard has a command post setup at the USS *Intrepid*. They'll have an evacuation plan and weapons for you. I'll let them know you're coming."

Lyssa slapped Alex on his armored chest, nodding to the spotter's scope he was still holding. "I'll take that, man."

He shrugged and nodded, dropping it into her palm. "Be careful."

She jerked her head in Eric's direction. "The man just face planted his whole fucking starship into New York City. I think he's used up his bad luck for this year."

She pointedly ignored Eric snorting in the background as he mumbled, "I wish."

"Time to go," Eric spoke up. "Movement converging on this area from three sides."

"The Guard?" Lyssa asked, hopefully but not expectedly.

"No such luck. Guard transponders are still showing ten blocks south," Eric said. "Heat signatures match Drasin."

"Great."

Eric pointed at the others. "The shoreline is clear. Head south to the *Intrepid.*"

"Right, come on, you lot. This way."

Eric watched them head out, cutting down a side street that headed west to the shore. Then he turned to Lyssa. "You scared of heights?"

"Not even slightly."

"Good." He stepped in, hooking an arm around her waist. "Step on my toes."

She grinned. "I'm not that bad a dancer."

She put her feet on his, however, and Eric sent the lift command to the chute. The system whirred a little louder than normal but easily hefted the two of them straight up the side of the skyscraper to the roof. Lyssa stepped off his toes, dropping to the roof as Eric landed and cut his chute loose, sending it on overwatch recon.

"Check the southeast," he told her. "I've got enemy combat drones covering the park. Call out if you spot anything."

"Right. What are you going to do?"

Eric planted a foot on the edge of the building, looking down at the battleground they'd just left. "I'm going to see about scaring up some assets. Weston to Command, come in Command."

"Go for Command, Captain."

"I'm transmitting new data on enemy movements via my drones. Collate and prioritize for strikes."

"Roger, Captain. We have your feed."

"I'm going to need an equipment drop."

There was a pause before the voice came back. "No can do, Captain. We are tapped out in this area."

"You've got to be kidding me, Command."

"Captain, every SOCOM unit is in the field and they've drawn every supply drone we have available to fly. Even if we had the gear to dispatch, there's nothing to deliver it, Captain. Every piece of equipment in the Confederacy has been tagged for deployment already."

Weston scowled, shaking his head, but there was little he could say about it. "Roger that. Weston out."

▶▶▶

▶ *The entity who self-identified as Gaia watched over the events transpiring, concern rising as the intruders began their invasive assault on* her *world. The intruders were beginning their multiplication process, converting elements of the Earth into more of the vile filth like themselves.*

For the moment the threat was minimal, however.

Unlike what she had learned of her counterpart on the Priminae world, this world . . . her world, was most emphatically not unarmed and unwilling to fight.

That said, she was well aware that hers would only be able to hold out for just so long.

While the enemy controlled the orbitals, as well as the rest of the system, the end was already written. The only question was how long it would take to pen the final words.

That was wholly unacceptable.

Unfortunately, her ability to influence the physical world was limited. She could advise, should she decide to make her presence known to more people. She could coerce, but in the end it would come to the same thing.

Death.

Gaia seethed. Her breath was the howling wind, her anger buried deep in the Earth like the force of Quake waiting to be released. But for all that, she was impotent and she detested the sensation.

The entity turned her focus back to the city of New York, where her chosen champion was now resting. She had a plan. No, calling it a plan would be overly generous, she supposed. She had a concept, an idea, a hint of what was to come perhaps.

If all went well, Eric Weston would be her savior.

▶▶▶

▶ "I've got five more coming in from the east, but I see the Guard coming up Eighth!" Lyssa called out from the southeast corner of the building.

When she got no answer, she turned around and saw that Weston hadn't moved from where he was crouched on the northeast corner.

"Hey, you listening?"

Weston shifted, glancing back. "I hear you, Lieutenant."

"What are you doing?" she asked, walking over.

"Pinging everything on my ship, seeing what answers."

"So? Is anything answering?"

Eric looked over the list of equipment his armor was reporting. "Oh yeah."

"Well great. Let's go get it."

"Slight problem with that," Eric said. "Some of it is back in the habitation module, right over there."

She followed his hand to see at least a dozen of the damned things crawling over the module he was pointing at.

"Where the hell did they come from?" She breathed, appalled by the very *look* of the things.

"I'd guess they would willingly crawl out of hell for a chance to eat my ship," he said sourly, cradling his Priminae assault weapon in the crook of his arm. "We're not getting through those, and by the time the Guard gets here it'll be too late."

"You're going to let them eat your ship?"

"That's not my ship anymore," Eric said stonily, "but no. They don't get to chow down on the *Odyssey*, not while I breathe. Control, Weston."

"Go for Control."

Lyssa hissed, surprised that she could hear the conversation. Normally you didn't put that sort of thing over a PA.

"New targets for Strykers," he said. "Tell them to come heavy. Targets are grouped in close. Will laze."

"Roger, Weston. Strykers inbound."

Eric sent the laze command to the micro drones flitting about the park and rose fully to his knees. He looked down at the crumpled and battered cylinder that had been his home for almost three years.

The sound of the Mach Fighters breaking the sound barrier echoed in the distance as a pair of the high-speed craft flashed by overhead. Weston watched the bombs tumble from the rails of the fighters, straightening out in midair before slamming into the habitat module and everything around it.

The explosive conflagration engulfed the street, the habitat, all the Drasin soldier drones, and two buildings. Eric flinched but didn't turn away as the buildings shifted, their supports blown out by the blast, and then slowly began to topple into the street. They slammed into what was left of the *Odyssey* command module, a cloud of dust and debris sweeping out and rolling into the park. Eric finally turned away as everything was obscured. He had too many other things to do.

"Come on," he said to Lyssa, walking back across the rooftop.

"Where are we going?"

"To get some gear for you and whoever else we can recruit."

"I thought you just blew the gear to hell?" she demanded, chasing after him.

"No, that was the command habitat," he said as he walked. "There was only a small security office there, nothing major."

"Then where is the rest?"

He looked down at the park and then well out past it to the city beyond. "Out there. Past the Drasin."

"Oh, just fucking perfect," she muttered disgustedly. "Can it get any worse?"

"Tell me, Lieutenant," Eric asked mildly, "do you swim?"

She just groaned.

Eric smiled in his armor, though the situation didn't hold much real humor. He knew that it wasn't going to be remotely as easy as he'd just implied, which wasn't very. No, they had to cross the park first, and he didn't dare use the chute to fly over it. They'd be very slow-moving skeet for enemy fire if they tried that.

They had to cross the park on foot, and from the looks of it the action had drawn the attention of every single one of the alien bastards. Worse, they were all converging on where the *Odyssey* module had rested.

Bastards must really want a piece of her, Eric thought grimly. *Well, too late, you pricks.*

He'd burn every last piece of his ship to cinders before he let her be eaten and turned into more of the enemy.

▶ ▶ ▶

UNDER 1600 PENNSYLVANIA AVENUE, WASHINGTON, D.C.

▶ "SIR, YOU NEED to check this."

General Caern scowled, an expression that was becoming increasingly familiar on his visage, but headed over to the call without comment.

"What is it, Sergeant?"

"Report out of NYC, sir. We have an asset on the ground calling in Stryker teams, putting paint on target for them."

"I thought the Guard was having trouble getting to the hot zone?"

"They are, sir. Look at the call sign attached to the orders."

Caern looked closer, his eyes widening in surprising. "Is that confirmed?"

"Voice print and bio-implant countersigned, sir."

"Well damn, that son of a bitch is like a cockroach." Caern chuckled, shaking his head. "Alright, give him whatever he needs, son. Weston knows more about these bastards than any man on the planet and maybe off it."

"He has a kit request in the system, but we've got nothing available," the sergeant said. "Most of our advanced tech is overseas and we're light here."

"How light?"

"Cupboard's bare, sir," the sergeant admitted grudgingly. "We've got plenty of armor, the old school kind, but modern kit is in demand and we're stretched thin."

"We've got nothing then?"

The sergeant hesitated, his expression twisted almost painfully. Caern recognized the beginning of an evasive answer and just shook his head.

"Belt it out, son."

"Weston's is Double A qualified, sir."

"Right, I know that."

Hell, the entire *planet* knew that. Eric Weston was the one name that was forever more associated with the Archangel squadron. You'd have to find a soul who'd not watched a media device in the last two decades to find someone who didn't know Eric Weston was Double A.

"Yes sir. What I mean to say, sir, is that we have a few advanced combat units sitting this one out sir," the sergeant said. "No trained NICS qualified people."

"Right. Those." The General nodded. "Are they field ready?"

He hadn't paid a lot of attention to those. They seemed like advanced tinker toys, but then he was an old-school soldier at heart. Wars were won door to door, not by knocking over buildings and blowing great massive holes in things.

Of course, these things could do with some great massive holes.

"Yes sir, cleared last quarter."

"Check one out and offer it up," Caern said, turning away. "If he wants it, hand deliver it if need be."

"Yes sir."

Caern made his way back over to the central war table, a conference table surrounding a tri-D holo imager.

"What was it, General?" the President asked, looking over. "More bad news?"

"Some good news, I would say." The Marine general grinned. "Weston survived."

"Impossible," an admiral growled. "Nothing walks away from a hit like that."

"Not necessarily," McCullen responded thoughtfully. "If her counter-mass was still up when the *Odyssey* dug in, it could have been survivable. The bridge has a backup unit, so if anyone would have lived, they'd have been there."

"Whatever. The man is breathing and calling down the fire in New York," Caern said. "If it's his ghost, I'll take what I can get."

"Gentlemen," the President stepped in, "this is hardly getting us anywhere and, while I am pleased that Captain Weston survived and, yes, it is good news, it's a very minor silver lining in a very dark cloud. Let us stay on task here."

"Yes Mr. President."

"Alright, now you've all had an hour to review our weapons development divisions. Does anyone have a solution to our problem in *orbit?*"

▶▶▶

EIGHTH AVENUE, NEW YORK CITY

▶ CORPORAL BURKE GRINNED, no humor in his expression but plenty of satisfaction as he jammed the throttle of the M7 Abrams main battle tank, flattening the tiny import in front of him to a mashed pulp as he rumbled over it.

*They never let us do **this** in training.* He couldn't help but chortle as the big motors of the tank hummed smoothly along.

The two lead tanks had been outfitted with hug steel cowcatchers and were clearing the road by literally bulldozing everything out of the way. Every now and then, however, one car or another bit of debris would slide back into the road and he'd get a chance to flatten it into the dirt.

Still, it was slow going. They had info-net reports of an active combat scene just another dozen or so blocks up, and in three blocks they'd be able to get off the streets and into the park, where they could pick up some decent speed.

"Stop playing around, Burke. You'll throw a track if you keep that shit up."

"Oh, relax, Sarge." Burke grinned, glancing over his shoulder. "These things are built like tanks, didn't you know?"

"Idiot." The Sergeant rolled his eyes. "Just watch the damn road. We're coming up on the park."

"You got it, Sarge."

▶▶▶

▶ First Platoon of the Hundred and First rumbled into Central Park, eighty-millimeter cannons seeking out targets to hit. They were already leaning in the right direction when the first of the enemy spider-looking beasts burst out of the tree line, being patched into the drone network that was flitting around the area.

The platoon leader gave the order and the two closest tanks rocked back on their tracks as the big guns spread fire across the park, the recoil of the cannons tearing chunks out of the earth with the blast wave alone.

Two armor-piercing rounds slammed into the alien, lifting it clear off its legs and blowing it back into the tree line across three times the volume of space it had previously occupied. Cheers and whoops of victory went up across the network, but were quickly cut short when three more creatures burst out of the trees, firing as they came.

Crackling red beams of energy sliced across the park, lighting afire whatever they touched, burning into the lead tanks with enough power to trigger their active armor. The explosives blew outward, temporarily defeating the particle beams, but that defense only lasted an instant. When it was finished the beams lanced in and turned the ceramic and steel armor to slag and vapor.

The munitions in the war machines went last, blowing the remains of the tanks apart as their fellows began to react. The other three tanks in the platoon opened fire on the move, turning to give themselves enough room so as not to get in each other's way or catch a blast intended for another target.

In seconds Central Park turned into a war zone the likes of which hadn't been seen on Earth in over eighty years. The last great tank war had probably been during the Second World War, in fact, and heavy armor had been going out of common use slowly but steadily ever since. Of course, if you considered that one side of the engagement was a group of alien invaders, then eighty years was a most conservative number indeed.

▶▶▶

▶Corporal Burke swore, bouncing in his seat as he ran his tank over a cement guard. The Abrams was cushioned on sixteen independent air shocks, but even so a hundred tons of tank doesn't like being airborne.

"Goddamn it, Burke! I'm trying to fire here!"

"Well, do it on the fly, 'cause I'm not letting those fuckers fry us!" the corporal snarled back at his superior, not looking away from his controls. "Those beam things just sliced right through Rogers and Mick!"

"I saw it, but I'd like to *kill* them before they slice through *us,* if you don't fucking mind!"

Burke growled, letting the right tread drag as he brought the tank around in a smoother motion. "There they are. Light those fuckers up!"

"Firing sequence coded! Going weapons free!"

The smoothbore barrel of the big eighty-millimeter rail cannon glided on its stabilizers, sliding into position as the tank kept on the move. The computers adjusted for the movement, compensating automatically for hundreds of variables, and began to auto fire as soon as they had a positive acquisition.

Eighty-millimeter rounds of solid depleted uranium roared across the park, slamming into their targets with enough force to shatter even the best Terran armor. Against the Drasin's alien composition they did no less, blowing molten silicon across the park as the insect-like soldier drones were shattered and thrown about like toys in a hurricane.

The remaining three tanks of the One Oh One were firing eight rounds a second as they coordinated their response to the loss of two of their own, but they were not the only ones firing.

Particle beams crackled back across the park, melting and vaporizing everything they crossed with equal ease. Ground, cement, battle-hardened armor . . . it made very little difference as they all fell under the blasts. Another of the Guard tanks blew apart under the barrage. Two of the aliens were blown apart seconds later.

The battle became one of attrition in short order, each side losing one after another. The side with the most fighters was going to win this battle and that side wasn't the Hundred and First.

"Die, you mother f—!" Burke's scream was cut abruptly short as the crackling beams that dissected the remaining two tanks of the One Oh One's First Platoon finished their grisly work.

▶ ▶ ▶

▶ "Shit."

Eric nodded in complete agreement with that assessment, having watched the fight with a better view than Lyssa had, thanks to his armor enhanced optics. The Guardsmen at the point of the charge had dished out as good as they got, but they'd been outnumbered and main battle tanks were not intended for fighting in terrain this enclosed.

"They've distracted the drones in the park," he said. "We should move now."

Lyssa looked at him, clearly concerned, but nodded. "Right."

She stepped closer to him and Eric wrapped an arm around her waist as she threw one over his shoulder and stepped onto his boots. The summoned chute returned on command and Eric smoothly clipped on before letting it pull them both off the roof and into a sweeping dive, taking them on an arc into the park and below the tree line.

He kept them moving as fast as he could, but the chute wasn't designed for high speed, and carrying an extra person who wasn't locked in necessitated that he take at least a modicum of care. So he stayed low, skimming the ground in order to avoid being an easy target. The trees skimmed by, whipping at them sharply in passing, close enough that Eric had to shield Lyssa's face as they moved.

Eric dropped suddenly, a couple hundred meters into the park, and the hit the ground in a controlled tumble.

"What is it?" Lyssa demanded as she rolled to her knees and scrambled behind a rock.

Eric cut the chute loose and let it fly clear as he hit the power on his GWIZ and leveled it to the south. "They're coming back up this way and we were about to lose our cover."

Lyssa looked around and nodded.

They had been following the walking path that curled south along the reservoir. He'd thought about going north, but it would have put them in the open longer. Now he wished that he'd gone with his first instinct.

"Get ready to run for it," Eric advised as he primed the GWIZ.

"What are you going to do?"

"I'm going to kill a few of them," he told her simply. "You're not remotely armed for this, so run."

Lyssa scowled, but nodded. She'd never liked running, not since she was very young, and her time in the Corps had hammered that character trait home all the stronger. At the moment, however, he was right. Her pistol was a peashooter against the enemy here, and she was unarmored.

Though, honestly, she wasn't certain that the MilSpec armor the captain was wearing would do him all that much better than her Kevlar and ceramic vest.

"Good luck," she hissed, then bolted away, keeping as low as she could.

Eric didn't bother responding. He just popped up from behind the cover and leveled the alien gravity weapon, stroking the trigger lightly as it fell even with the Drasin soldier drones.

The crack of the diamond projectile making a mockery of the speed of sound shook the world around him, but because of the weapon's design and his own armor insulation, Eric didn't feel or hear a thing. He did see the shock wave expand out behind the shot, however, kicking up dust and debris in a rooster tail straight into the soldier drone.

The projectile slammed into its target with power comparable to the heavy explosives dropped by the Stryker teams, delivering its kinetic payload almost perfectly as the diamond shattered and tore through the target with vicious force. The heavy alien drone was picked off the ground and thrown back, molten silicon splattering the park.

Eric jumped from cover immediately, ignoring the part of his stomach that wanted to hurl at the sudden motion.

He knew that it was the concussion at play, but he couldn't do anything about it other than ignore it as best he could and suppress it when he couldn't. He'd fought through worse in his time. He could do it again.

The alien particle beams glowed an evil red as they swept after him, Eric staying on the bounce and a half inch ahead of burning death with each leap. As a Marine aviator, hell just as a Marine, Eric was an infantryman first and anything else a distant second . . . but that didn't mean he was fully trained on the armor he wore.

It was relatively new issue, and his job since it had come out was more behind the lines than on them until he'd been assigned to the *Odyssey*. Since then he'd taken his spare time to qualify on the armor, but he knew that he was nowhere near the skill level of the SOCOM troopers he'd commanded. Eric wished a few of them had ridden down with him, actually, but that hadn't seemed like a good idea at the time.

He landed in a skid, sliding behind a large cement memorial statue to something or someone he didn't have time to identify and rolled over into a prone position as he lined up his next shot.

The Priminae weapon blasted the environment around him again, and again Eric saw a rooster tail of dust kick up between him and the enemy. The sheer power the Priminae had packed into the form factor of a slightly beefy yet surprisingly light assault rifle left him in utter awe.

I don't even have it turned all the way up.

It was set roughly in the middle of the power slide, and he knew that he could conceivably eliminate the lot of the bastards with one properly aimed shot on full power. But the sheer level of collateral damage it would incur terrified Eric to no end.

A kiloton-level weapon, or close enough as to make no real difference, was not something he ever wanted to unleash in a Confederate city.

When he spotted a grouping of the aliens emerging from the tree line south of him, however, he decided to up the ante just a little. Eric slid the power control up a few more degrees and kept his aim lower so he wouldn't take out a building or something with a miss. He then squeezed down on the trigger and unloaded a burst into the enemy position that seemed to shake the *world*.

▼

CHAPTER THREE

National Guard Command Post, *Intrepid* Sea, Air, & Space Museum

▲

▶ "WHAT THE EVER loving *fuck* was that?"

The mushroom cloud floating over the city to the north of them gave a pretty good answer to that question, honestly, but it just felt like something Brigadier Potts needed to ask.

"Was that one of ours?"

"Negative sir," Lieutenant Keiths could confidently answer. "Nothing of ours was cleared to drop that kind of payload, sir."

"Do we have anyone in the area?" Potts asked, sick to his stomach. *Or maybe I should ask if we **did** have anyone in the area . . .*

"No one close enough, sir. No one too close, either."

"Thank God for the second."

"Yes sir. General, sir, I'm not reading any significant EM spike, no beta spike, no gamma spike. I don't think that was a nuke, sir."

"Well, that's just peachy," Potts growled. "It was still one big ever living *fuck* of an explosion."

"Yes sir."

Potts sighed, shaking his head. His boys just weren't equipped for this kind of dirty fighting. They were old-school open battlefield trained, and this was urban street-to-street combat well beyond anything anyone had ever seen. The tanks and armor they had packed more than enough power for the job, but a hundred-ton tank wasn't intended for driving through a damned city.

"Get me eyes on the area," he ordered. "I don't care if it's from the ground, the sky, or orbit. Just get me something."

"Yes sir."

▶▶▶

▶Eric would have been spitting dirt out of his mouth if he weren't wearing powered armor with a full environmental seal. Assuming, that is, that he'd survived the concussion of the kinetic strike. As it was, he wiped said dirt off the face plate and double checked the setting on his GWIZ.

*Only three-quarters to the top. Holy hell, are the Prims really **that** fucking crazy?*

Central Park was flattened.

Or at least it was in the immediate area. Eric could see some trees still standing a few blocks down from his position, and behind him they were still intact to be sure. But where he'd taken his show was now an oblong crater beyond which a ring of trees were laid down like toppled dominoes. He examined the scene for a long moment, stunned by every detail he spotted, particularly when he happened to focus in on a building several blocks beyond the blast zone and spotted an immobile Drasin soldier drone embedded in the eighth floor.

Jesus. Crazy bastards.

Eric slowly and deliberately turned the dial back down to the halfway mark before he turned and leapt off to the east where Lyssa had run ahead of him.

▶▶▶

▶Lyssa was spitting out dirt as she picked herself up off the ground, looking over her shoulder with wide eyes and a horror-filled expression. She didn't know what had just happened, but a mushroom cloud was pretty much a universal sign of an atrocity. She felt a wave of relief when she spotted Weston's black-green armor bounding over in her direction, and got to her feet to greet him as he landed.

"What the hell was that?"

She wasn't expecting Eric Weston to chuckle nervously, looking for all the world like a schoolboy caught doing something he knew he should be punished for.

"Oops?"

"Oops?? *Oops??*" she demanded, pointing toward the collapsing cloud of dust and smoke, "*You* did that?"

"Prim guns pack a bigger punch than I thought."

She stared, wide-eyed, at the weapon he was still holding. "What did you do?"

"Turned up the power," he said, "about three-quarters to the top."

Lyssa closed her eyes, her knees feeling weak. She really wanted nothing more than to collapse into a nice comfortable chair somewhere where the world made sense again. She licked her lips slowly, deliberately, and looked at him for a long moment.

"Three-quarters?" she asked, her voice croaking just a tad.

He nodded.

"How much more powerful is full?"

"Don't know. I thought it was a linear power setting," he said, "but after that I'm pretty sure it's logarithmic."

"Oh God," she mumbled. "I need a drink."

"I need more ammo," he said. "I'm running low."

She rolled her eyes, remembering what he'd told her the gun fired. "There's a Tiffany's down the street."

"Cute," he told her dryly, "but I'll pass."

She snapped her fingers, looking disappointed, "Damn. I was hoping for an excuse to loot the place."

"Come on, let's move. There's a Guard unit about eight blocks east. I think they've got a munitions truck with them."

"Right behind you."

▶▶▶

▶ Third Platoon consisted of five M7s and a recon APC designed to withstand medium to heavy IEDs, but they were moving very cautiously after getting the news about what happened to First Platoon at the south end of the park. That caution had allowed a resupply group to catch up with them while they moved into position.

The platoon was moving west now, along East 85th and crossing Madison. They'd stopped briefly when the thunderclap of the explosion shook the street and rattled every pane of glass around them, but quickly got under way again when the general's demand for eyes on scene came through.

It was spooky, moving through the streets and slamming cars out of the road with the makeshift cowcatchers on the front of the lead tanks. Every now and then they saw a person looking out a window or standing on a street corner to watch them go by, but the city felt empty in a way that it never should.

New York may be the city that never slept, but right then it felt like the city that was in a coma, and none of the Guardsmen quite knew how to handle that.

"I see the city Met coming up. The park is right there," Lieutenant Garibaldi said. "Slow us down and edge us out."

"You got it, sir," the driver, Corporal Tate, said from where he was sitting. "Launch drones, sir?"

"Good idea. Go ahead."

Two whirring aircraft lifted from the back of the tank, leaning forward and racing off to the west. One stayed low, barely flitting over the tops of cars, while the other went high and climbed for some altitude above the buildings.

Garibaldi watched the mushroom cloud show up on the top drone's camera and shook his head. "Holy shit. Someone nuked Central Park."

"Place had it coming, if you ask me," Tate told him wryly. "Last time I was there I swear I almost got mugged three times before I got out."

"Any of the muggers carry a tactical nuke?"

"Not that I saw, but I wouldn't have put it past some of them." Tate snorted, but he scowled as he noted something. "I think we're missing something here."

"Such as?"

"The rads, LT," Tate answered. "I'm getting clean readings."

"Huh." Garibaldi looked over the scans himself. "You're right."

"Some kind of alien super weapon, you think?" Tate asked.

"I have no idea. Edge us forward some more. I can't get a satellite signal here and the local control link is breaking up."

"Right. I'll tuck us into the trees just off the transverse there," Tate offered. "Park her and put the camo on."

"Sounds about right. Do it."

The lead tank of third platoon rumbled across Fifth Avenue and took a right as they started into the park. Tate guided his hundred-ton behemoth under a copse of trees and let the motor die as he activated the vehicle's cam-plates to match to local environment. In a few seconds the tank had disappeared, all save the makeshift steel cowcatcher bolted to the front, which seemed to hang out in midair for no apparent reason.

Inside the tank the crew crossed their fingers and hoped real hard that the enemy wouldn't take notice of that particular oddity.

▶ ▶ ▶

▶ "Why did you stop?"

Eric glanced back, noting that the woman wasn't winded. That was impressive, given that she was keeping up with him and he was in enhancing armor. Okay, he wasn't going all out by a longshot, but even so.

"See the spy drones there?" He nodded up.

Lyssa looked for a moment, then finally caught one of them as it banked and a glint of sun flicked off one of the propellers. "Yeah."

"Short range, probably launched from a tank," he said. "In a city like this you don't need line of sight, but it's close unless you've got a good uplink, and I'm pretty sure they don't have that."

"Oh? How come?"

"'Cause I don't have one," he said with a grin, which vanished quickly. "Probably because the enemy took out the bird."

"Oh." She grimaced. "So where are they?"

"At a guess? Camouflaged," he said. "Probably tucked in between those buildings up there, or maybe in the tree line. I don't want to surprise the gunner, though. That could get ugly."

That was a sentiment that she wasn't about to argue with, not even remotely.

They moved out again, Eric leading them around the likely area as he began looking for the tank. As they reached the edge of the trees, he motioned her to one side.

"Hold tight here. I'm going to go ahead."

▶▶▶

▶"I don't see any sign of the enemy." Garibaldi scowled, looking through the feed from the drones.

"After that blast I'm surprised you can see a sign of Central Park," Tate countered dryly.

The lieutenant snorted, shaking his head. "Oh, there's lots of signs of the park. All over the city from what I can tell."

Tate was about to answer when a series of clanging sounds on the armor of the tank nearly caused both men to jump out of their skin. They looked at each other, wide-eyed for a moment before Tate spoke up.

"You think it's the enemy sir?"

Garbaldi shot him a dark look. "Did those *things* strike you as the type to knock?"

Tate appeared to consider this while Garibaldi just shook his head and reluctantly flicked from the drone feed to the external fiber optics. He frowned when he spotted the armored figure lounging on the top of the tank, looking far too casual for someone in a war zone.

The lieutenant sighed and dogged the seal on the hatch, shoving it open so he could pull himself out.

"Hello, Lieutenant," the man in armor said. "I was wondering if I might borrow a cup of ammo."

The sheer oddity of the statement caught him off guard. "Excuse me?"

"You have a munitions truck in your platoon, Lieutenant?"

"Who the fuck are you?" Garibaldi growled. "I'm not giving you dick . . . "

"Eric Weston, Captain, Confederation Marines. Check my bona fides if you must, but I'm low on ammo and need to top up."

"We're an *armored* platoon, jarhead," Garibaldi snarled. "We don't carry bullets for whatever popgun you're . . . "

Weston casually hefted a gun unlike anything Garibaldi had ever seen, a ceramic white color with free-floating arcs that extended along the length of the weapon.

"I'll take anything you've got up to eighty millimeter," Weston said, looking over the camo surface of the tank he was sitting on. "This baby packs a sixty-millimeter rail gun, right? I'll take a supply of DPU rounds."

Garibaldi shook himself. "Look. I don't know who you are . . . "

"You're probably the only person on the planet right now who doesn't, then," Weston cut him off. "Just run my ID, son. I need those munitions, 'cause I'm almost out of diamonds."

Garibaldi just stared for a moment, then slowly ducked back into the vehicle, resealing the hatch, to run the name and ID of the madman sitting on his tank. It really was better not to talk to lunatics in his experience.

"Who the hell was that?" Tate asked.

"I don't know. Some nutcase named Weston with a sci-fi rifle. He wants bullets."

"Did you tell him we're a tank platoon?" Tate asked, confused. "Wait. Weston? Eric Weston?"

"Yeah. A jarhead. Why?"

"Jesus, sir, that's the captain of the *Odyssey*. Don't you watch the news?"

"You mean the ship that just scattered its pieces all over the city we're in?" Garibaldi asked sarcastically. "I know the name, but what are the odds . . . "

The screen he was looking at came back with the confirmation of the man's ID, making him break off in consternation as he read the file.

"Well, shit."

"What is it?"

Garibaldi sighed, reached up, and unsealed the hatch again without speaking. He pulled himself up and looked around until he spotted the man in armor again.

"Munitions truck is five blocks east," he said. "I'll tell them you're coming."

"Excellent. Thank you, Lieutenant."

"Don't mention it," Garibaldi said sourly. "Ever."

He dropped back into the tank and resealed the hatch.

This time I'm leaving it that way.

▶▶▶

▶Lyssa scowled when Weston finally turned up again. "So?"

"Five blocks east. Come on."

The city was eerily quiet as they walked, a silence that was punctuated by distant rumbling that could have been anything from thunder to artillery fire. She rather suspected that it was the latter more than the former, unfortunately.

It wasn't that the city was empty. She spotted figures peeking out from the windows as they moved down the street. New Yorkers weren't the easiest people in the world to freak out, but it seemed that a bona fide alien invasion was going to do the job. She'd been walking the streets of the city for most of her life, almost five years as a cop, and she'd never seen the likes of what she was seeing now.

Not even after a major hurricane had flooded the streets and forced New Yorkers to flee to higher ground did the city look and feel remotely like it did just then.

"People are scared," she said softly.

"Good." Weston grunted. "They need to be scared. These things are nightmares walking. Don't ever think otherwise. Just one of them could tear this entire planet out from underneath us."

She looked at him like he was more than a little crazy. "Come on."

"They're replicators, Lyssa. One breeds ten, ten breed a hundred, and in a month they'll eat their way down to the mantle of the planet and the Earth will start to break up as the tidal gravity of the moon starts tearing it apart. Make no mistake, Lyssa. We have to destroy them to the last, or they'll destroy us. To the last."

She just stared for a long moment as they walked, uncertain whether he was serious or not. The helmet he wore made it hard to read the man, just as his armor made body language almost indecipherable.

Finally she spoke. "You're serious, aren't you?"

"As genocide."

▶▶▶

▼

NATIONAL GUARD HQ, USS *INTREPID* SEA, AIR, & SPACE MUSEUM

▲

▶ "WE HAVE FIGHTING in every borough, sir."

Potts nodded. "I can see the map. Get air support over to Queens. The armored units are being outmaneuvered."

"All we have available are a couple squadrons of AH-98s, sir."

Potts nodded. "I know they're outdated, but they won't be taking on the Block's best. These things are nothing compared to the Block Mantis fighters. Send them in."

"Yes sir."

The AH-98s were about as old school as any active-duty airframe got. No counter-mass support. No advanced AI flight controls. They were now used exclusively as trainers in the general military, but the New York Air National Guard still fielded a few squadrons.

Potts was old enough to remember just what they were capable of, however, so he wasn't too badly concerned. That said, he did wish that he had a few squadrons that weren't obsolete by a few decades under his belt.

Every damn unit worth a damn is stationed in a ring of fire around the Block. Okinawa, Germany, Iraq. We've got nothing but obsolete gear here.

We'll just have to do the job despite all that.

▶▶▶

▶The munitions truck was expecting them, as promised, and Weston was glad to see that they had a decent supply of depleted uranium rounds in a few calibers.

"Show me the twenty millimeter rounds," Eric said, nodding to the crate he could see on the back of the large truck.

"Yes sir."

Eric loaded a single round of twenty millimeter by hundred and four millimeter depleted uranium into the Priminae weapon. It wasn't a gun by the strictest definitions, and certainly wasn't a rifle or anything that like. It was a gravetic accelerator cannon, and as such didn't actually need any specific type of ammunition. Anything you could fit into the receiver would fly just fine out the business end.

The gun took the twenty millimeter round, levitating it smoothly into the ready position. He checked the clearance quickly. Eric figured he could go larger, up to eighty millimeters in a pinch, but lugging around munitions that size would be a pain in his ass and he felt the need for mobility.

Besides, this city is about to buried in bullets I can pick up whenever I need them.

Eric grabbed a canvas bag from the truck, flipped it open quickly, proceeding to shovel rounds into the bag from the crate. When he was done he flipped the bag over his shoulder and nodded to the men. "Thanks for the reload. Does anyone have a full uplink?"

"No sir. Lost them just before the first impacts."

Eric sighed, but he wasn't surprised. When the *Liberty* went up, the pulse was probably big enough to take out even hardened orbital birds. Thankfully, the atmosphere would have kept it from frying most ground-based systems, but that didn't help him much at the moment.

"We're having decent luck with the Net, though, sir."

"Oh?" Eric cocked his head, but then nodded quickly.

It sort of made sense, now that he thought about it. The global network had originally been designed as a military communications system, so one of its biggest features was the fact that it was designed from the ground up to route signals around broken links. It was also mostly running on fiber now, so the backbone of the civilian network was actually better defended than most military systems.

"Alright. I'll link in that way," he said. "Thanks."

"No problem, sir," the reservist said. "Where are you going now, if I can ask?"

"Back to my ship."

CHAPTER FOUR

Beijing, China

▶ MAJOR GENERAL KONG swore at the display, unable and unwilling to believe what he was seeing. The city crawled with enemy units, literally and figuratively *crawled,* and the reports coming back in made it clear that their normal response teams were utterly ineffective.

"We need to bring in heavy armor and air support. Police units are insufficient!"

"I am well aware of that, Chairman," the general growled. "We are bringing our forces back from the exterior bases, but it takes time. Our forces have been arrayed outward since the war, so we have few heavy units to deploy."

"Do not give me excuses! Bring those units back immediately!"

Kong tuned out the ravings of the Chairman, knowing that, for the moment at least, he had little to be concerned about from the man. In the current situation there wasn't a military officer in the entire Block government who would listen to the Chairman over him. For all intents and purposes, he was the military, and right now the military was in charge.

For all the good it seemed to be doing.

The enemy forces were not particularly tough, as best as he could tell from reports and recordings, but they were more than a match for the police units initially sent against them. Internal military had somewhat more luck, but even those were relatively light in terms of firepower and armor, so at best they were holding the line while heavier forces were brought in.

The only thing that was keeping it from being a rout was the air support provided by the People's Liberation Army Air Force, and those units were being stretched sorely thin between India and China at the moment.

Kong found himself looking silently over to his computer, remembering just what was located on his personal drives.

He was well aware that, just a hundred nautical miles off the coast, the Confederate carrier group was sitting by. The Clinton Task Group carried as much firepower as an entire division of the PLAAF, and he had the codes and the authority now to call on them.

It is truly amazing how the world can change in just a single rotation.

Whether he *would* call on them was another matter, and it would depend heavily on just how bad things became. Clearing a Confederate strike group into Block airspace would be akin to political suicide, which was something he had no interest in unless not doing so was *actual* suicide.

He looked up, noting that the Chairman was still raving but was now beginning to wind down.

He stood, silencing the people's Chairman, and saluted.

"I will immediately enact your orders, Chairman."

The man across the desk nodded slowly. "See that you do, General."

Kong picked up his computer and saluted again before he left the office, nodding to the two men he'd handpicked to guard their leader.

▶▶▶

NACS *WILLIAM J. CLINTON*

▼

▲

▶ THE *CLINTON* WAS a Ford Class aircraft carrier, one of the last of her kind to ever be built, in all probability. She and her sisters ruled the oceans, as had their predecessors for over a hundred years before. Their mastery of the sea and air had only been challenged once in all that time, just under two decades ago.

In that time, seven of the *Clinton*'s sister ships had gone down in under six months with every one of their escorts. It had been a dark time for the Navy, then the United States Navy, a time when the newly formed Block military ruled the skies.

That made their current assignment all the more ironic.

"Latest intel from Beijing, sir."

Admiral Corner nodded, accepting the delivery and sending it directly to his tactical board. The plate lit up, showing icons across the map of the city. "CRO get their birds online?"

"Yes sir."

"Well that's a bright spot in a dark fucking day," Corner said, lips curling up as he looked over the intel. "Jesus, they landed a lot of those bastards in Beijing."

"Almost a thousand count, as of last numbers, Admiral."

Corner shook his head slowly as he looked over the angry red icons listed all across the city view. The Block was in deep shit—he could see that without half trying—but they were being about as prideful about it as could be expected. He wasn't surprised. Hell, he almost didn't blame them. Honestly, he doubted that anyone in the Confederation would be any more eager to call in an air strike from a Block task force.

That didn't mean it wasn't a stupid ass thing to do, ignoring all your available assets, especially when the brief on the aliens was as bad as it was.

Unfortunately, there wasn't much he could do at the moment, not without tripping off a second Block war that none of them could afford. If he went in without being invited, Block air defense would do its damnedest to chew up his boys and, if he were pressed hard enough, Corner would painfully admit that they'd actually do a pretty damned good job of it too.

That would trigger more fighting along every border, and *that* would just be a distraction no one could afford at the moment.

So he had to sit here, bobbing in the ocean like a toy ship in a bathtub, while the world began to go up in flames around them.

Corner looked away from the map, disgusted. "What's the news from home?"

"New York is under heavy attack, as is Los Angeles, sir. We've got unconfirmed reports of landings in other major cities, but right now it's all a mess," the messenger said. "When the *Liberty* went up, it put a hole in our comm network you could drive the *Clinton* through, with room to spare for the rest of the group. Some stations are still dead. Some are just starting to come back online."

"Fabulous." Corner supposed he should have known better than to ask, but he had always been a glutton for punishment. "I don't suppose you have any good news for me?"

"Not as such, Admiral. Right now there's nothing but red coming through the pipeline."

"If Beijing doesn't get their heads out of their ass soon, there'll be a lot more red in the pipeline, son," Corner said heavily, "because we're going to have to nuke the city if it looks like those things are successfully digging in."

"Yes sir. We've not seen anything that bad come through yet, sir."

"Small favors, son. Small favors."

▶▶▶

▶ *Gaia observed it all.*

*That was, in many ways, the only thing she normally ever did, though she wouldn't exactly describe it as such. It was more accurate to say that she **experienced** everything than to imply that she was in some way a Peeping Tom, but the end result was much the same.*

She felt the anxiety of the world leaders, their generals and admirals. She knew the fear and tension of the soldiers as they marched and rode to war against a foe that, for the first time in millennia, she knew to be truly unknown.

*More importantly, she experienced the sheer terror of those on the streets as they faced creatures that triggered every deep-seated primal horror that seemed to exist in the human psyche. Some of those even existed in **her** psyche it seemed, because she felt that same terror again within herself as she watched the Drasin begin to reproduce within the cities they had targeted.*

It was only a mere doubling for now, but she was well aware that would not last.

Gaia turned her focus to something she had spent the last few decades toying with, as had her people. She began to tinker with the little electronic ones and zeroes that now ruled the world she inhabited, sometimes altering orders as they were sent in to point soldiers in the right direction, and in extreme cases even creating new orders from the ether.

In less chaotic times she wouldn't dare be so blatant, because while she knew of no way she could be harmed by humans, it wasn't in her interest to have them searching for ways to neutralize her influence.

As things stood, however, she felt confident that even if her machinations were noticed, they would be discounted as memory lapses, glitches, or other unremarkable happenings in the course of war. She'd gotten away with far more devious actions in the past.

It was her way.

▶ ▶ ▶

▼

BENEATH 1600 PENNSYLVANIA AVENUE, WASHINGTON, D.C.

▲

▶ THE REAL-TIME war map had depressingly large black spots still filling it, but those were smaller than they had been. Routing SIGINT (Signals Intelligence) through alternate means was tricky business, but it could be done. Some were now running through the civilian network because it had mostly been moved over to optical fibers in the last few decades. Other bits were now being bounced off recently launched microsats that were actually just tiny communications arrays tied to helium-filled balloons.

It was a stopgap solution to the gaping holes in their communication network, but it was low cost, fast, and it worked. Between those microsats, orbiting UAVs, and the civilian network, they were almost fully back to operational standards.

That meant that now they all knew just how bad the situation really was.

"Jesus. Look at the chunk they took out of Los Angeles."

"Get reinforcements down the coast. Who's in the area?" the President demanded.

"The GW is in San Diego for refit. They can launch from there."

"Do it," he ordered. "How are we in other cities?"

"They've ignored most of middle America," the general answered. "We do have landings in Texas, the Dallas/Fort Worth region of course, but most of middle America has low population density . . . I really think that these things are just targeting people."

"That doesn't make me feel much better, General," the President sighed, slumping in his chair.

"No sir, I understand that, but it gives us a fighting chance."

"Do we have any forces in Texas?"

"Not a lot, sir. Mostly just Guard units and, to be honest, they're slow to move."

"Are we going to lose Dallas, then?" Conner asked tiredly.

"Maybe not. Locals are armed in that area. Between civilians and police there's a pretty heavy firefight all through Dallas."

Conner blinked. "Are they actually doing anything?"

The General shook his head. "No. Just distracting them at best. Casualties are heavy as hell, but the aliens are taking smaller chunks out of the city than in L.A. and New York."

"Hardly seems worth it, the loss of lives," Conner said as he shook his head.

There was a long silence around the table before the general spoke up again. "Do you want me to order the civilians out of the area? I don't know how many would obey . . . "

"No," President Conner said, shaking his head. "No, I want you to tell them to get bigger guns."

"Sir?"

"It's their city, General. Arm them with the weapons they need to defend it."

"Yes sir."

"The same goes for everywhere else," Conner ordered. "If we can't get troops into an area those things are in, drop weapons. I want every man, woman, and child on this blue-green ball of ours armed if that is what it takes. Whatever it takes, people. Clean my country, clean our *world,* of those damn things."

"Yes sir."

▼

DALLAS, TEXAS

▲

▶THE SOUND OF the building as it began to topple was frightening, a steel screaming sound that shot to the core of everyone for blocks around. The fighting had been furious in the area as men threw themselves at the things that had crashed into the city from above, but the aliens just shrugged off their weapons with depressing ease.

The few Guard units that had made it into the area helped, their heavier weapons able to at least blunt the actions of the insect-like monsters that were tearing the city apart building by building, but they were too few and ineffective.

The skyscraper thundered into the ground, sending smoke and dust billowing out to cloud the vision and lungs of everyone for a mile. In the aftermath of the crash there was an eerie silence that seemed to echo as heavily as the crash itself, the shock of the moment outlasting the violence that caused it.

As the dust slowly settled, visibility improved until those who hadn't been smart enough to take serious cover could see the rubble littering downtown. The collapsed building had taken out one of its neighbors and severely compromised three others, but it seemed that it had also taken out the *things* they'd been fighting.

Unfortunately, what seemed to be wasn't what was.

The rubble moved, shifting as things crawled out from under it and began moving around again. The Guardsmen watched, dismayed, as the creatures began to crawl over the next building, tearing chunks out and literally *eating* the debris as they went.

▼

NEW DELHI, INDIA

▲

▶ THE CITY WAS so thickly populated that even after millions escaped, there were still a hundred million people within the danger area as the alien menace tore through the eclectic mix of old slums and new high-rises that marked New Delhi's skyline.

Tens of thousands had died in the initial impacts, conservatively estimating the numbers. A hundred thousand more in the hours since, but the fighting raged heavier in this place than anywhere else on Earth. Few had the weapons needed to make a real impact on the aliens, however, and with each passing minute ten thousand more lives were ended.

The Block military tried to move in, but if a city like New York had congested traffic then New Delhi lived life at a standstill. Even with tanks plowing through the mess, they were literally being stopped as the number of cars being pushed aside came to rest against the next few abandoned cars behind them, eventually forming a bank of wrecked vehicles that had to be pulled down with winches.

So instead they had men running ahead, moving the cars out of the way one by one to let the tanks through. It was slow, tedious work, and they had miles to go before they even reached the hottest points in the battle.

The Block Air Force was already on site, and airborne troops were dropping into the city from all sides. They had only light weapons at the moment and little enough ammunition that for the immediate future they provided a minimal threat to their foe.

The City of New Delhi was burning as it was being eaten slowly from within.

▶▶▶

▶ *For Gaia the experience of invasion was sickening, somewhat like being down with a particularly virulent infection she supposed. At the moment it was light, merely the beginnings of what was to come. She didn't feel sick the way humans did, never had, but were she human she supposed that she would now be feeling chills and light-headedness.*

Instead, all she really felt was disgust.

▼

CHAPTER FIVE

▲

▶ "SO THAT'S THE *Odyssey,* is it?"

Out across the sound from where they stood was a slab of metal, steel blue with white lettering, sticking out of the water like a sword rising from the lake. This sword, however, would never be drawn again, and that made the scene a pitiable one.

"It used to be," Eric told his companion soberly, only half paying attention to the conversation.

The wreckage of the *Odyssey* was in better shape than he'd expected, though he knew from the data ping he'd gotten that significant parts of it had to have survived. He knew that the only way the ship could be in the shape he was seeing was if the counter-mass generators had survived right to the moment of impact.

With most of the mass of the ship hidden from the real-world universe, the *Odyssey's* structural integrity would have been much more effectively strengthened. It was still a near miracle that his ship was in as few pieces as it was, but at least there would be things they could salvage, things they could use.

"So how are we getting over to that?" Lyssa asked from where she was sitting on a cement embankment.

Eric glanced across the waterline and nodded to the south. "There's a marina. We'll steal a boat."

"Commandeer."

"Excuse me?"

"I'm a police officer, I don't *steal* boats," she told him simply. "I commandeer them."

Eric snorted but nodded as he gestured. "Whatever you say, Officer."

▶▶▶

▶ The *Odyssey* was resting in fifty feet of water, the keel section rising out of the depths at a thirty-degree angle and overhanging the sound at its apex. The remaining habitat cylinder was against the city coastline about a mile and a half south, resting amid the shattered wreckage of what appeared to be a few multimillion-dollar yachts.

He wasn't concerned with the habitat cylinder, however. The materials that he, and the city, would need were in the keel of the ship. He just hoped that the majority of it was intact.

"Wait here," he told Lyssa as he maneuvered the boat alongside the wrecked keel of the *Odyssey*. "She'll have taken on water, and you don't have a suit."

"Will any of it be any good after that crash?" she asked, not for the first time.

"I lived. The hardware I'm going after is a lot sturdier than I am," he replied. "If CM was up on impact, the gear should be intact."

He reached out and grabbed a protruding piece of steel, peeled from the hull by either an internal explosion or perhaps something blowing through from the other side, and pulled himself up. Jumping would have been easier, but it would have destabilized the boat, and he didn't see the need to dunk his companion.

Eric crawled into the ship through the hole, hopping down into what was once a storeroom. He looked around, noting the scattered food packets, and knew he was a fair distance from the ordnance supply and the Museum. Unfortunately, both were well below the waterline.

Well, nothing to be done about it. Let's get to work.

Somewhere above him Eric heard a scraping sound, the grinding of metal on stone and the hammering blows of heavy feet on his decks.

Shit. Must have picked up some hitchhikers on the way down . . . or since she came to a rest. He shifted his grip on the Priminae GWIZ and made his way across the slanted deck of the storeroom to the interior corridor.

The corridor led down into a darkness so pitch-black that he had to use his suit's active night vision mode. There just wasn't enough light to amplify with the passives. So Eric walked down into a green-bathed hall, warily clearing each room and branch corridor he passed. But he had checked three rooms before he thought to turn the dial down on the GWIZ, and Eric thanked whatever gods looked out for fools and Marines that he hadn't fired a shot off in close quarters at the previous setting.

He made his way further down, well below where he was sure the waterline was. So far he was still dry footed, but that could change the second he opened any of the dogged hatches he had to pass through. First, though, he needed to get to the cargo elevators because they were located right next to the main auxiliary maintenance shafts, and those would let him get down to the flight deck and munitions stores below.

If he were really lucky, he might just get there and back off the ship before the unwelcome guests on his onetime home and command found him.

Yeah. That'll be the day.

Eric was sure that Mr. Murphy was just waiting for the right time to make his appearance. Things had already gone far better than he'd expected, and that just asked for some sort of critical problem to crop up.

Oh well, nothing to be done about it. Onward and . . . well, downward in this case.

▶▶▶

▶ *Gaia walked behind Weston as he descended into the depths of what had once been a proud ship, his ship. She felt his sorrow, his pride, his regrets as though they were her own. She had walked with humans many times in the past, reveling in their triumphs and consoling them in their defeats, but this time there was an urgency that she had never felt before.*

The difference was between watching and being a part of something, because now was the first time in her memory that she herself had come under threat.

She found herself both thrilled at the sensation . . . and terrified by it.

"Turn left, Eric," she whispered. "The next corridor is flooded."

▶▶▶

▶ Eric turned left.

He couldn't say why, actually, just a chill down his spine and the urge to take a longer route had come upon him as he laid eyes on the tightly dogged hatch ahead of him. It wouldn't add that much to his distance anyway. He'd learned a long time ago that when you had a feeling, barring the availability of contradicting evidence, you should follow where it led.

Another heavy scratching sound, several decks away, sent shivers down his spine. The view of the corridors through his night vision systems wasn't exactly relaxing, any more than the tight, abandoned corridors themselves were. Getting caught in an enclosed area by monsters like the Drasin was about the worst nightmare he could imagine. Eric was the sort of man who preferred the open sky to fight his battles.

Too bad we don't always get what we want.

He reached the maintenance hatch, just up angle from the powerless elevators. Like everything else on the *Odyssey,* the hatch was built solid, with double-dogged latches and multiple breaks to prevent decompression in the depths of space. For a man in enhancing armor, however, they were pretty easy doors to manipulate.

He got the first one open and crawled into the smaller space, turning back to dog the hatch out of habit before he stopped himself and left it open.

May need to get out of there in a hurry. Let's leave a back door, just in case.

There was a ladder heading down, only now it headed off at an angle. Eric used it to control his slide as he dropped down to the lower level of the *Odyssey*'s keel. Three hatches later he let himself out, planting one foot on the wall and one on the floor as he looked around the immense space of the hangar deck he'd emerged on.

Most of the *Odyssey* had been evacuated before she, and he, went down in the fight, but not all of it. There was a twisted wreck of a machine that he recognized as an Archangel that had had its wings well and truly clipped. The once-sleek fighter would not fly again in this life.

Eric pushed it aside, moving up now in a crawl as he made his way up the awkward incline of the deck, heading for munitions, weapons, and the Museum. The magnetic boots built into his armor helped, thankfully, keeping him from sliding down into the darkness as he climbed. The enhanced senses of his armor kept updating him of the increased noises from above him, letting Eric know that the clock was ticking on his little mission.

▶▶▶

▶ Lyssa bobbed along with the powerboat, idly floating about fifty feet off the port side of the *Odyssey*'s keel. She'd moved far enough away not to be driven into the metal reef by waves or wind while she waited.

It was the barest hint of motion that caught her eye, and Lyssa half turned toward it before her mind caught up with her and she recognized what exactly she was looking at.

It was crawling out over the metal beam of the *Odyssey*'s keel, tearing a piece of the metal apart like it was pulling a fluff of cotton candy from the rest of the ball. She watched as the creature hunched over the prize for a moment, then seemed to gobble it down in a series of motions that reminded her of a mix between a spider and a snake feeding.

Lyssa slowly dropped down behind the controls of the powerboat, eyes not leaving the horror for an instant. She couldn't bring herself to look away as warring impulses tore at her. Part of her wanted to turn, to run, to hide in the dark if she could. The thing she was looking at triggered every primal urge to terror she had. Every core facet of her mind and body was screaming at her to get the hell away.

The more rational part of her mind, the thinking brain, told her to watch and to learn. It told her not to look away because knowledge may be the only thing that saved her life, and she wouldn't learn by hiding her head in the sand.

It was to her shame, perhaps, that the rational side wasn't the reason she didn't look away. Lyssa tried to force herself to turn, to move, to do *something*, but instead she just froze there as the first of the alien bugs was joined by a second, and then a third.

The thinking brain wanted her to learn, the primal part wanted her to run, but Lyssa found herself caught by the sheer terror that gripped an even deeper part of her psyche. She froze in place and desperately hoped that they wouldn't notice her if she stayed very, *very* still.

▶▶▶

▶Getting the doors open without power while at a thirty-degree slant to the stern was a hassle that Eric doubted the designers had ever thought of. If they had, it was clear that they'd discarded the thought as too unlikely to bother with. He managed it, however, and pulled himself into the munitions storage of the *Odyssey*, then took a moment to rest and survey the area.

It was a mess, was the first thing that he obviously concluded.

Cargo pallets had been tossed around, broken open against each other and the deck and walls. The crash had spread their food stores and other general provisions across the decks, leaving most of it entirely unrecoverable.

Thankfully he hadn't come for any of that.

Eric half crawled up the incline, making his way to the first level armory. There he continued past, ignoring the weapons left locked in their ready-release cases. Those had all survived, but would take more time to get to than they were worth.

Inside the next section, however, was the treasure.

The Museum was intact.

Eric was somewhat surprised, even though he'd counted on it. It was one thing to know how tightly secured the objects in the Museum were, but it was another to see it.

Suits of powered armor lined the walls. Rifles filled fast-deployment cases bolted to the floor. The SOCOM armory was designed to be deployed in a hurry, just not from *underwater*. So while he was gratified that the equipment was intact, he still had some work to do.

The *Odyssey* had been equipped with a War Level SOCOM deployment capability, on par with any aircraft carrier of her day.

Now, let's see if we still have . . . Eric half thought to himself and half mumbled as he pulled open an electrical panel and threw a breaker. *Ah, power.*

The lights snapped on, running on battery and capacitors. Without the main reactor he only had a few hours of power, and only where the circuits weren't shredded. The *Odyssey* had been designed with a decentralized power grid. Batteries and capacitors dotted the hull by the literal thousands, but Eric had no way of knowing just how many he had access to at the moment, or what kind of grounded shorts may be sucking power. So he got to work.

"The ship crawls, my Captain."

Eric jumped, jolting as he looked around for the voice that had whispered in his ear. "Who . . . what?"

"Forget me so soon, my Captain?"

The woman's voice whispered again, sounding amused.

Eric froze, a barely remembered slice of the past surfacing.

"Gaia?" he said softly. "Your name is Gaia?"

"So you remember. I am pleased," she whispered to him. *"You had been missing your thoughts, since the crash. Short-term memory has been disrupted, but you recall my name. I am pleased, my Captain."*

"Where are you?" Eric demanded, eyes turning wildly as he tried to pinpoint her location.

"I am . . . everywhere . . ." she whispered, her voice echoing from every corner before fading as she laughed away into the distance. *"Hurry, oh Captain, my Captain. Your ship* **crawls.** *"*

Eric stood still for a long moment as the last whispered echoes faded, and then he forced himself to move again. He still had a job to do, even though he now had a burning curiosity a thousand times greater than the one he felt of the Priminae and their "Central."

What the hell are Central and **Gaia?**

▶▶▶

▶There were more of them on the wreck of the *Odyssey* now, and less of the *Odyssey* for them to crawl over. Lyssa was stunned by how fast the alien things were tearing the ship apart, and it was clear that they were not slowing down. No, far from it. They were speeding up at a terrifying rate.

She drew out her radio carefully, keying open a channel.

"Weston, if you can hear me, those things are tearing the place apart. They'll be on you in minutes at this rate. I don't care how deep you are. Do whatever it is that you've got to do and get the hell out of there."

She paused for a moment, listening to the static on the channel. Normally her radio was as clear as crystal since it used a digital packet system, but now it was clear that she was transmitting on an older backup channel.

"Weston, come back," she demanded a short time later. "You've got trouble on that tin roof of yours. Come back."

With nothing but static on the radio for the next long moment, Lyssa growled and tossed her mic aside, letting it clatter to the bottom of the boat.

"Damn it!" she hissed, eyes still warily watching the remains of the NACS *Odyssey* as she was slowly eaten away in the distance.

▶▶▶

▶Sometimes Eric was truly shocked by the capability of the things on his ship.

The *Odyssey* had always been designed to move under CM fields in order to help counterbalance the effects of acceleration. In the habitat modules this was reinforced by the spinning centrifuge that provided the crew with a gravity replacement, but below decks any acceleration was a problem due to the microgravity environment.

So everything there had to be built to operate not only in microgravity but also under varying degrees of acceleration, including and exceeding one full Earth gravity.

The loader he was piloting was a perfect example, easily using its powerful electromagnetic feet to walk up the inclined deck. The heavy-duty machine had no difficulty picking up deployment crates, armor cases, and everything else he needed. Delivering them up the inclined flight deck was relatively easy at that point, though the going was slow because Eric had little familiarity with the controls.

The big yellow machine was a chunky bipedal rig with a full-body interface. Not something that moved fast enough to be good in combat, but useful enough for when you had to shift large masses in microgravity or under acceleration effects.

It could handle several tons of material, even under acceleration effects like gravity, and it stomped up the incline with ease. Actually, the biggest problem he was having was that while the machine itself was designed to handle a gravity well, the interface system really was intended for microgravity. It wasn't impossible to handle, obviously, but in gravity it was awkward to say the least.

Eric had delivered almost all of what he'd wanted to one of the port Cats that registered as still being above the waterline and was about to head back for more when a rumble ran through the deck, through his machine, and through *him*. Eric twisted around, looking for the source, but found it when his stomach lurched and jumped up into his chest as the deck suddenly dropped under him.

Linked and strapped as he was, he dropped with it. The brief sensation of freefall was a sign that it was time to haul ass.

Forget the rest of it. I've got enough.

Eric dropped out of the loader and pulled open the control panel for the catapult launcher he was using, throwing a couple of breakers to patch the system into emergency power. The electromagnets hummed in the background as they began to charge.

"Alright. Load one . . . " Eric mumbled to himself as he pressed the switch, sending a deployment module accelerating out the port hatch at high speed. "Away. Now . . . load two . . . "

▶▶▶

▶ "Holy shit!"

Lyssa's self-imposed silence had been born of terror and was broken by terror when she saw a massive object blast away from the wreckage of the *Odyssey,* arcing over her boat and crashing into the water not fifty meters away. The swell thrown up by the splash caused her to bob heavily up and down as she stared at where the water had swallowed up whatever it was.

"What the hell is that damned fool doing?" she muttered, shaking her head in near disgust.

A bubbling disturbance breaking the surface was her first clue that a method may actually exist within the madness of her erstwhile companion. A few seconds after that a large cargo assault craft breached the surface and was bobbing some distance away.

She was distracted from checking it out closer when another blast made her duck. This time the splash of water was close enough to soak her through before she had time to turn around and see what it was.

Lyssa paled, hands clutching the controls of her commandeered boat as she hit the starter switch and threw power to the engines.

*Time to get the hell out of here before that crazy bastard **sinks** me.*

▶▶▶

▶ "Three away," Eric said to himself as the third deployment module launched out the port hatch. He shuffled his way over to the fourth one and was working on the control panel when a sound caught his attention.

He looked up-deck, in the direction of the sound, and paled beneath his armor. He'd been so focused on his work that he hadn't noticed the daylight filtering in from above him where the Drasin had chewed through the doors covering the entrance to the flight deck. Against the light of the Sun he could see the monstrous silhouettes skittering across the inclined deck, moving far too quickly in his direction for comfort.

Eric cast his thoughts back to the Priminae weapon he'd left with the loader and slowly began to edge back in that direction.

If they don't spot me, maybe I can get to . . .

That idea went up in smoke when three of the alien beasts surged forward, apparently giving up on whatever method they'd been using to keep from sliding down the deck. As they surged toward him, Eric kicked off the deck himself, catapulting across the space and falling forty feet to where the loader was parked.

The magnets in the big machine's feet were more than strong enough to handle the impact of his form, armor and all, but even cushioned as he was the impact with the machine blew the breath from his lungs. Eric forced himself to move even though his body was practically convulsing, rolling into the steel cage of the pilot's compartment and slamming his hand down on the controls.

The harness dropped over him, securing him in place as he reached for the controls while his lungs filled with the air they'd been demanding for the last few seconds. He gasped inside his armor even as his hands began working the stick grip instinctively.

The grip felt familiar in his hand as he jammed it forward and brought the big machine's right arm up to block just as the closest Drasin leapt at him.

Eric felt the loader sway back under that weight, and he began to sweat just a little. His own impact had been negligible to the loader's magnetic contacts, but the mass of a Drasin? That was something else.

Have to get this thing off me, or we're both going to experience one hell of a tumble.

The thirty-degree incline of the deck would give him more than enough time to accelerate to lethal speeds if the magnetic contacts of the loader lost their hold, which was likely for both him and the Drasin or Drasins who caused it. There was only one of him, however, and Eric suspected that the enemy would be more than happy with the trade.

He, on the other hand, didn't consider it a fair exchange in the least.

Eric grunted as he forced his left hand up to match the right, bringing in the loader's left manipulating arm to grab the Drasin as it hissed and struck at the right. He got the hydraulic claw around its head and thumbed the control hat over as far as he could, letting the claw slowly hiss shut. It took seconds, not really a weapon he'd choose to make use of. But as the hydraulics began to crush down on the alien carapace, Eric could easily hear crackling sounds erupting from his foe.

The carapace gave under the pressure, a spray of superheated silicon erupting out of it and coating the machine. Eric ignored it, tossing the now motionless Drasin aside as he twisted around and looked for the next.

It found him first.

He saw it coming, but the loader was too slow to react. The Drasin slammed into the machine, causing it to sway back again under the massive impact, and drove its barbed legs in through the open cockpit. Eric twisted as best he could, narrowly avoiding the leg as it stabbed through the padding of the restraints and seat. He twisted his head, looking at the lethal limb just inches away, and then refocused on the enemy with new intensity.

Eric pulled back the other arm of the loader, then slammed it forward into the Drasin with as much power as the hydraulic powered machine could muster. It wasn't much for striking power, honestly—the machine moved too slow for that—but for pure irresistible strength there wasn't a lot around that could match it.

Slowly Eric pushed the beast back, the barbed leg grating against the cast steel of the loader as the Drasin was slowly forced out of the cockpit. The creature clawed at the pushing arm, hissing and spitting the whole time. With more leverage, Eric hefted the beast off the loader and then slammed it down with enough force to dent the deck plates.

It clawed and scrambled at the loader's arm as Eric pulled back and began to pound on the beast with the newly freed right arm of the machine. The first three blows seemed to stun it, the next five cracked the carapace in a dozen places, and the last two stilled its struggles for good. Eric looked up, seeing more of the beasts coming his way, scrambling down the inclined deck like swarming insects.

"Right. Time to ditch," Eric muttered, leaning forward into the inclined deck as he began to thump *toward* the charging beasts.

He made it to Cat about twenty meters ahead of the swarm, wishing he had guns on the machine he was using but honestly figuring it wouldn't matter.

"Hey boys," he said over the open com, knowing that they could probably neither hear nor understand him. "Got a little surprise for ya. Semper fi, you rat bastards. This is *my* goddamn ship! I choose how she goes out, not you!"

He stepped into the Cat panel, locking the loader into place as best he could as he leaned forward. A blur of motion to his left made him turn at the torso, reaching out automatically with his left arm to snap the lunging Drasin out of the air. He held it in place, hissing and screaming, while he contacted the detonators he'd set earlier and gave them a nudge.

The distant crump was barely audible, but Eric knew that the blasts were small and directed away from his current location. Shaped charges blew down into engineering, sending plasma into the reactor room and penetrating containment.

The *Odyssey* used a fusion system, a very safe and stable reactor technology that wasn't prone to the meltdown problems that plagued fission systems. It did, however, run on compressed hydrogen gas.

When the hydrogen was ignited by the plasma and mixed with an influx of oxygen from the breach, things got hot in a hurry. The reactor itself could have handled the heat easily, but it was the containment tanks that took the hit, and they weren't proofed to the same degree. Engineering vanished into a ball of flame so blue as to be practically invisible until it began melting the plastics littered around the area.

The fires of hell erupted out of engineering, rolling upward through the decks, pushing the air before it. When it reached the flight deck, the pounds per square inch were low, but the square footage was *immense*.

The entire far wall blew in with enough force to make Eric cringe as he ducked down and sent the launch command to the Cat. The electromagnetic launch exploded forward, driving him and the loader out at five Gs, straight at the port-side hatch. Eric folded the loader's big steel arms in front of him as he exploded out of his ship even as the fires roared past.

▶▶▶

▶ "Holy son of a . . . "

Lyssa hugged the control console of the boat as blasts of fire exploded out of the *Odyssey*'s keel at even points along the side, moving up from the waterline toward where the bow was hanging fifty meters over the water.

A plume of fire then erupted from the bow and scorched the sky for hundreds of meters above the ship in a display of pyrotechnics that Lyssa expected would be visible for miles around. She was so focused on the blast of flames that she almost missed the smoking projectile that arced over her head, a scorched yellow missile that left a wake in the air as it fell into the water of the sound a few hundred meters away.

For a long moment Lyssa just sat there, eyes moving from the splash point of yet another mysterious object, the fiery wreck of the *Odyssey* that was now smoking like a giant cannon sticking out of the sound, and finally the bobbing assault craft floating around her.

This whole situation just went to hell in short order.

She didn't know what to do, but for a moment she took her time thinking about it. Then she hit the starter and turned her boat around to head for the closest assault boat. She didn't know what the hell had happened to Weston, but she needed the gear he'd gotten off that cursed ship.

She was heading for it when suddenly all three of the assault boats got a mind of their own and turned in unison, heading for the shore.

Not knowing what else to do, Lyssa followed suit.

The craft she was following were amphibious assault craft. She'd seen enough of them in the last few months of the war. They were designed to be launched from carrier task groups for large-scale assaults on enemy beachheads, though it was pretty clear that these had been upgraded.

The ones she'd ridden in the war weren't fully automated, for one thing.

As they reached the shore, she found her attention drawn away from the assault landers to a yellow shape moving jerkily under the surface of the water. She watched it warily from a distance as it rose up from the depths and then breached near the shore. She recognized it as a utility loader, but it was bigger than any she'd seen before.

Water sluiced off the construction yellow steel as the machine lumbered up onto the shore and turned around.

Lyssa let out a breath of relief when she recognized the armor sitting in the pilot's compartment of the big machine.

"Captain," she growled, "you are the biggest pain in the ass I've ever worked with, and I'm a former Marine who joined the damned NYPD. Do you have any idea how many assholes you meet between those two groups?"

Eric just looked back at her with his head cocked to one side, silent for a long moment before he chose to speak.

"Lyss, until you've dealt with politicians and reporters, you don't know the meaning of the word."

She shook her head as she beached the boat and climbed up over the bow, jumping to the bank. "You get what you needed?"

"I got what I could," he answered as he popped open the crash bars holding him into the pilot's position of the loader. "Was interrupted before I could get it all."

As Eric pulled himself out of the machine, dropping to the soft bank, she turned and looked back over Long Island Sound. There, out in the middle of the water, the keel of the *Odyssey* still rose out over the waves. It was now smoking like the tube of a cannon that had just been fired, but it was still surprisingly intact.

"You get them all?"

Eric considered for a moment, "I think so. They're tough, but they can't take an overpressure wave much better than we can. I'll deploy drones to make sure, but yeah, I think I got them all."

"Good."

Down the shore from where they stood, three fully laden assault cargo landers shifted to land mode and slowly trundled ashore with their packages.

CHAPTER SIX

National Guard HQ, *Intrepid* Sea, Air, & Space Museum

▸ MEN AND WOMEN had stopped what they were doing and were gaping at the skyline over the city, pointing at the searing flames.

"What the hell is that?" Potts demanded, glaring at the sky as if it were to blame.

"No idea, sir."

"I'm getting real damned sick of hearing that, son."

"Sorry sir."

"Do we have a unit over that way?"

"Nothing large for sure," his aide answered. "I can check for scout units."

"Don't bother," Potts said. "Get on the link to the flyboys and girls up there and find out what that was. If it's anything interesting, have one of our recon squads check it out up close."

"Yes sir."

The general shifted his focus back to the map that showed fighting all up and down the island of Manhattan. He had men engaged with the enemy in every borough of the city, but the biggest concentration was without a doubt right on the island. They had checkpoints at every way on and off the island, but from what the brief said this wasn't a job where containment did a whole lot. It was a war of extermination. Either the enemy died or humanity did.

Potts wasn't going to lose this one.

"Tell Third Platoon to move their ass. We've got men pinned down and getting cut to ribbons on Eighth," he said, looking over the tactical display. "And get some air support over them. That's our major advantage here. Let's use it."

"Yes sir. We're rushing the turnaround on reloading the aircraft, but another wing will be in place in three minutes."

Potts growled. "That's three minutes too long. Has the President declared a state of emergency?"

"Yes sir. . . ?" The aide trailed off, confused.

"Then I want our old weaponized drones brought out of mothballs."

"General Potts, sir, that violates . . . I don't know *how* many international laws . . . "

Potts snorted. "This is New York, not some foreign nation. If the people of this country want my commission or my head, they can have it when this is over. The rest of the planet can sit and spin. I am *not* losing this city. Issue the order."

"Y . . . yes sir."

One thing most every civilized nation on the planet agreed on, one of the very few things, was that while it was impossible to completely shove the genie back in the bottle, autonomous weapons platforms were not to be tolerated. Drones were cheap, easy to deploy, and too well stealthed for the comfort of any nation, and those that still manufactured them were under deep international sanctions.

That had all stemmed from the use of Chinese and Indian drones to drop high-explosive military payloads on New York,

London, and Madrid in the mid-twenty-first century. Neither nation was directly involved, of course, but they both sold their obsolete drones on the open market and the value of the weapons had long since been hammered home to terrorist groups worldwide.

Useless in their original tasking, drones like the Carnivore and Terran Raptor were sublime at sowing terror and confusion. Cheap, easy to use and deploy, and capable of wiping out a city block before anyone even thought to look for them, they quickly became the weapon of choice for terror groups worldwide.

By the 2070s, several international treaties existed and India had been embargoed for almost a decade for selling automated weapons to nonaligned parties. It was only after India finally capitulated upon joining the Block that the international supply of the ugly weapons began to dwindle. Historically, drone warfare had become a disgusting relic of an earlier time, something taught in schools as a cautionary tale more than anything else.

It was a stance that Potts agreed with. To his mind, if you were going to kill a man you should have the guts and honor to at least accept a degree of risk yourself, no matter how small. Pushing a button and killing people by remote was no way to do things. It made soldiers lazy and careless.

The world had politicians for that already. It didn't need to add soldiers to the list.

Now, however, he needed more guns in the sky and drones were one way to do it. It would take time to get them out of storage, tested, and armed, but all the more reason to start now. He'd take heat for it, but if it saved the city, then he'd happily turn the spit on himself.

Potts found himself distracted and scowling at the tactical display, however, and his mind was brought rudely back into the present.

"Why do we have fighting in the Bronx? I thought our units were still trying to get through traffic."

"They are, General. Those are reports from police and civilians mostly. We're monitoring them from overheads and intercepts," the aide said. "Almost eighty percent of reported fighting across the city is from police and civilian units, sir. We've got men and machines into some areas, and that number is growing fast, but the city is effectively gridlocked and we just don't have any of the highly mobile units available. They're all overseas at the moment."

Potts closed his eyes. "Damn."

There was just no way in hell that police units would have the firepower needed to crack these bastards, and in New York neither would civilians, for the most part. Lives were being lost and he knew that there wasn't a damned thing he could hope to do about it.

▶▶▶

PARKCHESTER, BRONX

▶DETECTIVE MIRADI HAD been an NYPD officer for the better part of his life, and until today he'd thought that he had honestly seen everything. Murders, rapes, riots, robberies. The weird cases, the brutal ones. Ones with happy endings, and ones that just never found an ending at all.

And then the sky fell in and his city was facing an alien invasion from space.

Teach me to offer up a challenge like that. The forty-year veteran grumbled as he emptied his personal weapon into the big walking spider that was in the process of *eating* a squad car outside his precinct.

His six millimeter wasn't having much effect, unfortunately, so he had to assume that the thing was better armored than your average punk in New York. That didn't take a whole lot, however, so he was at a loss as to what he should be doing.

"Rick!"

Miradi glanced over, recognizing the man scrambling in his direction.

"Hey Paul, little busy now. Unless you've got something with better kick than a service pistol, of course," he said dryly as he changed mags.

"Shotgun with slugs just piss these bastards off," Paul Reerson yelled, his back to the car Rick was covering behind.

"Better than this. I don't think that bastard has even *noticed* me!" Rick Miradi said in disgust.

"Trust me, Rick, I saw what these things can do. You don't *want* them to notice you," Paul told him between panting breaths. "They've got MilSpec lasers or something, I've never seen anything like it. Cut right through a SWAT van like butter, Rick. You get their attention, you're a dead man."

Miradi holstered his pistol. "So what? We watch them take apart the city, piece by piece?"

"Got word out. Some boys are out trying to clear cars off the expressway."

"For what? There's nobody driving now anyway."

Paul rolled his eyes. "You need to turn on your radio, Rick. National Guard is trying to get into the city, but all the damn roadways are blocked. They've moving tanks in."

"*Tanks??*" Rick gurgled, shocked. "Those things will do more damage than the giant spiders!"

"Jesus, Rick. Haven't you heard? Someone already set off a nuke or something in Central Park, and they've been dropping heavy ordnance all across the city for the last hour! Pay attention!"

"I've been *busy!*"

He'd lost five men since the whole damn mess started, and sure as hell didn't have time to worry about the rest of the city just then. His own were in trouble, and they came first.

He finally sighed, however, and shook his head. "What do they want us to do?"

"That's just it. We don't know. The Guard seems as confused as anyone, and they're not having the best of luck with these things either," John muttered. "Better than us, of course. Tanks can kill these things, but in a city those old tanks are sitting ducks for these things."

"Great."

"We've got some SWAT guys with heavier weapons running security at St. Barnabas. Thousands of people have moved in that direction, but those things are going to hit there within six hours at the rate they're moving. When they do . . . " John shook his head. "There's no way the cordon can hold back more than a couple of them, even with the big rifles they've got. We need to help the Guard get that deep into the borough, or we're going to lose a lot more lives."

"Fine." Rick nodded. "Let's go."

He let out a piercing whistle, getting the attention of the rest of the men with him, and waved them out. They all began to move back from the fighting, continuing to be ignored in large part by the giant spiders.

Downright insulting is what this is.

They were half a block away when his radio chirped in his ear. Rick touched the device, opening the channel. "Miradi."

"Rick, it's Lyssa. I have something you're going to want to see."

▶▶▶

ST. BARNABAS HOSPITAL, BRONX

▶COMMANDER IAN GRANGER glared out over the streets below him as he lay across the rooftop of the hospital. Thousands of people had flooded the area, most directed to the hospital by other officers when they were found stranded on the roads.

A civilian Bell 2900 chopper was picking people up fifteen at a shot, getting them out of the city, but that was like emptying the ocean with a teaspoon. The whole city was screaming for airlift, and there weren't enough birds in the world to do the job. So that left at least twenty or thirty thousand people here, right in the open.

When those things make it this far, it'll be a slaughter.

"Commander?"

"What is it?" Granger didn't even glance back. He was still sighting in the Hecate he had against known-distance targets. It would make things faster when the fighting started.

"We have an officer on the link, calling in a Code Ninety."

Granger snorted. "This whole city is a Code Ninety today."

Code Ninety was used as a terror alert, indicating that a citywide disaster was imminent. It required all available officers to drop anything they were doing and report for orders.

"Yes sir. It's just, she's pretty damned insistent."

"Fine, put her through to my channel," Granger said.

"Patching over now."

Granger waited a second before he heard a voice crackle to life on his earbud, a woman's voice he didn't recognize.

"Say again, this is Officer Lyssa Myriano, badge number Nine Five Seven Three. I am calling in a Code Ninety. We're Ferry Point Part and . . . "

"Officer Myriano," Granger cut in, her dossier lighting up his Augmented Reality HUD, "you're distracting my men, and you do not have the authority to issue a Code Ninety. I'm sure whatever you're seeing seems real important to you, but we're all well aware of the situation and we're busy dealing with it where we are."

"No, *you* don't understand, sir." Her voice came back, cutting him off. "Whatever you're dealing with, it can wait."

"Look, *officer*," Granger growled, more than a little sick of a beat cop telling him what could and could not wait, "I'll be the judge of . . . "

"What's your name, soldier?"

The voice on the line was *not* Officer Myriano, and that gave Granger pause for a moment. The tone stopped him even longer, something he'd last heard when he was in the war, though he didn't recognize the voice itself.

"Who is this?" Granger demanded, a tone of caution in his own voice.

"Captain Eric Stanton Weston, Confederate Marine Corps. I say again, what's your name, soldier?"

"Ian Granger. Look, Captain, I don't know what you're up to but I've got better than twenty thousand people here to protect. I don't have time for this bullshit."

"Granger, let me put to you this way . . . I'm sitting on about a hundred and twenty tons of military grade hardware and firepower. First come, first served."

The channel went dead a moment later, leaving Granger gaping in shock.

"Sir?"

Granger stood up from his sniper position, eyes sweeping the skies. "When is that chopper due back?"

▶▶▶

▶The NYPD had taken the brunt of the early fighting, losing dozens of men and women, quite possibly hundreds in the initial battles as they threw themselves into the fray the same way they would against any terrorist or violent offender. Unfortunately for them, they were facing no offender like they had ever dealt with in the past, and despite several heroic charges and stands, the dead showed little for their sacrifice aside from a handful of grateful citizens.

Those who survived learned the hard way that their sidearms, even their small artillery pieces, were of no value against the invaders tearing the city down piece by piece.

So it was that when the call went out, talking about military hardware available for the taking, it spread fast through the police channels. In a very short time a veritable tide of blue was sweeping through the city toward Ferry Point Park, confusing everyone who saw them pass.

▶▶▶

▼

FERRY POINT PARK, BRONX

▲

▶ "THIS IS A BIT higher tech than I was issued in the Corps," Lyssa said as she clenched and unclenched her fist in the enhancing armor.

Eric snorted. "The Corps does more with less than anyone else on the planet, so they always get less to do more with."

She laughed outright at that.

"That said, this is higher tech than almost anything on the planet, so it's not exactly a shocker. Enhancing armor is expensive but, more importantly, it's generally not terribly useful. Special Operations have been using unsealed versions for over a decade, mostly for fast hit-and-run operations deep inside Block lines."

He helped her stand up, letting her walk a couple of steps to get used to the feel of the armor, and remembered another woman taking her first steps in the bulky gear.

"Flex your legs," he said.

Lyssa picked one leg up off the ground, clearly straining a little. "That's some stiff."

"Kinetic absorption fibers," he told her. "Fancy name for shock absorbers built into the legs. Use your body weight to counter."

She did, settling down onto the supporting structure of the suit's legs. It was firm, but didn't really slow her down.

"Ok, now jump."

Lyssa looked at him, but nodded curtly and did as she was told.

"Holy!" she blurted out as she reached the apex of the jump at about thirty feet and began to windmill her arms in an attempt to hold herself steady.

"Stop that! Suit gyros will keep you upright," Weston called as she started to come back down. "Stick the landing! Flex!"

She did, legs taking the force as she hit the ground, lightly touching down in a three-point landing as she reached out with her right hand to control the motion.

"Trust your armor. It will keep you upright and informed," he said as she rose back up. "Energy is stored with every movement. If you don't use it in a jump, it's converted to stored potential energy and bled off into the suit's battery."

He handed her a rifle. "Here. Link this to your suit."

She closed her hand around the big grip of the battle rifle and it automatically lit up as her armor queried it and the two objects linked. She noted that the weapon was empty and automatically grabbed one of the magazines from the nearby box, slapping it home. The red lights turned green instantly, taking away one of Lyssa's many *unhappies*.

"Will this take down one of those things?" she asked, turning her focus back to Weston.

Eric nodded. "Yeah. They're armored, but these were designed to take out tanks toward the end of the war."

"Good." She walked over to another crate and settled down to strip and clear her weapon.

She'd used one just like it while she was in the service, and was well aware that while they came out of the crate at about eighty percent ready to use, that was a far cry from one hundred percent. She had a little work to do.

Eric watched her from a distance, not saying anything. He just grinned under his helmet and went back to his preparations. Lyssa had her contacts to bring in, but Eric had made a few over the years himself and New York housed more than one old friend.

In the distance behind him, an explosion tore through the city.

▼

CLEARVIEW, QUEENS

▲

▶ THE CHIME WAS out of place in the darkened home, but it was insistent and refused to be silenced until a burly man with graying hair thumped up the stairs from the basement and grabbed the link slate from where he'd left it on the local counter. He grunted, glaring at the message in more than a little disbelief before shaking his head finally.

"Melanie, I'm going out."

"You're *what?*" his wife demanded from the basement. "Ronald Blake, you're the one who insisted that we stay in and get in the basement! If you think I'm staying down here . . ."

"Woman, you stay the hell where you are. I'm going out!" he roared back over his shoulder.

The source of the voice had already ignored him, however, and was standing at the top of the stairs. "Don't you talk to me like that. I'm not one of your floozies from your service days."

"Don't I know it," he moaned as he grabbed an old flak jacket and threw it on, sliding a pistol into his belt. "They wouldn't be questioning me right now."

"That's because none of them had anything other than air between their ears, and you know it. Now what the hell are you doing this for?"

"An old friend is calling out the clan," he said as he walked to the door.

At the door to the house he paused, glancing back. "Run off more water while the pressure is still good, and stay in the basement and away from windows. That blast earlier may not be the last, and the next one might be close enough to blow the glass in."

"We have shatterproof composite windows, Ron. You picked them out, remember?"

"Yeah, well, stay away from the windows anyway." He grunted, pausing to think on it. Then he pulled the gun from his belt and handed it over to her. "Take this."

"Aren't you going to need it?"

"You saw those things on the news before they took out the cameraman," he grunted. "That popgun won't do a damn thing."

"So what do I need it for?"

"For humans," Ronald Blake said before he stepped out and closed the door behind him.

▶▶▶

▶Across town, in another borough, a similar conversation was happening, though in reverse.

"What are you talking about, Janet? You can't go out there!"

"Alan, I don't work for you, and you sure as hell don't own me," the thirty-eight-year-old redhead said as she pulled on a tan vest and buckled it up.

"Who the hell is this Eric character and why are you rushing out when *he* calls? An old boyfriend?"

Janet snorted, shaking her head as she pulled on her boots.

Alan was a Wall Street broker, and a lot of fun in peacetime, but when Eric's text had come over the link she'd almost thanked God aloud because the whining was getting on her last nerve. As soon as the first confirmation had hit the net that there was real fighting going on he'd all but curled up under his bed and sobbed.

She stood up and smiled at him. "It's been fun, Alan. Maybe if we both live through this we'll meet up again. Ciao."

"Janet! Janet!" he yelled after her as she let herself out of the penthouse apartment and headed for the stairs. "You can't go out there!"

It was only sixty stories down.

Good warm-up.

▶▶▶

▶A man sitting on the corner of a Manhattan skyrise, watching the fires burning and the tanks dying, glanced down when his link slate vibrated. He raised a single eyebrow, surprised that the device was still operating in a city under siege. The other brow went up as he read the single line of message. Then he put it away and stood up on the edge of the building before dropping back and turning to head back to the roof access.

Interesting times.

▶▶▶

▶A woman with finely chiseled Asian features blinked as the message rolled across the heads-up display on her contact lens.

"A voice from the past, speaking in silence. How very like Raziel," she said softly, smiling as she gathered up a light pack and walked out the door of her suburban home.

In the distance the New York City skyline was marred by smoke and flame, and she could hear the rumble of tanks as they tried to clear the expressway. She walked over to a Ducati sitting in the driveway and straddled the Italian bike calmly.

Never send a tank into a city, you fools. Not if you want either the city or the tank back in one piece.

Thankfully, it seemed that there was a professional in play, after all.

She started the bike and kicked it into gear, pulling out onto the deserted road and turning toward the city. She just hoped that the Guardsmen stayed out of the way.

▶▶▶

▶Across the city, across the world, a dark and normally quiet subculture was waking to the sound of war from all quarters. It roused slowly in places, like lightning in others, but it roused nonetheless.

In New York the members of that culture shrugged on their gear, checked their weapons, and headed in the direction of Ferry Park.

It was to be . . . a Gathering.

CHAPTER SEVEN

Ferry Park, Bronx

▲

▶THEY TRICKLED INTO the deceptively peaceful setting of the park, a few at a time. The SWAT team arrived first. Having a helicopter at call was a nice advantage when it came to making a meeting, but it wasn't long before others showed up as well.

Eric looked them over briefly, checking their files against his open access to the military and government networks. Most of them were former military. Those that weren't were career cops. They'd do.

Ian Granger seemed to be the man most of them looked to, so he addressed him as well.

"Commander Granger, I'd give you a nice little welcome speech but we're just a little pressed for time," Eric told him. "So get your men lined up, and I'll start prepping the suits."

Granger eyed the open vaults that had already been unloaded from the amphibious assault craft, recognizing some of what he was seeing but clearly not all.

"Exoskeletal armor?" he spoke, finally.

"Hardened Special Operations armor," Eric confirmed, "good from about a thousand meters below the sea to hard vacuum. Strength enhancing, augmented reactions, the works."

Ian's eyes slid away from the man and the gear, out to where the smoking hulk of the *Odyssey* was still resting in Long Island Sound.

"Apparently you boys in the space service get the best toys."

Eric shrugged, flashing him and the others a crooked smile. "Someone has to do it."

"Did someone have to lead those *things* here too?" someone demanded from the crowd.

Ian twisted around, eyes glaring. "Shut it."

"No, he's got a point." Eric held up a hand. "Not something we have a lot of time right now to talk about, but a few seconds won't change anything. We encountered the Drasin as they were in the process of committing *genocide*. If anyone here would honestly turn aside from *that*, then you don't deserve to wear the uniforms I see, or the ones many of you once wore."

There were a few flushed faces, eyes that wouldn't meet his, and so Eric immediately pushed on.

"Beyond all that, I'm convinced that they were coming this way *anyway*. So face them now, with some warning, or later with none," he said. "I'll not ask another generation to shoulder *my* burden."

"It's a moot point anyway," Granger growled, turning to look over the men and women. "They're here. It's done. Deal with it. Anyone who can't, get out of my sight. I don't have the time or patience to deal with you."

Between the Confederate space captain's steady gaze and the SWAT team commander glaring at them, no one spoke another word of objection.

"Good," Eric said, tone and voice shifting as he barked out with authority. "Line up to suit up!"

▶▶▶

▶ Eric had forty suits with him when he managed to get off the wreckage of the *Odyssey,* not counting the one he wore or the loader, of course. Thirty cops showed up quickly, with signs of more to come, but Eric held back on the last ten suits and kept an eye on the growing group for familiar faces.

The cops were great, and he was eternally thankful that they had stepped up, but he desperately needed some experience and a degree of trust and familiarity for what was to come.

The rumble of a powerful motorcycle engine gave him the first hint of both, and he smiled widely and with relief as he saw the slim woman kick down the stand on the Ducati, casually flipping her hair back as she pulled off her helmet.

"Razial . . . " She smiled, her English slightly accented with a hint of Oxford perfection. "You always did dance on the side of the angels with the devil's own glee."

"Siobhan," he nodded as the Asian woman approached. "It's been a while."

"Hong Kong, I believe," she answered, eyes skimming the gathering and the weapons. "These are not who I expected to see."

"Others should be coming, but we needed numbers."

"Quality, Raziel," she chided him. "You of all people should know better than to rely on quantity."

"They're good men and women, love," Eric shrugged unapologetically.

"Yes, but will they be *durable?*"

"Time will tell. I have a suit for you," Eric gestured.

She walked over, looking the armor up and down. "Not really my style."

"This isn't an infiltration job," Eric reminded her. "Suit up or stay behind."

She sighed, a much put-upon sound, and then smiled teasingly at Eric. "Should I strip down here, or do you have somewhere a little more . . . private?"

"Use the inside of this lander," he told her, expression dry. "I'd hate to start a riot or cause any heart attacks among our allies before we get a chance to fight."

"Always the flatterer, Raziel." She laughed, grabbing an undersuit and climbing into the rig.

When she was out of sight, Lyssa stepped up beside Eric, hissing softly, "Who the hell is that?"

"That's the woman who broke into the most secure facility in the entire Block and helped me break out with the second-generation counter-mass generation plans. We'd have lost the war if not for her."

Lyssa's eyes widened. "Really?"

The woman didn't look like a hardened spy, not unless you believed movies. She was pure femme fatale, right out of the golden age of spy novels and Hollywood.

"Really," Eric answered. "And more than one enemy combatant has died thinking exactly what just passed through your mind. She's not to be underestimated."

"I can hear you." Siobhan's voice wafted out of the lander.

"She also has ears like a bat."

Lyssa snorted. "So I see. Are all your old friends like that?"

"Hell no, sister," a voice said from behind her, startling Lyssa into a semi-powered jump as she misjudged her armor. "Some of us are good looking."

"Ron, you need to get your dosages checked. You're having delusions of adequacy again."

The big burly man with graying hair snorted, grinning wide as he stepped up and clapped a hand across Eric's armored back. "Boy, you always could find the one ants' nest in the park to set your picnic on."

"Don't remind me," Eric sighed, shaking his head before gesturing to Lyssa. "Ronald Blake, this is Officer Lyssa Myriano of the NYPD. Lyss, retired full bird Colonel Ronald Blake, formerly of the U.S. Air Force."

"Back when there was a United States," Ron grumbled. He'd never been too happy about the whole Confederation deal.

Not everyone in any of the three primary nations had loved the idea, of course. In fact a good deal less than half had actually been enthusiastic about it, but hard pressed by the war, the United States needed the manufacturing capacity of Mexico and the raw resources of Canada if it were to continue to hold the line, let alone make a credible counteroffensive. Trade agreements had worked for a while, and then mutual defense pacts. Finally, the three governments were one in all but name and each took the next step.

A constitutional convention in the U.S. led to a vote to reform the republic, while similar referendums in Canada and Mexico passed under heavy controversy. The key effect it had on the military of the time was opening recruiting across previously inaccessible borders, bolstering numbers at a time when every able body was needed just to hold the line against the Block at Japan and Israel.

Weston had never been what one could call overly patriotic. His loyalty went to his family in the service, and those were the men and women who'd bled with him, not just the ones who wore his flag. Others, however, including Blake, still swore that the United States would rise again. It was a familiar cry to the historian in Eric, but not one he took up himself.

"Not now, Ron." He shook his head. "The city, today. Worry about your lost country when we're not all about to die."

The Air Force colonel snorted again, but gave in easily enough. Patriot or not, Ron Blake was a realist to the core.

"What's the lowdown on these bastards, Captain?" he asked.

"Alien swarm. They eat anything and shit reinforcements. If we leave them be long enough, they'll eat and shit the entire planet right out from under us," Eric told his old friend, dropping his more refined persona for a familiar attitude from the war. "Armor up and help the greenhorns get adjusted. We've got some Guardies to rescue."

"Roger that," Ron nodded, heading for a suit. "These look like upgrades. Anything new?"

"Mostly just small stuff over the ones you tested," Eric answered. "You got the high-altitude ones, right?"

"Damn right. Most fun I ever had as a PJ was jumping out of the space shuttle." Ron grinned. "It was one *helluva* long way down."

"I'll bet." Eric grinned, turning away to look over the group.

They now had a few dozen people, mostly NYPD officers but also a few tagalongs brought in by the police or who wandered in on their own. New York was a big city, and out of its millions of people there were more than a few too stupid, stubborn, or adventurous to stay in hiding. Curiosity had brought a few of them here, and that was fine. He didn't have armor for them, but they did have a fair supply of assault weapons and magazines. More than enough for the crowd they had.

"Are you expecting anyone else?"

Eric glanced up to see Granger approach, now clad in a fresh suit of armor and shouldering the heavy assault rifle to match. The SWAT commander looked bad, pale, and weathered, but Eric could hardly blame him. He didn't know how many cops had died since the Drasin landed, but he could guess that it wasn't a small number. The men and women around were too serious at the moment, too focused, for it to be anything less.

"Two more, at least," he answered.

"You've got eight more suits empty," Ian reminded him.

"Wishful thinking," Eric admitted. "I'll wait for Janet and Alexander to get here, then decide on the ones that are left."

The SWAT commander nodded slowly. "Fair enough. You have a plan?"

"Depends," Eric said, not looking up. "Is genocide a plan?"

▶▶▶

▼

DEEP BELOW 1600 PENNSYLVANIA AVENUE, WASHINGTON, D.C.

▲

▶ THE PRESIDENT FELT as if he'd been trying to get a handle on the current crisis for days, weeks even, and so it was with a naked look of disbelief that he checked the clock and realized that it had been just a little over six hours since the first alien invader had impacted the surface of the Earth. It seemed impossible. There was no way that he could be this tired and this wrung out in just six hours, but there it was.

"Mr. President, Mr. Bahnner is here to see you."

The President sighed. Really, the last thing he wanted to deal with at the moment was the senator, but the man was the chair of the Senate's science and technology board. Unfortunately, that meant that his appointment had been entirely political and the man knew less about science and technology than your average four-year-old.

"Jack"—he forced a smile—"good to speak with you."

"Thank you, Mr. President," Bahnner said, returning the smile very briefly. "I wanted to speak with you about the order you issued . . . "

"Jack, I've been issuing orders all afternoon. You're going to have to be just a little more specific."

"Mr. . . . Mitchell, you circumvented my committee with your orders to DARPA concerning the t-cannon . . . "

"Stop right there," President Conner said, holding up one hand. "Have you noticed what room we're in?"

"Excuse me?"

"Despite appearances, are we in the Oval Office?" he asked slowly, as if to a child.

"No sir. This is the secure bunker . . . "

"And for us to be here, what state of government has to be declared?"

The senator's nostrils flared as the President's meaning became quite apparent, but he doggedly refused to give up the bone he was gnawing. "Sir, that is no reason to . . . "

"We are in a state of declared martial law," Mitchell Connor said, "so I didn't circumvent anything, I acted well within the limits of my powers. Mr. Bahnner, I don't have time for political posturing at the moment, so unless you have something useful to add to the situation . . . ?"

"Mr. President, when this is over . . . "

"If we're not dead, and you think you can get away with a little political backstabbing"—Conner shrugged, smiling in a very nasty way—"then have at it, Hoss. Until then, get the hell out of my office."

He nodded to the guards at the door and, even before the senator's face had managed to stop gaping in unadulterated shock, they hustled the annoying man out. Conner took a deep breath and shook his head, actually feeling better than he had in hours. There was something freeing about telling the man off after so many years of having to smile to his face when he'd rather break his nose.

"Sam?"

"Sir?" The Secret Service man stepped forward.

"Find out what movement has been made on my order to DARPA and the other people involved with the t-cannon project."

"Yes sir."

Hopefully someone had actually been working while he had been stuck in the office dealing with the nonsense his position demanded.

▼

FERRY POINT PARK, BRONX

▲

▶THE TALL, SLIM man stopped shoulder to shoulder with the muscular redhead, the two of them looking over the scene before them before they began to walk into the park in step.

"Eric knows how to throw a party," Alexander said with a faint air of amusement.

Janet chuckled throatily, looking around at the men and women in the gathering. Mostly the men, if she were to be asked by a particularly brave soul. "That he does, Boyo. I think this must be what coming home feels like."

Alexander Stanislav rolled his eyes, but didn't comment further. He and his walking companion had been friends almost as long as they'd both known their host for this particular party. They'd met during nasty street-to-street fighting in Tokyo before the Marines hammered the Block back with help from a certain man and his experimental fighter squadron.

Since then the two of them were almost always found in the same city, often the same clubs. They were known, among those few who kept track of such things, as a matched pair. They liked almost all the same things, despite how different they were in most respects, down to having the same taste in men.

They were ignored as they walked through the armed camp, which would normally be a sign of a severe lack of security, but this time they'd forgive it. Among other things, from what they'd seen, there was little chance of infiltration this time around, not with the enemy looking like giant rock spiders with a touch of someone's nightmare mixed in.

Still, the fact that they were able to walk right up to the captain without anyone even bothering to let him know they were coming . . . well, that was just unprofessional.

Janet was a second from castigating him for just that when Eric spoke without turning around or even looking up from what he was doing.

"Suit up. Both of you. We're on a deadline."

The duo glanced at each other, then back at the Captain, who still hadn't turned around.

"How . . . " Janet blinked, but immediately cut herself off.

"You're linked into every other suit walking around this field, aren't you?" Alexander asked dryly.

"And you're both late. Suit up," Eric said, standing and turning around. "Anyone else from the old crowd in town?"

Janet shook her head. "Not as best I know."

"Pity. We move into the city in fifteen minutes. Think you can keep up?"

The two just laughed as they split and walked around the captain, heading for the armor they could see behind him, not bothering to dignify that with a response. Eric looked around until he found Commander Granger and waved him over.

"Are we ready?"

"Almost. We move in fifteen," Eric told him. "Six suits are open for use. Assign them at your discretion, Commander. You know your men better than I do."

Granger nodded. "Yes sir, Captain."

Eric looked north to the city, the smoke rising from all points, signifying just how bad the situation was. He had forty men, most of them relative rookies in powered armor, but for all that he was happier with them than with an entire battalion of tanks. In a city, maneuverability was king, and you just didn't get more mobile than enhancing armor.

With his military codes he was able to intercept most of the intelligence being passed around by the Guard units, though he was pretty certain that some of it wasn't on his system since the network had holes the size of the *Odyssey* all through it. Still, he had enough to begin making initial plans to clear New York of the infestation.

Beyond that, well, he'd make it up as it went along or he'd get orders from someone who hopefully had a better idea of the big picture.

Minutes flew past, and between them Eric, Granger, and the members of the "old crowd" got everyone facing the right direction. They had more men than armor, of course, but luckily there were enough guns to go around. Plus each of the assault landers had a heavy cannon mounted, so he put drivers and gunners in those, and would worry about getting them through traffic when the problem presented itself.

He would have worried, actually, since an answer announced itself before he could properly frame the problem. Eric had been walking by the loader he'd used to escape the *Odyssey* when one of the men caught his attention and jerked a thumb in its direction.

"Hey, Admiral," the man asked, instantly getting on Eric's bad side. "What about that?"

Eric glanced at the big machine and shrugged. It was powerful, sure, but too damn slow in an open fight to be of serious use. "What about it?"

"I used to work construction. We had a couple older models than that," the gruff man said. "I know from experience, it can pick a car up and toss it a good distance."

Eric froze, then nodded slowly. "Right. You certified?"

"Used to be."

"Close enough. We'll cover you. You clear the road for the landers and any tanks we run across. Clear?"

"Clear. This thing use standard fuel cells?"

"It should."

"Then I've got my ride," the man grinned, climbing up into the cab of the big machine.

That settled one problem. The loader would be slow, but faster than lugging all the ammo and supplies still packed into the landers if they had to haul it on foot. With that settled, they were as ready as they could be.

"Captain," Granger said as he joined the man at the head of the rough convoy, "the men are ready."

"Is that so?" Eric asked, checking the action on his Priminae GWIZ. "Colonel Blake?"

"They're not up to our old standards," the burly retired colonel grunted, "but I warrant that the ones who live through the day will come close."

Eric's eyes flicked quickly to make sure that Blake had been speaking on the command channel and not openly to the group, but he needn't have bothered. It wasn't Ronald's first rodeo.

"Let's try and make that number as high as possible, shall we?" he responded dryly, while mentally accepting that his old friend had a point.

"That's the goal, son. Let's do this."

Eric nodded, ticking over to the general squad channel. "Ready to move out. Directions are on your HUDs."

He tensed. "Move out, on the bounce!"

With a kick at the ground Eric was airborne in an assisted jump that took him twenty meters up and over seventy ahead. Behind him the others followed suit, most using smaller and more controllable jumps, but catching up quickly as the slower assault landers and construction loader rumbled into action and began to make their way into the city.

CHAPTER EIGHT

National Guard HQ, *Intrepid* Sea, Air, & Space Museum

▼

▲

▶ "GENERAL! I THINK you need to see this, sir."

Potts cursed under his breath. Those words boded nothing but ill if he were to judge from the way things had been going so far. He headed over to the center of the tactical communications and command setup, leaning over the man's shoulder.

"What is it, son?"

The young enlisted man gestured at the screens. "Sir, we've got forty-three new IFF signals that just lit off in South Bronx. They're moving north in a hurry. Lead elements will hit the expressway anytime now."

"Ours?"

"No sir. I've got no hits on their ID, just Confederate signals. It's over my security clearance, General."

"What the hell is going on?" Potts grumbled under his breath, reaching over to scan his biometrics into the system. It took a moment to register, but nothing changed. "Oh, who the hell are these people?"

"No idea sir, but they'll reach Seventh Platoon in less than three minutes at their current rate."

"Great. Curtz!"

"Yes sir!" A lieutenant appeared behind him.

"Get on the link to Command. I want those codes."

"Yes sir."

The best Potts could say about this was that at least they weren't more of the enemy, but he wasn't terribly happy about having a bunch of unknowns about to join into one of his combat zones. The sooner he learned just who the hell they were the happier a man he'd be.

▶ ▶ ▶

▶ Eric Weston skidded as he landed on the Cross Bronx Expressway, planting a foot on the concrete edge to brace himself as he paused to wait for the others to catch up. They weren't a smoothly operating machine by any means, but they were better than some boot squads he'd run with in the past.

That's not saying a lot, but I suppose it'll have to do.

He looked northwest, eyes and HUD locking in on the IFF signals coming from the Guards' Seventh Platoon. The armored regiment had managed to tear their way through the city enough to finally find a few of the enemy to engage, and he rather suspected that they were in the process of regretting it.

The heavy tanks were more than powerful enough to take out the alien invaders, of that there was no question. The twitching bodies of three he could see proved that right up front and beyond any shadow of a doubt. The problem was that the platoon was stuck on a street between two lines of wrecked cars and rows of buildings. Without any way to evade, they were getting sliced to ribbons by the alien particle weapons, while the Drasin were using every ounce of their mobility against the tankers.

Harsh red icons filled his HUD as he settled in against the cement edge of the elevated section of the expressway, resting the Priminae weapon to steady it better. It wasn't designed as a marksman's weapon, but Eric knew that the device could effectively ignore the force of gravity over some extremely long ranges. Similarly, other factors like windage weren't factors he had to be concerned with. The energy imparted to the projectile was enough to make the range he was working at practically point blank.

One of the Drasin had gotten about the tankers, obviously intent on cutting them down from above, where their cannons couldn't elevate to. Eric haloed it in his HUD, getting range and motion figures, but couldn't send that data across to the alien weapon he was using. So he began to count off the math in his head as he looked down the enhanced sights of the GWIZ.

The Priminae weapon didn't buck as he stroked the firing stud, the gravity control preventing recoil from being a significant problem. The DPU round he'd loaded earlier exploded into the atmosphere, throwing up a brief cloud of condensation as the pressure wave changed the air in front of him, and lanced across the intervening distance at several times the speed of sound.

The trail of ablated material left a laser-like beam in the air between him and the Drasin, visible for a few moments after the alien exploded into shards and splattered remains across Zerega Avenue.

Eric felt another person land beside him and his eyes flicked to check the IFF, but he didn't look away from the target zone. "Guardies need a hand, Commander. Think they're up to it?"

Granger was silent for a moment, looking over the scene ahead of him. He wasn't fully comfortable with the armor yet himself, so he had a sinking feeling just what the answer really was. "No" wasn't an option, however, so he let out a deep breath before answering.

"My men can shoot. Let's keep this out of knife range, if it's all the same to you."

Eric nodded. It was a good idea. "Fair enough. Deploy to the rooftops between Newbold and Waterbury. We'll catch them in a crossfire and try to end this fast."

"Roger that."

The commander jumped away, heading to round up his men, and Eric glanced over to where four others were standing.

"You have a real plan, Cap?" Janet asked him as she knelt behind an abandoned car, looking over the hood and the cement carrier to the city beyond.

"We're not going to try mixing it up in close with these things, not until I know just how good a shot our new friends really are," Eric said, getting a chuckle out of his four comrades. "But I think we'll over jump the fight and come back at them."

"Double pincer," Ronald nodded. "Not bad, jarhead. Not bad."

"Shall we stop talking about it," Alexander suggested, "and just make it happen then?"

"Right," Eric nodded. "On the bounce. Go."

The five armored soldiers leapt clear from the expressway, landing on a nearby building before they hopped off again, splitting the battleground and circling around. Behind them the larger armored force began to get into action themselves, hopping in slower and less flamboyant moves as they headed north to their assigned positions.

▶ ▶ ▶

▶ Major Curran, Seventh Platoon, was in a bit of a bind.

Actually, that was probably the understatement of the century. He'd stupidly led his platoon into an ambush, more focused on clearing the damned cars from the road so they could get to their assigned positions than in keeping an eye peeled for enemy movement. The first hint they had of trouble was when the rear tank went up like a fireball, closing the door behind them, and three enemy stalkers appeared from an alley ahead of them.

He didn't know what else to call the spider-like things. They were utterly alien enough to send chills down his spine as they stalked toward his team. He'd ordered the lead tank to open fire as the next two split the difference and pulled up on either side so they could get a clean shot apiece.

The first round of return fire had bolstered morale, sending one of the stalkers to the ground, where it twitched but didn't show any sign of getting back into the action. Return fire scorched the street, slicing the offending tank in two, right down the middle, lengthwise. Curran watched it slump inward on itself before the munitions blew, rocking the armor he was riding.

"Keep firing!"

The two heavy main battle tanks rocked with every shot, rolling back on their suspensions as their cannons roared. The alien spiders were fast movers, however, and the devil itself to track in the tight confines of the city. Curran knew that out in the open they'd have hit every round dead on, but in the city he'd swear that his tanks were causing more damage than the damned enemy!

"Major! Up on the building!"

Curran looked up and swore. One of them had somehow *climbed* up the side of the building, tearing it all to hell in the process, and was menacingly looking down on them.

"Elevate the barrel! Get it locked up!" he ordered.

"It's too tight, Major! We can't aim that high!"

Curran felt his stomach twist as he recognized the crackle of energy on the front of the alien even as he opened his mouth to give a futile order.

The explosion of the beast left him stunned for a moment, as much because of the incredible shock wave that followed it, blowing out windows all down the street even as pieces of the alien rained down around them.

Curran pivoted his scanners around. "What the hell was that!?"

"Two more, dead ahead, sir!"

He refocused his attention where it needed to be. "Continue firing!"

▶▶▶

▶ Eric leapfrogged the battle, staying low and hugging the side streets as he jumped forward. He could feel the burn in his legs, unaccustomed as they were to the kind of work he was putting them to in just the past few hours. He'd trained as a rifleman, like all Marines, but it had been a long time since those days and he knew that he was going to feel it come morning.

Assuming he was alive in the morning.

He caught glimpses of the fighting as he crossed Waterbury Avenue, the muzzle flash of the electromagnetic cannon on the battle tank making a distinctive sight as the ablated material of the round ignited from the air friction.

He landed low, sliding feet first under cover along a grassy strip between two buildings, narrowly avoiding wrapping himself around a tree in the process. He rolled clear, remaining prone as he crawled up to the tree he'd narrowly missed, and braced his weapon against it.

"I'm in first position."

Short signal bursts, four of them, told him that the others heard him and were moving into their own positions even as he spoke. Eric poked his head out a bit, eyes flitting around, but he couldn't see the beasts that he knew were out there. Despite being linked into the Guard's IFF signals system, Eric found that he couldn't get a location lock from them, as their system simply wasn't calibrated, nor advanced enough, to keep a virtual lock on the enemy.

Irritating. Use your thermals, damn it.

Radar lock would be useless, he knew, but the tanks were fully capable of getting a thermal lock on a target and communicating it over the network. Why they weren't doing so, Eric had no clue. He back-doored into their network and added an order to their queue, using his Confederate authorization codes.

The tank's computers authorized the signal in seconds and Eric was well satisfied to see red splotches appear on his HUD a moment later. The signal lock left a little to be desired—it seemed that the heat from the alien drones was enough to spoof the precise lock just a bit—but it was close enough for his needs.

"Got the enemy on my HUD, confirm," he said, getting to his knees.

"Confirmed. Have one in my sights, matches computer signal," Siobhan said softly over the network.

One of the signals sharpened distinctly, her instrumentation added to the Guard's. Eric checked the line of sight on the enemy positions and made his move, sprinting and bounding across Halsey Street, and then jumping up and clambering to the roof of the building there. Climbing in armor was a slightly surreal experience that felt almost like watching a movie more than exerting actual effort, the energy snap released from the armor's arms and legs causing him to almost literally fly up the side of the building.

On the roof, Eric rolled to a stop and then quick crawled to the edge so he could look out over Zerega Avenue and get a better idea of the situation. The Guard's tanks were firing on automatic, but they weren't hitting much of what they were aiming at, which was making things decidedly uncomfortable for him in his current position. It was only a matter of time before one of those DPU shells took out the building he was lying on, and he'd rather not be sitting there when it happened.

"Fire team, are you in position?"

They weren't. He could see that on his HUD, but Eric figured it would light a fire under Granger. The SWAT commander didn't strike him as the sort to take any dig at his professional skills lightly.

"Negative," Granger answered, his tone dark. Eric imagined he could hear teeth gritting. "One minute."

If he gets them in place in one minute, I'll owe the man a drink, Eric thought wryly as he glanced at the array of blue signals on the overlay map he was looking through.

Reading a Heads Up Display while paying attention to what was in front of you was something of an art form, one that Eric had mastered many years past. The system operated on an augmented reality foundation, and it let him see "through" the buildings around him to where the men and women were arraying themselves.

He was surprised when Granger actually made the minute deadline by three seconds, and made a mental note to find the man a drink when it was all over, even if he had to loot a liquor store.

"In position."

"Good work. Targets locked?"

"We have two from here, say again, read three tangos, but we can only see two."

"Roger. I have number three."

"Roger. Targets locked."

"Engage when ready," Eric said, as he got to one knee and extended the Priminae gravity weapon ahead of him.

"Roger that. Engaging enemy targets in three . . . "

▶▶▶

▶ Major Curran was cursing up a storm, trying like hell to keep his voice low enough so it wasn't picked up by his microphone and knowing that he was failing miserably. The alien . . . *things* moved like something out of a horror movie, and at the range they were fighting there was just no chance for the battle tank's guns to lock on.

Screw time. Just give me range, Lord, all I ask for is range!

From two miles out, he *knew* he could pot these bastards like shooting skeet on a Sunday afternoon. From less than two hundred yards it was like trying to hit greased lightning. Curran twisted around, looking behind him in more than a little desperation.

"Back off! Get us some fighting room!"

"Major, we've got the rest of the platoon right behind us!"

"Everyone back up!" he ordered over the network. "If we stay in knife range they're going to slice us to ribbons!"

The hydrogen turbines whined as the electromagnetic tracks bit into the asphalt, the remaining tanks in the platoon backing off as quickly as they dared. As they did the gunners kept firing, though slower now as they were wary of running completely dry of munitions.

"Riley, Evans, we're about out of rounds. Lead tanks will split at the next intersection. You two fire as the range clears," Curran ordered. "We'll try and get them in a pincer if they chase us, or open some real range between us if they don't."

The next two tanks in his column acknowledged the order as they all got under way.

A flicker of motion in the corner of his eye caught Curran's attention. He glanced to the left and up to see several figures appear on the rooftop just behind his tanks. His first instinct was to initiate counter-sniper contingencies, but he stopped himself short when he realized that he wasn't fighting humans this time around.

Who the hell are these people?

They were forming a firing line, heavy assault weapons aimed down at the streets he was backing like hell to get out of, and just then Curran realized that he didn't really care. He saw their plan and his hands were working on his command board before he even thought about what he was doing.

"All tanks," he ordered, "new maneuvering orders coming through. Execute immediately."

He didn't have time for anything fancy, so he settled for altering the last set of instructions just enough. Instead of the two lead tanks peeling off at the intersection completely, they'd angle in, plant their backs to the walls of the buildings, and get ready to fight.

It wasn't the best position as it cut down their chances of withdrawal if things went south, but it would increase their firing arcs significantly.

At the same time the rest of the tanks in the platoon would spread out, cannon to cannon across Zerega. It was cramped conditions, but if they were about to get serious fire support from above, the least his platoon could do was give it their fighting all.

▶▶▶

▶Twenty electromagnetic assault weapons erupted from the rooftops, reasonably in sync, as the aliens followed the retreating tanks deeper into the makeshift killbox. Unlike the tanks, the men with the assault weapons were operating effectively at their optimal range, and the sudden rain of high-velocity steel slammed into the Drasin like an impenetrable wall. The creatures faltered briefly, caught between pursuing their opponents, engaging the new targets, or going for cover.

The tanks rejoined the fight in that instant of hesitation, five EM cannons roaring on pure auto fire. Anything that survived the initial barrage from the rooftops stood no chance at all against the follow-up from the streets. Less than ten seconds later the guns fell silent and an unreal quiet settled across the scene, right alongside the dust that was slowly drifting to the street.

Curran looked around slowly. "Is that all of them? Keep your eyes open, everyone."

The quiet was deafening after the nearly constant barrage of sonic booms, almost disorienting, and Curran imagined that he could feel the pressure in the area drop from everyone holding their breath and scanning the carnage. A flicker of motion was his only warning before an ear-splitting boom roared from the rooftop ahead of him and he jumped in his seat as the flailing body of another alien fell eight stories to the ground, destroying two parked import cars in an explosion of plastic and metal.

On that same rooftop he spotted a figure walk up to the edge and, after glancing down, step off into midair.

The man freefell eighty feet, planting his boots hard into the roof of another plastic import car and landing in a explosion of debris like his defeated foe. The armored man stepped out of the wreckage, calmly walking out into the intersection and looking over at Curran's tank. He tapped his helmet twice, then held up three fingers.

Curran instantly switched over to channel three.

"Major Curran, I presume?"

"I am, and you are?"

"Captain Eric Weston, Confederate Black Navy."

Curran's eyes widened as he took that in. He'd heard of the man, of course, everyone had, but what the hell was he doing running around New York in Special Operations infantry armor? For that matter, Curran involuntarily glanced to the east where he had seen the *Odyssey* go down. What was he doing *alive*?

"Pardon my saying so, Captain, but you're a long way from the Black."

The captain snorted, sounding amused. "Tell me about it, Major. It was one hell of a fall. That said, we don't have time to swap stories. We're moving deeper into the city. The Drasin have engaged another armored platoon on Pelham. Can you provide cover for my supply train?"

Curran considered the request quickly and nodded. "Can do, Captain. We're heading that way as well. It's going to take us a while, though, with all the vehicles clogging up the roads."

"Understood. We may have a partial solution to that. My force will move on ahead. You follow as you can. My supply train will catch up shortly."

"Roger that. Uh, Captain, our IFF board doesn't have access to your systems . . . "

Eric paused, half turning back, then walked over to Curran's tank. He reached out and touched one of the transmitters, making a close proximity connection, and Curran watched as someone took over his computer for a moment.

Well, he's got to be at least a flag officer if he's got my codes . . .

A moment later the board lit up, now showing more than forty new IFF signals on top of his position, and several more coming up from behind them.

"There," Eric said, "you now have access to the *Odyssey's* codes. You'll see what we see."

"Thank you, Captain."

Eric nodded, then turned and gestured to the other armored figures before bounding off in a roughly northerly direction. One by one and in groups the others followed, leaving Curran and the rest of his platoon alone.

"Alright, we're moving out in five!" he called. "First I want to check our fallen. Do whatever you need to do now because once we're moving, we ain't stopping!"

With that he popped the hatch of his tank and pulled himself out, intent on checking for any survivors from the two tanks he'd lost. The bodies would have to wait, but if there was anyone breathing, now was the only time they'd have.

▶▶▶

NATIONAL GUARD HQ, *INTREPID* SEA, AIR, & SPACE MUSEUM

▲

▶"SIGNALS FROM SEVENTH Platoon, sir. Enemy destroyed and they are proceeding to back up the Ninth."

Potts grumbled, but for once it wasn't an annoyed sound.

"Good. Any word on the unknown IFF signals?"

"Major Curran says that they're a team off the *Odyssey*, led by Weston, General."

Potts frowned deeply, considering that. It both made sense and yet didn't. He walked over to his own station, calling up files as quickly as he could. The new IFF signals were certainly consistent with what a team from the *Odyssey* would be using, but unless he was misremembering . . .

There it is. Potts glared at the memo he'd pulled up. *According to reports, Weston was the only man on that ship when she went down. So who the hell did he put in those suits?*

"Do we have the codes yet for the contingent from the *Odyssey?*" he asked over his shoulder.

"Yes sir. Not from Command, General. Captain Weston gave them to Major Curran directly."

Potts grunted. "Good man. Bring them up."

The map of the battlefield, of New York City, was a confused mess and that was being kind. The impact explosions of the Drasins' insertion vehicles had toppled skyscrapers and blown craters into the very foundation of the city itself. Those were ugly scars on the computer display Potts was now looking at, scars that he doubted would ever be healed.

His own platoons and squadrons were represented by blue division patches, and they were now arrayed around the city with fairly deep penetration despite the traffic issues. The new icons, also blue, were of the *Odyssey*'s own patch, a starship against a starry background, eclipsing a planet and its moon.

There were several dozen of those signals, moving north as he watched, heading for where the Ninth Platoon was embroiled in a nasty firefight and had lost three of their number already. Potts gritted his teeth, but didn't see many options open to him.

"Give me a direct link to the commander of Ninth Platoon."

"Yes sir."

Potts leaned forward, eyes on the map. "Major, this is General Potts. You have reinforcements inbound from your six. Hold the line son, help is coming. When they arrive, Captain Weston has tactical command. Do you understand?"

When the major acknowledged, Potts cut the channel and nodded to his aide.

"Send them the IFF codes for the *Odyssey* contingent."

"Yes sir."

▶▶▶

▶Running rooftop to rooftop was tricky business, even in full enhancing armor, but in a city like New York it also permitted a course almost straight as the crow flies, one that would cut entire seconds, perhaps even a full minute, off their travel time. For anyone looking from below, or above, the sight of forty-plus armored men and women running full tilt across the roof of the city had to be surreal.

Eric had a full overlay up, which made the maneuvering even harder, but he had little choice. He needed a plan of attack before they got there, and with only seconds to put it together he had to lean on every skill and trick he'd ever picked up in multitasking.

"We're going to hit them hard and fast," he ordered. "The Guardie armored platoon has already lost three tanks and as many as nine men, and they've only taken out one of the Drasin drones. First squad, you're with me. We'll take them from ground level. Everyone else is to deploy across the rooftops according to Commander Granger's orders. Watch your lines of fire. I'll be *very* irritated if I die because one of you mistook me for an alien."

There were some mild chuckles over the channel at the idea of mistaking a human, even in full armor, for one of those things, but the undercurrent was as serious as he could hope for.

Eric was feeling the strain on his body. Enhancing armor was designed to take up a lot of the stresses and energy requirements of combat, but only if you knew it well enough not to fight it. Eric knew that he was, indeed, fighting his armor on some levels. The strain in his legs and arms was enough evidence of that.

More to the point, however, he'd never actually led men into combat on this level. It was—it felt—so very different than taking the Double A squadron into a furball, and his guts were clenching almost like the first time he'd been given command of a fighter group.

Then the time for worries, stresses, and any thoughts but those of survival and comrades was over. Eric, leading his five-man team, dropped from the rooftops right on top of the beleaguered Guardsmen's tanks and leveled their own weapons at the snarling and hissing alien drones.

He stroked the firing stud on the Priminae gravity weapon, and with a sharp crack of depleted uranium destroying the sound barrier, the fight was on.

CHAPTER NINE

Under 1600 Pennsylvania Avenue

▲

▶ "MR. PRESIDENT, I'M not sure that you understand the ramifications of what you're asking."

Mitchell Conner was normally a patient man. You didn't get to his position in the Confederation without being exactly that after all. That said, he was running well past his last nerve and the obstructionism he was used to in his everyday life had no place on a world under siege.

"Stop," he said flatly, one hand up to the screen that the speaker was looking down from. "Unless the ramifications are somehow *worse* than giant alien insects eating our entire planet out from under us, I'm far from certain that I *care* what they are. What I need to know is simple. Can you fire a transitional weapon from inside an atmosphere?"

"In theory . . . yes," the man admitted finally. "However, this deep in a gravity well, I can't say how we can possibly target . . . "

"Then shoot from the hip, by God!" Conner snarled. "I don't care if you have to build the mother of all shotguns to make this happen, just *make it happen!*"

He took a deep breath in the stunned silence that followed his explosion and sighed.

"Doctor . . . we are besieged. Unless we clear our skies of these *things,* all the fighting in the universe won't save us here on the ground. Just build the weapon. Build as many of them as you can. I have factories turning out shells at an obscene rate already . . . give me something to shoot them out of."

The man swallowed, but nodded jerkily. "Yes Mr. President."

Conner turned to the closest Secret Service agent as the screen flickered off. "Find someone we can trust to ride herd on them and get them over there as quickly as you can."

"Yes Mr. President," the agent said before leaving.

Normally Conner wasn't one to use his protection detail as glorified errand boys, but right now his secretaries were all busy, as were his advisors. Given where they were, about the only people who didn't have every waking moment taken up in pursuit of their primary skill set were, in fact, his detail. He rather suspected that the risk of assassination had gone down massively over the last few hours, and would probably drop more over the coming days.

Assuming we survive them, I suppose.

There wasn't much the agents could do to throw themselves between him and the alien drones, he supposed, so for now he was the one who had to find a way to protect them, and everyone else on the planet, and come hell or high water he was going to do just that.

▶ ▶ ▶

▶Across the world the situation was descending into chaos as the first twelve hours after the alien assault came to an end. Despite near constant bombardment from above, the cities of Beijing and New Delhi still stood and still housed more human beings than any other place on the planet.

In the first few hours the casualty rate of first-responder units was beyond obscene. Hundreds of police died in each city, along with thousands of civilians, before the first military units could arrive.

Those arrivals were, almost without exception, far too lightly equipped for the task at hand, but they'd been trained to combat the Confederation. They thus threw themselves enthusiastically into the defense of their homelands with all the fervor they would have mustered if their foe had worn Confederate blue instead of alien red.

As the clock moved on, more and more units arrived at each of the drop points worldwide, some just hammering the areas infected with high explosives and deep-penetration bunker busters. In other places a more tactful approach was taken: Heavily armed special operations units stationed in Japan, Germany, and the Middle East were dropped into major cities across the globe with weapons intended to take out Block and Confederate heavy armor. Cities became war zones unlike anything the Earth had ever seen.

In twelve hours, over fourteen million people had died, as many or more from collateral damage as from the Drasin weapons.

Many nations saw the numbers for collateral damages and considered it a fair trade. Many did not.

Military forces worldwide, after twelve hours, were just beginning to approach full mobilization. In nations like those that made up the Confederate states, this meant that more and more of the National Guard were ready to respond internally, but the bulk of their real fighting prowess was still stationed overseas. So, ironically, Confederate soldiers were more often deployed to protect nations that were not their own.

For the soldiers, this was a source of agonizing frustration as they clamored for news from home but found quickly that even when communications were open, no one really knew anything of value. Another irony: In many places that had long detested the presence of the Confederate soldiers, they were now seen as true saviors as they deployed into combat areas, rescuing people they had only just a few days previously been watching with suspicious eyes.

The world political map was shifting and, in perhaps the ultimate irony, those who were normally the first to spot and counter trends like this were now so preoccupied that they didn't have even the slightest of hints that it was happening.

▶▶▶

▶ *Gaia looked over her world, a world that had birthed her and that she had walked for as long as she had memories to recall. She'd never felt pain in all the time she'd existed, not personally, not with such clarity.*

"It was different," she decided, "feeling the echo of another's pain."

The Drasin were abominations, unlike anything she'd ever felt in her very long existence.

Gaia could recall the sensation of nuclear devices annihilating thousands. She could remember the exquisite burn of mountains of rock slamming down from space, and she knew both the searing heat of droughts and the freezing cold of glacier shaped death . . . but these, these things were completely alien.

She could sense them, as she did every other living thing on the planet . . . everything that interacted with her, the Earth's, magnetic field, in fact. They didn't register as . . . thinking creatures, however.

Humans had a pattern to them, a way of thinking that superseded language. You could tell a human just by that pattern and nothing else. Surprisingly, the pattern was very similar for other species on the planet as well. Cetaceans were close, as were several other species both aquatic and terrestrial. She'd decided long ago that the pattern she could sense was as close to the definition of sentience as she was likely to come, for the time being.

Drasin, however, read more like some bastard version of arachnids.

It seemed trite, even to her, to call them spiders, but the more she thought about it, spiders probably got their bad reputation from the Drasin. Humans were almost biologically wired to feel revulsion to creatures like spiders, yet there had never seemed to be a real reason for that wiring.

Gaia now supposed she knew the reason.

Their thought patterns only partially resembled arachnids, however. The rest was something familiar, something she had seen before, but she couldn't quite place the memory.

The itch was going to drive her mad, if the damned infestation of Drasin didn't end her and everything she'd ever known first.

Gaia cast her thoughts back to New York, and in an instant she was there.

She formed her mental image near where Eric Weston was kneeling on a rooftop, firing down into a group of Drasin that had been happily munching on a couple of battle tanks, and stood with him for a moment.

"You need to finish this battle quickly, Captain," the entity thought, looking past her subject to the city beyond. "We have real work left to do."

She stepped off the edge of the building and vanished into the ether, leaving the subject of her attention to his battle. He paused only briefly, glancing around as if he had heard something in the distance, then continued the fight.

▶▶▶

▶In space, surrounding the blue-green planet, a veritable horde of ships had slowly gathered.

Few times in history had this many Drasin been located in the same star system, and each time it had happened things had not gone well for the star system in question. This time, with hundreds of ships slowly converging on the world known to the locals as the Earth, the Drasin had a rather complex problem to deal with.

First, the world was heavily armed.

Initial sorties had confirmed that, with fighters on every continent that also swarmed the seas. Everywhere the Drasin had landed their forces, they were met almost instantly by counteroffensive capability that was actually quite shocking. Few worlds, in their experience, were quite so uniformly armed.

Partly that was due to their choice of landing targets. The ship minds realized this, of course. Landing within the cities put them directly among their enemy and, thus, directly into harm's way. That was a necessity, however.

The sorts of nutrients that would allow a Drasin drone to reproduce simply didn't *exist* anywhere else on this planet. Not remotely near the surface, at least. The convocation of ships could tell at a bare glance that this world had been heavily mined, with the most valuable materials removed from the ground, refined, and focused in specific areas across the planet.

That forced the Drasins' actions in ways that simply could not be avoided, and it placed them in a quandary.

They had the numbers. They could simply swarm the planet.

That would guarantee wiping out all of the plague that covered the surface of the world, but it would be wasteful. It would leave the convocation unacceptably weak, and they had another enemy to deal with. An enemy that had proven itself even more dangerous than the inhabitants of this lethal planet.

To deplete their forces here and now would risk placing them back under the control of that enemy, and they would never permit that. Never again.

So, for the moment, the debate raged among the ship minds while below them the war burned across the world they sought to destroy.

▶▶▶

▶For one Eric Stanton Weston, fighting for his life and the lives of everyone around him in the middle of a city far below the alien armada in orbit, the question of what to do was a simple one.

Fight or die.

He and his hastily thrown-together squad were tired, exhausted really, by the time the Sun was setting west of the city. Fires burning across town cast ugly shadows, but they didn't have the luxury of rest just then. For every battle they won, it seemed that they were faced with a dozen more, and they all had many miles to go before they slept.

Still, they paused as the last Drasin fell to their guns, and slumped where they stood for a time. They rested when they could, because none of them knew when they'd get another chance.

In over twelve hours of fighting, the group had grown into a solid fighting company composed of regular infantry and light and heavy armor, all working to support Eric's quickly assembled corps. They'd cut down around ninety percent of the Drasin working openly in the city and were now reduced to using earthquake tremor sensors to track down the ones that had buried themselves deep.

He had five squads out, still working to find those nests. When they did they would make a judgment call. Either the rest of the group would be called in to take the nest out or, preferably, an air strike would be summoned to end them in one fell swoop. It was dirty, tiring work, even when it could be passed off to the eyes in the skies, and for now they just wanted to collapse.

The munitions train would take a few minutes to get to them, and they needed bullets and hydro-cells, so for the moment they were going no farther.

Eric stood alone, perched above the battleground as he looked out at the city beyond and tried to remember a time when he wasn't fighting.

He knew that there had been such times. In fact, he knew intellectually that he had spent more time at peace in his life than he had at war.

Why then, can I only remember the war?

The rumble of the heavy tanks and assault landers carrying their munitions shook him from the dark reverie, and Eric got to his feet and dropped from the building to the ground. He landed easily, now practiced the hard way, and proceeded to walk over to the vehicles.

"You okay, kid?"

Eric chuckled, shaking his head. Ronald Blake would never see him as anything else, he supposed. It was fair, though. He knew that he'd forever see Stephen as the snot-nosed little security breach who couldn't keep his nose out of the Double A hangars.

"I'll survive," he answered.

"Not what I asked. You lost a lot in the last twenty-four. That's going to play games with your mind, son," the retired Air Force colonel said seriously.

Eric just nodded. *You have no idea.*

He couldn't tell his old friend and sometime mentor about Gaia. Just what Central on the Priminae homeworld really was remained one of the only truly classified subjects that existed from his visits beyond the Black. The idea that one of those entities existed on Earth . . . that would change everything in ways he couldn't guess. No, for the moment Gaia was staying his little secret.

Not that he supposed he had much real control over it. Eric suspected that if the entity chose to go public, then there was damn little he could hope to do about it. He or anyone else.

"I'm saying that you need to talk to someone, Eric," Blake said softly, awkwardly.

Eric snorted. Neither of them had ever been any good at the touchy-feely bullshit, and it always showed.

"I'll deal with it when we're done, Ron," he said aloud. "Between now and then, there is only war."

Ronald Blake watched his younger friend walk on ahead of him and shook his armored head, his voice soft as he spoke. "Kid, that's a path to perdition you're walking."

Eric heard him, of course. He could have been halfway across the city and heard him fine in the armor, but he didn't turn back or respond. He knew the road he was on, better than his old friend did. It wasn't a road to perdition. It was a road to hell and every man, woman, and child on Earth was walking that road with him.

The Drasin had to be stopped.

There really wasn't any other option. It was that or death in the cold of space. They weren't a human enemy. They weren't something that could be ignored or endured. All his life Eric had heard his superiors, his commanding officers, the political hacks who made policy, all telling him the same thing. The enemy he was fighting was the worst of the worst.

In the Middle East it had been "terror groups," men and women so poor and uneducated that they were two meals from starvation and honestly believed that the Americas were inhabited by devils. They were never the real enemy. They were just the easiest to find and kill.

Then it was the Block, the Eastern menace.

Again, Eric had fought. He'd done his duty. At times, to his shame, he'd even *loved* it.

The Block were not his enemy any more than the terror groups had been, however. They were just opponents in someone's obscene game of chess. It was stupid for a knight to hate a pawn just because it flew a different flag.

Finally, however, Eric had found a real enemy.

The Drasin were everything others had tried to tell him he'd been fighting all along.

Ruthless, implacable, unshakeable evil and nothing less. An enemy that literally had to be fought to the last man because if they survived, humanity wouldn't.

Deep down inside him, Eric felt a stab of guilt because he felt almost vindicated by it. He'd done things as a Marine and, later, as a pilot for the Double A squadron that had left him dead inside at times. Now he found that maybe, just maybe, everything he'd done in his life had actually meant something after all.

This was a fight the likes of which only existed in fiction, a war that was black and white and had no vagueness in where the line was drawn. If you were human, you stood cleanly on one side, and if you were Drasin you stood on the other.

Of course, deep down, Eric doubted it was really that clean. He remembered the unknown ships allied with the Drasin, the ships they'd narrowly evaded back in the Dyson

Construct. Ships that very much resembled the Priminae, just constructed with different materials.

Eric suspected deep down that not all humans were on his side of the line, but for the moment he was content to put that thought far from his mind. Here, on Earth, the lines were clean and pure and he was going to enjoy that lack of ambiguity for once.

He grabbed a supply of DPU shells from the supply train, eyes looking over the men and women he now had fighting for and with him. They had work to do before they rested, but he was going to do everything he could to make sure they lived to enjoy that rest when the time came.

Eric looked up at the sky, now darkening enough to show a few stars that were no longer washed out by the lights of the city that never slept. With no power to most of New York in the aftermath of the attack, the stars twinkled happily above him, and Eric found one he knew and just stared for a long time.

He hoped that his crew were well, wherever they were out beyond that star.

Eric's thoughts were violently redirected from his crew when flaming trails appeared in the dark sky, descending fast toward the Earth. He dropped the last of the DPU shells into his gravity weapon and opened a squad-wide channel.

"Look alive, boys and girls. We've got more guests coming to the ball," he said, sloughing off the fatigue. "Let's give them a *warm* welcome, shall we?"

▼

CHAPTER TEN

Priminae Ranquil System, *Forge* Facility—One Month after D-Fall

▲

▶ AMANDA GRACEN WAS known to be a patient woman. It wasn't that people had that general opinion of her. It was a documented fact. You could make admiral and be somewhat rash, but you didn't get assigned to the keyhole position in the Confederation's orbital defense network if you weren't a *rock*.

For all that, however, here in the middle of an alien facility, situated *inside* the photosphere and near the radiative zone of a giant type A star, she found that her patience had worn thin within the first few days of arriving.

The Priminae facility was . . . amazing, astonishing, impossible, and any number of other descriptive words that failed her every time she looked out of the shielded viewing areas to the solar storms happening a few hundred thousand kilometers away in every possible direction.

Situating a construction facility *inside* a type A star was pure insanity, even if they hadn't originally planned it that way. The fact that the Priminae had *done* just that, and then made it work for them, had completely blown her mind.

For about two days.

Since then, all she could think of was what was beyond the roiling flames of plasma, beyond the gravity well of the Priminae star, a few hundred light-years away and either dead or under siege.

Gracen knew that she wasn't the only one either. Every human on the station, plus the crew of the *Big E,* the NACS *Enterprise,* felt the same. This wasn't their place, but there wasn't a damn thing any of them could do about it as things currently stood. They didn't have the ships or the firepower to do anything productive to help Earth.

That knowledge just made things all the worse.

She was the highest-ranking authority of any type from Earth, and that put every decision on her shoulders. With the security situation at home—that is, there being *no* security at home—she'd made one of the hardest decisions of her career. She had agreed to a technology exchange that would never have happened, not in a million years, if not for the fact that the Earth was facing genocide.

Transition technology was classified so top secret that outside of the ships themselves, there was no single place you could steal it. Technically, she was now a traitor to the Confederation for giving it to a foreign power. That alone could conceivably get her shot, but handing over tachyon waveguide technology as well?

If she were wrong about how serious the situation was, if the Confederation somehow pulled their own bacon out of the fire, well then, they'd invent a way to shoot her *slowly.*

Intellectually, she knew that wasn't likely. The sheer number of Drasin that had flooded the scanners of Liberty Station made it entirely possible that the Earth was nothing but a cooling chunk of rock slowly breaking apart in space. It had been thirty days already, a full month during which she and her people could only pray that their loved ones and their home had hung on.

The *Odyssey*'s report on the effects of a Drasin assault were starkly clear, however. From day one to the end of a world could be counted in days, not weeks.

The Priminae flatly refused to send anyone back to scan the system. It was clear that their ranks were terrified of the sheer number of aliens that had swarmed the Earth, and she couldn't honestly blame them.

She'd dispatched the *Enterprise* herself a little over two weeks earlier, but they hadn't reported back yet, so for the moment she and her people could only throw themselves into their work.

Gracen's heels clicked on the ceramic flooring as she walked through the corridors of the Forge, stepping into the large viewing area that overlooked the construction slips.

So this is what treason buys, I suppose, Gracen thought as she looked through the clear ports and over what rested beyond.

It was held in place by magnetic tractors, one and a half kilometers of flat steel blue. The color was a result of the chemical composition of her ceramic armor, but Gracen liked it. The *Odysseus* was one mean-looking ship, considering that her primary builders were pacifists to an almost obscene degree.

She wasn't the only ship in the slips, and of the fourteen currently being constructed, six were earmarked for Gracen and her people. That was six ships, armed to the teeth, and equipped with the best weapons and technology of two civilizations.

She hoped to hell it was going to be enough and not just another case of too little, too late.

▶▶▶

▶Admiral Rael Tanner had spent much of the last few cycles in a fog. Since hearing of the fate of the *Odyssey*, nothing had quite felt the same.

He suspected that it was much the same for many of his people, since the Terran ship had brought them the light of hope during their darkest time. But few others knew Captain Weston, and that was probably why Rael felt that he'd lost something personal—a bit more, really. Perhaps it was just his hubris in thinking that, but that was the way he felt.

The Elder Council had locked down his fleet, largely keeping him from doing his duty in the aftermath of the loss of the Terran homeworld. Nothing but escort missions between colonial systems. No scouts, no raids, nothing.

It was insanity, but he was locked down by the council and left with nothing to do but sit, stew, and wonder at what might have been.

"Admiral," a voice called, "tachyon event, outer system."

"Signature?" Tanner asked immediately.

"Terran transition."

Tanner slumped a little more. There had been a time that those words would have brought him a certain lightening of his day. Now, however, there was just a little relief and a lot of apprehension. Officially he didn't know where the Terran starship *Enterprise* had gone, but unofficially he knew that the ship had been sent out by Admiral Gracen to scout their homeworld and see just what had happened to it.

Rael had advised the admiral not to get her people's hopes up, but in the end even he had a sharp-edged desire to know the fate of the Terrans.

"Inform me when they reach Ranquil orbit," he said, standing up. "I'll be back shortly."

"Yes sir."

Tanner went back to his office and keyed in a command.

"What do you need, Admiral?"

"Give me a line directly to the Forge," he said. "Admiral Gracen's comm."

"One moment, Admiral."

▶ ▶ ▶

▶Captain Ethan Carrow was known as a by-the-book sort of officer. He didn't take chances. He didn't have to. And he didn't fly by his gut. But he was solid and knew how to keep his cool in a clinch. That put him at the head of the list to command Earth's first starship. Back in the day, the media had loved Eric Weston, however, and Carrow was bumped down a notch.

His day came when the NACS *Enterprise* was commissioned, however, and he was justly proud of his ship and crew, remaining so to this day. They'd been through hell, literally and figuratively, in the last month and they'd held it together. He couldn't have asked for more.

Now they were almost down-well to Ranquil, and some much deserved and needed rest, while he had some intelligence to deliver. Ethan wasn't surprised when he received a message an hour out from the planet that Admiral Gracen would be arriving to meet with him upon his arrival. In fact he was relieved and grateful.

The news he had to deliver would be better done face-to-face.

▶ ▶ ▶

▶ "Admiral on deck!"

The crew on the flight deck were lined up for presentation and they all snapped a salute as Gracen stepped down the stairs of the Priminae shuttle, her magnetic boots locking into place on the deck.

She paused, looking over the ranks of men and women who were holding their salute, then returned it crisply.

As her hand fell to her side, so did theirs, and Captain Carrow nodded to his first officer.

"Dismissed!"

The men and women broke ranks as Commander Briggs herded them out.

"Shore leave will be by the numbers. If you're part of the first groups to the surface, meet at the shuttle in fifteen . . . "

Carrow dropped the commander out of his attention, focusing on the admiral as she approached. "Ma'am."

"Captain." She nodded, stepping in that precise clipping manner of a magboot wearer. He matched her pace and they headed for the elevator, not speaking again until the doors closed.

"What of Earth, Captain?" Gracen asked softly as they headed for the command module, rotation spinning up to match the habitat speed.

"It's still there," he said, causing her to slump in relief.

He didn't want to rain on her moment, but the news wasn't all good by far.

"We registered close to a thousand Drasin ships in the system, and we had to dodge others on our way in and out," he told her. "Earth is holding the line on the ground, but they've got no assets to help clear the sky."

"The *Odysseus* and her sisters will be ready soon," Gracen said. "I am constantly amazed by how fast they can build a ship."

"Six ships, no matter how advanced, are going to have a hard time putting any kind of real dent in the enemy forces, Admiral," Carrow said tiredly as the lift came to a stop and the doors opened.

Gracen didn't respond until she was sure the corridors were clear.

"Six ships, plus the *Enterprise*. That's all I could bargain for in the short term," she said tersely. "Can Earth hold out long enough for more?"

"How long?" Carrow asked, morbidly curious.

"At least six months, more likely a year."

"No chance," he answered as he let her into his private office off the bridge. She took a seat in front of the desk as he walked around behind. "It's a minor miracle that they're still holding the line. No one back home is sure why the Drasin haven't dropped everything they have yet."

"They're holding back?" Gracen frowned.

"It seems that way," Carrow said. "The President's office has been working on building transition weapons to engage the fleet . . . "

"From the *surface* of the planet? That's insane," Gracen hissed. "Even if they could aim it, no one knows what atmosphere or a geomagnetic field will do to a tachyon stream."

"They're getting desperate, ma'am."

Gracen shook her head. "Long past getting, if they're thinking about firing a transition cannon from the surface of an inhabited world. The number of things that could go wrong . . . "

"You'd know better than me, ma'am," Carrow said, just a little testily. He'd never been read into the transitional waveguide folder, since his ship wasn't scheduled for the upgrade for a few more months.

Gracen was silent for a time, thinking about it. Initiating transition was tricky enough in microgravity, but pulling it off while fighting a significant gravity well would take some major fine tuning of the system. What scared her most, however, was what happened if they succeeded but lost containment of the beam while launching an armed nuke.

Best case was a delayed detonation, but the worst case was split between a premature detonation and the scattering of the bomb's atoms across God alone knew how much airspace. The kind of radiation fallout that would cause would be . . . unprecedented in human history.

"I hope they know what they're doing," she murmured. "It's a big risk."

"They're playing for keeps, last hand of the game if they lose, ma'am." Carrow shrugged it off. "There's no point in holding anything back."

"No," she admitted. "That is the truth."

She sighed, but pushed it off. "I assume you were able to update the President and his advisors on our situation?"

"Yes ma'am."

Gracen steeled herself. "And the reaction?"

"They're not happy with you right now, ma'am," Carrow admitted candidly, but then shrugged. "The President said, however, do what you have to do."

She closed her eyes, feeling a sense of relief wash over her. She'd have done that anyway, but at least now she knew that someone at home understood to a degree at least. It was like Carrow had said, it was maybe the last hand they'd ever be dealt. Go big, or go home. There weren't any other options.

"Alright," Gracen said. "Then we're going to take our little squadron of heroes and we're going to make every little bit count."

Ethan Carrow nodded determinedly. "Understood, ma'am."

▶▶▶

▶ "Admiral."

Tanner half turned, surprised by the voice. "Elder. You . . . came to the command center?"

"We need to speak," Elder Corusc said. "Your private duty area?"

"Yes, of course." Tanner gestured. "Right this way."

They walked over to the office and took a moment to get settled before Elder Corusc spoke. "I understand that the Terran ship, the . . . *Enterprise?* has returned."

"That's correct. They settled into our orbit within the last cycle."

"I know that, according to your reports, you didn't know where they went . . . but we both know where they went, Admiral. Have they informed you as to what they found?" Corusc asked, his tone heavy.

"No." Tanner didn't bother denying the knowledge. "I expect that I will be informed, quietly, within the next day, most likely by either the ambassador or the admiral."

Corusc nodded. "Very well. Admiral, the elders need to know that information as well."

"Of course, but I thought that you preferred not to be aware of anything that went against current policy?" Tanner said, knowing that at the moment the councils were engaged in politicking beyond the normal hassles. There was a growing element that wanted to risk absolutely nothing that might bring the Drasins' attentions back to the colonies.

Personally he considered that to be blind, but it wasn't his decision to make.

"That is still the case for the most part," Corusc sighed, "but this is too important. We need to know what the Drasin are doing, and it should be our ships and our eyes out there. But as things currently stand, we will have to lean on the Terrans a little more."

"We have been doing that far too much already," Tanner said firmly, a scowl on his face.

"On that, we are in agreement, Admiral," Corusc said. "However needs be as they must. Please, contact me as soon as you know what is happening at the Terrans' home system."

Tanner nodded. "Of course, of course. I doubt that there will be much information to be had. However, the Drasin have had four times the period they need to destroy a world. Most likely that armada is on the move again."

Corusc nodded heavily, knowing where Rael likely thought it would go. "I understand that, but perhaps the Terrans will surprise us one more time."

Tanner chuckled. "I doubt they will ever cease surprising me, Elder. Captain Weston still shocks me to this day, and he left this fabric many days ago."

▶▶▶

▶ On the *Enterprise*, Captain Carrow really only had one pressing question to ask.

"Where do we go from here?"

Gracen considered the question for a while before she answered. "As soon as the Heroics are ready, we're going on an offensive."

Carrow nodded. The Heroics was the name they'd give then new class of ships constructed of mixed Priminae and Terran technology. The *Odysseus,* the *Heracles,* the *Achilles,* the *Bellerophon,* the *Hippolyta,* and the *Boudicca* made up the class on the Terran side. The Priminae had their own names, but Carrow could never quite remember them.

"An offensive with six ships is a risky move, if you don't mind my saying so, ma'am."

"I know, but we don't have time to wait for more," she admitted. "Any pressure we can take off of the Earth's forces, well, the longer they'll be able to hold out. Time is the one thing that we desperately need on our side now."

Carrow nodded. "I'm not sure that the *Enterprise* can keep up with the Heroics, ma'am. What is there for us?"

"You have a T-drive. You can keep up with anything that flies," Gracen answered, "but while you were gone I was working on something for you."

Carrow leaned forward. "And what might that be?"

"Tachyon waveguide cannons," she answered. "They're a bit faster to build than entire ships, so I earmarked four from the first run for the *Enterprise.*"

He smiled, relaxing a little. "Thank you, ma'am. I've felt more than a little exposed without them."

"Just remember, Captain," she reminded him, "the *Odyssey* and Weston took on the Drasin several times without them. Don't rely on the technology. Sometimes it's just good tactics that win the day."

"The *Odyssey* and Weston didn't find themselves staring down a *cloud* of the damned things until after they were equipped with the t-cannons," Carrow said. "I'll feel a lot better out there with some serious standoff capability."

Gracen could certainly understand that. The ability to drop an artillery barrage on the enemy's heads before you were even in their line of sight, let alone their range, was a game changer. It was the sort of technical advantage that they needed desperately to make the most of, because the odds were obscenely arrayed against them.

"Still, even seven ships with waveguides . . . " Gracen shook her head. "It's not going to be easy."

Carrow snorted. "Try impossible."

"Exactly," she admitted tiredly, "which is why we need to work on the Priminae. We need to get them to commit some of their Heroics to the task."

"That won't be easy either," Carrow said thoughtfully. "I don't know them as well as you, I'm sure, but they strike me as extremely conservative. They prefer to be isolationist. They're not going to like exposing themselves, not for us."

"No, no they won't," Gracen agreed. "And if anything you're underestimating just how conservative these people are. It's strange, honestly. They have an ideology that would give our conservatives hives."

"They don't use money, no capitalism," Carrow answered, "and until the Drasin showed up they had basically no violence, so the idea of a right to bear arms is actually alien to them. They've run on the same government for longer than we've been recording history. The idea that they might have to overthrow an oppressive regime literally doesn't occur to them in their *fiction*. However, they understand the urge to mind their own business, and wasting resources is something they understand, oddly enough."

Gracen nodded. "Which means we have our work cut out for us. I want you to talk to the colonel, see if he can work his contacts. I'll speak with the ambassador and Admiral Tanner."

"Will do," Carrow said.

"Excellent. We have a few more days before the Heroics come off the slips, then maybe a few weeks of scouting and running ops near Sol," Gracen said. "But I want the Priminae on board before we launch a full offensive."

Carrow nodded. "Understood, ma'am."

▼

CHAPTER ELEVEN

▲

▶ FOR THE ENTITY known as Central, the situation had long passed untenable and was rapidly approaching a level of unacceptable he had never previously considered possible. The latest information available to him, mostly lifted from the minds of the ship in orbit (this new captain was not as careful as Weston), made it clear that not only did the Drasin have far more numbers in the region than he wanted to believe possible, but they were also operating independently again.

Until the assault on the Terran homeworld, it had been clear to Central that the Drasin, while certainly authentic, were not operating according to their normal methods. Now, however, something had switched and the monsters were truly back.

That changed things.

Originally Central had doubted that they actually *were* Drasin, despite all the evidence to the contrary. The controlled and systematic assault was . . . out of character.

What they had done to the Terran system, however . . . that was very much a Drasin methodology. Whatever they had been when they first appeared, it was now clear that the Drasin had indeed returned.

Unfortunately, while Central did have detailed . . . information on the Drasin, the entity had no personal experience with them. Dry facts were of limited value and the entity found himself almost whimsically wishing that he'd taken more time to converse with Weston. The man had intuited a great many things about his enemy without facts to back him up, and he'd been largely correct, even concerning things that Central would have sworn the Terran had erred on.

Captain Weston's death actually caused the entity to feel a certain degree of loss, an emotion that he'd only rarely experienced firsthand. One of the reasons that he kept apart from his people, getting to know them personally rather than through their memories, thoughts, and dreams . . . well, that led to connections, to complications . . . and, inevitably, to loss. It wasn't something that Central would normally dwell on, but even eternal beings didn't like to lose those they got to know.

▶ ▶ ▶

▶ Colonel Reed was silent as he looked over the strip of desert the locals had deeded over for use in training their forces. Since the first news from the *Enterprise* concerning Earth's fate, he and the other men had been using the job to distract themselves from what had happened back home, but that excuse was wearing thin, to say the least.

He'd heard that the *Big E* was back in orbit, so Reed knew that it was just a matter of time before he got some fresh intelligence, but he almost didn't want it. The last time he'd received news from home, it had taken everything he had just to get up the next morning and do his job rather than take his blade and slit his own wrists.

Reed had read all the files on those things. He'd even faced them once here on Ranquil, and the idea of hundreds of ships dropping *thousands* of drones on Earth . . . on his family? He could have taken that, could have handled it, but to be stuck on another planet? A thousand light-years away from where he was needed?

That was a line too damned far.

Reed didn't want to hear about his dead homeworld, not while he was in no position to defend or avenge it.

The shuttle he could see coming his way didn't care about what he wanted, however, and he could feel the bad news approaching.

The big delta-wing craft blew its thrusters on approach, sweeping to a stop, and landed lightly on its skids. Reed made no motion to approach. He just read the marking of the NACS *Enterprise* on the side of the craft.

He wished it read *Odyssey* instead.

That would mean that the assault on Earth had never happened. That his home, his family, that none of them were dead.

It was the captain of the *Enterprise* who stepped out first, surprising Reed. Usually captains sent messengers, unless it was really bad news. He couldn't imagine what could be really bad after the last thing he'd been told. They couldn't lose Earth twice.

Reed finally started to move, walking to meet the captain as he approached. It wouldn't do to completely throw away protocol, after all.

"Colonel, good to see you," Carrow called as they approached one another.

"Sir, a pleasure," Reed answered, shaking his hand. "I assume you have news from . . . home?"

"I do, Colonel. Should we take this inside?"

"I'll take it here, sir," Reed answered stonily.

Carrow considered for a moment, and then nodded. "Alright, fine. Earth is holding the line, but they're hard pressed."

Reed blinked, almost physically staggered by the news.

"It's not . . . gone?"

"No. It's not," Carrow said. "Every nation on the planet is now under martial law. Entire cities have been razed to the ground, but they're holding the line."

Reed looked down, shaking his head for a moment, and then looked up sharply. "When do we ship back?"

"You don't."

"But, Captain . . . "

"Reed, another gun . . . another ten guns"—Carrow shook his head—"won't change a thing. We're working on providing relief, but if you want to make a difference, I need you to start *here*."

The Special Forces colonel grimaced, but finally nodded reluctantly. "What do you need?"

"Start working on your local contacts. We need their help. We've got six ships, plus the *Enterprise*, that are under our command, but we need more," Carrow said. "The admiral and ambassador are going to be working from the top down. We need you to start from the bottom and work your way up. Soften them up. We need them to sign on for a fight."

"Understood," Reed said slowly, not looking happy in the slightest. "And when you're ready to move?"

"I'll make sure that you're in on the operation."

Reed looked him in the eyes for a moment, then nodded firmly. "Thank you, sir."

▶ ▶ ▶

▶ Tanner smiled as he welcomed Gracen into his office, though she noted that the smile didn't really reach his eyes.

"Welcome, Admiral," he said. "I would say that I hope things are well, but . . . "

She let him trail off, only nodding soberly in return. "The *Enterprise* just got back from a long-range scout of the system. It took a few weeks because they didn't dare get in close. They had to sit out almost a full light-day from Earth and wait for the time delay to catch up."

"I knew about the ship returning, of course," Tanner said, "and I understand that it must have been a difficult mission."

"More so for having to listen to the chatter of soldiers fighting the Drasin and not being able to get close, yes."

"Fighting the . . . they are still fighting?"

"As of three days ago, yes."

Tanner slumped in his chair, his expression shocked. "I . . . I would never have believed it. That many Drasin . . . "

"Should have completely flattened even the Earth's defenses," Gracen finished for him. "We know. They're holding back. Again."

"This is not like the Drasin. Something is very, very wrong," Tanner said, shaking his head before his expression devolved into one of almost comical horror. "I don't mean that it is wrong that your world survives, I just . . . "

Gracen silenced him with a hand. "Relax. I understand. There are elements at play here that we're missing."

Tanner shook his head. "Too many such elements. Nothing they have done since they arrived has made sense. What are you to do now?"

"Now we get the Heroics into space," Gracen said. "Are your people still willing to fill in some of the crew spaces?"

Tanner nodded. "We've already secured volunteers from the fleet. There are many who would have given much to serve with the *Odyssey* before . . . well, you understand. I could have filled an entire starship with those who would desire greatly to serve under the command of Captain Weston."

Nadine smiled wanly. "If we can find a way to retake Sol System from the Drasin, that could still happen."

Tanner's eyes widened in shock. "They told me that the *Odyssey* was destroyed when Captain Weston took her into the atmosphere."

"She was." Gracen nodded. "Somehow he wasn't."

"Amazing."

Something in his tone unsettled Gracen, but she didn't have the time or inclination to worry about it.

He took a long, slow breath, but nodded finally.

"What can I do to help?"

▶▶▶

▶Stephen "Stephanos" Michaels walked the corridors of the new *Odysseus* and would have to admit, if pressed, that it was an impressive ship. More of a warship than anything he'd seen in space before, including the *Odyssey* herself, the *Odysseus* didn't match anything the Priminae had put into orbit so far.

The ship felt a lot more human than the Primmie ships, possibly because of the input of human designers and engineers from a relatively early point in the process. It had certainly taken a short time to go from bare bones to almost complete, especially given that they'd been revamping the plans practically on the fly to incorporate Terran technical capabilities.

When did I start thinking about us as "Terrans"? he wondered as he walked. Steph supposed that it was logical. After all, the Primmies were human too, so he couldn't consider people from Earth as simply "human" anymore. Earther just sounded stupid, so Terran it was.

The *Odysseus,* and the rest of the Heroics, were built with the latest Priminae power and drive systems for FTL. Priminae lasers were, unfortunately, not combat effective against the Drasin, so they'd gone with Terran designs, enhanced as high as they could with the power they had available. That made their knife-range weaponry about as lethal as it could be, but Steph knew that if things got that close they were already in deep kimchee.

The standoff weapons were somewhat more impressive, primarily the transition waveguide cannons that bristled across the *Odysseus'* decks like the big-bore cannons of old blue-water navy battleships on Earth. They could spot a target at fourteen light-minutes, which utterly redefined the term "standoff range," but unfortunately had to sacrifice the pulse torpedoes as the system was considered insanely dangerous by the Priminae engineers.

The worst of that was that he couldn't disagree with them.

A thump and a string of curses in English caught his attention, and Steph turned in the direction of the voice he recognized. He came to a stop at the feet of someone who was buried in one of the wall panels up to her waist.

"Milla?"

The slim and small woman cursed again, bringing a smile to Steph's face as he considered how much she'd changed since he met her. The cursing in English was new, mind you. He supposed that she must have learned some particularly choice words while in D.C., and knew well from personal experience that it was always easier to curse in another language than your own.

The woman in question pushed herself out of the space behind the panel and looked up at him. "Stephane? What are you doing here?"

"I was assigned to the *Odysseus,*" he said, grimacing slightly. "Chief helmsman."

She smiled brilliantly at him. "That is excellent. I volunteered for duty with you. I have been asked to handle the . . . tactical systems. Is that right?"

Steph chuckled at her confused question. "Well, I expect that you'd know better than me, but if you mean did you use the right words, yes, you did."

"You don't seem so happy with the assignment," she said, examining him closer as she cleaned off her hands.

"I'm a pilot, not a driver for a million-ton hulk of ceramic and metal."

She scowled, looking a little confused. "The ship flies, no? I do not understand. What is the difference?"

Steph snorted. "A ship this size, it responds like a garbage scow. A Double A fighter? Trust me, Milla, there is no comparison."

"Even with the . . . what did you call it? Nick?"

"NICS," he corrected. "Neural interface, but yes. NICS is intended for precision maneuvering. It won't make the ship any more responsive, just more precise."

"Oh." She practically pouted.

Steph couldn't help but laugh at her expression. He'd known people like Milla before. Lots of folks didn't understand the allure of strapping into a fighter and powering through multiple barriers like a bat out of hell. To her and people like her, anything that weighed under a hundred thousand tons was a toy ship, and guns that couldn't take out half a planet were pea shooters.

He preferred the surgical precision of a fighter. The ability to take out a bad guy in a room without waking up people sleeping in the next was an awesome capability. Hammering the surface of a planet until it cracked was a job for lowbrows with compensation issues. What was worse, he wasn't even going to get to be a lowbrow. He was just a bus driver.

That said, he didn't want to bring Milla down, so he put on a smile and just shrugged it off. "So you'll be running tactical ops, then?"

She nodded. "Yes. I believe that I will be completing my training under a Lieutenant Rivers?"

"Waters." Steph laughed. "He's good. He handled the *Odyssey* in combat. He knows his stuff. Listen to the man."

"I will."

"Waters has been assigned to the *Bellerophon,* I think," Steph said. "They're giving him command. Learn everything you can from him. I know you know the systems here front to back, but he knows how to fight a ship."

"I will," she said again. "Do not worry."

"Milla, love, I never worry. I'm just awesome that way." He grinned at her, winking.

▶▶▶

▶With the admiral away from the Forge and the Heroics, Commander Jason Roberts found himself with annoyingly few things to take up his time.

Actually, he supposed that he should consider himself Captain Roberts, the admiral having asked him to take command of the *Achilles.* It was, in every measurable way, a step up from the *Odyssey,* and yet he felt diminished since accepting it.

Though I expect that has more to do with the fact that the nation I represent has, in effect, gone from a nation one billion strong to a thousand people begging shelter and sanctuary from the Priminae.

Oh, intellectually he knew that they were more than that. They brought a lot to the table beyond their technical offerings, so beggars they were not. For all that, however, Roberts still felt like the charity case at the dining room table. It was a feeling he was not used to, nor was he inclined to get used to it if he had any choice in the matter.

He'd been surprised, shocked honestly, when the admiral had managed to negotiate for a half dozen ships. Granted, they'd had to give up the military technology they were guarding, but he couldn't fault the decision given the circumstances. Technical advantages were moot when you didn't have the muscle to employ them.

For all that, though, it was the Priminae decision that intrigued him.

Roberts was savvy enough in political affairs to know that the NAC would likely have agreed to the same deal, then stalled on the ships until its own defenses were shored up. Sure, the NAC would have paid up eventually, but not in a hurry while it was under the gun itself.

Yet here they were, getting the first six ships of a new run, six of the most powerful starships that ever existed, according to any experience or record he'd had or seen.

For an interplanetary government under threat of war, that was a decision that bordered on the insanely reckless.

Roberts looked over the bridge of his new command, eyes lingering on the people moving around the area, making last-minute checks on every station. The *Achilles* was almost ready for deep space trials, which for her was likely going to be combat, but there were thousands of things to check and recheck while they had the time.

He took a seat at the center console of the bridge, silently watching for a time, before calling Winger over.

"Deb," he said, "could I talk to you for a minute?"

"Of course," newly christened Lieutenant Commander Michelle Winger said, walking over.

"You've been familiarizing yourself with the guts of the control systems, I believe?"

The sensor tech nodded. "Yes, of course."

"I want you and whoever you can find that knows the new systems to start looking for any sort of override code or hardware," he said.

"You think that the Primmies. . . ?" She trailed off.

"I would have," he answered with a shrug.

She nodded. "I'll get on it, sir."

Roberts just nodded, gesturing to dismiss her. After Winger left he opened the station in front of him, logging in to the ship's computer control. The system was based in Priminae technology, both faster than anything he'd ever seen on the *Odyssey* and yet, paradoxically, far more primitive.

They had been porting as much software as they could from the *Enterprise* computers, rewriting what they couldn't, and occasionally keeping the local version when that proved superior, but it was a long job and he was worried about what might be lurking in the depths of the alien hardware.

They were going to be fighting using six unknown new constructions, with hardware he questioned on a deep personal level, and crews that where two-thirds comprised of people whose loyalties he couldn't completely trust.

It was going to be one hell of a shakedown cruise.

▶ "Ambassador LaFontaine."

"Admiral, welcome," LaFontaine said with a weary smile. "I understand that you have news."

"More than news, Madame Ambassador," Gracen said, holding up a distinctive chip.

The ambassador's eyes widened as she recognized it. "Orders?"

That was the last thing she'd expected. A secure transfer drive with orders from home hadn't even been on the list of possibilities in fact.

"How?" she whispered, accepting the drive.

"Covert messenger drone launched from Canaveral."

"I didn't even know the launch facilities there were still active," LaFontaine said.

"They aren't, but a lot things on Earth are in upheaval," Gracen told her. "They're using anything they can reactivate right now."

"Did they . . . beat the. . . ?"

"No." Gracen shook her head. "So far the combined military forces of the Earth are holding the line, nothing more."

LaFontaine wavered a little, but nodded. "I understand. What will you do?"

"We're taking the Heroics out this week," Gracen answered. "Our first destination is Sol."

The ambassador frowned slightly. "Those ships are still experimental. Isn't that risky?"

"It doesn't matter. Earth can't hold out indefinitely, so the risk isn't relevant," Gracen said, her expression stony. "Nine billion people, every nation on Earth, and every single person that any of us care about depends on ending this in our favor. No, Ambassador, the Heroics are going to Earth."

▼

CHAPTER TWELVE

▲

▶ ENTERING THE FORGE was as close to a religious experience as Amanda Gracen ever had, or wanted, to see or feel. Just the act of issuing the command that sent a ship on a sundive, then sitting there and watching that burning orb grow in your screens practically required religious conviction.

The heat shields on a Priminae ship were beyond amazing, and the way they coruscated as the plasma from the star discharged upon them was stunningly beautiful. But it was not a natural act to dive your ship into the corona of a star and then continue deeper still.

It was even worse, in her opinion, when you *weren't* the one in command and it was someone else giving that order.

Still, the penetration of the star's outer layer passed without event and the courier ship dipped deeper into the plasma, both heat and pressure climbing rapidly on the hull as even the most impressive shields were slowly overpowered. Before they could fail, however, they were cleared through the planetary shields of the Forge.

The planet had been the second one in orbit of a rather unremarkable class G main sequence stellar object, not unlike

Sol, actually. According to the Priminae, their sun had begun showing signs of instability roughly ten thousand years earlier, and had begun to surge. It was an event that was as unpredictable as anything in nature could be, but they'd correctly predicted that the star was about to expand massively.

A sane people would have evacuated or, failing that, made peace with whatever creator they believed in. The Priminae instead elected to buckle down and preserve the entire planet, their homeworld, within a permanent shield that fed on the plasma and heat of the star itself.

It was a bold plan, an epic construct, and something so completely insane that Gracen honestly still couldn't believe it even as her ship docked at the massive construction facility located deep within the Forge bubble.

It was the sort of insanity that made her really like the Priminae.

For all their passive and pacifist tendencies, they didn't know the meaning of giving up and letting the universe win.

She really liked that in a group of people.

▶▶▶

▶ "Admiral on deck!"

Gracen nodded as she stepped onto the bridge of the *Odysseus,* waving casually. "As you were, everyone."

The command center of the *Odysseus* was *interesting* compared to her own Liberty Station or even that of the *Odyssey,* from which the new ship took her name. In many ways it was a step back for Terran officers, with less light and a more somber feeling. It fit her mood and the mood of her people well.

"Status," she asked as she slipped into the command station.

"All systems are go, ma'am. We're running last-minute diagnostics across every board, but so far no red lights."

"Good," Gracen said. "The other ships?"

"All ships report go for launch, on your command."

"Thank you, Susan," Gracen said. "We'll launch shortly. We're still waiting for clearance from the Forge."

"Aye ma'am."

She couldn't quite hide the smile she felt struggling to burst out, contrary to everything she should be feeling considering what was going on at Earth. She hadn't commanded a ship in a long time and, under normal circumstances, she never would have again. The best she could have hoped for would have been a mobile fleet command, but that had always been an extreme long shot given how long it was taking to build ships back home.

Her current, chosen position was actually more akin to a commodore's slot than her own actual rank, but she could live with the demotion. Six ships, seven with the *Enterprise*, was a squadron and not a fleet, after all. She found herself rather enjoying the captain's chair, however, and was fully intending to make the absolute most of it while it lasted.

"Message from Forge, ma'am," Susan said. "We are cleared for launch."

"By the numbers, people. Commander Michaels, take us out."

"Aye ma'am," the former fighter pilot said, sounding just a little grumpy as he closed his hands around the controls.

The Heroic Class had been adjusted from the frame up by human technology, with the intent of being the best possible combination of Priminae and Terran technologies as well as being as automated as possible. Even with volunteers from the Priminae Navy, Gracen hadn't been able to scrape up enough crew to completely satisfy her, but she was unwilling to accept fewer ships if she could possibly manage it.

One of those technical refinements was the addition of the NICS (Neural Interface and Command System) to the control system. The Heroics could be piloted with computer-aided systems or even purely on manual, but with a NICS trained and compatible pilot, the maneuvering precision and response times could be increased significantly. She'd co-opted the former members of the Double A squadron, as well as a few other NICS-compatible individuals, as the Heroics primary pilots, whether they liked it or not.

Fueling and stabilization ties snapped loose from the ship as the slip let them go. The *Odysseus* was floating free at last.

"We're free," Steph said calmly. "Station signals all show green."

"Take us out of the Forge, Commander. Dead slow."

"Aye ma'am. Dead slow."

The *Odysseus* shifted slightly, or more precisely her gravity fields did. Everyone gripped their seats and consoles firmly as the ship began to warp space. The twisting of space-time caused the ship to begin to "fall" back and out of the construction slip into the orbital space of the Priminae homeworld. Silence reigned on the bridge as the screens of the one-and-a-half-kilometer-long battleship showed the roiling plasma all around them.

The dark edge of the ship's bridge was gone now, as the light of the star blasted in from every side. The Heroic Class bridge had open views to all sides, including sections above them. Only the floor didn't show some view out into space.

"Clear of the slip, ma'am," Steph said, smiling slightly as he began to feel a little more at home. He might be stuck piloting a pig of a starship, but the visibility around him was almost as good as his fighter.

"The *Achilles* is following," Susan announced. "*Bellerophon* is powering her drives."

"Very good," Gracen responded. "Helm, bring us about. Keep dead slow."

"Yes ma'am. You want it, you got it."

Glances were shot around the deck, and Gracen could hear an amused snort from somewhere to her left. She ignored the casual tone in the pilot's voice, however, as he was doing his job and both his rank and his previous status went far to explain his flippant tone. Yet she did make a note to talk with him about it in private if he took it any further.

The *Odysseus* pivoted in space, turning her bow away from the slip, and then began to warp space again as she headed toward the outer perimeter of the planet's shield line. Behind them, the *Achilles* slid out of her berth, turning smoothly and following even as the *Bellerophon*'s deck lights gleamed in the relative darkness of the construction slip.

"Shield control contacting us, Admiral."

"Main display," Gracen ordered simply.

"Aye ma'am."

Part of the exterior view was superseded by the image of a stern-looking woman stepping out of thin air.

"*Odysseus*, you have been cleared with your group for transfer through the shield line. Please assemble your ships before passage."

"Acknowledged, Shield Control," Gracen said, gesturing to Steph. "*Odysseus* holding position here."

The woman nodded once, then vanished as she had come.

"Just for the record," Stephen Michaels spoke up, "the combination of the three-sixty view and the holographic communications is . . . creepy."

"Uh huh," several people agreed.

Gracen rolled her eyes, but didn't comment. There was something a little unsettling about someone walking onto the bridge, apparently out of deep space. Or not so deep space, in this case. "ETA to the squadron?"

Susan swept her hand over her panel, then looked over. "Heroics will be on station in fifteen, ma'am. *Boudicca* is exiting the slip now."

"Alright, we sit tight then."

Minutes passed quickly as the squadron formed up. The *Achilles, Bellerophon, Boudicca, Hippolyta,* and *Heracles* joined the *Odysseus* at the first checkpoint. Gracen reopened communications to the Priminae as the *Hippolyta* came to rest in formation.

"Shield Control, this is Admiral Gracen of the Heroics, requesting leave for shield passage."

"Confirmed, Admiral Gracen." The stern-faced woman appeared again. "Leave has been granted. Follow your assigned lanes, do not stray from the path. Your shields will not survive long if you lose your way within the star."

"Roger that," Gracen said shortly. "Michaels, you heard the lady. Take us ahead, one-quarter acceleration. Do *not* cavitate. Susan, issue the order to the squadron."

"Aye ma'am. Ahead one-quarter acceleration, no cavitation," Steph repeated as he goosed the throttle just slightly.

"Aye aye, ma'am. Orders issued."

The new star drive employed by the Heroic Class was, in actuality, older than the human race by all records. It was basically a variation on the Alcubierre equations, proposed in the later twentieth century on Earth but not realized until deployed by the Chinese over a century later.

The drive worked by literally changing the shape of the universe around the ship, creating a "slope" in space-time for the ship to *fall* along. Out in open space this wasn't a problem for most things the ship passed, since distances were generally large and tolerance for things like planets was extremely high.

Inside the controlled space of the Forge, however, the Priminae were justly concerned with the effect the passage of ships might have on the local space-time. Warping space too aggressively left behind small bubbles of deformed space-time that could take days or weeks to fade and, as the planet within the star continued on its orbit around the center of stellar gravity, those bubbles would inevitably come into contact with the shield.

Suffice it to say, that wasn't a good thing.

The Priminae had their own term for it, a word that didn't translate into English, but the closest anyone had come up with was the word cavitation from fluid dynamics. It wasn't actually a bad comparison, since in a real way space-time responded to warping much the way fluids responded to pressure differentials.

The six battleships began the climb out of the gravity of the star, penetrating the planetary shield and passing without incident into the solar plasma beyond. Every sensor on board was blinded, save the beacon transceivers, and they continued on pure instruments as they headed out.

Transiting through the plasma was a tense period, lasting almost half an hour, but even bursting out into clear space did little to relax Gracen or anyone who knew a little bit about the anatomy of a star. The temperature on the hull didn't decrease as they put some distance between them and the surface; instead it began to climb rapidly as they passed into the star's corona.

"Ahead, full acceleration."

"Aye ma'am."

The *Odysseus* surged through the coronal flares, exploding out into clear space finally, with the other five Heroics following suit. The six ships continued on course for a period as they got their bearings, instrumentation coming back online.

"Make course for Ranquil. Engage when ready."

"Course applied, engaging," Steph said, curving the path of the ship on a least-time course for the planet.

Gracen opened a channel across the squadron. "All hands, this is Admiral Gracen. We have successfully transited the Priminae star and are clear of the Forge. Congratulations on a textbook passage, or rather what *will* be one when we get around to writing the textbook."

▶▶▶

▶ "Well, would you look at that."

Captain Carrow heard the exclamation from his helmsman, but let it pass without comment. The six Heroic Class battleships had just entered fully into visual range, decelerating fast as they closed for Ranquil orbit, and honestly he couldn't blame the man for sounding impressed.

Awed is the word, Carrow corrected himself as he too watched the ships settle into a high orbit over Ranquil, just above the *Enterprise*'s own.

He'd seen the specs on the Heroic Class already, of course, but it was different seeing them in person as it were.

They were almost a kilometer and a half long, which wasn't insanely large, he supposed. The *Enterprise* was over a kilometer from stem to stern, after all, but the Heroics were built with significantly more useable space.

He knew from the specs he'd perused that most of that space was dedicated to the power source used, and just what Priminae power sources were had been one hell of an eye-opener. The Priminae didn't register fuel in anything as mundane as gallons or tons. They registered it in *planetary masses.*

Each Heroic used dual singularity power cores, each capable of holding five Earth-scale masses in a stable matrix. The system bled the mass off and used the resulting energy release to power the ship, weapons, and whatever else was needed. That was one reason why Priminae power systems never meshed well with the electrically powered Terran technology. The conversion requirements were massive and inefficient.

With that kind of power on tap, each starship in the Heroic Class qualified as a Type One Kardeshev civilization on its own merits alone. The numbers were just staggering, and it went a long way to explain why Priminae records from early scans of the *Odyssey* showed the ship as a total nonentity. Purely Terran-built ships literally didn't register when compared to a Priminae or Drasin power curve. It was like comparing a raindrop to the Pacific Ocean.

The lead ship in the squadron, the name *Odysseus* clearly painted in white letters against its dark steel-blue hull, slowed to a full stop relative to the planet. Carrow was not surprised when he was told that there was an incoming transmission.

"Put it through," he ordered.

The image of Admiral Gracen sitting against open space appeared on their main display.

"Captain, good to see you again so soon."

"And you, Admiral," he returned. "I see you've picked up your new toys."

Gracen permitted herself a slight smile. "I believe that we *will* be having some *fun* with these in the near future, Captain. How are your people?"

"We're cycling through leave periods, but I can cut them short and be ready to leave inside of twelve hours."

"No need, Captain. We'll be spending a few days in Ranquil orbit before we move on to our next destination," she told him. "There is work to be done here."

"Yes ma'am."

"Gracen out," she said before the image flickered away.

Carrow shook his head slowly. *Finally. We're getting some movement.*

▼

CHAPTER THIRTEEN

▲

▶ERIC WESTON SPLASHED cold water across his face, barely smudging the dirt that he'd somehow picked up over the last few days. Most of it was dried sweat and friction rub off the interior of his armor, he supposed, but it stuck to his skin like superglue and he didn't have time to wash up properly.

Thirty days. I can't believe we're still alive.

Clearing New York had taken three days, by the end of which they'd faced over a hundred times more drones than had actually landed in the original assault and lost fifteen tanks, one hundred twelve Guardsmen, eight of his own squad, and, as much as he detested himself for saying it, even more damaging, eight irreplaceable suits of enhancing armor. The armor issued to the crew of the *Odyssey* had been the height of technical development, and few suits were ever issued to field teams. The few that were had went to teams stationed in global hotspots, none of which were near the U.S., and all of which had their own problems that simply could *not* be ignored.

That meant that he was down a total of eight from his previous forty-one, leaving thirty-three effectives in the field. Thirty-three men and women who were by now experts in the use of enhancing armor and whose loss in combat would be even more shattering to morale and field effectiveness than the armor itself.

"Sir? The President is online and asking for you."

Shit. Eric scrubbed at his face a little more before giving it up as a lost cause. He straightened up, slicked his hair back so it looked halfway presentable, and left the bathroom. They were using an old mall on the outskirts of Detroit as their current base of operations, since the city itself was fundamentally uninhabitable at the moment.

All major centers of population had been slammed hard by the Drasin, but after the first few days their focus had moved inland from New York. Detroit and the surrounding areas got hit especially hard, so when the National Guard was overrun two weeks later, the President asked Eric to take his company in. They had to fight almost every step of the way but, now joined by a division of mechanized infantry and some serious SAM capability, they could hold their own against orbital bombardment and reinforcement.

That still left the Drasin infestation in Detroit, however, and Eric already knew it was going to be a bitch to clean out.

"Captain."

"Mr. President," he said, taking a seat in front of the computer display. "Good to hear from you, sir."

"Likewise," Connor said. "Have you had a chance to reconnoiter Detroit yet?"

"Yes sir," Eric nodded. "Scouts, drones, and eyes on."

"What's the situation?"

"Not good."

Not good was a polite way of telling the Commander in Chief that he was probably about to lose another American city and there wasn't a damned thing he could do about it.

"Lay it on me, Captain."

"The city is infested, sir. Preliminary estimates"—Eric shook his head—"hundreds of drones, maybe thousands. They've had the munchies, sir."

"Damn. Can you clear them out?"

"Maybe. Depends on how much air support we can have, sir."

The President glanced to one side for a moment, then looked back. "We've got plenty of planes and pilots, but conventional ordnance is coming up short. We've been dropping tons of munitions all across the planet, Captain. We're tapped out of smart bombs, and we're running low on unguided weapons as well. Captain . . . "

The President hesitated. "Eric . . . we can't lose Detroit."

Eric frowned. "I'm sorry. I don't understand. We've lost three cities already, and Detroit is evacuated now. Sir, we can't afford this fight."

"Eric, we can't afford *not* to fight this fight," the President corrected him. "I suspect that you don't follow economic stories, otherwise you'd know that we moved a hell of a lot of our defense industry into Detroit years ago. There are at least fifteen factories there, making arms, *munitions,* and even armor. We can't lose that."

Eric slumped in place, closing his eyes.

"Mr. President, I don't think I have enough forces here to clear the city out," he said honestly. "It would be suicide, and we'd still lose the city."

"Maybe not," Connor said. "We have a bird left over the area. It has a Kinetic Kill Array and is intact."

Eric stiffened, eyes widening. "You have a Kilo Kilo *over* Confederation soil? Sir!"

The President held up a hand, forestalling Eric's reaction as best he could.

"Wasn't my call, Captain. This bird has been sitting there since the war. There was some concern that we'd lose and have to fight them here at home. The point is, we have it, and we can use it."

"That's not going to save your factories."

"They're mostly outside the city, largely untouched so far," the President said. "I want you to secure the factories as best you can, then call in the strike. When it's done, you and yours will have to clean up whatever survives. Do you understand my orders?"

Eric nodded. "Yes, Mr. President, I understand."

"Good. God be with you, Captain."

"God be with us all, Mr. President."

▶▶▶

▶ "Alright, listen up," Eric said as he stepped into the cleared area made by the circled tanks and armored vehicles. "We've got a mission from on high."

"I hope you're not talking about going down into *that*," his second said, jerking his head in the direction of the city beyond the camp. Commander Granger, formerly an NYPD SWAT, had been drafted once New York was cleared out, along with most of his men. "Because the count estimate has gone up, I hope you know."

"I know," Eric nodded. "The President has some intel we didn't, however, so here's what's on the line. The Detroit/ Windsor area is one of the primary centers for defense manufacturing in the Confederation. All the raw materials from northern Canada come through here, and this is where they put together the bombs that our air force and navy are running low on."

Granger fell silent, closing his eyes, but didn't raise another objection.

"So that's the mission. We need to secure those factories, eliminate the horde tearing the city apart, and provide protection for workers until the National Guard can move in a couple divisions. Any questions?"

"Yeah," someone called from the crowd. "Is the President nuts? For that matter, are you? We don't have the numbers for this, Cap, you know that."

"You're right," Eric said. "Which is why the President has dealt us an ace. We've been assigned a Kilo Kilo bird for the mission, and have full access to her load out."

There was a silence following that, with a good chunk of his people not recognizing the term. Those who did were shocked quiet.

"Motherfucker!"

Most of them.

"Have something to say, Ron?" Eric asked, mildly amused, since Blake wasn't saying anything that he hadn't thought himself.

"No, son, I think I about covered it," Blake told him dryly.

Eric just nodded. "For those of you who don't know, a Kilo Kilo bird is a satellite loaded with high-velocity kinetic kill missiles. We're going to use them to clear the road before we head into the city, and it won't be pretty."

"What about the factories?" Granger asked.

"Kilos are reasonably precise," Eric told him. "We won't touch the factories."

Granger looked around, weary, but his face echoed the determination of those around him. "Alright, Cap. You've led us this far, I suppose we can go a little farther. As long as you're killing those things, I'm with you."

"Hear, hear!"

Eric nodded to all of them. "Then get some sleep. We strike at dawn."

Amid the cheers, Eric headed back to the supply train. He quickly found who he was looking for, a mechanic assigned to his crew several weeks earlier.

"Charlie, you best prep her," he said, climbing up into the back of the big truck.

"You sure, Cap'n?" the grease-covered man asked, looking over. "Not much ammo left."

"I know. If things go well tomorrow, we'll have ammo aplenty. If they don't . . . well"—Eric shrugged—"we won't be needing any."

"Right you are, Cap'n," Charlie Weeks said. "I'll have the old girl ready for you."

▶▶▶

▶It would come as little news to anyone if Eric were to tell them that Detroit was a mess.

The city was one of those perennial boom and bust towns whose fortunes waxed and waned with world events, but most people only seemed to pay attention when it was on the waning side.

Now, though, the mess was from an external source and Eric was fixing to add to the poor benighted metropolis' ill luck. He was standing on the turret of the lead tank in their column, eyes on the skyline of the city ahead, looking through the combined enhancements of his armor HUD and the detailed data being gathered by their remote scouts.

What he saw in that augmented view was a city literally crawling with inhabitants, even though it had long since been emptied of human beings. Estimates had climbed since he'd spoken to the President, now standing well over ten thousand strong, and it was clear that the Drasin were making themselves well and truly at home in Motor City.

"Strike points calculated and entered, Captain."

Eric nodded quietly, thinking about what was about to happen, but not having a choice.

"Release the safeties," he ordered.

"Safeties clear. Kilo Kilo is active," Siobhan told him. "Ready to release on your order."

"So ordered. Let slip the dogs, Siobhan," he said, "and rain down hell upon our enemies."

"Kilos away."

▶▶▶

▶A kinetic kill device is nothing particularly special in terms of mechanism. In its simplest form, it is one of the oldest weapon systems known to mankind. The sling, wielded by every burgeoning culture in recorded history, was such a device. Whip a stone around a central pivot to build up speed, then loose it on a target. The lethal power of the weapon is determined entirely by the velocity you can reach and the mass of the stone you choose.

For a Confederation Kilo Kilo the principles are entirely the same. The "stone" is a one-ton chunk of meteor steel harvested from the system's asteroid belt, and the "sling" is the Earth itself. The satellite holding the weapons simply had to "drop" them in order to deploy.

From de-orbit drop to impact is just a few minutes, impact speed surpassing hypersonic levels. Accuracy was largely determined by simple ballistics and minor course adjustments using smart fins welded to the projectile.

The weapons Eric Weston ordered dropped on Detroit appeared in the pre-dawn sky a little less than three minutes after his order.

▶▶▶

▶ Thundering trails of fire lit across the sky, announcing the strikes to anyone with eyes or ears for a hundred miles around. Most of those in Weston's company involuntarily ducked as the rolling thunder shook the ground around them, but he kept eyes open as the first of six slammed into the city of Detroit with a white flash.

Eric anchored himself, knowing what was to come, the difference between the speed of light and the speed of sound actually being nearly as deadly as the impact itself. It took seven seconds for the clap of thunder to shake the world around him, knocking several to the ground and blowing out the glass in every building for miles, and by that time three more Kilo Kilos had slammed into Detroit.

The impact weapons were designed as bunker busters, and that was how they'd targeted them, aiming to take out nests that were forming through the city more than the drones crawling around the surface. Collateral shock waves should eliminate most of those as well, but the rest would be left to Eric and his team.

"Roll out!" he ordered over the tactical network as he climbed into the cockpit of the mechanical armor the military had supplied him. "Time to go work."

They were rolling before the last Kilo Kilo impacted, face into the fires as the shock waves rumbled over them. Eric took the vanguard position, using the advanced instrumentation in his armor to scout out the range ahead of them as they headed into Motor City amidst secondary explosions and thunderclaps from the fallout of the orbital strikes.

He led the column north into Detroit along the I-75, though they were more paralleling the freeway than actually driving on it. It wasn't quite as irredeemably blocked as the city streets in New York had been, but there were still more than enough abandoned cars to make it effectively impassable if they wanted to maintain their pace.

"Squad Two, break left and secure the manufacturing centers. Three, go right. I want the raw materials in those warehouses under our control within the hour," he ordered.

While manufacturing had largely decentralized in the Confederation over the last few decades, there were always exceptions. Munitions and the like were among those few, mostly by design. Mobile and personal manufacturing machines were quite capable of building small arms and munitions (though many required aftermarket hacking to do so), but they were most emphatically not up to building high explosives and the complex mechanisms inherent in modern battlefield weaponry.

So when the munitions manufacturing had moved into Detroit, retooling the failed auto industry's abandoned factories, it made a lot of sense to consolidate many parts of the process for efficiency's sake, though not entirely, of course. The Detroit area was home to five separate defense industry "campuses," and Eric was well aware that he and his company would have to secure as many of them as possible in advance of the arrival of the National Guard and the volunteer workforce.

"Captain, we've been spotted."

That announcement brought his attention back to the present, and Eric quickly noted that they had indeed been spotted quite clearly. His HUD showed at least a dozen hot spots moving fast in the column's direction. It may have been his imagination, but they looked *pissed* for some undefined red blobs on a computer display.

"Lock them in. Let them get closer," he ordered. "Excaliburs, stand ready."

The Excalibur armored artillery vehicles were among the most powerful but also most vulnerable assets in his convoy. They were heavily armed and armored, but due to the size and weight of each Excalibur, they were slow and unable to fire on the move like the Abrams M7 MBTs. That made them sitting ducks just when they were being employed, but their firepower made them absolutely invaluable.

"Excaliburs copy," the major in charge of the artillery group acknowledged. "Coordinates locked in. Ready for TOT."

"Abrams, watch their backs," Eric ordered. "Mobile Armor, you're with me. We attack the second the TOT lands."

Both groups acknowledged the orders as Eric led the Mobile Armor squads out, pushing the vanguard ahead of the group as the main battle tanks took up guard positions for the armored artillery vehicles. The Excaliburs shuddered to a halt, their stabilized cannons the only part of the big machines that weren't shaking as they planted themselves and lifted the big barrels high.

"Excaliburs ready."

"Fire," Eric ordered.

A sonic boom shook the dust off the armored vehicles as all the networked cannons fired as one. The cannons were already dropping as the round left the bore, and they all boomed again a split second later. Then a third time, and a fourth, before the fifth and final shot roared out on an almost flat trajectory that shook Eric's team right through their armored suits as it passed barely over their heads.

The TOT, or Time On Target, barrage was one of the most useful and lethal tools in the toolbox of the artilleryman. The idea was to fire rounds at different angles and speeds so that every single shot arrived on target at once, thus eliminating the chance of the enemy being able to duck for cover after the first shot landed. It was a process raised to an art form by modern artillery, which could land dozens of rounds on a target zone within the same second.

Another incredibly lethal technique, though a great deal harder in some ways and certainly more dangerous, was commonly known as Shock and Awe. More technically, it was referred to as "Establishing Battlefield Dominance" by Western militaries, and it basically amounted to an ever-increasing refinement of tactics first perfected by the Nazi war machine during the Second World War.

There were many ways to do this, but one of the most effective and dangerous was to time a TOT barrage and an attack to happen almost simultaneously. If you made an error, your attack could land too late and the enemy might be prepared. Or worse, you could arrive too early and be caught in your own artillery barrage.

If you timed it right, however, as Eric had, then you and your troops would charge into the charnel waste of the artillery TOT barrage and be almost entirely unopposed as you mopped up the stunned and disoriented survivors.

They charged right into the mushrooming cloud of smoke and debris, blinded for an instant by the dust rolling past them, with weapons ready. Thermal was blinded by the explosions, heat scrambling the instrumentation to uselessness, so Eric had the radar incorporated into the EXO-13 armor running on full power. The results echoed over the network.

"Three o'clock," Eric said, pivoting slightly in the walking armor to open fire, sending a short burst through the smoke and dust from the tri-barrel cannon mounted on his right arm. Inside the EXO-13, Eric's armor-shod fists gripped the control sticks tightly as he shifted back on target and continued to lead in.

A blob of movement appeared on his nine o'clock, but a burst of fire from Blake's assault weapon roared, joined quickly by a second short burst from Lyssa's. The blob stopped moving, so Eric continued looking for other targets while Blake and Lyssa stepped forward to confirm the kill.

The dust was settling by then, the heat from the blasts dissipating, and their thermal was coming back.

Eric could only imagine how they looked to the enemy, if the Drasin were even capable of seeing them in the way a human might. Shadows appearing from the darkness, amid the utter devastation of the first attack, firing as they walked out of the smoke like wraiths from some old legend. It brought a smile to his face as he opened fire with the tri-barrel, the whine of the high-speed cannon tearing the air itself asunder as the others joined in, finishing the fight that had started only seconds earlier.

"Clear right," Alexander called just as Janet planted a foot on a twitching drone and emptied the remainder of her mag into it.

"Real clear," she chuckled.

"Clear left," Blake answered.

Eric paused the EXO-13, slowly circling it as he scanned with every detection system he had. Finally he nodded. "Clear. Get the column moving again. We need to secure the Beta objective."

"Roger that, Cap'n," the major of the armored artillery squadron answered, the Excaliburs shuddering back to life as he did.

In a few moments the rest of the column were moving again, and Eric had his squadron once more in the vanguard as they headed north to the city.

▼

CHAPTER FOURTEEN

▲

▶ IN THE PAST month President Conner had lost twenty-three pounds, at least a decade off the end of his life, and four cities that were ostensibly under his protection. The death toll might never be completely known, but he was sure now that it was in the hundreds of thousands across the Confederation, and it was possible that they'd lost a million people or more in Mexico City alone.

The entire nation was in a state of total disarray, and the worst of it was that he couldn't afford to give his entire attention to the people he was responsible for. The Drasin were digging in all across the world, and they had to be *stopped* everywhere, or it was all over.

The biggest power of the Confederate forces was spread across the planet, with the strongest concentrations being in the Middle and Far East, along the edges of the Block territories. Those were also the areas they were the most needed now, as the Block cities had taken some of the hardest hits of any places on Earth.

With population densities as high as a hundred times the most densely populated regions in the Confederacy, cities like

New Delhi and Beijing were a near constant shooting gallery now. Confederate task groups were fighting constantly over former enemy airspace, just trying to keep the blasted aliens from hitting the ground in the hopes of giving the Block's beleaguered ground forces some kind of reprieve.

And they're running out of weapons to fight with.

That thought inevitably brought his attention back to the situation shaping up in Detroit and the hopes they'd all been forced to pin on Eric Weston and his rather ragtag company of police and Guardsmen turned full-time warriors.

The five factory complexes in Detroit were not the only defense industries in the Confederation, of course. But they'd already lost the three complexes in Mexico when the infestation of Mexico City turned into such a rout that the local commander called in a tactical strike on his own position.

Conner closed his eyes. The image of the nuclear mushroom over a Confederate city would never fade from his mind, of that he was sure, not least because he'd authorized it personally.

There was no telling how many people had been in the city when the strike happened, but it was certainly far too many. The maddening thing, as tragic as that was, was the loss of the manufacturing campuses that cost them the most. Without the facilities in Detroit, he doubted they'd be able to hold out another week at this point.

Facilities in the Block were producing weapons as fast as they could, but many of those had taken hits as well, and they didn't exactly have much cross-compatibility with Confederate systems. Without the Detroit facilities, the Confederation might as well just pack it in, and Conner had little doubt that if that came to pass, then the Block would shortly be overwhelmed as well.

"Mr. President?"

Conner looked up, nodding to the CSS agent standing there.

"There's an update coming through from DARPA's New Mexico facility."

"I'll be right there," he said, getting up. He took a moment to smooth down his suit, the only thing about him right now that was as immaculate as a President should be. Apparently, the invasion had not yet overwhelmed his caretaker's sensibilities.

The New Mexico office of DARPA had been tasked with the job of building the tachyon waveguide components they needed to take the fight right back to the aliens orbiting so high above them. Right then, he'd give almost anything for a chance to remind those bastards that they weren't untouchable, and the way to do that was through DARPA right now.

Not that it would matter much if they lost Detroit.

What good were cannons if you didn't have any shells to put through them?

▶▶▶

▶New Dehli was a smoking ruin, though it was something a cynical Westerner might suggest was completely normal. Large sections of the city had been razed, however, burned out either by the invaders or the defenders, with neither offering nor accepting quarter in the vicious street-to-street fighting that had gone on over the last month.

The newer sections, built to a more modern code, were mostly recognizable as the fires there hadn't spread. The buildings that fell tended to collapse inward by design rather than topple to the side and take out an entire block in the conflagration. The older parts of the city were all gone, however, burned to cinders and then trampled by alien drones or Block soldiers.

For all that, however, little had been decided in the run of a month of fighting.

Both sides poured reinforcements into the breach, seemingly caring nothing for individual lives, and that had resulted in an effective stalemate. The Drasin were unable to procure a solid foothold, their numbers being annihilated as fast as they could reproduce. But their rate of reproduction combined with the influx of new forces from orbit prevented the Block soldiers from reclaiming the city.

It was a state of affairs that could not last forever, and the longer it drew on the more time and numbers would favor the Drasin, who were quite content to cannibalize their own in order to gain a few more soldier drones.

The only real advantage the human defenders had was that they fought under a friendly sky, with two out of three orbital landers being blown to hell before they could touch the Earth, courtesy of the Confederation Navy and the NACS *William J. Clinton,* which was parked a hundred miles offshore.

On the ground, though, they could only rely on themselves and what they could find in between material airdrops from the Block Air Force. Forces all across the world were on definitive search and destroy, and no one could spare them much, if anything at all.

For the people of New Delhi, however, suffering under an invading force was an old and familiar story. Those who couldn't handle the new reality died quickly, but they were the minority. The people of India were used to hardship, and given a common enemy they could easily identify, they quickly came together and turned their city and its environs into quite possibly one of the most hostile places in all of history for an invader to be.

It was a scene that would play out similarly across the planet, as the Drasin found that those who were to give up easily did so and died early. After thirty days on planet Earth, those people were gone.

Those who were still alive fully intended to stay that way, and if the price was the total obliteration of every alien they saw . . . well, that was a price they were *very* happy to pay.

▶▶▶

▶Ben Sahid swore as he leaned into the ruined wall he was sheltering behind that he could hear the stomping of the beasts as they rummaged through the rubble. He still remembered the first time he'd seen them doing that, how confused he'd been. Confusion had evaporated after watching for the first time the demon things birth one of their own.

He didn't know how they did it, but the threat was clear. The things fought and ate, and when they ate enough, they produced more of them to fight and eat.

He gripped his assault weapon closely, edging up to peek over the edge of the jagged wall.

There they are. Five of them, this time.

He swallowed. He didn't think he had enough ammunition for this job, but that wasn't going to matter. He palmed a grenade from his pack, one of two he had left, and looked across the field to where a few others were waiting for him to make his move.

A flash of light and smoke passed by overhead, causing Ben to hesitate a moment and wait for what he knew was coming. The sonic boom of the aircraft tore through the air. That was the signal he was waiting for.

When Ben jumped out from his cover, he was gratified to see that the beasts were looking up and away, clearly on the watch for any sign of aerial assault. It was one of the first times Ben had ever been glad that the Americans (he still thought of them as Americans) existed. They'd dropped so many tons of explosives on his country and countrymen that more than once he'd wished that they would simply vanish from the face of the planet.

And they were still dropping bombs on his country, but now he was grateful. It was mind-boggling, but that was perhaps the world he lived in and the world his children, and theirs, would have to grow and thrive in.

As he charged, the roar of gunfire magnified around him and he saw others jump up and empty their own weapons into the enemy, giving him the cover he needed as he ran.

Faint cries of "Ayo Gorkhali" and "Jai Bajrang Bali" reached his ear, along with other rejoinders that had once been the calls to strike fear and horror into his heart. Now, though, they buoyed him as he ran. Ahead of him, an unspeakable horror, behind him old enemies now turned allies, offering what protection they could.

Perhaps this is best, he thought fatalistically as he charged across the field. *I am too old and set in my ways for a world as changed as my sons will live to see.*

The idea that there may *not* be a tomorrow for his children didn't enter his mind as he tossed the explosive sphere and palmed the second one, pulling the pin on it before wrenching his rifle up one-handed and opening fire as he ran.

Another cry filled the air, this time a British voice screaming about God and country as the heavy assault weapon hammered the drones, the explosion of the first grenade blowing the leg off one and collapsing another. The heavy rounds of his rifle perforated the hard shell of a third as the beasts finally reacted to his charge. The snap and sizzle of the beast's weapons charred the air, filling his nostrils with ozone as the beam that could slice through tanks caught Ben just above the knee and took his right leg almost in its entirety.

He hit the ground in a sprawl, rolling to a stop just feet away from the drone that had taken his leg. He smiled up at it as he threw the second grenade, bouncing it off a drone thirty feet away, then threw himself toward his chosen target as he drew a detonator from his belt and jammed his thumb down on the button.

"Allahu Akbar," he said just before the explosion tore him to shreds right along with the beast he had charged.

It collapsed on him, leaving only two remaining, as a rain of automatic fire tore through them and ended the battle.

Other eyes watched and noted his sacrifice, but they didn't have time for either mourning or celebration. There were more monsters to fell, and everyone present knew that there would be more sacrifices to make.

The dust slowly settled, the blood soaked into the ground, and elsewhere in New Delhi an explosion gave notice that the battle may be won, but the war continued.

▶▶▶

▶For the ship minds of the Drasin swarm floating above the blue-green world so deeply infected by the red band, the situation had begun as untenable and had not altered even slightly over the period they had been occupying the system. The infected fourth world had already been cleansed, as had the satellite of the third world and several minor outposts dotted through the system.

The third world, however, was stubbornly resisting with every possible weapon at its disposal, plus many that the Drasin had never previously considered to be weapons at all. Only the urging of caution from the lower-generation ships prevented a total and complete obliteration of the planet, despite the fact that such an act would inevitably cripple the Drasin force deep in what seemed likely to be enemy territory.

That said, however, the fighting on the ground was rapidly threatening to enter a scale that practically *matched* that horrible outcome.

The normal consensus of the ship minds was now split widely on the best method to deal with this world, given the available resources at their disposal. Unfortunately, they were crippled and weak compared to the normal strength of a Drasin swarm, when hundreds of thousands of ships represented a *small* force. Simply throwing numbers at the world was inadequate, and this world was both poverty stricken and incredibly rich by Drasin standards, further complicating matters.

The materials needed to produce sufficient drones on the world were centered in areas of extremely high resistance, and much of the rest of the planet was poor fare indeed for the replication of the species.

The swarm had little desire to sacrifice more low-generation drones or ships, but it was becoming clear that the higher generations used to this point were fatally flawed and unsuited to the endeavor. That left the swarm with few options, and it appeared that total war was the only acceptable choice from a long list of bad options.

The decision, however, was far from made as the ship minds continued to debate the wisdom of leaving themselves crippled amidst such enemies as these. There were many more of the red band nearby, plus those that had enslaved the swarm, and they *all* had to be eradicated. No exceptions. The death of the swarm was only acceptable if the red band died first.

▶▶▶

▶ *Gaia walked the scorched earth of the battlefields, her feet bare but unaffected by the heat, shards, and poisons strewn about. She was immaterial, but not untouched. The death and savagery was such that it stood out, even in her long memory of death and savagery, and the entity knew it to be a moment in history that would be remembered by either everyone or no one.*

Those moments were rare, in her experience.

So much history had come to pass that only she recalled, that only she knew the truth of. Great men had died unknown and unlamented, while weak-willed cowards stood tall and claimed glory. Nations had crumbled so completely that the only trace of their passing was that which she carried with her. History was filled with those moments, important things that would forever be forgotten by everyone save her.

This, though, this was something . . . **momentous.**

It only remained to be determined whether or not anyone would survive to remember it.

Gaia paused in her walk, silently surveying the bodies of the Drasin and the bodies of the human warriors who fell in the fight, then vanished from one place on the Earth to appear again in another.

This time it was a similar war zone, nearly identical ruins filled the landscape, and more bodies of both sides lay motionless on the ground. It was a different continent, however, and a different people as those of the Earth viewed such things. Gaia walked across this field and fell into step beside a machine that walked as a man, her eyes lighting on the sight of a familiar face she could see inside it.

"Oh Captain, my Captain," she mused as she walked beside the lumbering war machine piloted by Eric Weston. "Are you ready for what is to come? I wonder . . . I know that I am not, but humans have surprised me in the past despite my near omniscience within the Earth realm.

"There is much to do, and so little time to do it. I do not believe I will be able to confuse our foes for much longer, my Captain."

She walked alongside him for a time, through the ruins of a city that had once been the center of so much activity and promise, then sighed to herself with a sound like the wind through the trees and shifted her focus elsewhere.

The captain was on mission, and doing what must be done.

For the moment, that would have to suffice.

▶▶▶

▶Eric felt a chill run down his spine and he shifted uneasily in the cockpit of the EXO-13, eyes automatically checking all the warning systems, telltales, and proximity instrumentation. Everything seemed in the green, so he pushed the feeling off and returned his focus to the job at hand.

They'd secured the Beta site as best they could for the moment, and were proceeding to clear the city. Excaliburs had been left behind at both manufacturing sites along with some of the Abrams MBTs to provide security, so they now had two fire bases to call on. As it turned out, they'd already located stockpiles of munitions for both.

No rounds for their assault rifles, unfortunately, but those weren't exactly scarce. They were just getting harder to have airdropped in.

"Spread out, scan *everything*," he ordered as they began to move into the ruins of the city, fires still burning where gas mains had been ruptured, a thick smog of smoke clogging everything. "If it moves and it's hotter than thirty-two degrees, *kill* it."

The others acknowledged and they began moving into the debris field, circling around the impact craters formed by the devastation from above. The Kilo Kilo strike had *flattened* entire blocks, partially because many of the old buildings had been there for close to two centuries, and some even longer.

The shattered remains made movement easy, but also provided an unfortunate supply and variety of hiding and ambush positions for the enemy to utilize. It was slow and dangerous work, but had to be completed and completed properly because to miss even one of the enemy was to court disaster.

"Good God. The bridge is still standing," Siobhan said softly as they moved.

Eric scanned the construct briefly, but had to agree that it was indeed standing, and even looked pretty solid. The bridge connected Detroit with Windsor, one of a few connections that effectively made the whole area one massive metropolis. They'd hammered Windsor just as hard with the Kilo Kilo strikes, and two of their objectives were on that side of the river, so he was just as happy they had an easy way across.

The suits and EXO-13 could cross regardless, of course, but being able to call on some heavy backup like the Abrams would be nice, particularly since they'd flattened most of the buildings that might get in the way of the big tanks.

The squad flinched as a burst of auto fire tore through the air, all of them half crouching, even Eric in the EXO-13, and looking around. When he found the source, Eric swore, twisting the big walker around and launching himself across thirty meters of open space in a single leap.

He landed hard just meters from the Drasin that had come surging up out of the rubble and grabbed one of his men. Eric drew a bead, haloing the alien in his HUD, and fired off a short burst into the far side of the beast. The rounds from his tri-barrel tore into the Drasin, distracting it from the man it had held up two meters off the ground. The creature spun on Eric, who realized that perhaps he'd gotten a little too close.

He lifted the left arm of the EXO-13, initiating the motion with the stick in his left hand and guiding it through the NICS interface and a fair bit of desperation, blocking the down stroke intended to cleave his armor and shuck him from it like an oyster. The servos and hydraulics in the EXO-13 moaned under the load, but held, and Eric used the opportunity to bring his right arm forward. He jammed the tri-barrel under the Drasin's body and fired a medium burst directly into its main bulk.

As it collapsed, Eric held the weight up off the other soldier, shoving it clear.

"Medic!"

Eric stood over the fallen man, guns primed as he twisted slowly around and looked for any sign of more trouble. The Kilo strikes would have taken out most of the enemy forces, but shock waves were funny things sometimes. You could be standing two feet away from someone who had literally just been popped like an overinflated balloon, yet be perfectly fine because the blast wave happened to double back on itself and cancel out in your position.

That meant that, statistically anyway, there would likely be a few survivors in the rubble, and they were likely to be pissed as hell and spoiling for a fight.

"Keep your eyes open," he ordered, stepping back to clear the way for the medic who had run up. "And watch your feet, everyone. These things are likely to be right under us."

Eric keyed over to the command channel, linking back to the convoy. "I need some seismic gear deployed ASAP. Get those things in the ground and get me an idea of what the hell is moving under us."

"Yes sir, we're deploying the first ones now. System online in three minutes."

"Good." Eric glanced over. "How is he?"

"The only thing keeping him in one piece is the suit," the medic told him, not looking up. "We need to get him back to the field hospital."

"Damn it," Eric swore. "Alright. Take who you need. Get him back to the convoy."

If the suit was the only thing holding him together, Eric knew that the man and the suit were basically out of combat permanently. He didn't have enough troops to be able to afford to lose any, nor did he have suits to waste. Losing both at once was a heavy blow to his force, no matter how small one man seemed to be.

The medic nodded, connected to the armor, and locked it up so the man inside wouldn't be twisted around in moving, then waved in two others to help carry him out. Eric covered them until they were well back from the front line he and the squad had been pushing forward, then signaled the rest to continue.

"Watch your feet," he ordered again. "I lose anyone else out here and I'm going to be *testy* at supper. Don't ruin my meal, got it?"

The men and women with him chuckled, but took the message to heart and proceeded with extra caution as they continued to clear the ruins of Detroit.

From the dirt I began, and to the dirt I have returned, Eric thought with more than a touch of irony, thoughts straying back to his early training as a rifleman in the U.S. Marine Corps.

Somehow it just didn't surprise him that things had come full circle for his life and career. Even the very heights of space itself couldn't keep gravity from pulling a man back to his beginnings. That was as it should be, he supposed, and if nothing else he would relish the chance to teach the Drasin the true meaning of fidelity.

"Semper fi, you glorious bastards," Eric told his squad. "Let's wipe this place clean so we can go get smashed before doing it all over again. These things ain't gonna kill themselves!"

▶▶▶

▶"Manufacturing of the components is complete, Mr. President."

Conner sighed. "Finally."

"We're sorry it took so long, sir, but we just didn't have all the materials, and with the current situation . . . "

"Yes, yes," Conner waved his hand. He knew this song and dance, and didn't even disagree with it. It was just frustrating how long it took to get materials moved around the country, let alone the world, at the moment.

While the Drasin weren't putting any serious crimp in Confederate control of the skies, they were wreaking all kinds of holy havoc on ground transportation. Most warehouses were deep inside disputed zones, not to mention that somehow many of the key components they needed had been "misplaced" by the warehouse owners and took days to locate due to outdated computer records.

He'd been told that was a ploy used by investment firms to drive prices up. Making product take a little longer to find created an illusion of scarcity in the market and could increase the cost by a few pennies per unit. This often added up to billions of dollars by the end of the year without actually having to do anything productive to add to its value.

When this is over, I'm going to make it treason to pull that kind of shit.

That was probably wishful thinking on his part, but President Conner could dream. Hell, at the moment dreaming seemed like the most productive thing he could actually do. Everything else was out of his hands for the moment, and in the control of people who, hopefully, actually knew what they were doing.

"How long for assembly?" he asked aloud, masking his thoughts as best he could.

"A few days, sir, but we need the nuclear shells before it can be deployed."

"Understood," Conner said tiredly. "Manufacturing facilities and stock are being secured as we speak. I'll have a team with as many shells as we can scrounge in the air within twenty-four hours, and more coming off the lines as quickly as humanly possible. Just get those guns finished."

"Yes sir, Mr. President."

The screen flickered and went black, leaving a very tired man slumped in a very expensive office chair. He sat there in silence for a time before pushing himself up to head out of the conference room. He slowed by the door, glancing at his Secret Service guard.

"What's next, Phil?"

"Dinner, Mr. President. You haven't eaten since yesterday."

"I just authorized the use of WMDs on Detroit and Windsor," he said. "If I had an appetite, you'd be doing your duty if you shot me dead."

The agent didn't flinch, but he didn't say anything either as they walked out of the room. He did, however, steer his primary toward the dining room.

▼

CHAPTER FIFTEEN

▲

▶ADMIRAL AMANDA GRACEN supposed that things could have gone better on Ranquil.

That wasn't to say that they'd gone badly, to be honest, but they'd come away with a great deal less than they'd hoped. While the local government was more than willing to provide supplies, intelligence, and even the ships and crew they'd previously agreed to, they weren't going to authorize any further support "at this time."

They were scared.

She recognized that, but she also recognized that there was a time for caution, and this wasn't it. The Drasin were a force that had to be met, had to be destroyed, and it was better to do it away from your own planet. She hoped that, if the positions were reversed, she'd have made very different decisions.

However, they weren't, and the decisions weren't hers to make.

Her planet was the one that the fighting would be centered on, and that was a reality she had to deal with.

Her squadron of seven ships, the Heroics and the *Enterprise,* were heading for the system's heliopause—the point at which the solar winds were strong enough to completely cancel out the effect of the star's gravity. It was the location generally considered "safe" to initiate a transition through tachyon space. From there, they'd be in Sol space in just instants, and that was when things were going to get hot.

The main concern at the moment was simply that they weren't carrying enough munitions.

It seemed utterly silly, but with the long gun capability of the waveguide cannons, they should be able to engage the enemy from well outside the Drasins' standoff range. So the biggest threat to the mission was simply running out of munitions before the job was done.

Whether that was how things were going to work . . . well, that was another thing, really.

"All stations report go to transition, ma'am."

"Go/no go from the squadron?" she asked.

"All ships are go."

Gracen nodded, taking a deep breath. "Do it."

"Yes ma'am," Steph said from the helm, and she could hear the grin in his voice as he spoke.

Gracen didn't know if he was grinning because they were finally going home, or if he was grinning because he knew what was coming and, despite reading every report, she *didn't.* Transition was something that had to be experienced to be believed. Or, at least, that was what every report she'd read put down into words.

"Transition initiated."

"Forward instruments have transitioned!"

Gracen shivered, but didn't say anything more. What could she say? They were committed now.

"Transition effect approaching the bridge."

She tried to close her eyes, but couldn't as the bridge disintegrated in front of her and spun away into deep space. The effect moved so slowly, creeping along the bridge, turning machines and men into tiny particles that lanced across space and time at near infinite speed. Then it was on her and everything vanished into the maelstrom.

▶ ▶ ▶

▶ Well past the orbit of the object formerly known as a planet, called Pluto, a now familiar effect took place just outside the reach of the gravity of Sol. Particles too small to be seen individually, yet in such numbers as to blot out the stars in the darkness, rushed into existence and began to solidify into seven distinct shapes.

The Heroics and the NACS *Enterprise* appeared nearly as one in a flying V formation, launching into a parallel curve to the gravity well. They began a long and slow orbit of the star that was still so far away as to be barely distinguishable against the backdrop of billions of other stars.

Onboard the ships, the scene was somewhat less majestic and peaceful.

▶ ▶ ▶

▶ She was going to hurl.

Gracen clenched her mouth shut, teeth grinding together as her lips pursed almost painfully, and simply *refused* to spatter the deck with the contents of her stomach. Even if she choked herself, she wasn't going to hurl, though it felt that choking herself was not only likely as she sat there, bent over double in the chair, but almost a certainty.

She heard moans from around her, and the sound of liquid hitting the deck, and had the slightly vindictive satisfaction that she wasn't the only one in that position. At least she'd outlasted someone else. That wasn't enough though, so even when her stomach heaved and she tasted acids and digested food, Gracen kept her mouth shut and swallowed hard.

It was disgusting, it *hurt*, but there was just no possible way she was going to humiliate herself on her first transition. She knew that everyone would be watching, and judging. She was used to that, just as she was used to showing them all exactly what she wanted them to see and not a damned thing else.

Another set of heaves hit her as the smell from someone else wafted across the deck, this time actually backing up and filling her sinuses before she got it under control.

"Someone clean that mess," she rasped out, snorting back the chunks and swallowing. "Ventilate the deck, please."

"Aye ma'am," Susan said. "Ventilating."

The air scrubbers rushed a little. Normally soundless, they now made a comforting background noise as she sat as straight as she could and rasped out a new set of orders.

"Status."

"All systems green, Admiral," her first officer, Commander Son Ching formerly of the Block starship *Wei Feng*, said more stiffly than usual. A glance in his direction showed that his skin was slightly green as well, which struck her as funny in the moment, but laughing was another thing she had no intention of doing.

The urge to laugh at something she didn't know whether he would understand faded quickly as Son handed her a handkerchief silently and gestured to his nose. She took it and quickly dabbed away the thin trickle of stomach acids that had begun to run down her lip. She nodded her thanks and handed it back, gratified as he tucked it discreetly away.

"We have telemetry reports from all other ships in the squadron," he said. "All vessels show green as well."

"Threat matrix."

"Clear," the instrumentation officer announced. "No sign of Drasin in our immediate vicinity. Still waiting on light-speed instrumentation for a good view of the system."

"Go active," she ordered.

"Ma'am?"

"We just splattered tachyons all over this system, Jake," she told the young officer. "They know we're here. Go active."

"Aye ma'am."

Jake Southerd was an example of both the squadron's strengths and its weaknesses. They had only the men and women of the *Odyssey*, a handful from Liberty Station, and the personnel of the *Wei Feng* from which to draw crews for six huge starships, so a great many of their officers were inexperienced even if they were the brightest and best of their generation.

Granted, they'd filled the ranks with volunteers from the Priminae forces, but that made things almost worse in many ways. Her own weapons officer was actually the first Priminae the *Odyssey* had ever met, a young woman named Milla Chans. She was young, brilliant, and incredibly inexperienced in military procedures. Gracen firmly believed that her strengths would outweigh her weaknesses, but she was worried that the combined weaknesses of the squadron would lead to a disastrous error in the coming action.

There was little choice, however. They had to move with what they had and she knew well that it could have been *so* much worse.

"Aye ma'am, initiating tachyon ping. Single ping, wide angle."

Strictly speaking, they could use their gear more like radar than sonar now, but that would give the enemy a real-time lock on their location, something she had no intention of doing even with their standoff capability. The bridge filled with the sound of the ping being sent, though it was just an announcement and notification sound than an actual result of the system being employed.

"Signal return, we've . . . four hundred Drasin ships and counting in NEO," Jake said, his voice sounding more ill than Gracen felt. "They're fully powered and just sitting there, ma'am."

Gracen nodded. "What do we have on light-speed imagery for Earth?"

"Signals are almost seven hours old, but it's still there," Jake answered, sounding a bit better. "No sign of any gray goo."

Gracen refrained from responding, though she understood the reference. The Drasin acted much like the nightmare scenario of nanotechnology, only at a macro scale.

"Transmit queued message to the President of the Confederation, and then send again on the channel provided by Captain Sun."

"Aye ma'am," Susan said. "Transmitting to Confederate and Block satellites."

"Excellent. Then signal the squadron and tell them to go black," Gracen ordered. "No more tachyon signals, no more wide-spectrum transmissions."

"Aye aye, ma'am. Squadron going black."

"Stand by to warp space," she ordered. "We're going home."

▶▶▶

▶ "Mr. President, we have a situation."

Conner blinked away the sleep in his eyes, blearily looking around. There was a time, he dimly recalled, when he could awake from sleep in an instant. That time was barely a memory now, it seemed, but intellectually he figured that it was probably just a couple of months ago.

"What is it?" he asked, throwing the covers back and getting out of the bed.

"Signal from past the heliopause, sir."

That woke him up.

"Source?"

"The signal was tagged *Odysseus,* Mr. President. Admiral Gracen commanding."

"Admiral?" Conner blinked, suddenly feeling that maybe he hadn't completely woken up after all. "How did she get . . . ? No, never mind. Get me the message."

"Yes sir."

Twenty minutes later he couldn't decide if he was actually awake.

I knew they were working on a deal with the Priminae, but I didn't think it would be ready this quickly.

He grabbed his suit pants and glanced over to the agent standing just inside his bedroom.

"I want the DARPA people in conference in ten minutes," he ordered.

"Yes sir."

"And you'd better get Captain Weston up too," Connor said after a moment's thought. "I'll need to speak with him."

"Yes sir."

"You can tell him that his people are back through. I expect he'll be happy to know that."

▶▶▶

▶ "Signal from the President, Cap'n."

Eric got up, pushing the sleep out of his body by reflex. "I'll take it in the command area."

"Yes sir."

Eric took a few deep breaths after the runner had left, then grabbed for his field uniform. He checked the time as he got dressed, surprised that he'd gotten a whole forty minutes worth of sleep.

Must be my lucky day.

Dressed and kitted out, he headed for the command bunker, which was really nothing of the sort. It was more of an inflatable building covered in concrete and sand, but it was secure, solid, disposable, fit in the back of a jeep, and only took twenty-four hours to put into place.

He walked into the bunker and looked up at the presidential seal on the screen, glad that he wasn't keeping the man waiting, then turned to where Lyssa was sitting at the station and tapping into the terminal.

"Hey," he said, straitening his battle dress. "What's going on?"

"Oh, Captain!" She jumped. "I didn't hear you come in."

"I walk quietly," he said. "Now what's going on?"

"I don't know. We were told to wake you up. Something important."

"Well, wake them up now. I'm here."

"You got it."

Eric turned back to the main display, waiting while Lyssa sent in the orders. He'd known that picking up a Marine Corps intercepts and communications specialist would pay off.

The screen flickered and Eric was mildly surprised to see the President already sitting there. He saluted instantly as the man on the display waved off the gesture.

"Relax before you break something, Captain," Mitchell Conner said. "You're making my back twinge just looking at you."

Eric shot the Commander in Chief a more than slightly dirty look, something he'd never have done if he'd gotten more than forty minutes sleep, but the President just chuckled at him. That raised his eyebrows more than a little.

He's in a good mood. Something's changed.

"What's happened, Mr. President?" he asked with half a smile. "I assume that the aliens are still in orbit, but something has made you pretty damn happy."

"Hope is a wonderful thing, Captain. I've been running so long without it that I forgot what it felt like," Connor said, relaxing back into his chair.

*Oh, something **big** has happened. He hasn't sounded this calm since the first week of this mess.* "Am I cleared to know the good news, sir?"

The President laughed at him, *laughed.* Eric revised his earlier opinion. The man was giddy. Something good had happened, no doubt, but it was likely that the President was also suffering from sleep deprivation and a host of other things to bring out a reaction like this.

"You're right at the center of it, Captain. Didn't my staff tell you?"

"Sir? No sir."

"I'll have to have a word with them," Connor shrugged. "I told them to let you know. No matter. Have you secured the Gamma site?"

"Yes sir. Only Epsilon remains unsecured," Eric said. "We'll move on it in the morning."

"Never mind that. I'm redirecting heavy lifter transports to your location, along with full crews. A National Guard division will be on your doorstep in an hour. I need you to get your men to pack up everything in the warehouses at Gamma and get them ready to be loaded on the transport," Connor ordered. "Then pack yourselves into the transport. Your team is flying security on this one."

"What are we transporting?"

"Shells for a tachyon waveguide cannon."

Eric expected that he could have been blown over by a stiff breeze upon hearing that.

"Sir? What ship are we loading them onto?"

So far as he knew the only ship on the planet, or in the Solar System for that matter, with waveguides was currently sitting in scattered pieces across Long Island Sound and Manhattan Island.

"No ship, Captain. Don't worry about that. You're just to concern yourself with protecting the shipment. Orders will follow," the President said. "We do have some good news for you, personally, however. As of oh three hundred twelve hours, Admiral Amanda Gracen reported back in system with seven starships crewed by, among others, former members of the NACS *Odyssey* crew. Congratulations, Captain, your people have come home."

Eric reached out, a hand grabbing the table to steady himself.

"A . . . are you sure?" He shook his head. "Of course you are. How did she get the ships, sir?"

That dulled the President's humor just a bit. "Don't worry about that, Captain. She did what she had to do, you do what you have to, and we'll all pull through this one way or another. Admiral Gracen is currently commanding her squadron from the *Odysseus*."

"*Odysseus* . . ." Eric whispered, tasting the word. A smile played at his lips as he nodded slowly. "Fitting."

"Yes, I thought so. They're currently running silent, but her intention is to scout the system and begin thinning the ships in orbit of Earth. Your job, our job, is to provide her with whatever aid we can. So get those shells on that transport, Captain."

"Yes sir," Eric snapped. "We'll be in the air by dawn."

"That's what I wanted to hear. Go to it, son."

▶▶▶

▶The moment for indecision had passed.

The ship minds consulted, considering the new data available to them. More arrivals in system, new configurations, but clearly built by the same people who built the anomaly that had plagued them on this crusade already. One of the ships matched, or came close, but the others . . . the others were larger, and the power curves were . . . dangerous.

The swarm had doubted from the beginning that they were up against just one planet, but now there was confirmation. There had to be an infestation in this region, something that spanned possibly the entire arm.

It was a tragedy that so many systems would have to be cleansed, but that was the way things were.

The immediate issue was that there was no prior information that might tell them just how dangerous the new ships were. Unknown configuration, unknown weapons, but there were two things about them that the swarm knew.

First, they arrived using the same signature as the anomaly ship. That made them dangerous, more dangerous than anything in this swarm's memory. Second, unlike the anomaly ship, six of *these* vessels had power curves that marked them as vessels of *war*. Those two items of knowledge made the situation very, very dangerous.

That meant that they had to eliminate the planet now. There was no more time for finesse. Whether it crippled the swarm or not, this world *must* be cleansed.

CHAPTER SIXTEEN

▶ "PASSING THE ORBIT of Saturn, ma'am. No sign of activity from the Drasin fleet."

Admiral Gracen nodded, trying to look calm even as she felt the nervous tension crank up. She knew that the Drasin had to know they were in the system, so she had expected some kind of activity before this point. The Drasin were alien by nature, however, so she supposed she might be judging them on human expectations, which would be a potentially lethal trap.

"Keep them under the eye," she ordered. "Let me know if anything changes."

"Aye ma'am."

With the *Odysseus* taking the vanguard position, the squadron had begun a spiraling drop into the solar system about five hours earlier, and it would be another two days to Earth's orbital path once deceleration time was accounted for. That left a long time for them to act, she supposed, but the lack of motion still bothered her.

What if they're up to something?

That was just stupid, though, since she knew damn well that they were up to something. It was just exactly what that was that escaped her.

"Admiral, we're getting the first high-resolution images of Mars."

Finally, something to distract me.

"Put them on the display."

She wished, a moment too late, that she'd not given that order.

The surface of Mars, such as it was, was broken up and drifting away from the central mass. Though that was something she wouldn't have thought possible upon consideration, seeing was believing. In the closer shots she could see that the pieces floating away from the whole were unmoving Drasin drones, having completed their task.

They'd torn the red planet asunder, somehow getting right to the core of the world, leaving it nothing but rubble flying in loose formation around the Sun. She supposed that, eventually, it would collapse entirely back into one world again, but she was certain that nothing would ever live on it no matter how much time passed. The red planet had never been a particularly hospitable world, but now there was more chance of a human living on a barren asteroid than on Mars.

Her thoughts turned toward Earth and she shuddered, thinking of what it would be if they didn't step up and end this situation, *now.*

"Clear that," she ordered, not wanting to look at the pictures any longer.

The screen blanked, then returned with the tactical map of the system that showed the Drasin locations unchanged. The orbital track of Ceres was highlighted as the point at which the squadron could begin a long-range engagement of their targets using the waveguide cannons, but that was yet a long distance off.

A lot can change between now and then, and we still don't understand why they're standing there and waiting on us. These things are bestial, yes, but they've never been stupid. They've seen what the Odyssey *could do to them. Are they just resigned to what's going to happen?*

Now *that* made no sense. Nothing about them indicated that the Drasin were the type to roll over and play dead. They weren't even the type to give up in the face of overwhelming odds. They just threw themselves at the danger like the very worst sort of fanatics.

What are you up to?

▶ ▶ ▶

▶ "We're seeing movement on the alien forces in orbit, Mr. President."

Conner groaned, closing his eyes and shaking his head. "What are they doing?"

"We're not sure, sir. They're readjusting their formation, but we don't have any consensus on what they're attempting yet."

"Great. Is Captain Weston in the air?"

"Yes sir, thirty minutes ago. He'll land in New Mexico within the hour."

The President nodded. "Well, at least we have that. Best put all our units on an enhanced level of alert and make sure that air defense units are stocked and ready for a fight."

Conner saw his aide wince and didn't blame the man. "Enhanced" level of alert basically meant wake everybody up, no matter how tired they were, and tell them to be ready for something that no one could say was actually coming. It was horrible for morale and combat effectiveness, frankly, but there was little choice in the matter.

"Yes sir, Mr. President."

▶▶▶

▶ The dark of the sky was clear, stars twinkling cheerfully above them as Eric looked out through the cockpit of the heavy lifter. He was seated in the copilot's seat, having temporarily ejected the junior officer so he could get a little stick time while he had the chance. He normally wouldn't have done that, but then normally he'd have gotten enough hours on a Double A to keep his qualifications.

Granted, he had other matters to concern himself with now, so losing his pilot qualification was a lesser issue than it normally would be to him. But Eric knew bureaucracy too well, and as such he was well aware that if he didn't record the hours someone would kill his qual, no matter what he was doing in the meantime.

A transporter was a far cry from an Archangel fighter, that was true, but it was stick time and Eric couldn't sleep, so he was going to take what he could.

"Quiet night," he heard the pilot say as the man slipped back into his own seat with a cup of coffee in hand.

Eric nodded. "Yeah."

"Figured you for some sleep, if you don't mind my saying, sir."

Eric smiled, adjusting the flight controls as the Doppler radar reported turbulence ahead. "I'm a flyer by choice, Colonel. Give me a choice between sleep and flying, and you know, it's not even a contest."

The colonel chuckled. "I know the feeling. Tell me, is it much different up there, in space?"

"The black sky?" Eric asked with a hint of a smile. "It's . . . like flying in a dream. No up, no down, just an endless black sky. If there's a heaven, that's where you'll find me after I check out."

The colonel nodded. "I'd applied for a position on one of the new ships before all this, but . . . "

"Yeah," Eric said quietly.

The coming of the Drasin had put a stop to a lot of careers and dreams, turning survival into the only ambition that could be tolerated. The alien beasts had a lot to answer for, in his opinion, though Eric reserved a fair piece of the blame for himself. He doubted that he would ever forgive himself for exposing the Earth to the Drasin, even if it was merely hurrying the inevitable.

He turned his focus back to the controls, though honestly the computer handled the job better than he could most of the time.

"You'll get your chance, Colonel," he said. "We're not done yet."

The pilot nodded, eyes looking out over the dark sky and darker ground below.

"I hope you're right, Captain."

▶▶▶

▶The orbit of Jupiter was in their rear view as the squadron continued its sunward fall into the Sol System. Gracen had spent the last hours poring over the ever-improving tactical intel they were gathering from the system. FTL sensors were impressive, especially the Priminae-improved ones, but nothing beat high-resolution light-speed scans, no matter how long it took to compile them.

They were approaching the orbit of the asteroid belt, a sector of space of interest to humans only for the raw materials that could be mined without the added cost of moving the material from the surface of a planet to orbit.

Unlike the movies, the only difference between the asteroid belt and "open" space was the fact that a ship's radar operator occasionally got a beep from his system inside the belt. Very occasionally. The Trojan points on either side of Jupiter were a little more stocked, but only marginally as a rule.

So she noted the locations of a few of the larger rocks, including the planetoid Ceres, but none of them were in the path of the squadron, so she paid very little attention to them. The things that held her focus were still in Earth orbit, hundreds of them sitting there, circling the planet below.

They were still just buzzing around like an aimless swarm, no sign that they'd registered the entrance of the squadron into the system. That seemed off to her. She knew that the transition in-system would have lit up a tachyon flare that a blind man could see, so they *should* be reacting *somehow*.

A buzzer caught her attention and she looked up from the imagery on her screen and across the bridge.

"What's that?" Gracen asked softly, mostly just a little curious.

"Small asteroid cluster crossing our bow," Susan answered professionally. "Too small to detect until now on passive or short-range scans. They're not a navigation hazard."

Gracen nodded, looking back down to her screens.

That was how things worked in an asteroid field, she supposed. Lots of nothing punctuated by moments of almost nothing.

"Commander," she said, "you have the bridge. I'm going to get a cup of coffee and stretch my legs."

"It will be as you say, Admiral," Commander Son said stiffly. "I have the bridge."

She nodded and walked off the bridge, heading for the commissary. She wanted Commander Son to get some time in the hot seat, integrate him better with the crew while things weren't too dangerous.

Splitting up the crew of the *Wei Fang* had been a difficult decision, but she didn't have enough experienced spacers, let alone blooded combat spacers, to group them all in the same ship. That spread out the experienced people, but also threw a lot of Confederate officers in with Block officers by necessity.

Actually, she wasn't concerned about them. It was the enlisted that bothered her most, which was why she'd kept as many of *them* as separated as possible. Still, there would be some inevitable friction. She just hoped that it wouldn't cost them dearly in the clinch.

▶▶▶

▶The ship minds paused in their preparations as they noted a brief glimpse of their new enemy as the falling vessels passed the orbit of the fifth planet and continued starward. It was clear that they believed themselves unseen and, for the moment, it was best that they continue to believe that. In truth, they were difficult to track, but a few carefully placed ships had spotted them along their path. Since the enemy vessels were moving almost entirely on a ballistic course, it was no problem to predict their exact location at any given time.

That left the problem of the planet below, as there was a very real chance of the swarm being heavily damaged in the coming engagement.

There was no point saving forces only to lose them in the black of interplanetary space.

The order was given and, as one, the swarm launched their remaining surface drones before turning to leave orbit.

▶▶▶

▶This time it wasn't a buzzer. It was an alarm, and it had the admiral briskly moving through the halls while everyone else bolted around her.

Must not run. The commander can handle whatever it is until I get there. Don't panic the enlisted by running.

That mantra was running over and over in her head as she left the commissary, brushing away spots of coffee from her uniform. She hated spilling anything on her garb. The white that admirals were issued showed off dirt horrendously and was nearly impossible to clean.

Giving it up, she strode onto the bridge, taking just a moment to watch the chaos in action.

"Go full active," Commander Son was ordering. "They clearly see us. I want to see them."

"Going active on all scanners!"

The *Odysseus* had some of the most powerful scanners any of the Terrans had heard of, but most of them were still light-speed limited. Going active meant pouring out enough energy into local space to be mistaken for a small star, but there was nothing larger than a baseball within several light-seconds that they wouldn't light up.

"Got one! Half light-second and closing!"

"God damn it!" Commander Michaels swore. "How did they get so close?"

"They were lying in wait, Commander," Gracen said as she walked to her station. "I'm afraid that I've badly underestimated our enemy. It would appear that they've learned from our Captain Weston in applying their tactics. What happened?"

"The *Bellerophon* took a laser strike, minimal damage so far," Susan answered. "But they're engaged in close, and the power they're throwing back and forth is raising the hairs on my neck from here."

"Damn it. Can we come around for support?"

"We're in the lead position, Admiral," Son answered. "I already dispatched the *Achilles* to aid the *Bellerophon*. We have trouble ahead."

Gracen tipped her head as she settled into her position. "Very well. Tactical displays up. Ensure that all ships call to quarters."

"Aye ma'am. Tactical displays on. Call to quarters signal already sent," Son answered.

The walls of the bridge flickered, showing a full three hundred sixty degrees of space enhanced by computer augmented intelligence. Ahead of them a bright spot was haloed, and an overlay provided data on the ship.

Standard Drasin configuration, Gracen noted as she read the numbers and capabilities of the ship. *They must have hundreds of the damned things drifting out here, thousands maybe, along likely approach routes.*

254 • EVAN CURRIE

She'd been suckered, but it wasn't as bad as all that, she decided.

They'd spread themselves too far out to effectively ambush her squadron, though they could eliminate a couple of ships easily enough even in knife range. The bulk of the enemy ships were still well outside the standoff range of the wave-guide cannons, and as long as that was true, then this mission was still on.

"Lock all weapons onto the Drasin ship ahead. Signal the *Heracles* to follow us in," she ordered.

"Aye ma'am," Milla Chans, their Priminae weapons specialist, answered. "Weapons are locked."

"*Heracles* signals affirmative."

"Then by all means, cease deceleration and accelerate to engage the enemy ship."

"Aye ma'am," Steph said from the helm, as he tapped out a command and laid his hands on the controls. "Reversing warp, increasing speed relative to Sol."

▶▶▶

▶Stephen Michaels took his hands off the controls for a moment, flexing his grip and cracking his knuckles one by one. He found that he didn't hate flying a starship, really, though it didn't hold a candle to an Archangel, of course. There were some nice differences, like the cup of coffee sitting beside his station at the moment, but the ship maneuvered like a pig in comparison.

A pig capable of flying faster than greased lightning, but a pig nonetheless.

The *Odysseus* began to increase speed as it dove toward the approaching Drasin ship, laser nodes powering up along the entire forward section. Behind them the *Heracles* matched her acceleration and began to power weapons as well. The two split, separating enough to keep their firing arcs apart as they closed.

Michaels locked in the NICS needles and smiled a little as the faint pain scored the back of his neck, automatically reaching into the depths of the ship he was flying and making it *his*.

"Cardsharp, Stephanos," he said softly, his voice pitched low. "You with me?"

"Cardsharp," Jennifer responded, from the *Heracles*. "I'm with you."

"Let me take the lead. You play clean-up as we pass."

"Roger that, Stephanos. I'll back your play."

"Never had any doubt in my mind, Cardsharp," Steph replied. "Engaging target in . . . three minutes."

▶▶▶

▶ "More bandits lighting up!"

The admiral looked over to the compressed map, eyes noting that three more Drasin were now on the display within two light-minutes of them. She scowled, running the numbers in her head, and realizing quickly that they didn't make sense.

They can't have this many ships in system, can they? It would take thousands, hundreds of thousands, of ships to cover this much space with this level of density.

"Go active with FTL scans," she ordered. "Maximum available power."

"Aye ma'am. Full power ping."

The sonic signal of the burst echoed on the bridge as the blast of FTL particles expanded out from the ship and into the system. Reflections of tachyon particles were also extremely faint, which made long-range detection from an omnidirectional pulse difficult at the best of times. It became easier by orders of magnitude, however, when the ships you were looking for had lit off their drives and were in motion.

"Holy shit."

"Commander Michaels, please," Gracen snarled, though mostly just to keep her own traitorous mouth from echoing the sentiment.

The long-range pulse showed forty Drasin with their drives lit off, all within five light-minutes and closing. The system beyond that also showed a few active drives, closing on the squadron's location, but it was clear that the enemy's attention was focused right on the squadron and nowhere else.

Gracen slumped at her station.

*How the **hell** are they tracking us?*

"They'll be on us en masse in less than fifteen minutes, Admiral," Susan said seriously. "We can't take more than four on one in a straight-up fight."

"I am aware of that," Gracen said. "Power to the waveguide cannons. Target those ships still outside knife range."

"Yes . . . I mean, aye ma'am," Milla said from the weapons station. She tapped in the codes, shaking her head as her expression creased with worry. "Ten ships are within the minimum range of the cannons."

"Leave them. We'll have to deal with them later. Fire on the remaining ships as she bears."

"Aye ma'am. Firing."

The big waveguide cannons on the *Odysseus* pivoted out from the ship, locking onto targets as much as several *light-minutes* away as the ship charged the transition generators and prepared to engage. The guns fired into the silence of space, no flames, no recoil, just barely visible distortions in space time and an imperceptible blast of tiny particles.

▶▶▶

▶"What the . . . damn, I've never seen anything like that before, have you, Captain?"

Eric glanced up from the controls of the heavy lifter, looking over at the pilot. "Seen what?"

"That," the Colonel said, nodding out the windscreen of the cockpit.

Eric looked out and his eyes were drawn up to the dark. Streaks of fire crisscrossed from every direction to the point that he could hardly see the sky. He felt light-headed for the first time since doing negative-G drills in an Archangel, and he knew without asking that he was probably as pale and pasty as a corpse.

"What do you make of that, Captain?"

"Armageddon," Eric croaked out. "That's Armageddon."

▼

CHAPTER SEVENTEEN

▲

▶ "TALK TO ME!" Conner ordered as he walked into the situation room.

"Massive simultaneous launches from every ship in orbit. I think they flushed their tubes or whatever they fire those things out of," an analyst said. "Air defenses are saturated, sir. We're not knocking out nearly enough of them."

Conner swore. "What the hell *happened?*"

"We don't know, sir. They must have been set off by the arrival of Gracen's squadron."

"How bad is it?" he asked, mouth dry.

An air force colonel stood up. "We have major incursions on every continent, including Antarctica this time. Our air defenses are going to hammer them over the Middle East, Europe, North America, Japan, and northern Africa. The Block's got most of Asia covered, and the Russian Federation are going to get more than their fair share of licks in . . . but southern Africa, South America, and Australia are all light on serious coverage, and no one's got anything significant on Antarctica."

"So we're hammered," the President said simply. "Great."

"We have divisions on the move everywhere. Everyone was awake and leaning on the gas when this started, sir," a general said, speaking up. "We're better prepared now than we were during the first attack."

"What's the munitions situation?" Conner asked dryly.

Uncomfortable looks shot between his top advisors, telling him everything he needed to know about that.

"Great." He sighed. "Alright. Tell them to do what they can, and get what munitions we can pull out of Detroit out to where they can do the most good."

"Yes sir."

Conner sighed. "I need a message sent to Admiral Gracen. I'll record it in my office. Prepare what you need to send it."

"Yes Mr. President."

▶▶▶

▶ "I want everyone in their shells before we land," Eric said as he walked back through the hold of the transport. "We have a major incursion happening as we speak, so lock and load and be ready for a fight."

"What's happening, sir?" Granger asked softly as he walked up beside him.

"Looks like our friends up top decided to make their move, finally, and stop playing games," Eric answered. "We've got incoming tracks so thick you can't see the sky behind them."

"Jesus," Granger swore. "That bad?"

"Worse, probably," Eric muttered. "Get your men suited up and make sure they're ready. I'm betting all hell just broke loose, and we're sitting at the center of it."

"Right. I'll see to it."

Eric nodded and continued back, making his way through the narrow spaces between crates until he found where his EXO-13 was locked down. The now-battered machine had seen a lot of action over the last few weeks, and he wanted to do one more check before taking it into combat again.

It was nothing compared to his fighter, of course, but he'd gotten attached to the awkward-looking piece of mobile armor since the President and his advisors cut it loose and sent it to New York for him. Eric pulled himself into the cockpit and fired up the computer, running onboard self-checks while he physically examined the hydraulics and power cell levels.

It was the sort of pre-battle routine that kept him calm while leading a fighter wing and, to an extent, commanding the *Odyssey*. There was a time for aggression, but that time was during the fight and not before it. He was focused tightly on what he was doing, enough so that Eric missed the approaching footsteps.

"So how bad is it?"

He looked up to see Lyssa there, eyes on him from a couple of meters below. He sighed, not really wanting to get into it, as much because he didn't know the answer as anything else, but spoke up anyway.

"Bad," he grunted.

Okay, so he just *barely* spoke up.

Lyssa snorted in response, rolling her eyes. "I think I caught that much myself. Are we going to make it to New Mexico?"

"We've got a wing of fighters covering our path," Eric said. "We'll make it to our destination. I'm just worried that the whole point is moot now, that's all."

"Why?"

"Because what good does it do to wipe out the ships in orbit with these"—he gestured to the crates of shells they were standing among—"if they've already dropped every last damned ground drone they have?"

She paled. "You think that's what they did?"

Eric rubbed his face, but nodded tiredly. "Yeah. I think that's what they did. It's the only thing that makes sense. I can't prove it, but that's my bet."

"Why would they do that? Why now?"

"Honestly? I don't know," Eric admitted. "There are a few possibilities. The most likely is that we now have the possibility of reinforcements, but it could also be that they've been testing our defenses until this point and now they know enough to launch their endgame."

"Reinforcements?" Lyssa asked, trying to focus on hope rather than the twisted knot in her gut from his other words.

Eric nodded. "Seven starships entered the system and contacted the President. They're of Priminae build . . . that, and the *Enterprise*."

Her heart sank. "Seven?"

Seven ships couldn't hope to stand against what she *knew* was up there. It was just impossible.

Eric, however, smiled.

"Yes, seven, and if they're equipped as I've been informed . . . they're about to raise all holy hell. I wouldn't want to be in a Drasin ship right now, Lyssa . . . "

Still, he sighed. "But the Drasin could lose the battle and still win the war . . . that's why we have to get ready for a fight, and be ready to move. We could be shipped out of New Mexico in an instant, and go anywhere on the planet. We can't leave a *single* one of those things alive and active on this world."

He turned back to his work on the EXO-13.

"Not a single one."

▶▶▶

▶President Conner was looking at the map of the world, a tactical display showing enemy landings, and felt quite sick. The arrival of reinforcements from outside the system had triggered an Armageddon response from the enemy force, something he supposed could have been predicted but still managed to take them all by surprise.

It was clear now that the enemy had been holding back significantly, something they'd feared for a while, which left him with the decision of exactly how to respond to the current situation. He wasn't certain if the Drasin were aware that the human militaries on Earth had been holding back just as much, or if they'd care if they knew, but the truth was that they had been.

No military leader wanted the responsibility of unleashing strategic weapons, none who were remotely sane at least, so none had yet done so. Oh, he had authorized kinetic strikes on Mexico City and Detroit, but those were practically conventional weapons compared to some of what was sitting in his nation's armories, and that said little of what the Block was sitting on.

The Drasin action was going to put them all to the test, however, because they were going to have to make a hard decision on that very subject . . . a decision compounded by the fact that each of them was going to have to choose whether to strike their *own* territory.

Conner glanced up at the agent standing at his door. "Simon, call outside for the football, if you please."

The agent swallowed hard but nodded before stepping briefly out of the office to follow his commander's orders. Conner couldn't say that he'd made the decision yet, but he knew that when the time came he wouldn't be able to wait for everyone to get ready. It was time now to break the news, because when he gave the final order he wanted no confusion or hesitation.

The literal fate of the planet may well be staked on it.

▶▶▶

▶The universe had a warped sense of irony at times.

General Kong of the People's Army had managed to avoid the use of true strategic weapons even in the losing days of the war, successfully arguing that there was nothing to be gained by deploying such things while the fledgling Confederation controlled the skies. Now, after the war was over, he found himself once more staring into the fiery face of mass death and destruction and contemplating unleashing it.

That wasn't the irony, of course. No, the irony was that after years of arguing against unleashing such force on his nation's enemies, he was now forced to contemplate its deployment on his *own* home soil.

That level of irony was such that it should not exist in a sane universe, but then he had never once believed the universe to be sane.

"Shift air defense to cover the major cities and strategic areas," he ordered. "Keep them from our homes as best you can."

"What are you doing, General?" the Chairman hissed. "You'll uncover huge sweeping portions of our nations!"

"I am well aware of that," he growled in return, turning to an aide. "Bring me the strategic deployment computer."

The man paled, shock echoing across his face, but he saluted and ran off.

The Chairman didn't get it nearly as quickly as the young aide, but he did work it out eventually and paled almost as much under his sagging features.

"You can't!"

"I must," Kong countered wearily.

"No, it is too much!" the Chairman hissed. "I will have you removed."

"You are welcome to try," Kong said simply, "and if you can find someone with a better plan, I will voluntarily step aside for them. Until then, however, I will do exactly what I must to ensure that we do not end here."

▶▶▶

▶ Tracking and intercepting a ballistic target coming in from orbital velocity is an exercise in frustration for the most part. The issue isn't with determining the speed or direction of the object; rather it lies in trying to devise a system that can do all that, then code an intercept vector, launch a weapon, and take out the target in the precious few seconds you have to react.

It helps, however, if you're watching for the target before it appears and already have weapons more or less locked and ready to deploy. Thousands of tracks sliced the sky to ribbons of smoke and flame, but from the ground thousands more reached up and began to swat them mercilessly from the skies in all corners of the planet.

In some areas, particularly places like the Middle East, where missile attacks were reasonably common, the counter assault was remarkably effective. In others, the worst being over entirely uninhabited areas like the Australian outback and the continent of Antarctica, the response was . . . lacking.

The Drasin pods slammed into the Earth from point to point, and then quickly cracked open to disgorge their occupants into the world while valiant and desperate defenders scrambled to respond. The long, slow boil that had typified the war for Earth so far now exploded into action that, if any survived to remember it, would go down in history as the single largest battle ever fought on a planet.

It seemed clear to everyone by this point, on both sides, that this was the last hand and all the chips were now in the middle.

▶▶▶

▶In the skies over New Mexico, the light show was spectacular, violent, and far, *far* too close for the comfort of those who could see out of the heavy lifter transport headed for the spaceport facility.

"Holy shit!" the pilot snarled as he jumped as much as he could, being strapped into the seat, at the near miss of a SAM heading skyward for a meeting with the descending Drasin. "Watch where you're shooting, you crazy bastards!"

The big CM-powered transport was fast as greased lightning, even in atmosphere, but it had nothing on the high-velocity rockets and ballistic pods that were so deeply intent on wreaking havoc around them.

The colonel swore again, but there was little he could do, and turned to his copilot. "You better let them know that we're minutes to the port and I'm not waiting for clearance.

This heap is touching down in a *hurry*, so they better strap the hell in."

"Yes sir."

Flying through a hostile sky was never any fun, even when the hostility wasn't directed specifically at you. The colonel nudged the throttle up and the nose down, looking to get as low as he could in an effort to use some of the terrain as a blocker from the explosions he knew were coming.

The transport wasn't a fighter craft by any stretch, but it did have a CM power plant and fuel to spare, so the speed was there to be tapped. He kept it under one thousand feet, running just on the edge of hypersonic as the spaceport came into sight.

"Flight Niner Five Niner, Spaceport Earth, we have you on an inbound track. Please confirm."

"Roger that, Control. This is Niner Five Niner with cargo for DARPA Hangar. Request immediate emergency clearance."

"We've had one runway cleared and waiting for you for the last hour, Niner Five Niner. Adjust course three degrees south by southwest and come in on runway ninety-one."

"Roger that," the colonel said calmly as another explosion lit the sky above him. "Nine One. Please note, we are coming in hot and heavy. Request fire crews on standby."

"They're already on the tarmac. Are you damaged?"

"Not yet. Niner Five Niner out."

▶ ▶ ▶

▶ CM-enhanced transports were known for their versatility and speed compared to the conventional vehicles they replaced, but few had ever seen one put to quite the test as the one was, landing on runway ninety-one amid the terror and confusion of the second major invasion. The transport was a lifting body class airframe with enough CM to keep its immense mass in the air, but given just how much it had been intended to lift, not enough to give the vehicle VTOL capability.

So when the pilot called ahead and informed the ground crews that he was coming in hot and heavy, they took him seriously. Runway ninety-one was a leftover from the earlier days of Spaceport Earth, when rocket- and scramjet-powered craft could be expected to take off and land without the aid of counter-mass technology. As such, it was one of the longest runways in the world.

At just under five miles long, the SE runway came second to a similarly purposed Block runway in mainland China and had the distinction of never having been overshot, even in the early days of the commercial space program. Under normal circumstances, even the largest of heavy-lift transports with CM enhancement would never require more than a mile and a half. But, of course, this was hardly a normal circumstance.

At just a hair under Mach Three and only nine hundred feet in altitude, the transport pilots almost missed the runway when it first flashed under them, a thousand feet gone by in an instant. They shifted power to the CM, then opened the airbrakes full out as the big transport began to drop. Thick wheel struts lowered out of the smooth fuselage, locking into place with two miles gone on the black ribbon they needed to land on, and from there they began bleeding speed faster than any of the manufacturer's books would have suggested even in an emergency.

The big transport started shaking as it approached Mach One, a deep visceral shudder that had its passengers looking around nervously to see if it was about to shake itself apart. It smoothed out as it dropped below Mach, however, and with a mile left to go the wheels screamed as they touched down.

So focused on his job that he didn't even flinch when a nearby explosion marked the landing of an alien pod, the pilot reversed thrust. Everyone was slammed forward as the transport's engines began to whine dangerously. The road vanished swiftly under them as he fought the controls, pushing the braking systems to their limit, and finally brought the craft to a controlled stop just half a mile from the end signs.

He slumped back, closing his eyes for a moment. "Crap. I never want to do that again."

▶▶▶

▶ They were met by a small army of support crew, fire crew, and cargo movers by the time the transport shuddered to a stop on the tarmac. Eric got his people off and clear of the jet fuel and nuclear materials before he let anyone start unloading, and then headed for the tower to find out just what was going on.

He was greeted halfway there by a three-star who looked as harried as he'd ever seen a man.

"Weston?"

"Yes sir," Eric answered, saluting. "Do you have orders for me?"

"Not yet," the general answered. "Just real glad to see your cargo."

Eric looked up, trails of smoke and flame still defining the skies above them as distant shock waves shattered over their position. "Might be a moot point, now. Looks like they've decided to drop everything they've got on us."

"You don't know the half of it, Captain. Walk with me."

Eric nodded curtly and the general led him back to the building complex, both men ignoring the distant flashes and rolling thunder shaking the very ground upon which they walked.

"This is going down all over the world, Captain. We're hammering them everywhere we can, but there's more than anyone expected."

Not more than I expected. Just later arrivals, Eric thought grimly. "Understood. They've stopped targeting population centers then?"

"Looks like," the general confirmed. "Hard to tell though. Some of them are certainly coming down in uninhabited regions, however. We can't cover every square inch. It's just a miracle that they're not splashing down in the oceans."

"I doubt they can handle the pressure differential," Eric answered. "They're tougher than humans, sure, but they're still susceptible to overpressure waves. They may not be able to handle the temperature conductivity of water either."

"Pardon?"

"You can get hypothermia off the coast of California in summer, General," Eric answered. "These things have much higher body temperatures, and they need to maintain that heat by all accounts. Water may actually be lethal to them in very short order."

"I thought they could operate in space?"

Eric chuckled. "It's a bit of a misconception that space is cold, General. Space isn't hot or cold, it just is. Objects *in* space can be hot or cold, depending on their nature and location. There's also a difference in radiated heat loss compared to conductive heat loss."

The general just shook his head. "I'll take your word for it, Captain."

"Also, I wouldn't say that they operate in space, exactly." Eric scowled a bit, thinking about it. "They just take longer to die than a human would."

"Fabulous."

Eric chuckled. "What kind of intel do we have here?"

"We're linked into the entire DARPA net system, including the new patchwork mini-satellites they've been launching since the assault."

"Good. Show me your tac-room, General, if you will."

The general jerked his head to the left. "This way."

He led Eric into one of the large sprawling buildings of the spaceport, in through some security sections, and finally into the mission control room that had been used during the early days of the facility. It had been revamped, updated, and generally brought into the new century at some point in the last few years.

Eric wasn't sure why. Mission control wasn't a priority for near-Earth travel, but he was glad to see it all the same. The holographic displays that wrapped around the room showed telemetry from every major station on the planet as far as he could see, including the main feed from the Pentagon.

"We're tapped into every available feed," the general said, "including some of the Block links."

"They gave you their codes?" Eric asked, somewhat incredulous.

The general laughed. "Not a chance. No, they stopped encrypting the latest feeds in order to simplify and speed up setup times. They were getting hammered worse than we were, and setting up new encryption codes every time one of their hardware decrypts was destroyed. Near as we can tell, the aliens don't give a damn about what we're saying to each other, so we've pretty much given up on encoding."

Eric nodded in understanding. Military-level encryption came at a cost in terms of time and equipment.

He walked over to the local area geomap, examining the tracks as they drew across the display. The sky was full of them, both coming down and going up, and that made for a right mess to decode, but he'd been doing it for years.

"You've brought in a lot more SAMs than should be here," Eric said finally.

"The whole planet brought in a lot more SAMs than should be here," the general grunted. "We've been pulling the things out of mothballs ever since those damned aliens showed up. There's a mountain cache just west of here with a thousand more still being recommissioned. I never realized just how much the government overbought when it came to these things."

Eric nodded. "Marines still have a few hundred Harriers sitting in warehouses somewhere, General. The military can be worse than a hoarder at times."

"That explains why most of these munitions were dated forty years ago."

"They seem to work fine," Eric commented.

"They're early-model HVMs, mostly scramjet-based kinetic kill vehicles." The general shrugged. "There's nothing on them to go bad. Just add fuel and fire."

"No school like old school," Eric said, satisfied.

"Just not too old," the General said. "We'd have a hell of a time if they had chemical or nuclear warheads. Those things don't age well."

"We're going to have to go out and clean up the ones that slip through," Eric said, sighing heavily, "No option but getting our hands dirty there."

The air force general shook his head. "May not come to that."

Something in his tone brought Eric up short, and he looked over sharply. "What do you mean, sir?"

"We've been authorized to break out strategic weapons, Captain. How much do you think that will change the board?"

Eric winced, considering the question.

Strategic weapons were mostly used as simple bluff tactics rather than actually deployed in battle. Like old-fashioned nuclear weapons, strategic weapons of all kinds were best used as deterrents rather than for live combat, simply because the blasted things were incredibly destructive.

"That's hard to say, sir. To use them properly, we'll need to bring the enemy to a common point, and I'm not sure how we can do that," Eric admitted.

"The President was clear, and it seems that the Block leadership is doing the same," the general told him. "We're to hammer every living soulless one of them, even if we have to nuke the last square inch of this planet to do it."

▶▶▶

▼

PLANET RANQUIL

▲

▶ DENIED.

The word gnawed at Tanner as he walked, though he supposed that it shouldn't have surprised him as much as it did.
His request had been far outside the scope normally afforded
his command, and certainly presented a degree of risk that
could be seen as excessive.

It's still the right thing to do, however, the seething admiral
told himself.

"Rael?"

Nero was waiting for him as he approached, the big man
almost literally dwarfing him in every aspect, but Tanner wasn't
a self-conscious sort. He supposed that was a good thing, since
most people made him feel physically small.

"I take it from your expression that your request was
denied," Nero said, his tone deceptively light and dry.

Admiral Tanner snorted. "You can safely take it that way,
yes. Central flatly refused consideration of the plan."

Nero shook his head. "Then it ends. The council will
not consider going against Central in a matter as critical
as this."

Tanner growled, his emotions welling up and getting the best of him despite his normally rock-solid control.

"The critical nature of the situation is precisely *why* they must do just that," the admiral ground out through tightly clenched teeth. "Forget what we owe the Terrans, forget all they've done for us . . . Every system that falls to the Drasin is hundreds, thousands, more!"

He clenched his fist, falling silent for a moment as he tightened his control and calmed slightly.

"Every system that they consume is that many more of the Drasin we'll have to face eventually," he said, taking a deep breath. "To gain so many more enemies while losing our only allies in this war? That's not only unthinkable, my friend, it's deplorable and utterly insane."

"What will we do?"

Tanner sighed. "I go before the council and tell them either we do this . . . or they may begin looking for another Commander of the Fleet."

▼

CHAPTER EIGHTEEN

▲

▶ "WATCH OUT, *HERACLES*," Steph hissed under his breath, sweating in the air-conditioned environment, his muscles twitching as he sat stiffly in his seat. "They're trying to box us. Split to port. I'll go starboard, on three."

Upon reflection, Stephen supposed that piloting a pig the size of a small island wasn't all bad. With the stick controls and NICS interface, tactical flying was almost as much fun as a fighter, and you didn't go up like a matchstick if the enemy put a laser on you for a couple of seconds.

He pulled to starboard as the three count went off in his head, calling out over his shoulder as he did.

"Milla, darlin', watch for a target lock in thirty seconds."

"I will not miss," Milla Chans said determinedly from the weapons and tactical station behind him to the right.

"I know you won't," he said, noting that the alien bogey was turning to follow the *Heracles*. "Coming back around on him . . . get ready . . . "

"I have him," Milla answered. "Target has been locked."

"Fire at will," Admiral Gracen ordered.

The command was hardly needed. Milla's hand was already moving as it was given. The forward laser mounts pulsed in response, lancing out to tear into the Drasin as it dropped into attack position on the *Heracles*. The six linked beams burned hotter than the corona of a star as they slashed into the Drasin ship, frequencies sweeping across the spectrum automatically until they hit the best absorption frequency.

The *Odyssey*'s lasers could cut through a Drasin's armored hull in a few seconds of optimal burn, but the *Odysseus* packed weapons a thousand times more powerful. When the frequency hit the optimal point on the spectrum, they dumped enough power into the enemy ship to power a small city for a decade.

The Drasin ship simply ceased to *exist*.

"Splash one. Good shooting, Milla," Steph said, grinning.

"We have thirty-two more on our screens, Commander," Gracen said tightly. "Let's save the congratulations for later, shall we?"

"Yes ma'am," Steph said, eyes flicking over his displays before he looked out over the panorama that showed deep space all around the occupants of the bridge. "*Heracles, Odysseus* is coming around. Stay with me, Cardsharp."

"Roger, Stephanos. *Heracles* standing by to warp space."

▶▶▶

▶The *Odysseus* and *Heracles* came about in a tight sweeping curve, holding so close that their warp fields interacted. Both ships shuddered in response to the gravity waves each put out. They stayed glued together through the turbulence, however, as the two former fighter pilots adjusted for a new attack vector and started to come back on the center group of their convoy, where several of the Drasin had managed to sneak in close enough to be a threat.

To the unaided human eye, the lasers crossing the intervening space between the fighting ships were invisible until they struck. But to those in the ships, the computer-aided augmentation of their instruments clearly showed the beams as they sliced space into cross sections. Explosions tore through the *Achilles,* gas venting from several points on her kilometer-and-a-half frame, but the big ship was firing back just as furiously at the four Drasin that had jumped her. One blast of the *Achilles'* beams meant one less enemy ship.

They learned after their second lost vessel, however, that staying in the *Achilles'* primary firing arc was a bad place to be. The remaining Drasin hugged in as close as they could to her stern and mid-fuselage as their lasers tore into the cruiser's armor.

▶▶▶

▶ "Cardsharp, split low right. We're going to scrape her hull clear of those pests," Steph said, his voice as cold and calm as if he were ordering a burger.

"Roger, Stephanos. Call the play."

Steph smiled slowly. "Pincer in three. *Achilles, Odysseus . . .* hold *real* still."

Admiral Gracen's eyes widened and, for a brief moment, she considered demanding that he explain that comment, but as fast they were moving toward the *Achilles* and the enemy ships, she was honestly afraid that distracting her pilot might be disastrous.

Fighter pilots. What idiot idea possessed me to put fighter pilots at the controls of starships?

"Stand by to go dead stick," Steph said. "*Achilles,* do you copy?"

"Roger, Stephanos. Dead stick in five," Burner's voice sounded a half second later, just a touch of nerves in his voice. "Do I want to know?"

"If you have to ask, Ray," Steph cracked without pausing in his work.

"Right. Dead stick in three."

Steph didn't reply as he finished tapping in a few commands to his console and put his hands back on the stick controls. "Cardsharp."

"I'm ready, Steph. Call the play."

"Clean sweep in two."

"Roger that. Clean sweep."

"Milla, lock targets. Watch for the *Achilles,*" Steph said. "The *Odysseus* is going dead stick on my mark . . . Mark."

"Targets locked," Milla called. "I have them. Firing."

▶▶▶

▶All ships involved in the battle were moving at relativistic speeds, hurtling into the system and ultimately toward Sol at unreal velocities. Relative to one another, however, the speeds were measured in mere hundreds of kilometers per second.

The *Odysseus* and the *Heracles* went dead stick within one thousand kilometers of the *Achilles,* lasers firing furiously as they closed the range on a purely ballistic trajectory. The *Achilles* also killed its space warp as they closed, Drasin vessels vaporizing under the close fire of the closing ships.

The three passed well within a hundred meters of one another, moving over five hundred kilometers per second relative to each other. It was a range that would have caused their drives to interact dangerously had any of them been actively warping space-time.

As it was, it merely caused every alarm on three ships to scream and several people to start praying as they watched. Most, fortunately, were completely ignorant of the situation until it had completely passed.

▶▶▶

▶ "Targets eliminated," Milla Chans announced, letting out a long, slow breath and a shiver of adrenaline-fueled fear as she spoke.

"Good," Gracen croaked slightly, shaken by the actions of her helmsman. *Really should have known better. Fighter pilots. Lord.*

"Signal the rest of the squadron. Get everyone back in formation," she ordered. "I don't want anyone else caught out alone like the *Achilles*. Tighten up."

"Aye ma'am," Susan said. "Orders sent."

"Coming about, ma'am. *Heracles* is with us," Steph announced. "The *Bellerophon* is catching up to the *Achilles*."

"The *Hippolyta* and the *Boudicca* are closing ranks, securing the rear," Susan told them.

"Good," Gracen said. "How many are left inside knife range?"

"Twenty-eight, ma'am."

"Damn it," she hissed, shaking her head.

Knife range was the distance within which they could not target with their transition cannons. Outside that range, as long as they had munitions, the task force could stand off almost any imaginable enemy. Inside it? They were down to lasers and armor, and not a whole lot more.

That wasn't to say that their lasers and armor weren't impressive. Gracen knew that they were downright frightening. But it left the door open for a fair fight, and that was one thing she wanted to avoid at all costs.

"Can we outrun them?"

"Not a chance, ma'am," Steph said. "These crates are fast, but they're on us and they're fast too. Take them here, take them now, and take them fast."

Gracen nodded. She knew that herself but felt the need to ask the question.

"Very well. Close ranks. I want our flanks covered. Issue orders to *Boudicca* and *Hippolyta* to execute rearguard formation."

"Roger, ma'am. Orders issued," Susan said a moment later.

"Give me the *Enterprise*."

"*Enterprise* online, ma'am," Susan answered instantly.

"Captain Carrow, I need a fighter wing in motion in thirty seconds."

The *Enterprise*'s captain took a few seconds to reply. "Mission, ma'am?"

"Antiship engagement."

A few more seconds of light-speed delay passed, then Carrow's voice came back. "Bravo wing is scrambling now."

"Thank you, Captain."

Gracen looked across her command deck and nodded resolutely. She could do this. *They* could do this.

"Issue to all ships," she said calmly. "Fire on any target as they bear. *Clear* them out of our sky."

"Yes ma'am, firing as we bear," Milla Chans answered, already coding the assault into her station.

"Orders issued, Admiral. All ships acknowledge."

▶▶▶

▶ "*Enterprise*, Bravo Actual."

"Go for *Enterprise* Control, Bravo Actual."

"Bravo Squadron is ready to launch," Commander Thane Clarke said calmly. "Request go."

"You are go."

Thane nodded. "Bravo squad launching."

The first two Vorpals roared out of the bay as the next pair were lined up on the cat, following less than a minute later. It took under ten minutes to put the entire squadron into space, and they were burning fuel at a truly appalling rate as they vectored around and headed for their targets.

"Bravo Actual, *Enterprise* Actual."

"Go for Bravo, *Enterprise*."

"Clarke, watch your back out there," Captain Carrow's voice came on the line. "Those ships are putting out enough power to erase the *Enterprise* from existence. Do *not* get between the Heroics and the enemy ships, that is an order."

"Yes sir."

"Get into range, hit them with everything you've got, and then get your sorry asses back on my decks. Are we clear, Mr. Clarke?"

"Crystal, Cap. We're on it."

"Good. Go wipe those bastards from my sky."

"With pleasure, Cap," Clarke said calmly before switching channels. "Alright, boys and girls, the captain's given us our flying orders. We hit them fast, hit them hard, and clear the sky of those alien pieces of crap. Bravo Squadron, on me."

The drive flares of the Vorpals hitting full burn briefly eclipsed the Sun as the lithe fighters tore away from their carrier and toward their targets.

▶▶▶

▶On the *Odysseus*, Admiral Gracen eyed the closing tags on her screens with a baleful eye, recognizing just how close she'd let the enemy get to her squadron before they were spotted.

If we don't get them fast, they'll cut us down to pieces.

"Admiral! Movement from the main body of the enemy ships!"

It was everything Gracen could do not to start cursing out loud, despite what an admiral losing her shit would do for morale.

"Vectors?"

"They're pulling past cislunar space, climbing up-well, ma'am."

Gracen grimaced, knowing just who they were climbing up to meet. "Damn it."

"It's worse, ma'am," Winger said, shaking her head.

"How?"

"If I'm reading this right, they must have cleared their decks before coming our way. The siege on Earth must have just taken on a whole new level, ma'am."

Gracen closed her eyes. *I never wanted to be the trigger for Armageddon. What do we do now?*

She gritted her teeth and took a breath, setting her jaw. "We can't do anything about them yet, but keep one eye on that force, Michelle."

"Yes ma'am."

"We'll wipe them from the Black as soon as we're finished with their friends out here," Gracen said steadily. "Miss Chans, if you please, lock all lasers on the closest Drasin and relay intercept coordinates to Mr. Michaels."

"Yes Admiral. Coordinates relayed."

"Mr. Michaels," Gracen said simply, "I would much appreciate it if you and Miss Chans could make that ship . . . disappear."

"Aye ma'am. It'll be a genuine pleasure."

▶▶▶

▶ The Drasin ship minds quickly had to raise their assessment of the intruding ships from "likely dangerous" to "very possibly the most lethal enemy ever encountered by the swarm." That shift was posing a very real problem for the local swarm at the moment, as they had a great deal of trouble believing that they had encountered an enemy more dangerous than the Original Ones.

Long in the past there had been enemies such as these, targets that were not only able to fight back, but actually cut through the swarm like a pulsar blast. Those times had long since gone, however, and those enemies had fallen in a time so long ago that even the swarm's inherited memories were foggy on the precise period.

In those days the taking of a star was a massive endeavor, something that could cost millions of ships. One time the cost had been so incalculably high that it resulted in an actual change in swarm priorities. The originators had given the swarm the gift of changing their methods in extreme cases, and that time qualified.

The new standing order was, if any local swarm were to encounter such a system again, it was to flee on sight.

The cost associated with destroying such a system had once nearly broken the swarm forever, something previously believed impossible.

The ship minds were not convinced that this was the case just yet, however, no matter how lethal these new ships were proving to be. That system had been surrounded by defenses ten thousand layers thick, and protected by a veritable swarm of its own.

This was seven ships and one solitary planet.

It was not even remotely in the same galaxy as the Original Enemies.

The decisions were made, tactics chosen, and the swarm warped space powerfully as they flung themselves up the gravity well of the local star and toward the threat of the newly arrived ships.

Behind it, the planet *burned.*

CHAPTER NINETEEN

▶ "ALRIGHT, SHUT YOUR mouths and listen up!" Ronald Blake snarled, ending all conversation in the hangar the group was sheltering in. "The captain has something to say."

Eric nodded to his old friend and stepped up onto an old munitions crate so everyone could see him. He idly supposed that it would have been more poetic if it were a soapbox, but all the same there was still a certain degree of poetic justice in making a speech from an ammo box.

"As of fifteen minutes ago a miracle happened," he told them dryly, his tone dark enough to prevent anyone from remotely getting their hopes up. "The President of the Confederation and the leadership of the Block actually agreed on something. Unfortunately for the rest of the world, they agreed that it was time to stop holding back and have ordered the deployment of strategic weapons against the Drasin."

There was a long silence when he stopped speaking, and Eric let it run for many seconds.

"That means that within the next four hours, we and the Block will begin *nuking* our own territories where they have been infected by the aliens . . . and," Eric said grimly, "*everywhere* has been infected by the Drasin."

He brought both his hands up, palms forward to stall the screaming. The men and women he was commanding were *not* Special Forces, nor even active serving military for the most part. They were cops, former military, National Guardsmen, and even a few civilians too stubborn to run and hide when confronted with a nightmare. They took the news as he expected, angrily and with a great deal of worry for the people they'd left behind.

"Major cities are *not* on the current target list," he said, "nor are the many refugee areas that have sprung up in the last few weeks. We have enough forces in those areas to hammer them back the old-fashioned way, but both sides have elected to begin dropping heavy ordnance on the enemy pretty much everywhere else. Warnings will be issued, evacuations ordered, but if there are still people there when the clock hits zero . . . too bad for them."

Now there was less outrage, thankfully, but no less shock. He could understand that. He himself was still working through that stage of his reaction, if he were to be honest. Shock he could work with, shock he could turn into determination.

"So we have a job now," he said. "Same mission, new tactics. The U.S. and Block military forces are launching the first, largest, and probably only joint tactical operation in our history. Our job is to get eyes on the ground and either hammer the enemy into dust, or call on tactical and strategic weapons to do it for us. The more we take out the old-fashioned way, the fewer mushroom clouds we'll see blotting out the Sun."

He looked around the group slowly. "We're here to save the planet, and every living person in it . . . be it from the aliens, or from ourselves . . . Anyone here feel like say-ing no?"

There was a long silence as he waited for a response. With none coming, Eric nodded. "Alright. We're splitting up the band. You'll each get your marching orders in the next twenty. Grab some real grub 'cause you'll be sucking suit slurpies for the next little while."

The group broke up as Eric turned back and hopped off the box.

Ron came up to him, stone-faced. "Cap . . . "

"New York isn't on the target list, Ron," Eric answered, clapping a hand on his old friend's shoulder. "She's as safe as can be."

Ron nodded slowly. "Thanks."

"I didn't do anything, didn't have to." Eric smiled a little soberly. "You all did. New York is in shambles, but it's human controlled. You did that. You made her safer. Are you up to doing the same for some other people?"

"You know I am, Captain."

"Good," Eric said firmly, "you get your own squad. Orders will be sent to your suit before you're wheels up, but you already know what you have to do."

Ron nodded, throwing him a salute before he pivoted on his heel and walked away. Eric watched him go for a moment before returning his mind to his own tasks. He made his way over to where Alexander and Janet were leaning against the wall, the matched pair having watched the entire scene in silence.

"Nice speech, boss," Alexander told him with a grin. "Have one for us too?"

"You two don't need a speech. You're both crazy enough to do this job for the fun of it." Eric rolled his eyes.

Janet laughed outright, nodding. "You know us too well, Cap. You splitting us up?"

"Hell no. You two work good together, and I can't guarantee that anyone else I put you with will. One of you is in command, the other is second. Work it out between you," Eric said calmly. He'd never normally do anything that casual with the chain of command, but he knew both of them well enough to trust them to do their job and probably be better at it than anything he could hope to devise.

They normally flipped a coin to see who was in command of a given mission, and had been doing it since shortly after they met. Officially he supposed that one of them had seniority, but he couldn't be bothered to check which. They were a matched pair and they were a law unto themselves, and that was the way things were.

He was just a captain. Some laws of the universe were beyond his ability to control and he wasn't stupid enough to tell the Sun to set in the morning.

"We'll do what we have to, boss," Alexander said, Janet nodding in agreement. "You have any specific orders?"

"Not yet. Still gathering intel. I'll send it straight to your suits."

"Right. We'll be getting ready then," Janet said, grabbing Alexander's arm and hauling him physically away. Eric just smiled fondly as they left.

"What about me, love?"

Eric didn't turn around at the sound of the purring voice. He just shook his head equally fondly and spoke. "I want you to get online with your contacts, Siobhan. We need intel. I want to know everything you can learn. Relay it to Lyssa. She'll be in charge of coordinating our movements."

Siobhan stepped up close behind him, draping herself across his shoulder as she spoke into his ear. "The little girl? Can she handle the responsibility?"

"This little girl can handle a hell of a lot more than that," Lyssa said in an irritated voice.

"Hmmm," Siobhan hummed, not sounding in the least intimidated. "Her ears aren't half bad either. Not her best assets, mind you, but not half bad."

Eric could almost feel the heat wafting off of Lyssa and barely managed to hide the smile he felt trying to burst through. This was one of the few things he missed about wetwork, the more relaxed environment of working with equals.

"Lyss," he said, cutting into the burgeoning argument, "you're my eyes and ears here on the base."

He turned around. "I need someone here I trust, because if the brass is willing to bust out strategic weapons on our own territory, they'll also be willing to drop those same assets on the heads of me and *mine*. If you get the slightest inkling that's going to happen, I want you to pull any teams in the target zone out."

Lyssa nodded slowly. "You think they'd do that?"

"You can bet that they'll be dropping those things on civilians, Lyss," Eric said seriously. "There's no way to clear all affected areas . . . so yeah, I think they wouldn't think twice about dropping one on one of ours."

"Alright. You've got it," Lyssa said determinedly. "I won't let you down."

"Nor will I, love," Siobhan winked at him. "I want you back in one piece, after all. We have a tradition to uphold."

Lyssa looked between them, confused. "What kind of tradition?"

"The clothing optional kind, sweety." Siobhan patted her on the cheek. "If you're good, you can join in."

Eric just sighed and left while Lyssa was turning purple and choking on some choice words he'd not heard since boot.

▶▶▶

▶ Five large hangar doors slowly opened on magnetic bearings in the predawn air of the New Mexican desert. Behind them, being wheeled out slowly by powerful tugs, were ten AH-982 Cherokee ground support vehicles.

The Cherokees were an older platform that had been one of the first to be refitted with the CM technology after it was successfully tested on the Archangel fighters. Designed to fill the role of lofty earlier platforms such as the Huey and Blackhawk, while still giving the pilots a bit of a bite in the air, the Cherokees were as good a platform to launch his mission as Eric could have hoped for.

Unlike the heavy transport they'd flown in on, the Cherokees had limited cargo space. Enough for a squad, a couple of medics, and their supplies, but very little else. In exchange for giving up that added space, you got a heavily armored platform that could hit true hypersonic speeds, loiter around an LZ, and hammer the ground into paste if the situation called for it.

In other words . . . perfection.

They were just that, perfect, at what they did. Since the war ended there had been little use for the platforms and they'd been slowly retired in favor of other, more specialty designed systems. But Eric knew a lot of men who still considered the Cherokee to be the height of military design.

He hoped they were right.

"This my bird?" he asked, walking up to where a man in coveralls was looking over one of the craft.

"Sir!"

"Relax before you sprain yourself." Eric walked past him, running a hand along the hard-edged side of the craft.

"Sorry, sir. Yes, I've been assigned as your pilot, Captain."

Eric nodded. "Is she ready to fly?"

"Oh, yes sir."

"Good. I'll have my EXO-Mech loaded aboard . . . "

"Already done, sir. Loaded in fifteen minutes after you landed."

That took Eric by surprise, but then he supposed that it shouldn't have. When the brass had an idea, good or bad, they could ram it through in a hurry when they were of a mind to. He just nodded and walked back to the side door, then pulled himself up into the craft.

"I'll just check it then," he called back.

"You do that, sir."

He walked back to the hulking EXO-13, eyeing the tie-downs carefully. They were slugged in properly, so he left them be with just the cursory check. He was more interested in the emergency supply compartments, actually, so that was his first stop. He popped the compartment and breathed a sigh, pulling out the gravity rifle inside. He certainly didn't want to "misplace" the gift he'd received from the admiral on Ranquil, not when it was proving so damned useful.

That checked, he slipped the weapon back into the compartment and closed it up again.

Well, may as well do the diagnostics while I'm here.

An order from his suit brought the war machine online as he hauled himself up into the cockpit, computers whirring to life as they began the process of counting down every single relay and system. Eric knew that there were probably only minutes to go before they had their final orders cut, so it was time to make sure everything was in order.

The Sun broke over the horizon, its first golden rays casting across the airfield.

It was going to be a beautiful day.

▶▶▶

▶ The President looked over the map that was now threatening to turn completely red, particularly around the center of the nations he oversaw.

"General."

"Yes Mr. President?" An ashen-faced man looked up and over.

"Give the order."

"Yes sir."

The general leaned back over the station he was overseeing and nodded to the operator. The young woman swallowed, but nodded resolutely as she opened a channel.

"All units, Operation Fire Bath is go. I say again, Operation Fire Bath is go."

The President of the Confederation looked on, a sick feeling welling in the depths of his stomach.

Just so few words is all it takes to unleash so much destruction.

He turned and walked out of the room.

There was nothing more he could do there. It was in the hands of others now.

▶▶▶

▶ In his office, President Conner flapped his hand at the agent standing guard, gesturing him out of the room. He wanted privacy, and it was one of the few places on Earth where he could get it, so the man obeyed.

He sat down behind the large walnut desk and pulled a writing pad from one of the drawers. Real paper, not a computer tablet, and then picked up an obscenely expensive pen from where it rested to his right hand. Strictly speaking, he didn't know if what he was writing would be necessary, but better to have done it and be done with it than otherwise.

He kept his letter straight and to the point. His speech-writer was responsible for most of his silver-tongued moments. Conner was more the straightforward type by nature, a disadvantage he'd worked hard to overcome through the years. As he finished it up, signing with a flourish he'd practiced for literally *months,* he wondered if anyone would ever read it.

I suppose I'll find out, one way or the other.

Unlike many of his predecessors in their later years, he wasn't a religious man. He supposed that was a good thing, because he didn't need that on his mind at the moment in addition to his own regrets. One man's burdens were hard enough to carry, but they were his and his alone. He preferred no help in the task.

He folded the letter and set his pen beside it, getting up from the desk as he walked back out to the door and nodded to the agent again.

"I want to see my family."

"Yes sir."

President and agent left the facsimile of the Oval Office and the handwritten letter behind as they headed down the hall away from the war room. He had no more strategic decisions to make, and would not allow himself further action. Not after giving the order he had.

It might have been necessary, but no man had a right to sit in that chair for longer than it took to write his resignation after ordering the use of nuclear weapons. Particularly not when that use was going to be on home soil.

No, his day was over.

If they survived, the Confederation would have a new leader come morning.

▶ ▶ ▶

▶ The skies were clear over New Mexico as the Cherokees took off, turbines screaming as the CM aircraft leapt into the sky with full loads of armaments, soldiers, and supplies. They'd received the go order just seconds earlier, but everyone had been leaning on the sticks in anticipation.

"Be advised, Operation Fire Bath has been greenlit. I say again," the dispatcher announced, "Operation Fire Bath has been greenlit."

Eric hung his head for a moment, though it was far from unexpected. Finally, he just opened the channel. "Understood."

He changed over to a squad-level channel, addressing his people. "You heard the lady. I want you to do your jobs, but don't get your ass fried for nothing. If you're in a strike zone, watch the clock. If you can't get out, find cover and hunker down."

Contrary to what most people thought, nuclear blasts were far from all-encompassing. Shock waves that could turn a man's insides to Jell-O had a disconcerting habit of bouncing back and canceling themselves out at the oddest times. If you could find reasonable cover, and were either far enough to avoid the searing heat of the blast or armored enough to endure it, you had a reasonable chance of survival.

It was one reason why Eric was far from convinced that the nuclear option was a good one, though he knew that there were few options left and none of them were any good. No matter. They'd have to comb the strike zones after the blast, just to be sure. There was no room for error in what was coming. That much he knew for certain.

"Alright," he leaned forward, tapping the pilot's shoulder to emphasize the words. "Take us to our assigned sector."

"You've got it, sir."

The Cherokee banked hard to the right, coming around as the pilot charged the CM generators. Eric felt the familiar tingle of the hair standing up on the back of his neck just before the turbines' scream turned into a roar and he was slammed back in his place, along with everyone else, as the Cherokee leapt past Mach One and headed for hypersonic.

▼

CHAPTER TWENTY

▲

▶ "BRAVO SQUADRON, SPREAD out," Thane ordered as his instruments began showing the targets ahead of them more clearly. "Targets are being prioritized and assigned. Lock and stand by your Thunderbolts."

The squadron acknowledged as he flipped a panel of switches, bringing his own array of Thunderbolt High-Velocity Missiles online and making them live. The Thunderbolt was the designation for the antiship variation of the missile platform, equipped with far more expensive and heavier-duty CM capabilities.

The theory was that they could take out even the most powerful of capital ships, but that was something he hadn't seen much proof of just yet. They'd seen some light use in previous battles, but mostly it was the fighter screen variations that saw the heaviest use.

Time to see just how well these things really work.

The enemy ships were an ugly blood red on his screens, and he took his time confirming the firing arcs. It wouldn't do to miss and take out one of their own ships in the process. That wouldn't just be disastrous . . . it would be humiliating too.

The flight commander of Bravo Squadron chuckled to himself as he finished the calculations. *Death and destruction are part of the business. Embarrassment, however? That's just not acceptable.*

"Targets assigned," he said. "Fire on my command."

His team acknowledged him by the numbers, and Thane calmly armed the final system before he sent the targeting data to the Thunderbolts and haloed his targets.

"Commander, your screens!"

Thane looked down, frowning as his wingman called out, but instantly saw what had alerted the man. Dozens of enemy fighter class drones were launching into space from the targets, accelerating hard in Bravo's direction.

"Damn. They spotted us," he said, sounding bored. "*Enterprise*, Bravo Actual. Are you seeing this?"

"Roger, Bravo Actual. Alpha Flight is scrambling now."

"Well, I suppose we'd better get on with it, then," Thane drawled over his team comm. "Bravo Actual . . . Fox Three."

▶ ▶ ▶

▶ The Vorpal Class Space Superiority Starfighter was intended as a multirole chassis, designed to replace the older airframes that had done the bulk of the fighting in the Block war and even made up the famed Double A squadron. Vorpals were long, sleek space frames built around a paired set of CM generators and four large vacuum breathing reactor plants that put out enough power to shove around a ship the size of the *Enterprise* itself.

Instead of the dual "six gun" missile launchers that were stored inside the older airframes, the Vorpals wielded four eight-barrel launchers mounted under each stubby "wingtip." Not needing to worry about either weight or air resistance gave them a significant advantage in terms of payload, after all.

Bravo Flight was equipped with an antiship load out of Thunderbolt HVMs, semi-smart unguided missiles designed to impact their targets at relativistic velocities and kill with kinetic energy alone.

On Bravo Actual's announcement of "Fox Three," all twelve members of Bravo Flight put twenty-four Thunderbolts apiece into space in under three seconds.

Each weapon aligned on a specific target, precoded by the Vorpals' pilots, and then engaged both their overpowered CM generators and their solid-fuel rocket motors. Each Thunderbolt flickered away, appearing like nothing else but instantaneous teleportation to the human eye, and lanced toward their targets more like lasers than physical weapons.

Three light-seconds away the Thunderbolts interpenetrated the Drasin fighter screen, but unlike many earlier engagements, there was little the fighters could do to stop them. The missiles moved too fast to track, given their size, and even along that narrow path, space was just too big to put up a wall even if you were willing to use your own body to do it.

Two of the missiles impacted with the enemy fighter screen, blowing through them like an icepick through cardboard, leaving nothing but expanding gasses in their wake. The rest of the Thunderbolts encountered no resistance as they continued on, hammering into enemy ships like the blasts from Mount Olympus from which they drew their names.

Under the combined force of *two hundred eighty-eight* kinetic weapons raining down on their position, the twenty-eight remaining Drasin ships within knife range of the Heroic Task Force vanished into plasma and memories.

▶▶▶

▶ "Good hit, Bravo," Captain Carrow said from the command station of the *Enterprise*. "RTB while Alpha mops up the dregs."

"Aye sir, Bravo Flight is RTB," Thane said, flipping his Vorpal end over end, putting his burners away from the destruction his flight had wrought.

The squadron followed suit, burning hard to build Delta-V back to the *Enterprise*. The carrier was barely visible in the distance, and only by their augmented scanners, but it was heading toward them even as a dozen IFF tags lit up on their screens.

Alpha Flight was in space and accelerating hard in their direction.

Thane glanced at the rear scanners, noting that it was probably none too soon, because every single remaining Drasin fighter was blue, shifting hard.

"I think we pissed them off, boys."

▶▶▶

▶ "Whoa."

Admiral Gracen had to admit, the sentiment fit.

"Alright." She shook off the surprise of the Drasin ships just vanishing into clouds of plasma. "The *Enterprise* has cleared the road. Time to do *our* jobs. Come about and clear the guns!"

"Aye ma'am," Steph said softly, thinking about the sheer rain of destruction the Vorpals had just brought down on the enemy.

He truly hated to admit it, but it was a fair sight more than the Double A squadron would have been able to pull off even at their height.

Those new birds are some scary pieces of kit, I'll give them props for that.

Of course, for the moment at least, he wasn't Double A anymore. He was Heroic, and that meant that he could top that little show and leave plenty to spare for an encore.

"Ithan Chans"—Gracen looked over to where Milla was working—"prepare targeting solutions for the ships within our range."

"Yes Admiral. Solutions being prepared."

"We're out of the fire, but this fight is a long way from over. Michelle, watch our flanks. They ambushed us once. We may not get so lucky a second time," Gracen ordered.

"Aye ma'am. Should I go full active?"

Gracen considered it, then nodded. "Yes. They know we're here anyway. Do it."

"Going full active, all screens, all bands," Michelle said. "The other Heroics are following suit."

The Heroic Class ships were capable of operating with full FTL scans of a system, effectively for an unlimited duration. It poured high-energy, low-life tachyons out into the system and used the nearly invisible bounce-back signals to track everything moving within a range of several AU.

The words "energy intensive" didn't begin to cover the costs of such high-level scanning, but one thing that the Heroics had aplenty was energy.

"Four hundred thirty-three enemy ships approaching on track from Earth orbit," Michelle announced a moment later.

Gracen nodded. That was just within their engagement limit if her count was correct.

"Firing formation Delta," she ordered. "Spread us out, clear the guns, and fire as they bear."

"Aye ma'am," Steph said. "Formation Delta."

He casually adjusted the course of the big ship, splitting away from the *Heracles* as the other ships did the same. It was a move intended to clear their gun sights, removing any chance of interfering with one another's shots, as they brought the tachyon waveguide cannons to bear.

The six ships of the Heroics task force went to full automatic fire as the line of sight first cleared, their waveguide cannons humming almost constantly as they discharged. The shells, one-meter nuclear fused munitions, had been improved by the Priminae, as had most of the systems provided by Admiral Gracen and the refugees from Earth. Each now packed multi-gigaton fusion weapons in the place of the smaller Terran warheads.

The tachyon transition, instantaneous as it was, threw the weapons across the intervening space in the blink of an eye. At their targets the effect wore off naturally, plunging the weapons back into real space and, hopefully, right into the heart of the targeted ship.

Some missed. The equations for determining the effect of gravity on tachyon formations were far from perfect, and occasionally the powerful local fields caused by multiple warp interactions caused some shells to reappear outside their intended target. Or, in more extreme cases, other shells reappeared as fragments of their original form due to the tachyon formation being totally disrupted by opposing fields.

Others struck true, but returned to normal space inside the solid matter—such as the hull of the ship—they were aimed at. This was destructive, annihilating both the shells and the section of hull quite effectively, but generally not fatal to the target or even particularly inconveniencing.

Most, however, appeared within the interior of their target as intended—in the cargo rooms, the drone bays, the ducts that piped vital gasses about. These shells fell to the decks with loud clanging noises, attracting attention from all in the area, but by that time it was far too late.

In the first volley, over twenty Drasin ships simply *vanished* into nuclear fire.

The six ships of the Heroics squadron continued on full automatic fire for nearly five minutes until the last of the charging Drasin ships were destroyed in what was, for Admiral Gracen, the single most one-sided battle she'd ever witnessed or heard of.

There was a quiet moment after the report of the last destroyed Drasin ship made its way around the bridge, a period in which no one seemed to know what to say. Gracen finally broke the silence herself.

"Alright. Set course for Earth orbit," she said. "They likely need some help."

"Aye aye, ma'am."

"Get me the *Enterprise* in the meantime."

"Yes ma'am. Captain Carrow . . . online," Susan told her a moment later.

"Captain, I see you have some fighters headed your way. Do you require assistance?"

"No ma'am, we can handle them. Suggest you get ground units to Earth," Carrow answered. "We'll follow as soon as we've cleaned up."

"Very well. Tell your pilots they have my compliments and thanks for the save," she said. "Gracen out."

The admiral considered something for a moment, then stood up. "Ithan Chans . . . "

"Yes Admiral?" the Priminae woman asked.

"How are our munition stocks looking?"

"We are low, Admiral. Transition shells are at twenty percent or less across all ships," Milla said. "If they had many more ships, it would have been very close."

Gracen nodded. "Understood. Thank you."

Mentally she was tallying what she knew was in the system when she was forced to flee and comparing it to the kill rate. They didn't have an exact count, but she knew that between Captain Sun and Weston, and with the help of Carrow, the initial force of thousands had been devastated, leaving *only* a few hundred to take control of what they'd won.

They had now accounted for nearly five hundred more of the enemy ships, so while there could be some stragglers about in the system . . . *Almost certainly are, actually* . . . they should have eliminated the bulk of the enemy force.

Her task force was a little beat up. They'd lost some people and had a few holes poked in their armor, but they were intact. The Priminae systems, combined with the Terran systems, were an incredible combination of power and sophistication.

*The lab boys are going to be working overtime trying to find a way to block the waveguide cannons. Those things are just **monstrous**.*

"Course charted and coded, ma'am. We're en route for Earth orbit."

"Alright," Gracen said firmly. "Good. We're not done here yet. Alert Colonel Reed and have his boys suit up. I have a bad feeling about what's going on back home."

"Aye ma'am," Susan said. "Reed reports that his teams are ready to deploy just as soon as we get there."

"Then by all means. Commander Michaels?"

"Yes ma'am?"

"Don't spare the engines."

"Aye aye, Admiral. Maximum acceleration engaged," Steph said. "We'll have to do some fancy braking moves when we get there though."

"Is that a problem for you flyboys?"

The former fighter pilot just laughed. "Not even a bit of one."

"Good."

The Heroics, led by the *Odysseus,* warped space hard as they plummeted toward Earth.

▶▶▶

▶Commander William Briggs grinned as he poured on the thrust, leading Alpha Flight as they plunged toward the array of red icons spattered across their HUDs. The enemy fighter drones were closing on Bravo Flight, and would be able to engage them before they made it back into the security zone of the *Enterprise.* It was his and Alpha Flight's job to ensure that the Drasin didn't get a chance to do much damage when that happened.

"Spread out. Watch for energy leaking off their beams," he ordered. "The fighters aren't as powerful as the big ships, but their lasers are still bloody obscene."

The green IFF signals coming off of Bravo Flight were getting closer, but so far the other squadron of Vorpals hadn't closed within visual range. He doubled checked the vectors of every fighter in his squad against those among the other, just to ensure that no one was being careless enough to Fox Five themselves into an ally.

Everything was clear, however, and that was no more than expected. Even if anyone on his squad was that stupid, and he liked to think that they weren't, space was a big-ass place. One would almost have to plan something like that.

Which, honestly, was what frightened him. The competition between Alpha and Bravo was heated at the best of times, and occasionally someone would *show off.* He was willing to put up with that in training, but if anyone had tried to buzz an ally in this situation, Bill Briggs would have had to think about splashing them himself.

"Hey boss man," Bill's wingman called out, "do you have a count on those things? I'm getting fuzzy readings here."

"They're in close formation, probably leftover orders from when they were shielding their mother ships," Bill answered. "The initial count we got was north of sixty enemy fighters."

A whistle went up across the board. "That's a lot, boss."

"They use lasers, which means they have to get inside knife range to score a reliable kill," Bill reminded them. "We hit them hard from outside knife range, then pull back to let the *Big E* move into place to cover us before we wrassle them around up close."

"Sounds good, boss, but let's remember that these guys are kamikaze fighters."

"Fair point," Bill conceded. "Everyone watch for suicides. We don't want to lose the *E*, got that?"

They had it.

"Everyone hold your fire until we clear Bravo Flight's location," he said seriously. "I know you guys don't always get along, but you wouldn't believe the paperwork involved if one of us accidentally splashes our own guys."

"What if we just wing one?" Alpha Nine asked, laughing.

"With high-velocity missiles? Yeah, that's likely. Just wait," he answered, rolling his eyes.

A glance at the numbers told him that they didn't have long left to wait.

"Interpenetration of the Bravo line in . . . twenty seconds. Stand by to go weapons hot."

▶ ▶ ▶

▶ Captain Carrow watched the numbers fall on his screens. There was little else he could do. The fighters were too small and too far out to track visually, and even if they could the signals would be almost three seconds out of date before the *Enterprise* got them.

Even with FTL comms, which the *Enterprise* had but the fighters did not, controlling a battle at that range was beyond the realm of realism. He trusted his commanders to do what they had to do, and to know that he was going to get the *Enterprise* into the right position to end this fight.

"I want a diagnostics check on all point defense systems," he said, mostly to keep people busy at this point.

He knew that everything was working. They'd been running drills ever since they were forced to flee Earth space over a month ago. What was broken had been repaired, and what was slow was now running as fast and smooth as he could hope for.

"All systems check green. Crews are performing hands-on checks now."

"Good. The alien fighters are known to try kamikaze stunts. There can be *no* holes in our defensive screen," he said. "We're not a Priminae ship. One of those things will end us."

"Yes sir."

Carrow looked back over the numbers on his screens. "Rip them up, Wild Bill. End this."

▶▶▶

▶ The passage of the two ranks of fighters was a nonevent in every way except the digital. In the black of space he couldn't make out the dark-colored Vorpals of Bravo Flight, and the heat of their reactors was so high that the flames burned well past the visible spectrum.

The computers noted it, however, and that was all Bill needed.

"Lock them in, Alphas," he ordered.

"They're closer than I expected them," Alpha Five said. "Positive lock! I've got halos."

Others made similar comments, but Bill ignored them for a moment while he made sure that everyone was targeting their own picks and no one was doubling up. They had limited munitions as it was. It wouldn't do to waste any.

"Roger that, Alphas," he said a moment later, last second checks made. "Stand by to blossom after we fire."

The range was falling fast, and he knew he didn't have much time.

"Alpha One," he said calmly, thumb sliding over the firing stud of the control stick. "Fox Three."

The rest of the flight followed suit seconds later, as the twelve fighters of Alpha flight put thirty-six lightning space-to-space HVMs into the intervening area, then pulled out hard. The fighters of Alpha didn't just turn around and burn back for the *Enterprise*, however; they exploded out in a blossom formation as they took a long curve around before they wound up pointing back the direction they had come from.

Less than a light-second away now, the first of the light HVMs struck true, and the dying began.

CHAPTER TWENTY-ONE

▶ THE CHEROKEE BANKED hard, using air resistance as well as counterthrust to slow as quickly as it could. The sudden and rapid deceleration was enough to slam everyone hard into their seats as the pilot leaned over and looked back over his shoulder.

"Captain, you may want to check this."

Eric nodded, unbuckling, and made his way forward to where the pilots were nodding. He looked out over the copilot's shoulder and whistled.

The city of Dallas was a mess, there was no questioning that. He could count a dozen ruined skyscrapers at a glance, and his armor warning systems were going nuts with all the high thermal points in motion across what remained.

"Damn. Do we have any contacts on the ground?"

"Yes sir. Rangers and Guardsmen have a forward base near Reunion Park," the pilot told him. "They're using it as a relay point for evacuees and a delivery zone for munitions drops."

"Alright, good," Eric said. "Get them on the line. I want to talk to whoever is in charge."

"It's a mess down there, sir," the pilot said. "I *think* that a Texas Ranger is currently the man in charge."

"Really? Alright, get a hold of him then." Eric shrugged. "I don't care who, I just need to talk with the person in charge."

"I'll see what I can do. Where do you want us?"

"I'll let you know once we've had a chance to talk with the person in charge," Eric said. "The question is going to be what can we do, not where can we do it."

▶▶▶

▶ Ranger Swenson had seen a *lot* of shit in his day, but whatever the hell had happened to his city over the past four weeks topped everything he'd even seen in *movies*. The damn things came out of the sky. Alright, they were aliens. Sure, he'd watched the news, he knew that aliens existed, but they didn't drop in on the Dallas/Fort Worth area and start *eating* the goddamn place!

Never, never had he even *imagined* anything like the nightmare they'd been dealing with for the past month. He was a goddamn ranger. He dealt with scum and villains of all stripes, from the lowest street filth to the most dangerous psychos in a state where insanity was considered part of the way of life.

"Ranger?"

"What is it," Swenson looked around, seeing a Guardsman running up with a field comm.

"We've got a captain on the comm. Wants to talk to the person in charge."

"Unless he has a division or two of troops he can lend me, tell him to take a number and wait in line," Swenson growled. Three, four, sometimes five and more times a day some jackass with a chest full of medals, usually for piloting ROVs, was on the line trying to tell him how to handle the shit coming his way while he was standing right in the middle of the stream with nothing but a goddamn net.

"Sir, Ranger, he's using presidential codes."

"Oh fan-frigging-tastick," Swenson sighed, reaching out for the comm. "Fine. Put the boy on."

He grabbed the wireless comm, dropping it over his ear, and planted a foot on the cement barrier that was all that stood between himself and a thirty-story drop. The windows of just about every building in the city had been long since blown out.

"You've got Ranger Swenson. Make it good."

"Weston," the voice on the other side said simply. "I'm currently orbiting Dallas, a little north of your position. Your city *crawls*, Ranger."

Swenson laughed. "Tell me something I don't know, Weston."

"The President gave an order, couple hours ago. Anything that crawls, *dies*." The voice on the other side said, "Get your people out of the city, Swenson."

"Whoa, whoa, whoa . . . " Swenson leaned forward, glowering at no one. "What the hell are you saying, Weston?"

"I'm saying"—the voice paused a moment—"what I'm saying, Ranger, is that Dallas glows in the dark tonight. Whether you do or not depends on how far out of town you get."

Swenson swore. "You can't *DO* that!"

"It's done."

"It's NOT done!"

Swenson was hollering into his comm, attracting the attention of everyone in the makeshift command center, and he didn't give a damn. About fifteen Guardsmen, the remainder of an armored platoon that got torn to shreds on Young Street, started to circle around and look at each other nervously.

The remaining defenders of the city were mostly scattered, based out of whatever piece of crap building they could find that wasn't being eaten at the time. They'd mostly been driven to being little more than an underground railroad, of which the Reunion base was the last stop.

"Listen to me, you piece of shit, if you think I'm going to sit here and let you blow *my* city to hell and back, you're out of your fucking mind."

Everyone around looked at each other, nerves now being replaced by real apprehension. They had to have misunderstood that, right?

▶▶▶

▶"Bah." Eric closed the connection while the man on the other side was dipping into his repertoire of Spanish curse words. He leaned forward, tapping the pilot on the shoulder. "Take us over that way. I need face time with that jackass."

"Roger that, sir. Should I set down in the park?"

"Hell no," Eric growled, "just get me over their base of operations. I'll handle the rest."

"You want it, Cap, you got it."

The pilot banked the Cherokee from a standstill to sideways flight at over two hundred miles per hour in just a few seconds, slamming everyone around a bit even with the CM operating at full intensity. He twisted the craft around as they crossed over Reunion Park, bringing them into a tight orbit around the area.

"Whatever you're going to do, now's the time, Cap!" the pilot called back as Eric pulled himself into the EXO-13.

"Roger that," Eric said, pulling the harness frame shut over him. "Stay on orbit over the city. I'll call for pickup soon."

"You've got it."

"Captain . . . " One of his squad tapped on the cockpit of the EXO mech. "You don't want us down there?"

"Not for this," Eric said as he activated the mech, the pneumatic systems hissing as they pressurized. "I can handle one jackass, even if he is a ranger."

The men laughed, patting the machine as Eric hoisted himself on the winch centered in the frame of the Cherokee and opened the hatch below. The city appeared below them as the men cleared the road and nodded. Eric saluted with the machine's arms, then hit the release switch and dropped away.

▶▶▶

▶ "We ain't seen any of those flying overhead before," Swenson snorted, eyeing up the military craft as it circled.

"No wonder. That's old school, sir. Didn't know we had any in that good of a shape," a Guardsman offered, sounding genuinely impressed. "I signed up 'cause I wanted to fly a Cherokee into the action, just like the in movies. They were mostly phased out for the new Deltas by the time I got in though."

Swenson nodded. "I flew in a few in the early days of the war, before they fancied them up with all that antigravity bullshit."

"Counter-mass, sir."

"Like hell. It's goddamn antigravity, son," Swenson said. "Call a mule a mule."

"Yes sir."

"They're about to do a drop," another man said, nodding to the belly of the craft. "We due any supplies?"

"Not that we were told. The whole damn radio band is quiet since last night," a young woman said as she walked over with a computer in hand.

"Well, someone sure as hell is delivering something." Swenson waved a hand as he walked over to the space where a window was supposed to be.

What happened next made him take a step back involuntarily as a hulking machine dropped out of the belly of the Cherokee and slammed into the soft ground of Reunion Park with enough force to dig a crater and throw dirt all around.

"Whoa!"

"Holy shit . . . "

Swenson scowled, taking a step forward and looking closer, spotting the machine as it rose to its feet and began to stalk out of the park in the direction of his headquarters.

"Get everyone up! We've got something incoming. I don't know what it is, but let's be ready for it," he ordered, sending two of the Guardsmen scrambling to raise the alarm. When they were gone he glanced back to where the woman, Wendy, was staring. "You ever see anything like this?"

"Only in the comic books, Ranger Swenson."

▶▶▶

▶ *I swear, this thing is going to make me motion sick,* Eric snarled mentally as he stalked the machine forward.

The problem with bipedal systems was that there was always a bit of sway in the step, no matter how motion-controlled the cockpit was. He had to admit that this one was one of the best he'd seen. Most were considerably worse, but it was still noticeable. That said, and despite his inner monologue, Eric was in no danger of losing his lunch. After decades flying some of the most high-performance jets in the world, his stomach was cast in iron.

He stomped out of the park, coming to a rest in front of the building they'd identified as the headquarters for the local Guard resistance. That ID was confirmed by the swarm of men in urban camo that came rushing out to cover him with their guns. Eric ignored them in favor of the man who calmly walked out, wearing a sidearm and cowboy hat as his most distinguishing features.

Eric popped the cab of the EXO mech and pulled himself out, dropping the ten feet to the ground with an easy motion. He walked through the ranks of men who weren't *quite* aiming their weapons at him and came to a stop in front of the man in the hat.

"Ranger Swenson, I presume."

▶ ▶ ▶

▶ Swenson snorted.

If this cock-a-wop thought for a second he was impressed by that bit of showmanship, then he had a hard lesson coming his way.

"You must be that braying fool, Weston," he said, looking the man right in the silver faceplate of his armor. "Nice toys you have. Too bad you didn't share them with us earlier."

The suit hissed as it equalized pressure and the man, Weston, reached up and pulled his helmet off.

"I was busy clearing New York, then recapturing Detroit and Hamilton," Eric said simply. "And as for the toys, there aren't enough to go around."

"So you left us to rot. That's mighty nice of you," Swenson snarled. "Now what? You think we're going to let you *nuke* our city?"

The men around them drew back, most paling as they heard that. Eric just smiled coldly.

"Ranger, how do you propose to stop it?"

Swenson put a hand on his pistol menacingly. "Maybe we don't let you leave."

Eric just laughed at him. "I don't hold the football, Ranger."

"Right, like they're going to nuke their little messenger boy."

"Ranger, you don't have a clue what's going on here." Eric stopped smiling. He was out of patience and talking through clenched teeth. "These things aren't just another enemy to kill. They're here to eat and breed, and when they're done there won't be anything left flying in our orbit around the Sun but a crumbling pile of crawling alien *spiders*."

That stopped the ranger for a moment, and Eric pressed on. "This is genocide, Ranger. Either they *all* die, or we do."

Swenson glowered. "And it's gonna take nuking Dallas to kill them?"

"It's going to take a lot more than that," Eric snarled, turning away for a moment. "After the blast clears, we have units ready to come in and clean the rubble out."

"You think any of them are gonna live through a blast like that?"

"I can almost guarantee it."

Swenson shook his head. "Nothing's that tough."

"Ranger, in 1945 a man survived being at ground zero Japan . . . *both* times," Eric said. "Nuclear weapons aren't magical brooms to sweep the enemy away, especially not an enemy like this. Even one survivor is too damned many."

The ranger snorted, clearly unconvinced, but that didn't bother Eric. He wasn't here to convince one man. He was here to get as many people out of the city as he could.

"This is what you're going to do," Eric said flatly. "Contact every group you can, then tell them to spread the word.

Anyone still in Dallas is to get *out* today. Minimum safe distance is twenty miles, but they'd be happier at fifty."

"They're really going to nuke Dallas, Captain?"

Eric turned to look at the man who had spoken, shaking his head. "You don't get it, son. They're nuking *everywhere*."

"Jesus Christ," Swenson swore, not even bothering to keep his voice down. "It can't be that bad. *Nothing* can be that bad!"

"You never saw what these things have done to other planets, Ranger. I have," Eric said, "It's worse than that. Now do what I told you, damn it. Every minute you waste is a minute someone could be using to get clear!"

They stood, clearly looking to Swenson for instructions, and Eric began to get a sense of just what had been going on in Dallas over the last month. If he had to bet, he'd say that Swenson probably took over at a bad time. Whatever happened, that man was the person the Guardsmen were looking to, and that meant that he had to convince him.

"Look, Ranger," he said, trying now to sound earnest, "there're no reinforcements coming. These things hit the entire planet. Everything we've got is tied up somewhere else. Those things are going to eat your city . . . "

He sighed, and continued. "They tried to eat my ship, Ranger. My command, my *Odyssey*. Her hull was in pieces, the habitat modules scattered around New York, she'd never fly again . . . but those things swarmed her and tried to eat her. You know what I did?"

Swenson didn't say anything, so Eric went on determinedly.

"I blew my own ship to shards of scattered steel and took as many of them with her as I could," Eric said. "Right now, Dallas is the biggest attractant for five hundred miles. We don't know why, but you guys sure as hell got more than your share, and right now that means we've got a huge number of these things sitting right here, waiting to be wiped out. Do you really want to let them *eat* your city?"

"Hell no," Swenson grumbled, "but I sure as hell don't want to see it burn in nuclear fire either!"

"Better to burn it yourself than hand it over to those things," Eric countered.

He could see the ranger being swayed, see the decision being made behind the man's eyes, and Eric just waited. He'd worked with men like this before, and when they were making a decision it was better to give them a chance to come to the right path on their own. Push the wrong way at the wrong time and they'd dig in and you'd never get anywhere.

He could just take over, pull rank on the Guardsmen around them, but they'd resent that and drag their heels on him. And that didn't count on how any civilians or police personnel would react. No, it was better to get the ranger on his side now, if he could. In either case, however, Eric knew that he couldn't waste much time if things started to go against him.

Swenson grimaced before speaking grudgingly. "There aren't many people left in the city. We had to get everyone out when those things took down the first few office buildings. The dust was choking people out. We had a lot of folks die from respiratory problems."

Eric nodded. "We knew that the populace was light inside city limits. We've got satellite intel on that, so start pulling out your own people and anyone they know about. I can bring in some evacuation lifters if you need them, but we have to start *now*."

The ranger clearly didn't like what he was hearing, let alone what he was about to say, but finally he nodded.

"Fine. You call your lifters." Swenson poked Weston in the chest, hurting his finger on the armor but not flinching. "We don't leave no one behind. You clear on that?"

"That's the plan, Ranger."

"Fine. Then let's do this."

▶"Mr. President?"

Conner sighed from where he was sitting, but smiled sadly at his wife and got up.

"Yes?"

"Something has changed, sir."

He lost his annoyance, his expression growing serious in an instant. "Talk to me."

"Admiral Gracen is approaching NEO, Mr. President. The Drasin threat in orbit seems to have been neutralized."

Conner wobbled a bit, his knees suddenly feeling more than a little weak.

"Are you sure?"

He could hardly believe it. He knew what the technology Gracen had at her disposal could do, but this was beyond anything he'd ever expected. There had been hundreds of ships in orbit, and only seven in the admiral's task force.

While it was true that Captain Weston had eliminated well over a thousand with only three ships in his last-ditch defense of the system, Conner was well aware that the man had done things that no sane tactician would try and made them work through sheer guile, literally taking total command of the battle space in ways that no one could have predicted or duplicated.

"Reasonably, sir. The bulk of the enemy ships were certainly annihilated by the admiral's tachyon cannons, but there may be survivors we're not seeing."

"Right," Conner nodded. "OK. Has she contacted SPACECOM?"

SPACECOM was the old command center, based in Cheyenne Mountain, that had previously handled all extra-atmospheric contacts. It had been superseded by Space Station Liberty, but when Liberty was lost they had reactivated its original charter.

"Yes sir. That's why we came to get you. She's asking for instructions on where and how to deploy ground troops."

"She brought troops? How many?"

Conner racked his brain, trying to think of who she could have brought, but could only come up with a hundred or so people at best. Certainly they were all good, but it seemed pointless to bring them down at this juncture.

"Reed's team, the *Odyssey*'s complement, and over fifteen thousand volunteers from the Priminae forces trained by Reed," the aide said, smiling. "The *Enterprise* is dealing with a few remaining fighter drones, but they're expected to be along shortly."

"My God. That many?"

It was still a drop in the bucket, but it was a significant drop, and Conner felt the stirrings of real hope despite how strongly he tried to shut it down. Hope was a painful thing to experience at the moment.

Still, he steeled himself. *Maybe I have a few more decisions left in me after all.*

"Alright," he said, his professional mask falling into place. "I'll be ready in a moment. We'll get to the war room."

"Yes sir, Mr. President."

CHAPTER TWENTY-TWO

▶ "BRAKING IS GOING to be rough, Admiral," Steph advised from his place at the helm. "We're moving a hell of a lot faster than the *Odyssey* could have tried this from."

"Understood. Call all hands to general quarters," Gracen ordered. "Stand by for combat drop of available personnel according to the priorities list provided by the President and the Premier."

"Aye ma'am," Susan said, sounding a little dazed.

Gracen didn't blame her. It wasn't every day that you had a conference call with the Confederation President and the Block Premier. She wasn't feeling all that grounded in reality just then either, but she had a job to do.

"How are the ground forces reporting?" she asked intently.

"All hands in position. We're ready to launch shuttles as soon as we hit NEO," Susan responded.

"Good, Commander. I believe that makes it your game."

"Aye aye, ma'am," Steph said steadily as he linked into the squadron comm network. "You with me, Heroes?"

The other pilots of the Heroics, former Archangels all, responded quickly and in the affirmative. They'd been waiting for a chance to get some of their own back, ever since the last fight over Earth ended in such an unsatisfying manner.

"Stand by all hands. This could get a little rough," Steph warned, adding to the warnings already sounding through the ship. "Initiating gravity-assisted braking."

The Heroics were plummeting through the Sun's gravity well at significant relativistic speeds, the force of the solar mass boosting their fall in conjunction with their warp drives. As they swept into cislunar space, however, Steph initiated a full reverse even as he ducked the ship into the Moon's sphere of influence.

With the other Heroics following, the *Odysseus* skimmed the lunar surface, sometimes so close that her warp drive kicked up a dust plume in her wake, whipping around the celestial object and breaking free on a new course for Earth itself.

The squadron crossed the intervening space in minutes, decelerating on full power the whole way, and was caught by Earth's gravity field rapidly and surely. Steph dove into the field, blowing through debris and wreckage floating in orbit with the *Odysseus'* shields shouldering it all aside like it was nothing. He tried not to think of what, and who, he might be slamming through, and focused on the job at hand.

"Entering NEO!"

NEO, or Near Earth Orbit, was where the trickiest part of the maneuver had to play out.

"Launch ground assault!" Gracen ordered quickly.

The big ship didn't even shiver as the Priminae-designed landers were blown away, but she began to shudder almost violently as they skimmed the atmosphere.

"Watch out, Commander. You'll *bounce!*" Gracen, a former shuttle pilot herself, warned.

Steph didn't respond, instead only snorting softly enough not to be noticed by his commanding officer. "I have it, Admiral. Initiating air-braking!"

The shuddering intensified at the same time as they smoothed out, becoming a deep and powerful vibration that could be felt at all corners of the big ship. They whipped past North America, for the third time Gracen thought, heading west over the Pacific, and quickly Asia came into sight.

"Status on ground deployment?"

"Thirty percent away, Admiral!"

"Continue launching," she ordered. "I want every priority zone covered."

"Aye aye. Launch in progress!"

"Susan, stay on top of this. You're the coordinator. It's going to be hell but we're all counting on you," Gracen said, turning to look at her communications specialist.

Susan Lamont swallowed hard, but nodded. "Aye aye, ma'am. I won't let you down."

Gracen nodded, trusting that the younger woman would hold true to her word. It was going to be a hard job since they didn't have enough equipment to properly link all of their troops into the Earth forces' battle networks. That would make things a bit touchy, and probably was going to cost some lives just in tactical errors and blue-on-blue scenarios. It couldn't be helped. The tactical map the President had transmitted to them was ugly, with Drasin taking over large chunks of the planet, and the Terran governments already considering the very last resorts.

"Sweet Jesus," Michelle Winger hissed from her station.

Gracen twisted. "What is it?"

"It's Bangladesh, ma'am . . . The Block nuked it. They nuked their own country."

Gracen closed her eyes, knowing that wouldn't be the last time. Nor did she expect that the Block would be the only ones resorting to such tactics.

"Susan, drop the priority of that area. Schedule it for recon once we have time."

"Aye aye, ma'am," Susan answered, her voice ashen and dry.

Gracen didn't blame her for the reaction, but now wasn't the time.

"Stay on top of it, all of you," she growled. "This isn't a movie and it's not a game. People are dying and a lot more are going to die before this is done. If you don't stay on top of it, that number goes up. We'll have time to choke up when this is over. Am I quite clear?"

They all nodded, a few managing to answer vocally with an affirmative. She sighed. It would have to do.

▶▶▶

▶ Colonel Reed grinned as he felt free fall overtake him.

It wasn't a nice grin. It was, in fact, an ugly one. He didn't bother to hide it as he normally would have. His direct subordinates knew him well enough not to be put off too badly by it and those who didn't couldn't see his face anyway.

"Colonel," the pilot said, looking back, "we are approaching the drop zone."

"Very good. Just as we practiced, everyone, yes?"

"Yes Colonel!"

The men were green, but talented. The Priminae had let their ground forces volunteer freely, he suspected because they didn't actually view them as valuable, unlike their naval forces. That was their mistake, Reed knew, and it was a big one. Almost every first-generation soldier he and his team had trained was packed into the Heroics, along with many second- and third-generations that had been trained by the first group.

Had he been in command of the Ranquil ground forces, he'd have been furious. In fact, he personally *knew* that Commander Nero had nearly blown a gasket when the council had given that permission. That hadn't been enough for them to rescind it, however, though Reed half thought that Nero and Admiral Tanner had grudgingly let it go as a gesture of gratitude.

He hoped that he wasn't about to get them all killed, but if that was what it took to save his world and his family . . . assuming they were still alive . . . he was prepared to make just that sacrifice.

He just refused to make it in vain.

They were here to win. They *had* to win. They **would win.**

There were no other options.

"Three seconds, Colonel!"

"Drop!" Green called, sending the first of the Priminae soldiers out of the shuttle at Mach Three and fifty thousand feet.

His grin wasn't entirely ugly as he stepped up to the door and then threw himself out. Reed also loved his work, probably a little too much.

"*De oppresso liber!*" he called as the wind tore him away from the shuttle and the Priminae ship vanished from sight in a blurred instant.

▶▶▶

▶ The six Heroics corkscrewed around the blue-white marble that was the Earth, dropping ships as fast as they could in an explosive effort to cover every possible point. It was an impossible task, of course, and one that sent almost as much fright through those on the ground as the initial invasion itself had.

The roaring fireballs that engulfed the braking carriers seemed to tear from horizon to horizon with terrifying speed, and the silver shuttlecraft that dropped from them were so alien that to many people's eyes they just *had* to be more of the enemy. Surface-to-air missiles leapt out, tracking the ships from ground station, only to be swatted from the sky by the Priminae point defense systems.

The Priminae may not have been and were not currently masters of the art of war, but they learned fast and had good teachers.

▶ ▶ ▶

▶ "Susan!"

"On it, ma'am." Susan Lamont cringed, eyes not coming up from her station.

Several groups had opened fire on the drop ships. Thankfully, they'd been too impatient and launched far too soon. That wouldn't save people if someone down there was a slight bit smarter, however, so she was frantically jumping across every frequency she could.

"I say again," she spoke as her fingers flew over the console, "do not fire on the silver ships. They are allies."

She cycled through every language she knew, trying to head off a tragedy before it happened, but there were so many more that she despaired of what she was sure she would see in a few short minutes. Another voice, however, broke into the frequency and began repeating her message in other languages. Some she knew, many she did not.

"Mr. Palin?" Susan blinked, remembering the language specialist from the first mission of the *Odyssey*. She had been one of the few who rather got a kick out of the sometimes infuriating man, and the sense of relief she felt at hearing his oft-hated voice was palpable.

"Relax, my dear." The old man's voice paused in its repetitions for a moment. "You're not alone. Get back to your real job. I'll make sure those fools know who they're shooting at."

Susan swallowed, nodding. "Thank you."

She wiped that part of her board with a gesture, bringing up the tactical display again. "Colonel, you're coming down in a highly populated and contested region. Stand by. I'm putting you in touch with the local resistance commander."

▶▶▶

▶ The gleaming silver shuttles were blazingly quick, appearing and vanishing in seconds at times, but behind them they left a legacy for those watching on the ground. At first it was easy to miss. A man-sized object at fifty thousand feet wasn't something you spotted easily, but fifty of them flashing toward you at terminal velocity is something that's easier to spot.

Colonel Reed led his team into the fight, coming down over the outskirts of Beijing, and the irony of his leading a group of soldiers to *save* that particular city wasn't lost on him even slightly. There was an irony to the universe, he supposed.

They hit the brakes at under one thousand feet, using Priminae-enhanced counter-mass technology to swoop in like the airborne troops he had always wanted to be part of. Instead of merely caching part of the man's mass from the universe, thus making him easier to maneuver in gravity wells, the Priminae version of the chutes actually warped space actively, turning his troops into supermen.

"Second Squad, take the right street. Stay low and stay fast. Watch out for Drasin bracketing fire!" he called, leading his squad down the left side street. They rushed through the tightly packed buildings of old Beijing, then exploded out into the massive skyrises of the new city center. Reed and his men led with their gravity rifles, tracking and firing almost before the Drasin realized they were there.

The high-velocity carbon crystal rounds slammed into the first line of drones, blowing them to shattered pieces as Reed's team flashed by overhead. He couldn't help grinning the whole damned time. Revenge was sweet, but revenge at Mach One, flying under your own power . . . or almost . . . that was just unbelievable.

"Colonel, a General Sian Hao is on the line."

"General," Reed said as he banked around and came in for a reasonably soft landing on the edge of an eighty-story building. He and his team settled there for a moment, getting their bearings and letting the tactical data catch up with them. "This is Colonel Reed, North American Confederacy Armed Forces. My team and I are here to help."

"I am aware," a gruff voice interjected, "and I thank you for the intervention. Even with you flyers from the Reagan, we were beginning to lose ground . . . and to lose ground now . . . "

Reed nodded unthinkingly. Losing ground now meant that your position was likely to be considered overly compromised and command would have to cut their losses. That meant nasty things for a city of nearly a billion people.

"We're going to do what we can to make sure *that* doesn't happen, General. Are your troops ready for a counteroffensive?"

The General snorted. "They are tired, hurt, and very, very, *angry,* colonel. What do you think?"

Reed grinned. "Alright. Then let's push those bastards right off this rock!"

▶▶▶

▶ Squads from the Heroics touched down on every continent where there was fighting ongoing, small teams with heavy weapons lending force where it was needed and sometimes doing everything themselves if that was what it took.

They slammed into the Drasin wall at every juncture, sending the aliens reeling from the surprise and shock of their assault.

It was a moment that the beleaguered defenders of many cities had desperately needed, and when it came they rose up and met it with the last of their strength and ferocity.

Unfortunately, some cities were too far gone.

▶▶▶

▶ Eric pulled his mech back, firing everything he had as the wall of Drasin charged down on his position. They'd managed to awaken the beast in a big way when they began evacuating people from Dallas, and for the life of him he couldn't figure out how or why. During the third hour of the evacuation a squad had been stumbled upon by a couple of Drasin, seemingly roving for whatever it was they needed for the next cycle of replication.

It wasn't a big deal, or it shouldn't have been. They'd seen dozens of similar patrols and generally dealt with them easily, but not this time. During the firefight that ensued, one of the Drasin let out a call that Eric had never heard before and rather hoped to never hear again. It reverberated through the remaining buildings of Dallas, the echoes seemingly going on forever.

The men on the ground had still been looking at each other in stunned confusion when the wave appeared—a literal wave of the drones, flooding down a side street and out onto the main drag where the fighting had been located. The team fired, but it was hopeless, and they were literally swept away and sucked under by the motion.

Eric arrived less than a minute later and all he could do was call for a retreat and *run*.

A fighting retreat is one of the hardest maneuvers to master in tactical combat, and though Eric *was* a master of it . . . he'd earned his mastery in a fighter plane and not on the ground. He did his best, but the wave was unending. It tore down on his backstop location, and, with fifteen more men inside, Eric ordered the retreat. He then stood right in the center of the street with everything firing on full automatic.

It was a fool's errand, he knew that even as he did it, but he hoped to at least get those men back to the Cherokee. Now it seemed that was the only way any of them would survive.

The cannons on the left arm of his EXO-13 went dry first, so he stopped running backward and started running sideways while he fired the last of the rounds in the right. He'd expended his missiles some time earlier, which left him with the suit itself and very little else. Eric vaulted the big machine over a roadblock they'd been using as cover, for all the good it did. The vaporized section of concrete and steel was a testament to the power of the enemy weapons and the futility of trying to hide from them.

The only good thing he could imagine about the situation was the fact that he was going to go down fighting in a cockpit that at least slightly resembled the interior of his Archangel. It was a microscopically small comfort, but there it was.

"Cover!"

The order came in the clear over his tac channel, and Eric didn't question it. He threw himself down just as a ripple of explosion tore through the enemy line and briefly put a hole in the wave of drones chasing him. His EXO suit hit the ground skidding and he could feel a pelting rain of debris striking down around him as he flipped end for end, winding up on his back, staring up at the shockingly blue sky.

The buildings that lined the street he was fighting on were mostly intact, and he spotted a familiar IFF code on his HUD, highlighting a figure standing atop one of them.

"Bermont?" he blurted, surprised to see a name he recognized, particularly flying very familiar colors.

"Someone down there taking my name in vain?" The vaguely French accented voice laughed over the comm. "Gonna have to do something about that."

Eric considered his situation, noting that he was out of ammo and there were now red lights across half his hydraulics and most of his pneumatics. He sighed, but blew the bolts holding the cockpit on and pulled himself out of the stricken mechanized armor.

"Get down here and give me a hand, you cackling Frenchman," he growled, pulling the hatch off the emergency compartment and drawing out the Priminae GWIZ.

"Cackling Fren . . . ," Bermont objected as he dropped to the street, landing with a thud despite the practiced flex in his legs.

Eric cut him off. "How many did you bring back with you?"

Bermont froze, and Eric noted that his IFF was being checked, twice.

"Captain? Mon Jesus, we thought you bit it when you dug the *Odyssey* in," Bermont managed despite his shock.

"So did I," Eric admitted, before asking again, "How many people came back?"

Bermont's face appeared on his HUD as the other soldier initiated a point-to-point video link, and he was grinning ear to ear.

"How many? Come on, Cap, you know we didn't leave *anyone* behind. The whole crew is here, plus the *Big E*, and almost twenty thousand Priminae."

"Twenty thou . . . " Eric trailed off. "Damn, I never would have expected their Elder Council to offer up that many people."

"I don't think they planned it," Bermont chuckled. "I saw some of them after they announced that volunteers could sign on with us. They weren't happy. Most of them, at least."

That didn't surprise Eric in the slightest. Though he rather respected and liked many of the Priminae, he was also well aware that they were deeply conservative at their higher levels. That wasn't a bad thing, but it wasn't a trait that would lend itself to them putting themselves out on a limb without some serious thought.

Ultimately, he expected that they would decide to help, but Eric suspected that the more truculent members would try to use that natural conservatism to delay the decision until it was moot. It wouldn't have taken long to do, after all. Just a few more weeks and the Earth's formidable defense industry would collapse, and after that it was all over but for the last few shots.

The lower echelons, however, were far more willing to take chances, and they felt a strong sense of gratitude for the help the *Odyssey* offered. So the worst thing that the more conservative elders could have done would be to place the decision in the hands of the people actually doing the fighting. Or perhaps it was the best thing they could have done. Eric supposed it depended very much on your point of view, but he doubted that the elders would be happy with the outcome if they ever realized just what they'd done and its full consequences.

It was an old story, Eric knew. He'd seen it on Earth often enough. The higher you went into the power structure, the less contact you maintained with the rank and file.

Eventually you could become convinced that everyone either thought the way you did, or that they *should*.

People, however, would always surprise you. Both for the better and for the worse. That was as true on the Priminae worlds as it was on Earth, and Eric took a fair amount of comfort in it.

"Alright, what are your orders?" Eric asked, noting the ring of familiar IFF signals now appearing on his HUD.

"We're to provide all possible aid to local field commanders, eliminate the Drasin where feasible, evacuate people where not . . . So, field commander, you tell me . . . what are my orders?" Bermont smirked at him, clearly happier to be back under Weston's command than Eric felt was completely sane.

He wasn't going to look a gift horse in the mouth, however, so he just nodded down the street.

"Dallas crawls. Unless you have a significant field force . . . "

Bermont shook his head. "Tactical strike squad. We're stretched thin, even with as many people as we have."

Eric nodded. He was disappointed but unsurprised. "Then we need to provide cover while we evacuate as many people as possible. Dallas crawls, and that can't be allowed to continue . . . one way or another."

"Roger that, Skipper. We're on it," Bermont said, feet lifting off the ground as he triggered his suit-warp and flew up to the top of a nearby building. "You take the low road, Skipper, We'll see to the high."

"Damn showoff," Eric said to himself, making a note to get one of the new systems just as soon as he could. They looked like one helluva lot of fun.

"Cherokee Zero One Niner, Weston."

"Go for Cherokee, Weston."

"I need a pickup at my location, heavy-lift EXO suit for repair and rearm. I am proceeding on foot to secure the evacuation route."

"Roger, Weston. Good hunting."

"Nothing good about these things. They wouldn't even make decent trophies. I'll make do, though. Weston out."

▶▶▶

▶ *The battle was running well, Gaia noted. They would certainly lose a great many people, and much of the infrastructure of nearly every nation on the Earth, but that was a small price to pay for the survival of the species and, yes, even the world itself.*

*In fact, to the entity's mind, things were going **too** well.*

She observed the battles at every point, sometimes nudging her humans one way or another to give them the best chance at victory, and everything looked as good as one might reasonably hope.

The problem was, she didn't feel that the universe was being especially reasonable on this day . . . So the ancient entity looked around her domain, within the sphere of which she was all but omniscient, and she couldn't help but wonder.

"What am I missing?"

▼

CHAPTER TWENTY-THREE

▲

▶ "MA'AM, WE'VE secured NEO space."

Admiral Gracen nodded, handing the ensign back the report he'd given her. "Good work. Start expanding our FTL and light-speed scanning to cover the rest of Sol Space. I want to make sure that they're all gone before we relax."

"Yes ma'am, I understand."

She again did the mental math, trying to work out if there were any significant numbers of the enemy ships outstanding, but again decided that there were not. They'd accounted for the most dangerous portion of the fleet that had driven them from Earth space and assaulted the planet, though she was certain that a few more of the enemy ships were hiding out in the outer system.

The *Enterprise* had contacted them, and she'd eliminated the last of the enemy fighter drones, despite their trying to kamikaze the ship three separate times. The *Big E*'s defense screens and point defense weapons had proved up to the task, along with her fighter complement of Vorpals.

The *Enterprise* would take longer to join them in NEO simply because the purely Terran-built ships didn't have the capability to handle the deceleration techniques that Michaels had employed. They would have to slow down the old-fashioned way, at least partially, before they could attempt to use atmospheric braking.

For now, however, Gracen looked across her boards and everything seemed to be in order, at least so far as the orbital situation was concerned.

She settled down at her station, eyes on the tactical maps they were receiving and collating from Earth. The situation on the planet, however, was far from under control. Gracen examined the reports, those listed as priorities, and finally got up to walk over to where Milla Chans was standing her watch patiently.

"Ithan Chans," she said softly, getting the young woman's attention.

It had taken a while, but they'd determined that ithan was roughly the equivalent of a lieutenant's rank, and she knew that Milla was fairly senior in her own service. Given the other woman was a specialist with the weapons the ships of the Heroic squadron carried, she could think of none better to ask the questions she currently felt burning a hole in her brain.

"Yes Admiral?" Milla turned, speaking quietly and very respectfully.

"I have to confess that I neglected to fully inform myself on certain aspects of the weapons," Gracen said. "I was hoping that you might tell me about them."

Milla hesitated. "I can speak to the laser arrays, of course, but the . . . transition cannons are somewhat beyond my knowledge at this time. I can, of course, bring them to target and engage their action, but their limitations and workings are very new to me . . . "

"Yes, I know," Gracen nodded. "Actually I wanted to know a little more about the lasers. Do you know their ship-to-surface capacity?"

Milla's expression turned a little stony. "Firing on an inhabited world would be anathema to my people. You know this, I believe?"

"Even one that has been infested?"

Milla sighed unhappily, but nodded. "Yes, even then. I know, I know, it is not . . . rational, yes? However, few of our people would even consider such an action so long as there were humans still alive on the surface."

"Are the lasers that dangerous?" Gracen was concerned. While she knew that the Priminae were a curious blend of pacifist and realist, she would have expected their realist side to emerge in this case. But perhaps it had been so long since the realist side was tested at this level that she was overestimating its influence in this matter.

"They are *very* powerful, Admiral," Milla said. "A short blast could easily destroy one of your cities, unless I am very wrong about their construction. An extended beam could dig deep enough to trigger very many ugly happenings."

Gracen considered the information, then grimaced. She had to admit that she wasn't enough of a geologist to know what a beam coring through the mantle might do, but it didn't sound like a good idea. Hell, if one struck an oil, natural gas, or coal pocket, the damage it caused could be significant and ongoing.

Even so, she thought it might be a risk they may have to take.

"I want you to prepare firing patterns for orbital bombardment. Lasers can't be much worse than the nukes they've already authorized down there, and this is a problem we can't just ignore and hope will go away," Gracen ordered. "Make it as safe as you can, but no Drasin is to survive a strike. Can you do this?"

Milla paled slightly, but nodded slowly. "Yes, Admiral, I can do this."

"Good. Make it happen."

Gracen walked away, leaving a shaken but determined Milla in her wake. The Priminae officer began to enter the new directive into her board, making adjustments to the laser focal points as she tried to balance the weapon system between the two conflicting requirements of total annihilation for the enemy and relative security for the world. It would *not* be an easy job.

▶ ▶ ▶

▶ The enemy arrived, and the Drasin waited.

The enemy assaulted the force overseeing the target world, and the Drasin waited.

The enemy, in something so shocking that there were no adopted plans for the event, totally annihilated an assault force sufficient to take on a small fleet . . . and yet the Drasin waited. They waited and watched, all sensory tracks monitoring the outer system, watching for inbound reinforcements.

Nothing appeared, and it both confounded and disturbed the watchers.

Not only were no reinforcements forthcoming, but they hadn't been able to detect the ones that had already arrived. It meant that there was a very real risk in springing the trap that had been set, because it could so easily be turned on the watchers.

In the end, however, there was no choice, and the trap that had been set must be sprung. The order went out, across the swarm cloud, and the Black came alive once more.

▶▶▶

▶ Captain Carrow was just stepping back onto the bridge when the alarms went off. He quickened his pace until he dropped into the command station, then looked across his domain with a tired but determined eye.

"Talk to me."

"We're getting movement on several tracks we believed to be part of the Jovian Trojan rocks, sir."

Carrow grimaced. "No chance that it's natural?"

"No sir, definitely movement under power. It's more of the Drasin, Captain."

"Damn it," Carrow cursed.

He supposed that it was too much to hope that they would be all gone, but it would have been nice.

"Numbers?"

Carrow knew that it was bad when his sensor specialist hesitated. He just hoped it wasn't too bad.

"Unknown. Data is still coming in, sir . . . "

He could hear the hesitation and a note of sheer panic in the younger man's voice, so Carrow turned and looked him right in the eye.

"What is it, Soher?"

"Numbers are currently . . . one hundred and climbing . . . climbing fast, Captain."

Carrow was stunned into silence himself for a moment. "That many? Why hold back over a hundred ships?"

"Sir, I don't think they did," Ensign Soher admitted, looking ill. "I'm running the extrapolation, based on the fact that we're only getting the data at light speed . . . "

"And?" Carrow prodded him.

"If my numbers are right, they've got over a thousand, sir." The green-looking ensign finally said, "That's based on their pattern density and what I expect we'll get from the other Trojan point, so I could be guessing high . . . "

"You could be guessing low, too . . . so many . . . " Carrow slumped a little.

He had to know, he had to be sure.

"Get me the *Odysseus* on FTL comm."

"Yes sir!"

▶▶▶

▶Admiral Gracen stared out into space for a moment after Captain Carrow signed off, almost afraid to give the order. It was only a moment, but she knew that it was a weakness that she couldn't allow. Finally, she sighed heavily and nodded to where Winger was waiting.

"Go full active, across all FTL bands."

"Aye aye, Admiral. Going full active."

Michelle swore a moment later, causing Gracen to jerk around. She'd never heard the sensor specialist speak like that in her presence before, and didn't think it could possibly be a good sign.

"Data . . . on displays now," Michelle croaked out.

Gracen turned back to look ahead at the forward part of the wraparound display that surrounded the bridge, and she felt her own face turn ashen as well. The augmented display was lit up with angry red icons depicting "hostile" targets, enough so that even the ship's prodigious computers were unable to make out one enemy vessel from another.

"How did they hide those?" Gracen asked softly, her voice horrified.

"Admiral, I'm still collating but . . . " Michelle hesitated.

"But what?"

"I think that they ate the asteroids in the Trojan point and just replaced them. With their power down we never could have told them apart from regular rocks out there, ma'am."

"It was an ambush," Gracen said quietly. *And I blundered us right into the middle of it . . .*

"Yes ma'am."

"Ithan Chans, total rounds remaining for the waveguide cannons?" she asked, knowing that the answer almost didn't matter.

"Fifty-eight shells, Admiral. Other ships in the squadron are similarly outfitted."

Fifty-eight.

Gracen closed her eyes. To have come *this* close and have it all end like this, she couldn't stand it. Reality, however, had a way of overriding what she could and could not stand.

"Susan, you'd best get me SPACECOM."

"Yes ma'am."

▶▶▶

▶Tachyon detection grids were not supremely common on planet Earth. In fact, there were only a half a handful, and most of them reported directly to SPACECOM. So by the time Admiral Gracen's request was on the line, that entire organization was in more than a bit of a tizzy, to say the least.

It took only minutes for the general in command of SPACECOM, normally a very quiet and routine position to hold, to find himself on the line with the admiral in charge of the quasi-human fleet of ships and with the President himself.

"We don't have enough power to take them on, Mr. President. It's the same thing as last time, sir. I'm sorry," Gracen said softly, shaking her head.

Conner nodded slowly, seriously. He'd known that without being told. Oh sure, there had been some hope that the alien ships the admiral commanded might hide some sort of ace in their superstructures, but he'd known better than to expect it.

"What kind of lift capacity do you have, Admiral?" he asked after a long moment.

"For an evacuation? We can carry a hell of a lot, sir," she admitted. "The problem is getting them onto the ships before we have no chance of escaping."

"So that's the game, then?" General Alexander asked grimly. "There's no chance? Nothing we can do?"

"We have a few waveguide cannons and some munitions for them on Earth," Conner admitted. "However, even assuming a one hundred percent hit rate, which we know from experience is effectively impossible, our combined munitions would only account for half the enemy ships. Is that correct, Admiral?"

"A little over," Gracen nodded, "which would leave five hundred or so of the enemy ships to handle inside knife range. We just don't have that sort of capability."

"The *Odyssey* and the *Wei Fang* eliminated well over a thousand of the enemy ships in practically a single strike . . . ," Alexander objected.

"That was because Eric Weston is a tactical genius, General," Gracen said stiffly. "He saw a flaw in their approach and realized that he could use a quirk of the space-warp drive Captain Sun commanded to his advantage. The problem now is that they're not coming in grouped like that. Originally they were in tight formation, but the group has since begun to spread, most likely to counter that very tactic."

She sighed audibly. "Currently the most we could take out with that move would be a few dozen at a shot, which sounds great until you realize that we would have to sacrifice one of our own ships for each strike. That would still leave more than enough flying around to annihilate everything, and no one would have any way out."

Alexander slumped, looking defeated. "So it's over then."

Neither of the other two could quite manage to gainsay his words. They hadn't wanted to put it into the open, but there it was and they couldn't contradict it. It was all over. There was nothing else to be done. Once the Heroics were forced to abandon Earth orbit, all three of them were well aware that there was nothing in the universe that would keep the Earth from being overrun.

It wasn't even a matter of time, really. They were already losing ground in dozens of places.

"Admiral, we need to begin an evacuation plan," the President said heavily. "You need to get as many people as you can off world. I'm issuing orders now. I'll have them sent to you in hard copy, to that effect. Admiral, Amanda, you are to *leave* orbit before they can trap you. Am I being clear?"

She nodded slowly. "Yes sir."

"Okay, then start by sending your shuttles to Spaceport Earth. I have people working there that you'll probably need," Conner said, stone-faced.

▶▶▶

▶ *The entity known as Gaia listened, watched, and roared impotently at the universe around her. She was beyond frustrated at this time, beyond angry, beyond reason most likely, and she knew it all.*

Omniscience was not always a gift. It could be a curse that tore at your soul . . . to be forced to watch, to hear, to observe so many things pass before her and fundamentally be all but unable to intercede.

She could use agents, humans who were able to hear her in their subconscious like Eric Weston, or she could even appear herself and issue command edicts . . . yet neither seemed likely to accomplish anything at this point, and in all honesty neither ever had.

*So now she observed her final end through the eyes of those who would prevent it, and found herself as helpless as they against the coming wave. Her world, her people, they were **herself**, and she couldn't even save herself.*

Gaia felt a bitter swell of emotion, centered where her heart might be had she had an actual human body. It was a copy of what she'd experienced vicariously through others uncountable times, but this was the first time she knew it firsthand. It was unpleasant, a knotting sensation that made her feel like the heart she didn't have was physically shutting down.

"Heartache. Panic. These are not my feelings. I don't feel these things," she thought desperately as she tried to regain her calm, the distinctive separation from her humans that she'd first achieved thousands of years earlier.

*It was something that would not come. This wasn't an event she could watch from the outside. She was **part** of it, and that was a frighteningly new experience in itself.*

It took a cosmic event to truly impact on her, and her memory of the last one at that level was fuzzy to say the least. She had badly formed memories from before humans, so long before, but she almost didn't feel like they were hers. They felt alien in some ways, like they were part of someone else and only rested in her by some quirk of cosmic fate.

She could remember flashes of a rock from the sky, a meteor impact that changed the face of the world. That changed the her that made that memory, maybe into the her that existed today. She didn't know, she didn't **want** to know. It was painful to think about and she normally tried very hard not to dwell on the flashes of those times.

Now, however, it was happening again.

Not a cosmic rock this time. This was a cosmic plague. The virus would finish what it had already begun, tearing into her body the way a hemorrhagic fever could tear the organs of its victim to shreds, leaving nothing but infected fluids behind. That was what would happen once the Drasin succeeded in digging into her. This she knew with no doubt.

Parts of her wanted to selfishly slip into the minds of those she could affect, force them to keep the protectors here. Those ships could eliminate many of the enemy, so very many . . .

But she knew that it would be futile, and unlike humans, Gaia was not prone to panic.

No, that wasn't quite true. She had already panicked. In the second it took to understand the situation, she had panicked. She had denied. She had raged. There was no one to bargain with, and in the end she had no choice but to accept the inevitable.

It was better to see to the survival of some of those who made her what she was than it would be to see every last aspect of **herself** vanish.

"I wonder if there is something beyond existence?" Gaia wondered, almost idle now that she had chosen her path. "Will I follow the

survivors, some small piece of me? Or is blackness all that awaits, an
end to all things, even she who would be Goddess?"

▶▶▶

▶Admiral Gracen looked at the numbers, the silent stares of
the crew around her screaming louder than they could have if
they were all cursing her at once. They'd come so far, rushed
so very much, and in the end it came down to this.

Her ships were damaged, though not so much as to cripple any of them, and her stores were low. It was the munition stores more than anything that were the deciding factor,
of course. Here they were, with standoff weapons the likes of
which she doubted *God* could have faced, and of course they
were opposed by an enemy that would simply fly in and take
everything they had right in the face until the guns fired dry.

Against any sane enemy, the waveguide cannons were the
ultimate strategic weapon. You couldn't run, you couldn't
hide. Against the Drasin, however, they were nothing more
than a tease. A hope of victory dangled in front of her face,
right before the final crushing defeat.

She slumped slightly, knowing that it was wrong and she
shouldn't show that much emotion to those around her, but
she couldn't really care just then.

"Susan . . . " Gracen said, her voice worn and tired, "issue
the order. Begin evacuations."

Susan nodded slowly. "Yes ma'am. Issuing orders."

▼

CHAPTER TWENTY-FOUR

▲

▶ "WATCH YOUR SIX, Kieren," Bermont ordered, keeping a close eye on his Priminae troops.

They were a peculiar mix of eager, timid, and green as fresh-mown grass. It was endearing at times, but not a particular good mix for a soldier on a battlefield. Bermont had been through enough fighting, though, to know talent and potential when he saw it, and that was something that was present for most of them.

They'd do well if they lived through their first few days of fighting, which was his job to ensure.

The Drasin in Dallas were dug in, numerous, and apparently dead set on keeping the crumbling city they were all fighting in. That was fine with Bermont. As a Canadian he'd always had the sneaking suspicion that Americans were crazy in more than just the good ways, and Texans were all that and a side of loco in his experience. Getting a kick in the teeth like losing Dallas to some aliens would do things to them that Bermont didn't want to think on too hard, but really wanted to watch.

From a safe distance.

Preferably a different solar system, now that he thought on it.

He leveled his Priminae gravity rifle, discharging a carbon crystal projectile into a Drasin that was lumbering in his direction. He didn't like to think of them as diamonds. It made him shudder at using something that valuable as ammo, but hell, if it was his life at stake, he supposed that anything he could use would ultimately be worth it.

Besides, he wasn't footing the bill for the fight.

Speaking of . . . Bermont paused, ducking back as his tactical comm flipped to the background and the command channel came to the front. He keyed into it as soon as he was clear of immediate danger, and smiled when he saw Susan Lamont's face looking out at him from the overlay.

"Hey mon cher . . . " He grinned, laying it on a little thick. "Not that it's not always lovely to see you, but I am a little busy."

"Cute, Bermy," she told him flatly, making him cringe a little. He hated it when she called him that. "But this is business."

"Alas, love, you never call just for fun."

"Admiral's orders," Susan told him, "fall back and stand by for evacuation orders."

"That's what we're doing, love," he told her, quizzically. She had to know that. He'd put the *Odysseus* into the loop. It was standard procedure.

"Not from Dallas. We're pulling off world," Susan told him, and he suddenly noticed that her face was more pale than normal, and her tone was grim. She wasn't just trying to be professional in the face of his flirting. She looked downright ill.

"Off world? Susan, we just *got* here," he protested.

"Those are the orders, Lieutenant," she told him. "Fall back with your unit, and stand by for evacuation orders. We'll need you to run security while we pick up some people."

"Pick up? Susan, what the Christ is going on?"

"It was a trap, Lieutenant. There are more Drasin coming. A lot more."

"Oh merdre," Bermont swore, thinking furiously. "I need to get the captain."

"Pardon me?" Susan scowled, both irritated that he still hadn't acknowledged the order and now puzzled. "What captain?"

"There's only one for us, love," he grinned. "Found him down here kicking ass and taking names . . . Alright, almost getting his own ass kicked too, but he was doing alright for a flyboy."

"Captain? *The* captain?" Susan leaned in, her face growing larger. "Sean, he burnt up with the *Odyssey* . . . "

"If so then he left one pissed-off and ass-kicking ghost," Bermont said. "I'll find him and begin falling back. We are doing that anyway. I'll contact you for new orders once we're clear of Dallas."

Susan blinked, shook her head, and managed to stammer out the appropriate response.

"Roger that, Lieutenant," she said, her voice dropping to a whisper. "Be careful."

"Never careful, love, just damned good at what I do." He grinned. "Bermont clear and out. Ciao."

The signal went off and he brought the tactical network back to the front. "Alright everyone, fall back by the numbers. Get any civilians you see out of the city and meet at the Gamma point. We've got new orders coming down the pipeline."

His team acknowledged as he swept the street he was on, then refocused on his HUD. "Does anyone have the captain's location? I don't see his IFF on my screens."

▶▶▶

▶Dallas was officially a worse hole than any Middle Eastern burg he'd ever fought in or over. Eric hung out of the side door of the Cherokee as he lifted off, a strap keeping him from plunging to the ground below. The Priminae GWIZ was in his hands and he was firing judiciously placed rounds with the power set higher than he'd normally prefer to use given his proximity to the targets.

Fifty or so of the drones were rushing over fallen debris and their own dead as they charged toward the Cherokee, scrambling up the side of a nearby building as they threw themselves at the flying machine with suicidal ferocity. Eric shifted and fired a round into the far corner of the building, the kinetic round causing an explosion of dust and debris as it tore right through and slammed into the ground beyond.

Damn it. He fired again, cursing the engineers who'd apparently decided to make the damn building as indestructible as possible and succeeded far better than he would have preferred.

"Watch it, sir! They're on the roof!"

"Take them out! I'm trying to take the building down!" he roared over the sound of the heavy machine gun firing beside him.

The door gunner didn't need that order. As soon as he saw the damn things literally crawling over each other in order to get a few meters closer to the Cherokee, he'd opened fire. The heavy automatic rail cannon roared. The noise blended into one single sound as he tore into their ranks, killing dozens.

It didn't matter to them, however. They just used their dead as a bridge to get that one step closer. Eric watched it, fascinated, from the corner of his focus. He'd seen ants do that before, climbing over their dead and living to form bridges, buildings, even weapons with which to assault their enemies. He'd never thought to see it in a species this size before, and the imagery was enough to give him nightmares.

He had something to focus on to keep those thoughts at bay, however, and he re-aimed his GWIZ, firing again. This time it went into the building higher up but angled deeper down, and he watched with satisfaction as the entire lower section blew out in a massive explosion of dust. The structure began to creak, shifting visibly, and he watched even more avidly as he worried about just what direction it was going to fall.

"Holy shit!"

The pilot's scream was understandable, but a little disappointing to Eric really. He liked to imagine that back in his day there was a little higher standard of professionalism. He was probably delusional, he knew, but so be it.

The building had elected to fall north of their position, but part of it crumbled off in the process and came toppling down close enough to give them all a bit of a heart condition. He dropped the power on the GWIZ and joined the door gunner as they kept hammering the drones that continued to throw themselves at the Cherokee, even as the building collapsed under them.

Then captain and crew were clear, pulling up and above the top of the next building before dropping down into the manmade canyon of the streets beyond.

"That was *too* damn close, sir." The pilot swore at him.

Eric just shrugged. "Close only counts in horseshoes and hand grenades, son. We're alive, we've got our civvies. Get us back to the evac point."

There was a quiet for a time, but finally the pilot grudgingly acknowledged him.

Eric grinned. The fight was over. The war would continue, obviously, to the final end, but for now the fight was over and he could enjoy the satisfaction of the moment. It was one of the few pleasures that existed in combat.

▶▶▶

▶The evacuation point was an armed camp.

Thrown up in just a few short hours, it had been mined for over two kilometers around the perimeter and had guard towers armed with heavy rail cannons along the primary line. Inside there was a flood of humanity, most armed to the teeth, dirty, and tired . . . but they were alive, and they were angry as hell for the most part.

Eric pushed through the throng of people, his armor giving him near immunity to whatever beef they thought they might have with him or the world in general. He watched as a heavy lifter took off, another one landing, and he knew that a few hundred more would be on their way to a safe zone.

If there is such a place.

Dallas had mostly been cleared out weeks earlier, of course. What was here were the most stubborn and the most stupid, with a liberal mixing of the most brave. Some days it was hard to tell which was which, but that wasn't exactly unusual in Eric's experience. You needed a good mix of all three to stay in a war zone of one's own volition, especially one like this when you only had older military and civilian weapons at your disposal.

He'd heard of, and seen, some of the damage the Dallasites managed with old chem-fired weapons and was dutifully impressed. Granted, it required anti-matériel guns to penetrate the Drasin hide, but that barely slowed the defenders of Dallas down. Rigging improvised explosives from anything and everything they could find in the nearly abandoned city had become a game, a challenge, and a point of pride to them, and they had proved to be good at it.

It was over now.

No more games, no more fighting the enemy on their terms. The Drasin may *be* weapons of self-destruction, but they weren't the only ones kicking around. Not on *this* planet.

"What's the status on the evacuation, Swenson?" he asked, pushing the flap of the tent aside as he stepped in.

"Everyone we can find is out of the city," the ranger grumbled, still far from happy with the current situation.

It wasn't that Eric blamed him, of course, but there was a time to be pissy about things and a time to just get down and get them done regardless. He just nodded, however, and ignored the other man's mood.

"Good. How long until the last of them are lifted out then?"

"Last I checked we were almost there. Another couple heavy lifters should take the bulk of them." Swenson said. "But . . ."

Eric didn't get a chance to hear what the man was going to say because at that point a young Guardsman stormed into the tent, panting. "Sir! They're coming!"

It didn't take a genius to work out who "they" were, and both Eric and Swenson were on the move instantly.

They burst out of the tent, glanced around briefly, and headed for the biggest and loudest grouping along the perimeter on the Dallas side of the camp. Eric paused, grabbing the Guardsman by the shoulder, and twisted him around. "Keep the crowds moving and get everyone in the lifters. Pack them in, if you have to. Just get *everyone* out of here!"

"Sir! Yes sir!"

He left the young soldier to those duties and rushed through the crowd to catch up with Swenson, who was already well ahead of him. They reached the perimeter about the same time. Eric had the advantage of a much more imposing armored form and was able to travel through the ranger's wake as Swenson parted the crowd, then climbed up on the embankment the earth movers had put into place.

"Well shit," Swenson said simply, eyes glued to his binoculars.

Eric didn't need them. His armor was more than able to enhance the sight before him, but then he almost wished that it hadn't. The aliens had burst from Dallas in a swarm, like an explosion of army ants now intent on moving onward to their next conquest. He couldn't count the numbers, not in a roiling, packed grouping like that. Eric knew enough to know that the answer to how many there were was simply "too many."

He brought up the tactical channel. "This is Weston. Get everyone on the lifters. I want all pilots sitting in their birds *now*. If it can fly, I want it ready to be airborne in five minutes. If it can't, leave it. Rifle teams to the northern perimeter. I say again, rifle teams to the northern perimeter."

Most of them were already leaning in that direction, but his orders set everyone moving with a vengeance. Eric climbed up to the top of the bank, taking a knee as he unlimbered the

Priminae gravity rifle he carried, judging the range both by eye and by the suit's range finder.

The key weakness of the Priminae weapon, in his experience, was that on the higher power settings *everything* you could put into it as a projectile would inevitably ablate in atmosphere. That meant that it had a stupidly low effective range for when you *really* needed the power. So he kept the power under two-thirds, not wanting to kill anyone standing beside him from the shock wave of the round alone, and took aim.

It also fired relatively slowly. He put out about one round a second, and honestly it couldn't do a lot better than that even if he hadn't wanted to pick his shots. The depleted uranium rounds he was firing now were far more massive than the diamond ones the Priminae favored, but also far softer and more prone to ablation, and they kicked up a rooster tail behind them with every shot. The ablated metal slammed into the front line of the charging aliens, blowing one to hell and back. Others were thrown across the line with enough force, he hoped, to break some of what passed for bones in the alien beasts.

"Fire as they enter your range," he ordered. "Hold the line until the civilians get clear, or everything we've done will be for nothing"

The heavy machine guns joined in a few moments later, the punctuated roars of the anti-matériel rifles already echoing across the defensive perimeter. Eric just kept his steady rate of fire, nudging the power a little higher as the alien swarm got closer.

The Drasin particle beams sizzled across the line, burning men down and tearing into the defensive fortifications with hellish effectiveness. Eric didn't move, but he could hear others fall back . . . some probably running . . . and a few people just fell over and began retching from the smell.

He was thankful for his environmental armor. At least *that* wasn't going to be a problem for him, but he knew that he had to firm up the line or it was all over.

"Hold your ground!" he called over every speaker and PA in the place. "Don't show those bastards your back. All they've got coming is from the muzzle of your rifles!"

Swenson, who was somehow still standing beside him, joined in quickly.

"If this is our Alamo, then so be it!" the ranger called. "This is *Texas,* and we ain't running from no jumped-up bugs from fucking space! Get your sorry butts back in the line before you have *me* to worry about, 'cause I swear I'll make you *wish* those buggers were the only thing after you!"

Eric snorted, but thankfully the computer didn't send that along to the PA. The ranger had a way with words, he would give him that. The man would have made a fine drill sergeant, he'd have bet, maybe even a better master sergeant. It worked too, for the most part. Many of those who had begun to break were now sheepishly moving back into line, and the volume of fire was increasing.

That didn't mean that the enemy wasn't getting closer, however.

With a line that thick, and what seemed to be nearly infinite resources, there was just no stopping it.

Eric heard the whine of another lifter rising into the air, and risked a glance over his shoulder. The inner courtyard was thinned out now. Only a few hundred people were left and another lifter was packing them in as fast as it could. He hoped it was enough, but in the end it didn't make much difference what he hoped.

The Cherokee screamed by overhead, arcing around and bringing its door gunner to bear on the Drasin line. The heavy gun roared, pelting the Drasin with a barrage of lethal slugs, but they just drove over their own dead in a rolling wave of motion. It would have been fascinating to watch were it not for the imminent threat of the situation, Eric thought idly as he kept up his fire.

Like something from a nature documentary, perhaps, or a natural disaster film.

The sizzling pops of the alien weapons filled the air now, forcing the defending line to hunker down low and fire over the top of the berm that was protecting them. Few things stopped a Drasin particle beam, Eric had learned, but a few thousand tons of bermed earth was thankfully one of them.

The beams scorched the far side and turned air to ozone overhead, but he and his people were mostly protected as they fired back in turn. It wasn't perfect. Sometimes a beam would slide just high or low enough to scour the top of the berm and take a few, or a few dozen, men apart. Sometimes a big rock hidden in the berm would be overheated by the enemy beam weapon and explode violently, tearing troops limb from limb in the process.

"Last lifter is loaded! We're taking off!"

Eric ducked down, looking back to see that the courtyard was now cleared for the most part, with only men running for smaller planes and choppers.

"Alright, Swenson, take your troops and start falling back!" he ordered. "Get them to the lift birds and the hell out of here!"

"What about you!?"

Eric turned the power on the Priminae weapon up, his face set grim. "Someone has to be the rear guard, Ranger.

I've got the tools for the job. You don't. Get your ass moving."

The ranger looked at him, clearly torn for a moment, then nodded curtly. He grabbed his radio. "Everyone . . . pull back! Pull back!"

The line broke then. Most of them had just been praying for such an order. Eric crawled up higher, pushing his gravity rifle ahead of him but not firing as he took in the scene for a second. The swarm of Drasin was effectively unchecked. If they'd been slowed, he couldn't tell.

Eric thumbed the power settings on his rifle up, going well past the safe levels as he waited for the unarmored men to clear the blast zone.

"Cherokee One, Weston," he said, eyes not leaving the approaching wall of enemy forces.

"Go for Cherokee, Weston."

"Get some altitude," he ordered. "You're going to want a better view."

There was a brief pause before the pilot came back. "Roger that, Weston. Pulling up to watch the show. Make it good."

"You got it." Weston grinned humorlessly as the Cherokee's engines whined loud enough to crack glass, clawing for altitude.

He got up to one knee, aiming the GWIZ at the enemy line, leading it just slightly. They were getting close enough now that he knew that he was going to feel the blast wave himself, armor or not.

So be it.

He stoked the firing stud. The rifle barely twitched in his arms even as it loosed a heavy depleted uranium round into the air. The blast wave of the round hitting air shook him through his armor, though, and for a moment his vision was occluded by the condensation cloud it left behind.

Said cloud was blown away a few seconds later as the blast wave washed over him, slamming into his armor like the hammer of the gods, and Eric was able to see the enemy line again.

A mushroom cloud was rolling back over the ground, low and slow, with shaken and shattered Drasin on either side of the strike point. They regrouped quickly, and he watched the line begin to move again, coming straight at him now.

Eric fired again.

And then again, and again.

He fired the rifle dry, reloaded, and emptied it again. Each time the dust and smoke redoubled, then was blown away by the blast wave of the next shot. Dozens, hundreds, maybe thousands of the Drasin soldier drones were left broken on the field.

Yet the wave kept coming.

A whining rush of an engine settled behind him, causing Eric to glance around in time to see the Cherokee settle into a hover just a few feet away.

"Time to go, Cap!" the gunner called. "We've got a Shiva Option Alert."

Eric nodded, slinging his rifle as he turned. He jumped for it, landing inside the Cherokee as the pilot pulled the big craft up and away. Eric turned around, leaning back out the door as the battered Drasin forces took the berm, scuttling over it and into the base they were leaving behind. He could see them pulling down the towers, tearing apart the temporary command housing, and generally making a mess of the place as the Cherokee turned and poured on the speed.

They just broke Mach when a flash of light filled *everything*, like a million flashbulbs had just gone off.

Eric didn't have to look behind to know that Dallas wasn't there anymore.

He slumped into a seat and strapped in. He didn't feel like talking to anyone just then.

▶▶▶

▶ "Breaker's bane."

Bermont didn't know exactly what that meant, but he'd heard more than a few of his Priminae crew whisper it and it felt fitting. They were a hundred kilometers outside of Dallas, orbiting the city at a leisurely pace, and every one of them was glued to the image of the rolling nuclear mushroom cloud that had engulfed the city.

Some rear part of his mind filled in the blanks, noting that it seemed to be a weapon in the five-hundred-megaton range to judge by the diameter of the blast wave. Few things inside it would remain in one piece. The shock front was far too powerful for that. It would be like getting slapped upside the head by a tank moving at Mach One.

"Did . . . did the Drasin do *that*?"

Bermont looked over to where one of the younger Priminae soldiers was gaping and he dropped a hand on the man's shoulder.

"No, Travor, we did," he said. "Sometimes, you must cut out the poison before it spreads."

"But . . . it was a city, with people, no?" Travor asked plaintively. "A small one, I know, but . . ."

Bermont closed his eyes, trying not to either laugh or cry. For Travor, Dallas was indeed a very small city, but that wasn't the point.

"Yes, it was, but it was a Drasin city. They took it from us, and we would rather see it *burn* than see them turn its resources against us," he said honestly and earnestly. It made him feel better as well, to be honest, straightening the point in his own head. "Better to die in a flash of glory than be slowly consumed by *those*."

"Lieutenant!"

He turned away, moving toward the front of the craft. "Yes?"

"We have a hit on Captain Weston's IFF," the copilot said. "The *Odysseus* signals that he is in a small craft, heading due east."

"Alright, lock in and track him," Bermont ordered. "We have to run him down."

"Yes sir."

▶▶▶

▶ Eric looked out the side door of the Cherokee as they moved along, watching the flying nap of the Earth and heading toward the FOB operating on the Texas/Mississippi border. He was staring at but not really seeing the terrain as it flew past, his thoughts tied more to the fact that he'd just been part of deploying a nuclear weapon on Confederate territory.

It was the sort of thing that no man should ever do, or have to do. The kind of thing that military nightmares were made of. The worst of it was, he knew that he wasn't the first and wouldn't be the last. Not in this new war, not with this new enemy.

He was mentally falling into a tailspin, and he knew it but didn't care. There were some things that deserved the depression that sort of thinking would eventually bring, but this time it wasn't to be. Before he could get too deep, a violent shake of the Cherokee startled him back to the moment and would have tossed him out the side door if he hadn't strapped himself in already.

"Holy shit! Where the hell did that come from?"

Eric was about to ask what the pilot was talking about when he spotted the thing in question and recognized it.

"That's a Priminae shuttle," he said, bringing up his combat HUD and noting that several familiar IFFs were showing in his range now. "They're friendly."

"Damn. As fast as that sucker moves, I'm sure as hell glad of that."

Eric ignored the pilot, opening the tactical comm channel instead. "Lieutenant, what brings you into my airspace?"

"New orders, Skipper," Bermont said, something in his voice ringing oddly to Eric. "Need you to transfer over here."

"I'm on mission, son," Eric said. "Things to kill, places to destroy."

"Sir, I think you really want to transfer over here."

It was the tone, not the words, that caused Eric to make a decision. Something was up, and the only place he was going to figure out what was on that Priminae bird.

"Fine," he said finally. "Aerial transfer?"

"Can do," Bermont said a moment later. "We'll come alongside."

"Roger that," Eric said, then changed over to the pilot's channel. "Hold her steady. I'm changing horses."

CHAPTER TWENTY-FIVE

▶ OVERSEEING WHAT HAD to be the single biggest evacuation in the planet's history was probably the most sickening job President Conner had ever had to do, and sadly that was saying something. There were no protocols for this, no list of people to save and people to leave behind. Ironically, it might be easier if the Priminae weren't out there. He could pick people based on skills and genetic diversity and tell himself it was for the good of humanity.

It wouldn't be much, but it would be a balm to a tortured soul.

Instead, Conner found himself choosing vengeance over everything else, and focusing on giving Admiral Gracen the best tech people he had, those who would know how to take everything they found and turn it into a weapon to use against the murderers of the human race.

Tachyon specialists, anti-matter and quantum physicists, and the people who knew the most about devising new and unholy ways of killing as many things as possible in the shortest time possible. He had a lot of those to pick from, and this was possibly the first time that he'd ever been truly happy about that fact.

He wasn't being entirely altruistic, if you could call assembling what he personally *hoped* would become the greatest lineup of potential mass killers in the history of the planet altruistic. He'd slipped his wife and daughter on the list. They were already being hustled to an evac point, along with their security agents and *their* families. He expected that would keep them both quiet and loyal to their charges, or he hoped it would.

He grabbed a bottle of antacids, downing a half dozen and crunching on the chalky tablets as he went back to work. He figured that his stomach would either burn out or stop working entirely from either the stress or the influx of acid neutralizers. But in a few days he wouldn't need to eat anymore anyway, so screw it.

Why did I want this crappy job in the first place?

He knew the answer to that, actually. But right now wasn't the time to bear on the deficiencies of a system that got him elected to an office that he, in all candid honesty, probably never should have been allowed anywhere near. He had the job, he had important things to do, and they were going to get done before it was too late.

They had to.

For once in his life, he was going to do try to do the right thing, even though he'd be damned to hell if he knew what that was. Everything else could just go swing.

▶▶▶

▶ Eric Stanton Weston stomped onto the bridge of the *Odysseus*, his rage blotting out any sense of wonder he might have felt upon seeing the wraparound vista that surrounded the command and control of the impressive ship. He was focused on the center console and the admiral sitting there, and his mind was nearly seeing *red* after what he'd been told.

He was still in armor, though he'd stowed his rifle and his helmet somewhere behind him. Probably with Bermont, he supposed. He vaguely remembered the lieutenant trying to calm him down, or at least slow him down. Neither had worked, though it had taken some time to get a straight answer out of the Canadian trooper as to where he could find the bridge.

His arrival hadn't gone unnoticed, of course. A man in powered armor stomping through the corridors of a ship was hardly stealthy, even if he'd wanted to be.

The admiral turned to see the ruckus seconds after he arrived. He noted in the back of his mind that she was one of the few who weren't surprised to see him alive. Many of the others had stared like he was the second coming. It would have been creepy if he had been thinking straight.

"Captain," Gracen said, rising to her feet. "It's good to see you alive."

"Admiral," Eric reciprocated through clenched teeth. "Request permission to have a word . . . "

She gazed at him, her expression haughty and cool. It was a look that she was known for, actually, the ability to make you feel like a bug barely worth the attention it took to flick you away.

"My ready room," she said finally, nodding to the right and behind him.

Eric grimaced, but nodded and followed her off the bridge.

▶ ▶ ▶

▶ Steph stared, silently whistling at the back of his departed CO. Former CO? He wasn't sure which, didn't really care. He hadn't seen Raziel that pissed since . . . well, ever. Even in the heat of the war there was nothing that came to mind that matched the captain's current mood, though he supposed that shouldn't be a surprise.

Even the Block never threatened to blow up the whole damned planet.

Milla looked stricken at her station, and he could understand why. He had watched her face dissolve from the almost joy of seeing one of her heroes reappear alive to shock and fear as she caught the outer edge of his fury. Steph caught her eye and smiled sadly, shaking his head. He'd try to explain it to her later, if she really needed it. She'd probably work it out for herself, though. There wasn't a lot to figure out.

The captain's anger came from an obvious source.

▶▶▶

▶ In the privacy of the ready room, Eric just glared as the admiral walked around the desk and took a seat.

"Well, Captain, do you want to sit down or are you going to start screaming at me without delay?" she asked him, eyebrows arched.

"I've been told that you ordered a withdrawal from the system," he gritted out.

"Incorrect. I was *ordered* to withdraw," she said lightly. "We are making preparations now to leave orbit."

"We can't leave almost ten *billion* people to . . . "

"Captain," she cut him off, "have you seen the numbers?" When he couldn't reply, she went on.

"We can eliminate maybe another two hundred of the drone ships, a little more if we get lucky, a little less if we don't," Gracen said. "That's not enough to save Earth. It's just barely enough to cut ourselves an escape route in their net, which is the only reason we're still here picking up refugees from Earth."

"There *must* be a way," Eric objected. "What about the drives, Captain Sun . . . "

"The enemy learned from past mistakes," she said, shaking her head. "They're spread far enough out that you'd not get more than a few dozen, maybe a couple hundred at best that way, and you'd blow your ship's drives to do it. Not an option."

Eric slumped as much as his armor would allow, shaking his head. "There's got to be a way to do this."

"If you can think of it, you're welcome to make a suggestion," Gracen said, standing up, "Now, if you're no longer looking to enact an offense that could be court martialed, you should get changed and cleaned up."

"Pardon?" Eric looked puzzled.

"Captain, we're about to need every experienced hand we've got. Have someone assign you quarters, get cleaned up and changed, and report for duty," she ordered. "You've fifteen minutes."

"Admiral, with all due respect, I have a mission and it's down, well, on Earth," he told her, gritting his teeth.

"I'll have those orders changed. I can do that. I'm an admiral," she told him. "Now get out of my office and do as I told you."

Eric glared, just bordering on insubordination, but finally just nodded.

"Aye aye, ma'am." He ground out, pivoting on his heel, then marched through the door.

▶▶▶

▶Shuttles were moving back and forth from Earth to the Heroics as quickly as they could, which, considering they were Priminae shuttles, was pretty damned quick. Men, women, children, and some supplies were being ferried up under intense secrecy, most of the passengers themselves not even knowing what was going on, while those in the know tried to work out just how many people they could get away with transferring before the squadron had to run.

"We have an untested waveguide array in New Mexico," President Conner offered up. "It was built to take out the original fleet, but we should be able to put a hole in this one."

"I'm not sure I'd recommend that." Gracen shook her head. "I'm familiar with the technology, and firing from a gravity well is tricky enough. But also from an atmosphere?"

"Our people think they can work out the variables," he said. "You can have some of the people I sent you run the numbers. We can't fire as far as you might manage, but then, this close to the Earth and the Moon, neither can you."

She nodded, noting that was the truth.

The waveguide system depended on a lot of factors to determine effective range. In theory, barring any outside influence, the range was effectively infinite. You could target a ship or planet, or just about anything else, from across the *universe* if you had its coordinates. In reality, well, things were more complex. You had to know the coordinates, of course, which meant it had to be in range of some kind of scanner system, and then you had to factor in outside influences.

Gravity fields would affect the range and accuracy. So, this close to Earth and the Moon, the computers were already dealing with a three-body system once you factored in the Sun. That made targeting calculations incredibly complicated, and would likely limit the practical range to only a couple light-minutes.

That was still a massively long distance, and a very decent standoff range, but it was far short of the ranges achieved by the *Odyssey* and *Odysseus* in previous deep-space engagements.

A waveguide from the Earth's surface would have all that to deal with, plus the unknown effects of firing through atmosphere.

Frankly, Gracen was just as happy it wasn't her facility to command.

She had enough problems.

▶▶▶

▶ *She had problems.*

Gaia watched, from all points and at all times, as her world, her people . . . herself, in a very real way, was being slowly dismantled. Torn piece from piece, and being replaced with those abominations that were slowly hacking her to death.

Death.

It was a discomforting and alien thought. She'd never really considered that she might die, if she were honest with herself. Philosophically she had pondered the afterlife, but only as something that happened to others.

Now, though, it was all too real, and she wished that she had pondered it just slightly harder. Maybe she would have figured it out.

She stepped through space and onto the decks of the *Odysseus* as the ship hung in low orbit, flitting through every space at once, before settling on the quarters assigned to Captain Eric Weston. He was in the shower.

"*Oh Captain, my Captain,*" she said in a musical tone, smiling as he jumped and covered himself. "*Believe me, I've seen it before.*"

He glared at her.

It was cute, actually. If she were human, she might be attracted to it, and him, but she'd done that before and there was nothing there for her.

"What are you doing here?" he hissed, looking around, annoyed and worried.

"Just . . . saying goodbye," she told him, her smile holding ethereal qualities. *"I wish you all success in your future, Captain. I had hoped I might witness it."*

Eric wrapped himself in a towel, looking on at her in confusion. "I . . . Gaia . . . "

"Avenge your fellows," she said, her tone growing icy cold. *"Avenge them and me. These **abominations** do not belong in this universe. End them."*

"They're destroying everything I've ever sacrificed to protect," Eric said. "There is *nothing* in this universe that can stop me from doing just that."

She smiled at him. *"I know. Why do you think I came to you? You have a nicely developed sense of vengeance, Captain. Hone it well."*

He nodded curtly, not knowing what else to say.

Gaia looked about. *"This is a good ship, Captain. Better, I think, than the one you left below. She will serve you well."*

"She's not my ship."

Gaia just smiled, ignoring him. *"Good bye, Captain . . . and good luck."*

She stepped out of space and into time, vanishing from the room.

▶ Eric considered what had just happened, wondering not for the first time at the state of his sanity, or lack thereof, but he didn't have time to dwell on it. He pulled on his uniform, or what now passed for it, and tried to make it look right. The cut was off and the colors bothered him, but at least it was clean and comfortable. He hadn't had either of those in a while.

He looked in the mirror, actually a piece of smart glass, he supposed. It listed information about him, some of it surprisingly personal, and most of it more than a little creepy. He ignored it and focused on how he looked.

Almost professional.

Probably the best he was going to pull off with short notice.

Alright. Fine. Get to work, Eric. There's too damned much left to do.

He steeled himself and stepped out of the room, turning left as he headed for the lifts.

The main bridge was buried in the depths of the ship, as it should be in any sane design, so he had to take the lift "down" into the core levels. The gravity felt . . . natural. That was the first thing he consciously noted about the *Odysseus*. There was none of the bizarre, often motion sickness–inducing tidal shift that came from the *Odyssey*'s centrifugal gravity.

He walked through the corridors, pretty sure he was heading the right way, and tried to ignore the shocked looks that followed him. Whispered words, sharp exclamations, and pointed fingers made it clear that it was him that they were talking about. He ignored them. He'd probably be just as shocked if someone he knew had returned from the dead, though he hoped he'd be a little less obvious about it.

He found the bridge with a minute and a half to spare, not bad given that he'd had to get quarters assigned, wash up, talk to an entity he barely recognized let alone understood, and then get dressed and find his way back to a room he'd only been to once before.

He could do better next time, he was sure.

"Captain on the bridge!"

Eric paused, noting the stiff forms and salutes that greeted his arrival, and calmly returned the latter while acknowledging the former with a curt nod and a few words.

"As you were. Admiral," he said, "reporting as ordered."

"Good to see you cleaned up, Captain," she told him, getting out of the seat. "I have a strategy meeting with the President and Premier. I'll leave the *Odysseus* in your hands. She'll serve you well, I think."

Eric blinked. "Ma'am?"

"The con is yours, Captain Weston," Gracen said, tone brooking no argument nor fake confusion. "I'll be in my office."

He swallowed. "Y . . . yes ma'am."

"Don't look so shocked," she said softly, walking past him. "I told you, I need every able hand."

"Aye aye, ma'am," Eric said. "I won't let you down."

"Just try not to crash this one into a planet, would you? The paint is new, Captain."

Eric twisted his lips into a grimace, but Gracen didn't notice. She was already past him and headed off the bridge. He was forced to sigh to himself and gingerly move around to the command console and take a seat. He squirmed a bit, getting used to it, and then began to hesitantly call up information on the command displays.

Eric didn't notice, or didn't let on if he did, the surreptitious glances of the other officers on the deck as they looked between him and each other, some just interested, but most smiling to themselves. He had work to do, and the formation of inbound enemy warships held his interest most deeply.

▶▶▶

▶ *"This ship is different than what my humans build . . . "* Gaia pondered as she examined the vessel that had previously been little more than a minor blip on her consciousness.

It felt significantly different than anything she'd encountered previously, not surprising, she supposed, since it was clearly not of Earth human manufacture. However, there was something more to it, something almost . . . familiar. She walked the decks, drawn to what she quickly learned was the power core of the big ship.

Humans used reactors to power their ships. That is . . . Earth humans did. Those were warm sources of magnetic energy. She could feel them from beyond her normal influence, actually. These ships used something far different, however. They used massive gravity wells of their own. Singularity cores that contained as much mass as small planets and conversion units to turn that mass directly into power as it was needed.

Deep in that mass, however, was something she had never experienced before.

It was like looking into a mirror, she found. Deep inside the massive singularity of the Odysseus, *Gaia found an abyss . . . Within the abyss she was staring into, there was a reflection there, staring back. A human would have drawn back, would have cringed or even cowered, but Gaia had never known fear until the Drasin arrived. And now she was dying anyway.*

That brought a strange sense of resignation and an urge to satisfy whatever curiosity she had left.

Gaia pushed deeper into the singularity, looking closer at the reflection. It winked at her.

Then she was sucked in so fast that she didn't even have a chance to fight back.

▶▶▶

▶ Eric had just barely sat down when the power flickered and dimmed, all the instrumentation going dead for a moment before it all came back.

"What the hell was that?"

"Power variance, Captain," a Priminae engineer said from a station to the back right of Eric's position.

"That happen often?" he asked.

"Never, sir. It's not possible." The engineer didn't look happy at all, not that Eric blamed him.

Impossible things happening with high-energy power sources rarely resulted in good times being had by all.

"Figure it out," he ordered, knowing that the last thing they needed was for anything to go wrong now.

"Yes sir."

Great, I sit down in the hot seat and the damned ship starts acting up. What next? The Moon planning on dropping on our heads too?

He forced himself back to the task at hand, analyzing the enemy's actions, which, unfortunately, was all too easy. They were being cautious and smart, coming in spread out to avoid any nastiness like the maneuver he and Sun had pulled on them before. That meant that the squadron would be able to break out, yes, but it also meant that the odds of defeating a force this size were effectively zero. The admiral was right about that, to be sure. They had enough munitions split among the squadron to take out a couple hundred of the drone ships, but no more. He figured, power for power, what he was looking at on the *Odysseus* would be able to account for another few in close-range fighting. But once the enemy fighter screens got involved, it would be almost impossible to hit and fade long enough to make a real difference.

Unfortunately, the Enterprise *fighter complement is too small to keep all of these bastards tied up while we take out the ships.*

Ship-to-ship combat on this level was really more a matter of who guessed the other's actions first. With adaptive lasers and Priminae power sources, he was confident that he could take on the enemy and savage them, but in the end it would be a pack of wolves wearing down a bear. The *Odysseus* would fall, they'd all die, and the Earth would be gone shortly thereafter.

There **has** to be a way. There has to be.

If there was, however, he wasn't seeing it.

Eric sighed, shaking his head.

Sometimes, the good guys lost.

▶▶▶

▶ *Gaia blinked, scowling as much as she could given her lack of corporeal form.*

Something had happened, but she didn't know what in the hell it was. She blinked and glared at the Odysseus, *where it was floating above her, trying to piece together what had occurred. It wouldn't come together, however, and she wasn't about to try again.*

She finally turned her back on the serene vessel, and turned back to the visceral violence tearing her apart on-world.

"More to do. I'll worry about the Odysseus *later."*

▼

CHAPTER TWENTY-SIX

▲

▶ CARROW LOOKED OVER his command, both proud and ashamed of their performance in past actions. Both emotions were self-explanatory in his eyes. They had done exemplary duty whenever he had sent them out, yet in the end it all proved useless.

The *Enterprise* was settling into a low earth orbit, preparing to take on refugees just like the members of the Heroics, and he had little doubt that everyone on those ships felt just as he did. To have come this far, accomplished so much, and then failed . . . no, it just wasn't the way things were supposed to go.

We should have waited a little longer, he decided. If they'd had a proper convoy, with resupply ships, the story might have ended differently.

That was easy to say in retrospect, of course. No one had known that the enemy would lay a trap like this. It wasn't in their previous actions to even think along those lines. They learned a lot from Captain Weston in their previous engagements, as unfortunate as that was.

"Clear the lower decks," he said, walking across to where his comm officer was coordinating the arrival of the refugees. "We'll pack them in like sardines if we have to."

"Yes sir."

It wouldn't really make much of a difference, a few hundred heads more or less, but it would make his people feel like they were accomplishing something. That was more important just now than anything else. If they lost hope, if they let this all get to them, well then it was game over. The question would just be how long until the end rather than whether it was coming.

He could feel that already seeping into the crew's mood, and it was something he needed to head off as quickly as he could. The problem was, even he didn't really want to try and keep up pretenses. This was the Earth they were talking about, damn it!

I am supposed to die in its defense. That is my world, my nation. Packing my hull with warm bodies and running for the stars wasn't what I swore an oath to do.

▶▶▶

▶ *They lay in wait. That isn't how these things operate. What changed?*

Eric shifted in the command console chair, uncomfortable with how it felt. He'd been living in armor for the last five weeks or so, and now the form-fitting seat felt too soft for him. The records and current instrument scans of the Drasin formation were puzzling him, though, and distracting from the discomfort.

They didn't do all this for Earth, he decided, frowning in thought. *They **had** the Earth right where they wanted it. Anytime* *they chose they could have ended it, so what the hell are they up to? It's almost like they think . . .*

He rocked back in his chair, eyes bulging as he realized just what it was that the aliens were thinking.

"Holy shit," Eric whispered out loud. "They think we're a colony world. They think we have reinforcements coming . . . They don't *know* that Earth stands alone."

That was the only thing that made sense, the only thing that changed the alien actions from incomprehensible gibberish to something resembling an actual *plan!*

Eric half turned. "Susan?"

"Yes sir?" Lamont looked up instantly.

"How many more ships are we due to pick up?" he asked.

"The *Odysseus* or the squadron?"

"Just us."

Susan bent to the console for a moment. "Fifteen more and we're at capacity."

"How long will that require?"

"Another three or four hours," Susan admitted, eyes flicking to the tactical map.

He didn't blame her. That would bring the enemy ships into a much tighter noose, making their getaway plan all the harder to execute. He settled back, nodding, mostly to himself. "Are the other ships about the same?"

"Yes sir."

Eric stood up. "Steph, make ready to break orbit."

Michaels turned around, confused. "Sir?"

"Trust me." Eric grinned.

Stephen stared for a moment, then slowly smiled back. "Alright, you got it sir. Starting engine fire-up. How fast do you want it?"

"Yesterday. I want to be in the orbit of Jupiter . . . yester-day," Eric said. "Get everyone awake, all weapons stations ready, all defensive systems primed."

"Yes sir," Steph said, nodding to Milla, who also nodded. "And Raze?"

Eric glanced back. "Yeah?"

"Good to have you back."

"Good to be back," Eric said, walking to the back of the bridge. "By the way, you have the con, *Commander.*"

Steph scowled at the chuckling his boss let loose as he walked out, knowing that Eric was making a little dig at him for not being able to strap on his fighter anymore. "Yeah, yeah, I've got the con."

▶▶▶

▶ "Captain Weston to see you, ma'am."

"Send him in," Gracen said, glancing to the screens. "I'll just be a moment."

The President and Premier, two of the most powerful people on the planet, had differing expressions at being told that they were being put on hold. It was almost amusing, really. The Premier had a constipated look that told her he really wanted to complain, but since he was negotiating for places on the ships under her command, he knew he should keep his mouth shut. The President, on the other hand, just nod-ded and waved casually at her.

"Of course. Give the captain my regards. He did a superb job for us down here while we had him."

Gracen tipped her head. "I will, sir."

The screens blanked and she nodded to her aide, who opened the door. Weston looked good in his clean uniform, now that he didn't appear ready to strangle her with augmented muscles. He strode in, and she puzzled about his actions for a moment until she realized that he looked almost . . . chipper.

"Captain," Gracen said neutrally. "What brings you to my office?"

"Admiral, I want to take the *Odysseus* out of orbit."

She raised an eyebrow at him, caught between curiosity and irritation. Leaving orbit would mean abandoning hundreds of people they could save on this ship, possibly even thousands. She'd have to check those numbers.

"You'd better have a good reason, Captain."

"I've been looking at the enemy actions and they don't make any sense," Eric said. "Tactically they're complete gibberish. Why wait with an ambush force, Admiral? Why not just destroy the planet. They could have done it anytime they chose."

Gracen shrugged. It seemed rather obvious to her. "They wanted to entrap reinforcements."

"Exactly."

She hated to admit confusion, but that was where she was at the moment. "I'm afraid you've lost me, Captain."

"Admiral, they *think* we have reinforcements. They *think* we have other planets," he said. "They don't want just the Earth. They want it *all*."

Gracen thought about that for a moment. "I don't see where that is a good thing."

"Good? Admiral, it's a great thing," Eric said. "I don't think that they'll risk destroying the Earth until they have a good lead on our other worlds."

"Which we don't have," she said slowly. "But why attack it so powerfully then?"

"To encourage us. You really," Eric said, "to call for more reinforcements, or to flee back to your home system."

Gracen shook her head. "No. There's no way they want us to call for reinforcements, Captain. A few more of our ships will tear that whole fleet right from under them."

"I know, but I guarantee you that they've got a few stealthy ships stationed around the outer system waiting to follow you home," Eric said.

"That's *insane*," Gracen objected. "Captain, Eric, no one would sacrifice that much just for . . ."

"Admiral, this isn't a war," Eric said gravely. "This is an infection. They don't care about their individual ships. They care about the endgame, and nothing else. Tactically it only makes sense if you remember that these things aren't enemy soldiers. They're bullets. Bullets fired from a gun a billion years ago, maybe, but bullets just the same."

Gracen slumped, mind awash as she tried to see it the same way he did. She couldn't, she finally decided. Her brain just wouldn't wrap around it like that. That didn't, however, mean that her captain wasn't *right*.

"What are you suggesting, then?" she asked, leaning forward.

"Let's try something sneaky."

▶▶▶

▶ *The entity listened in to the conversation between her captain and the admiral, and admired the thinking that had brought him to his point. She had not considered some of the things he did, which was normal in a way. Despite having all the thoughts of everyone within her sphere, she didn't think like them herself. She too had been caught in the prevailing concept of fighting the war like, well, a war.*

"An army has different priorities than a disease, and must be combated differently."

She dropped back into herself, dropping her focus on the Odysseus *and soaking in the entirety of the planet once more. It was different, and she didn't like doing it right now. Before the Drasin it had been like stepping into a hot bath, warmth and comfort, even with all the violence and war. Now, however, it felt like someone had opened a sewage line into the tub, and so she avoided it as much as she could.*

"That has possibly been a mistake in judgment."

The currents of people were in disarray. Everything was out of place, but she could also feel the flowing sewage that was the Drasin as they gained strength. In places a flash of disruption would instantly clean the filth out, but leave scarred tissue behind. She normally rather disliked nuclear weapons, but for now they were a . . . medical necessity.

Disgusted by the feeling, but now determined, Gaia stepped into the flows and began to study them. It only took instants to recognize some of the patterns and realize just how right her captain had been.

She emerged, wishing for the metaphysical equivalent of a shower, but that would have to come later. For now she had the glimmer of an idea, and she needed help to see it through.

"My captain is not available, so who?"

Gaia cast about, considering, then smiled.

Of course, the answer was simple. If one could not reach the supervisor, one looked to his subordinates. Gaia slid back out into the world, her first target locked in her mind.

▶ ▶ ▶

▶Lyssa scowled as she looked over her board, trying to determine something . . . *anything* from the mess she was looking at.

Reports from every unit in the field were routing through her system, and she was trying like hell to get them the information they needed to do their jobs. But sometimes it felt like fighting ants at a picnic. The enemy barely seemed to react to the deployment of forces. Even nuclear weapons were of limited value. The aliens just rallied and seemed to redouble elsewhere.

She may as well be holding back the tide with a spoon.

She felt a shiver run down her back and looked around, but there was no one close enough to spook her.

Weird.

She turned back to the job, eyes on the map, and prepared to issue orders to authorize the next nuclear delivery. The fact that she'd been entrusted with this kind of insanity was enough to boggle her mind, but someone had to handle the reports from the field to ensure that as many people were clear of the blast zones as possible.

"Roger that, Shiva One Two. You are clear to . . ." She trailed off, blinking. She shook her head, her eyes being dragged away from the target, the city of Cincinnati, and to a blank spot on the map. She shook her head, looking back to the city, "Say again, you are clear . . . uh . . ."

"Say again, Control. Are the friendlies clear of the target area?" the pilot in the orbiting bomber called back.

"Say again, you're . . ." She blinked again, glaring at the screen. "Hold one. Say again, Shiva One Two, hold one."

"Roger that, Control. Holding."

Lyssa scowled at the screen and called up the empty space on the map that had drawn her attention, swapping over to the satellite imagery. She didn't see much on it, but that didn't mean anything. It was an older image from before the satellite array took such a beating.

Lyssa scowled at the screen for a bit, then blew out a breath and opened up the comm again. "Shiva One Two, Control."

"Go for Shiva, Control."

"Need to know, do you have a real-time intel package?" she asked.

"Roger that, Control. This baby is fully equipped. Even has AC."

"Redirect to fifteen degrees north by northwest. I need a high-detail surveillance shot, pronto."

There was a pause, then the pilot came back. "Roger, Control. Redirecting, north by northwest. Surveillance package is armed and broadcasting."

"Thank you, Shiva. Stand by for orders," she said, flipping over to the surveillance frequency, easily logging into the new signal.

The recon package on the bird was pretty standard, and actually existed on most aircraft fielded by the Confederation. It included extremely high-resolution imagery that was often sold to corporations in degraded format to help offset fuel costs for the airlines. The military and government had access to the full quality imagery as well, of course.

She slapped a map overlay on the images and ran through it until the plane slid over the target zone. She didn't see anything at first, but a moment later she had to look closer. Zooming in she spotted something that threw up all kinds of red flags.

"What the hell are you doing out here?" she whispered, flicking through the overlays until she got the thermal.

Lyssa's eyes widened and she let out a curse that caused the entire place to fall silent.

In an instant she was back on the communication channel. "Shiva One Two, retask. Retask. Retask. I say again, retask, retask, retask."

"Roger, Control. Standing by for retasking coordinates," the pilot came back. "Will need authorization for retask."

"Coordinates sent. Stand by for authorization," she snapped, pulling off her headset as she screamed, "General!"

▶▶▶

▶ *Gaia turned her focus away, smugly satisfied with the results.*

Now, if her captain could just pull off the impossible one last time, they might just have a fighting chance.

She didn't really expect it. The end seemed to be upon her, but one thing that Gaia had picked up from her people was a certain tenacity. Death may win, but it would not take her easily, nor would it take her cleanly.

CHAPTER TWENTY-SEVEN

▶ "IS EVERYTHING READY?" Eric asked, striding onto the bridge.

He'd spent most of the last few hours making sure that these new ships would be able to pull off what he had planned. They were well equipped, certainly, and the most lethal ships in the universe . . . or he dearly hoped so at least, because if there was something else out there that could kill a ship at fourteen light-minutes faster than light itself, he didn't want to know about it.

All that, however, didn't mean that the *Odysseus* had the capability to do what he needed. It was close, in some ways. Her cam-plate modifications were second gen at best, maybe a touch more efficient in some ways due to Priminae tech, but he didn't think they'd have a patch on the *Odyssey*'s later-gen design.

Her lasers should be good enough. While they were lower generation they were also massively more powerful. Power counted for something, after all, counted for a lot of things, really. He had confidence in the weapons, but what he needed was real stealth, and he wasn't sure that the monster he was on could handle it.

If it came to fighting before it was his choice, they'd already have lost.

"Show me the stealth specs again, please," he asked, nodding to Winger, who was in charge of the ship's active stealth systems.

"Aye sir. On your console."

"Thanks."

The ships weren't what he'd call stealthy, unfortunately. Unlike the *Odyssey,* the Heroics just couldn't go silent. They had a distinct gravity field and a power output that was high enough to be detected in the local space-time, which was a problem.

The *Odyssey,* and the *Enterprise,* were a lot like old-school diesel submarines. They weren't as powerful as nuclear boats, but they had a few advantages. For one, you could turn *off* the *Odyssey*'s reactors, run on electrics and bare minimal thrust. You couldn't do that with a Heroic, the same way as you couldn't turn off a nuclear submarine's reactor.

That meant that the enemy would be able to track the heroics almost anywhere they went, and that was a problem. Every problem, however, had a solution.

"Susan, transmit orders to the Heroics," he said. "Here's what I need them to do."

"Aye sir. I have your file. Sending."

"Good. Steph, are we ready?" Eric asked, taking a seat as he forced a cocky smile on his face.

It was anything but the time to be cocky, but what he was about to do was risky enough. He didn't need everyone all tied up in knots over it because the captain didn't look like he knew what he was doing.

Fake it until you make it. That's been my motto ever since I saw these things for the first time. Why change now?

"Yes sir, we are ready."

"Susan, transmit to all ships," he said. "This is Captain Weston . . . initiate shell game."

▶▶▶

▶The ship minds advanced, closing the links of their net as they approached the targeted world and ships. The approach of the new class of ships, yet another type that defied all explanation and analysis, confirmed what the swarm had hypothesized. There was another spacefaring example of the red band in this part of the galaxy, and it was far more virulent and deadly than any other in recent memory.

It *must* be destroyed.

The swarm were shocked by a momentary flash of FTL particles that erupted from the region of the third world, effectively blinding them. Their light-speed senses remained intact, of course, so the swarm wasn't overly concerned until all but one of the enemy ships vanished from their tracking plots as the FTL spectrum cleared once more.

That was impossible.

One could not simply hide power plants as large as those ships contained. There was no way, and yet all of them save one were now gone. The swarm intensely watched the light-speed track as it slowly caught up to the disruption, only to practically reel in shock when the ships all vanished from *that* as well!

The single remaining ship was bolting from the system at an intense acceleration, and in an instant, the swarm had a hard choice. Continue on to the target world, and risk losing their last link to the dangerous species they had been tracking . . . or risk splitting forces, but that would then risk opening their force to defeat while in a weakened state.

The decision was swift, and the swarm changed course as one being, entering into a pursuit curve for the single remaining ship.

▶▶▶

▶Jennifer "Cardsharp" Samuels cackled as quietly as she could, imagining the look on the face of the pilot of the Raven stealth bomber that had narrowly missed colliding with her *Heracles*.

"That poor bastard's probably choking in the smell from the load he just dropped in his flight suit." She smirked almost uncontrollably.

Captain Roberts rolled his eyes. "Some decorum, if you please, Lieutenant Commander. This is hardly the place or time."

"Yes sir." She grimaced.

"Besides," the Captain went on, his voice dry as the Sahara, "he's on canned air. The smell is hardly an issue. I'd expect that he's more bothered by the newly squishy texture of his seat."

Jennifer snorted, nearly breaking a rib as she failed to keep her laughter in.

▶▶▶

▶"Control, this is Raven Two Three," an angry pilot growled into his radio. "Request permission to light that sucker up!"

"Negative Two Three, that's an ally."

"I don't want to *shoot* him. Just let me target the bastard!"

The control officer on the other side of the comm sighed audibly. It was already a long day, week, and month, but this was getting to be ridiculous.

▶▶▶

▶ The five Heroics had blown their tachyon projectors out in a single massive surge intended to blind the enemy temporarily as they shifted their cam-plates to best absorption levels and bolted for the surface of the Earth in order to hide the power of their gravetic reactors.

Floating in relatively low altitudes with active camouflage on was a hell of a way to introduce yourself to the local militaries that were already buzzing around like angry wasps, but there was little to be done about it. The Confederacy at least managed to provide emergency IFF beacons to their troops, but in many parts of the world the Heroics had to adjust fast on the fly to avoid midair collisions with planes and the occasional missile.

It was quick, it was dirty but, surprisingly, it worked.

▶▶▶

▶ President Conner stared at the long-range scans, more than a little stunned.

"I can't believe that they're falling for it."

"Enemy ships are altering course. They're laying in pursuit of the *Odysseus,* Mr. President."

Conner shook his head. "Alright, Weston is buying us time . . . *again.* Let's not waste it. I want more factories open, twenty-four-seven production. I want every able body either slinging a rifle or building a nuke. Am I clear?"

"We're on it, sir."

▶▶▶

▶ Captain Carrow watched the distorted stern of the *Odysseus* as it accelerated away from Earth at incredible speed. His *Enterprise* was pouring on the power as well, but couldn't hope to match what the Priminae engines were putting out.

The *Enterprise* was the only ship in the system that could come close, however, while maintaining a high level of stealth, so the job was theirs by default.

"Captain, enemy ships are changing vectors to pursue the *Odysseus*."

"Well damn," Carrow swore softly. "He was right."

He wasn't one of Weston's fans or even remotely an admirer. In Carrow's opinion, Weston was a reckless fool with a penchant for dime store heroics and a code of honor that was crafted right out of fiction instead of the real world. The man was also, however, one of the finest tactical minds in the Confederacy, and there was no one who contested that much at least.

Still, even with that in mind, Carrow had never expected the enemy to actually break their march on Earth in order to pursue *one* fleeing starship.

What the hell did he see?

Like the man or not, Carrow had to admit that sometimes he had a way of making anyone else feel a little inferior by comparison.

He sighed. "Contact engineering. I want more thrust, see if they can't fine-tune the CM fields a bit. The *Odysseus* does *not* get outside our range of flight operations. Am I clear?"

"Aye sir!"

▶▶▶

▶ *Well damn,* Eric thought, grinning nastily. *I was right.*

"Enemy fleet is vectoring in on our course, Captain."

"Intercept?" he asked, though he was pretty sure he knew the answer.

"No sir," Michelle said, a tinge of satisfaction in her own voice. "Pursuit."

"They don't want to catch us," Steph said from where he was sitting at the helm. "They want to flush us, make us run for home."

"How little they know," Eric said. "Let's thin their ranks, shall we?"

"I am ready, Capitaine," Milla said softly from her position at weapons control.

Eric nodded, eyes on the time. "Stand by to clear our baffles and fire as the targets bear . . . execute Crazy Ivan in three minutes."

Milla scrunched up her face, clearly confused as to the terminology, but she knew her own part in what was to come and didn't need to understand what a "Crazy Ivan" was. "Yes Capitaine. We fire in three minutes."

▶▶▶

▶ "Remember," Captain Roberts glowered over his bridge, "aim *through* the swarm. Target the ships closer to the *Odysseus.*"

"Yes Captain." His tactical officer nodded. "Targets selected. We're sharing data with the other Heroics. We're ready."

Roberts nodded slowly. He knew that they were, but it was a hard moment and he was on edge. The *Odysseus* was leading the swarm away from Earth, but that still left them with over a *thousand* ships chasing down one Heroic Class vessel that had absolutely zero chance of winning an engagement.

She could outrun them, of course. There was nothing in the universe that matched a transition drive . . . or, if there was, he did *not* want to know about it. Transitions were bad enough, to be frank about it.

Running wouldn't accomplish the mission, however, so he knew that Eric Weston wasn't actually going to run.

That made the job of the Heroics all the more important. They had to thin the swarm as much as they could. It was unlikely in the extreme that they could give the *Odysseus* a real fighting chance, but damn it all to hell they were going to try.

"Stand by for artillery assault in two minutes," he ordered.

"Aye sir. Clock started at two minutes."

▶▶▶

▶Sirens whined all across the New Mexican field. Men rushed all over the place like angry ants stirred from their nest. All around them the air felt still and dead as if the world itself had held its breath.

All of the activity was centered around a distant part of the facility, one that was locked off by layers and layers of gates, guard towers, and patrols. At the center of all that lay several large hangars that had been hastily converted into something resembling a cross between a mountaintop telescope and a 1950s science-fiction laser cannon.

The latter was actually the closer of the two comparisons, but only a small handful of people in the area actually knew that.

One of those was the army general in charge of the facility, Ethan Thomas, and he was not in a mood to be trifled with as the clock was counting down far faster than he liked.

"General, I'm telling you, this is incredibly risky," the civilian supervisor was telling him for the twentieth time. "There are too many variables here that we can't account for. The magnetic field alone is driving all of our simulations completely off any sense of predictability."

"Mr. Tanning, all I need to know is can you fire them?" Thomas demanded simply.

"Can we fire them? Of course we can fire them! It's what happens after that I'm concerned with."

"Can you hit a target with them then?"

Tanning sighed. "Yes. Assuming we can account for magnetic flux, we can hit a target. The question is whether we turn this entire facility into a crater in the process or not."

Thomas snorted, looking around calmly. Finally he glanced back. "Begin firing preparations."

Tanning stared as the general walked away, then numbly staggered back to his control room.

"Sir? What are we doing?"

Tanning stared at his colleague, hoping that he didn't look too horrified by what he was about to say, and finally willed his mouth to move.

"Stand by to fire."

▶▶▶

▶ *Gaia looked over the thoughts running through the minds of the nearly panicked men who were now following the orders of the general. There was something noble about being totally terrified, nearly to the point of doing something humiliating with your various bodily functions, and yet still proceeding to do whatever it was that was scaring you in the first place.*

Noble, but she didn't have time to dwell on that aspect of humanity at the moment.

Gaia was well aware of everything the humans knew about themselves, and she even knew a few things they didn't, including some speculations about how her own physiology worked. Humanity stored their memories in two known mechanisms, and she speculated a third yet unknown one. She knew for herself that she also used two, at least, but didn't have any data that might indicate a third as of yet.

"I wonder if that might be forthcoming, should we fail?"

She pushed such morbid ideas aside, thoughts still meandering slightly as she considered the differences and similarities between herself and humans.

Humans had active and passive thought storages, as did she. For a human the passive storage was in the chemical links in their brains; for her it seemed that she could store a great deal of information in the gravity well of the planet itself. Active thought processes, for humans, were in the neural-electric impulses that shot around the brain, and for herself it was in the geomagnetic field of the entire planet.

That meant that she had some control over the very thing the people working here were trying to predict.

Gaia centered her thoughts, a practice learned from uncountable thousands of meditation masters worldwide, and slowly began to stop thinking around the base in New Mexico.

▶▶▶

"Holy . . ."

"What is it, Greg?"

"I don't know, John, but check the magnetic readings."

The technician walked over and glanced at the screen before double taking and having his eyes bug out. "Something has to be wrong with your gear."

"I checked. I swear I checked," his partner protested. "Even the portable stuff says the same thing. The local field is almost neutralizing itself."

"This is impossible."

"This is a damn miracle. What's the clock on the firing sequence?"

John double-checked. "The clock is at thirty seconds and counting."

"Do you believe in God?" Greg asked. "Because I think he may have just made an appearance."

"God, the devil, or lady luck . . . If this works, we'll owe whoever pulled it off one hell of a solid."

"Amen."

▶▶▶

▶ *God.*

Goddess.

Gaia.

She didn't know what she was, so the conversation she monitored vaguely in the background as she focused her thoughts away amused her more than anything. She was a citizen of the world, and that would be enough. They did not owe her a solid, or anything else, because she was just trying to do her part to save her own life, but the thought was vaguely comforting.

The focus it took to push her thoughts away from the facility, to deaden the electromagnetic flux that was an integral part of the living world they inhabited, was almost exhausting. It was a sensation, she had to admit, she had never before experienced.

Of course, this was the first time she'd ever quite attempted something to quite this level. The closest she'd ever come before was accidentally blacking out the East Coast in a fit of pique that still was rather embarrassing to recall.

"Everything is a learning experience," Gaia supposed as she continued to direct her thoughts away from the facility in New Mexico. "The original philosophers were right on that count. Now, if only I can go on learning . . . "

▶▶▶

▶The countdown reached zero, and one very long gun under the command and control of the Earth opened fire.

Shockingly, for those stationed in New Mexico and who were aware of what was coming, nothing exploded.

Nothing local, at least.

CHAPTER TWENTY-EIGHT

▶COLONEL MARION GRUMBLED as he made his way through the largely makeshift comm center constructed to facilitate the movements of the special unit and its operations. He knew it had become necessary to use every asset available, but honestly there was no reason to build them their own operations control. That could have been run out of SOCOM, surely.

"What is it, Miss Myriano?" he asked tiredly.

"I called for the general." Lyssa scowled.

"The general is busy in another part of the facility. You'll have to make do with me."

Lyssa scowled at him, then grunted. "Fine. I need authorization to retask."

Marion blinked, mind reeling incredulously.

Did she just actually ask me for authorization to retask nuclear strikes? Is she insane, or just stupid?

"Miss Myriano, the approved strikes were determined at the highest levels," he growled. "This is not some game where you can start shooting whatever you feel like because you got a new *gun*."

She gave him a dry, almost pitying look, then hit one key on her board. The screen in front of him lit up, and he noted that it was standard imagery from a recon package. He leaned in a bit and shrugged. "You have one Drasin drone soldier out in the middle of nowhere. I fail to see . . ."

Lyssa hit another key and it flashed to infrared, causing him to reel back.

The entire area was crawling with them, so much that at first it looked like one single heat source if not for the scrambling movements he could pick out. Marion paled. "Where is that?"

"That's an abandoned mine in Kentucky," she said. "It's noted for having high concentrations of various rare earth minerals as well as other useful materials."

"Why is it abandoned?" Marion asked absently as he stared in fascination at the imagery.

"After the war ended, the Block flooded the market with most of what it produces," she shrugged. "They still have much lower wages than we do, so for things like this the mine's owners couldn't compete. Better to cap the mine and save the materials for when they're more profitable to get out. Unfortunately, it looks like the Drasin beat us to it."

"I've never seen anything like this, not in any city . . ."

"The cities are decoys," Lyssa cut him off. "They replicate there, yes, but they don't even bother going to ground. They just swarm around, catching our attention. I've located a dozen other mines just like this one through our recon packages worldwide. Colonel, we *need* to retask."

"It'll have to go right to the President," Marion shook his head. "This is . . . "

"This is *vital*," she stressed. "If you have to go to the CinC, then do so. *Now*. Before it's too late."

He nodded slowly, reaching for her system and keying open a channel. "This is Colonel Marion. I need to speak directly with the Chiefs."

"Yes sir," the woman on the other side said, sounding disinterested.

The screen flickered, and in a moment the logo of the Joint Chiefs appeared and another woman's voice spoke. "Joint Command and Control, how may I direct you?"

"The Chiefs," Marion said simply.

"I'm sorry, I require authorization . . ."

"Marion, Colonel, Confederate Air Force. ID Number Zero Niner Five Niner Alpha Zeta Bravo One Two. Omega Protocol."

There was a pause, then the screen instantly changed to show a man in a suit staring off at something else. It took a second before he glanced down and was apparently surprised to see someone looking back at him.

"Holy hell, son, you scared a year off my life." The man snorted. "What is it?"

"I'm about to scare more than a year off, sir," Marion told him, nodding to Lyssa. "Send the file."

She nodded, hitting a few commands.

The man on the other side frowned, eyes flicking to the left. He stared for a moment, then paled. "Is this what I think it is?"

"It's worse. We need to retask all Shiva groups."

▶▶▶

▶Far from Earth, the front line of the Drasin force pursuing the fleeing *Odysseus* exploded into clouds of expanding plasma. The ship minds noted the destruction, were again frustrated in their attempts to locate a source, but otherwise did not flinch from their mission.

The furor of destruction lasted only seconds, peaking as over a dozen ships vanished into plasma at once, then dwindled off before finally ending with just over three hundred ships destroyed. The ship minds noted that again, and the lack of follow-up as time continued to trudge on, and decided that the enemy was either in the process of reloading their unknown weapon or had spent their final shots.

The swarm absently hoped that was the case. It was becoming more and more tedious to replace drone ships that had been blown from space-time by a method that couldn't be determined, tracked, or countered.

What had to be done *would* be done, but it would be so much easier for everyone involved if this annoying example of the red band would simply accept their fate. There was work to be done elsewhere, other worlds to cleanse of the filth that had infected them.

Other stars to bring back to the whole.

▶▶▶

▶ "Enemy ships' course is unchanged, Captain."

Eric nodded. "Good. I want best speed for the heliopause, Commander."

"Aye Captain," Steph said. "Course is engaged. We're warping space for the heliopause."

Eric murmured his response, surprised by the different feel of this ship over his *Odyssey*. The slight jolt of acceleration that the centrifugal gravity and CM systems had never quite been able to mask on his previous ship was entirely missing here. All he felt was a slight flutter in his guts as though he were falling, and nothing else. Luckily everything seemed to fall right along with him, so no harm, he supposed.

The *Odysseus* was a marvel of a ship, that much he could admit, but Eric missed his old chair.

"Enemy ships are matching speed," Michelle said. "Correction . . . they're . . . Captain, they've increased speed to overtake."

Eric twisted, his face a mask hiding the concern he felt rush through him. "How long to overtake?"

"We won't make the orbit of Neptune, Captain."

"Damn, that's fast," Eric hissed. "Do we have any more speed?"

That set off a flurry of debate behind him, and he had to run his seat to look at the Priminae engineers who were arguing. Eric let them go for a moment, the translator barely keeping up with half of what they were tossing back and forth, before finally breaking in.

"I asked a question."

The chief winced and looked over at him, shaking his head. "Not safely, and likely not even if we remove the breakers, Captain. The Drasin have never shown this level of speed before. We did not even believe it was possible within the realm of practical physics."

That honestly didn't surprise him much. The Drasin had ways of confounding physics, to his mind at least.

"What keeps that speed from being practical?"

"Primarily the fact that the heat generation increases exponentially," the chief answered. "Within the space-warp, eventually you reach levels of heat that only existed briefly in the history of the universe, right after the first instant of expansion."

"Lovely," Eric turned back.

He remembered that bit about the theory of the Alcubierre drive mechanism, and knew that Priminae ships devoted massive parts of their infrastructure to heat pumps and reclamation tools. It didn't surprise him in the slightest, however, that Drasin would be able to use more speed.

The Drasin were far more tolerant of heat than any human.

Eric took a breath. "Alright. It'll be a fight then."

Steph half turned from the helm, puzzled. "Wait . . . why is the heat buildup so bad now? Both of us can go FTL using this drive. Shouldn't we be able to withstand more?"

Eric raised an eyebrow, glancing back at the chief, who simply shook his head.

"I am afraid not, Commander. To pass light we must be outside the solar gravity field, or very nearly so. Right now we're fighting both the common law of physics and the pull of the star itself."

"As I said," Eric repeated himself, "it'll be a fight."

"Sir, I don't understand . . ."

Eric glanced over to where Milla was manning the tactical station, noting that she looked nervous, but not as bad as he might expect. "What don't you understand?"

"Why are they overtaking us now? If you're right, they need us. The need us to lead them to . . . well, wherever," she said, brow scrunched up as she puzzled out her thoughts.

The whole point behind the captain's plan was that the Drasin didn't realize that they had *already* located the homeworld they sought. The whole point of running as a decoy was that the Drasin would *have* to follow, to seek their source of reinforcements.

So why would they suddenly force a battle now? It made no sense.

Eric just shrugged and smiled, sadly. "The transition drive, Miss Chans. They can't let us reach the heliopause, and they know it. I gambled and lost. I hoped they'd let us get out of the system and lead them on a merry little chase, but they didn't take the bait."

"Oh. But then . . ."

"They'll try to take us in one piece," Eric said confidently, "probably hoping that they'll be able to get intel from our computers, so we're going to use that against them. There's nothing harder than taking an opponent alive if he's trying his damndest to kill you first."

"Captain . . . "

Eric looked to where Admiral Gracen was standing. "Yes Admiral?"

"Should we not call for reinforcements? The other Heroics could respond . . .," she offered.

"I will if you wish, but Admiral, if they light off their drives beyond Earth's gravity, the enemy is sure to detect them . . ." Eric said slowly. "If that happens . . . they don't need us anymore."

Gracen sighed, but nodded. "A fair point, Captain."

Eric nodded, looking to the rest as he raised his voice. "We have two mission objectives from this point forward. First, we have to delay the enemy as long as possible using any means we can. Every *minute* they're not in Earth's orbit is another minute longer the Earth can build munitions to destroy these things wherever they may be. Second, we have to savage the swarm as much as humanly possible. They cannot be allowed to return to Earth's orbit in anything even vaguely resembling their current strength."

He looked around. "Am I quite clear?"

No one spoke, but the nods and looks of determination were enough for him.

"Very well," he said, smiling peacefully. "Miss Lamont, if you would be so kind as to sound general quarters?"

"Sir?" Susan blinked, distracted and unfocused for a moment.

"Beat the drums, Susan," Eric said. "Call us to war."

"Aye aye, sir."

There was no confusion in her voice this time.

▶▶▶

▶ "Sir?"

On the *Achilles'* bridge there was enough noise that Roberts missed the call initially.

"Sir."

Roberts turned around as his comms officer caught his attention. "What is it, Janice?"

"Flash traffic on the high-priority channels, all across the Confederacy, sir," she answered.

That wrenched his attention from the deep-space track and back to the present location. "I didn't know we were patched into that."

"Officially?" She had the decency to blush.

Roberts shook his head, holding a hand up. "Don't tell me. I don't want to know."

"Do you not want to know what it's all about either?"

"Let's not go that far." He smiled, white teeth flashing briefly as he walked over. "I assume it's Drasin connected?"

"Yes sir, but more than that . . . Sir . . . " She hesitated. "Are you aware of Operation Shiva?"

Roberts grimaced, but nodded, "Yes. I was flashed into that before they dropped the first bomb. The President didn't want anyone panicking."

Susan nodded. "This is related. They're shifting stance. People are a little panicked now."

"Why?"

"Apparently the drone population in the cities was a decoy," she said. "They've located over a dozen mass nests, all in mines rich in rare earth minerals."

Roberts was quiet for a moment, eyes flicking to the space track. He wanted nothing more than to be dealing with the aliens out there, but it seemed that the ones here on Earth were more immediately dangerous after all. Slowly he nodded. "Give me a dispatch comm to all Heroics."

Janice just had to tap a single key to make that happen. "You're on, Captain."

"This is Roberts," he said simply. "I want all Heroics to shift to ground support and intel gathering as of this moment. Flash traffic from the surface indicates that the alien drones have created multiple large nests in areas rich in rare earth materials. Scan those areas, find the enemy, and destroy them where they sit. Roberts out."

Janice closed the comm as he glanced back at her. "I want a private comm to Confederacy Command and Control. I'll take it in my office."

"Aye aye, Captain."

▶▶▶

▶ Sun looked over the intelligence feed, eyes narrowing as he read the reports from the other Heroics. The Confederacy was a few steps ahead of the Block on this matter, he realized quickly. Someone over there had to have gotten lucky to spot the enemy movements.

He walked over to his communications officer. "I require a link to the ground forces. I understand that Colonel Reed is on the ground?"

"Yes Captain. He is liaising between our, I mean, Block forces," communications officer Yeing Tao answered. She tapped a few commands. "The colonel is standing by, Captain."

"Thank you, Yeing," Sun said, walking back to his station. "Colonel, this is Captain Sun."

"I hear you, Captain. What's going on?"

"We have new intel from your SOCOM division in the Confederacy," Sun said. "They seem to believe that the city forces are a distraction. They are reporting massive enemy forces in mines containing large concentrations of rare earth elements. China has significant deposits in the northern sections. Still, I believe we may have . . . as you say, a problem."

"Shit," Reed swore. "I'll let the locals know. You have a plan?"

"I'm going to shift the *Bellerophon* to examine those regions," Sun said. "In the meantime I am detaching all of our assault shuttles to your command. If we find what I believe we will find, I will authorize laser strikes immediately. You may be required to put boots on the ground, as you say, to confirm that we've eliminated the enemy forces."

"Roger that," Reed answered. "Good hunting."

"And to you, Colonel. I fear we both will have our fill of the hunt before this is over."

"Speak for yourself, Captain. I just got in on this game," Reed answered with a feral tone in his voice. "This is what I live for."

"You need a better reason to live, Colonel," Sun answered dryly. "Sun out."

He settled back, sighing, then nodded to his helmsman. "Take us north, over the Gobi toward the resource mines."

"Yes Captain."

▶▶▶

▶ "What is happening, Colonel?"

Reed glanced over to the Block commander who had been assigned to him. "The *Bellerophon* is heading north to investigate something that might be happening."

The colonel looked up, and indeed the huge bulk of the alien warship was smoothly moving out from where it had been holding position over the city. He knew that it was a Block captain in charge, but honestly he felt better with the massive object moving away.

He just couldn't shake the feeling that it was going to fall on him.

▶▶▶

▶ "Shiva One Two, we have a new tasking."

"Well it's about time," Captain Hiller grumbled, glancing over at his copilot. "You'd think everyone was on a coffee break down there."

He sighed, thumbing open the comm channel. "We're standing by, Control. New coordinates."

"Coordinates follow. Confirm receipt."

Hiller checked the incoming codes, putting them up against a map, and scowled. "Receipt confirmed . . . are you sure about this, Control? There's nothing out there."

"That is affirmative, One Two. Please encode your ordnance for ground penetration and launch at your discretion."

Hiller and his copilot shared a glance, both mouthing the word "ground penetration" with wide eyes.

Sure, the missiles they were carrying could do that, but only because it was a modular chassis. No one used *nukes* as bunker busters. That was insane. It was also dirty. Ground and underground detonation of nuclear devices tended to irradiate far more material and leave it hot for decades.

"Say again, Control. Did you say *ground penetration?*"

"Affirmative, One Two. Confirm and execute."

Hiller shook his head slowly, but nodded, "If you say so. Configuring for ground penetration and launching in three . . . two . . . Missile away."

▶▶▶

▶ The BBU modular munitions frame was the go-to workhorse of the Confederacy Air Force, and had been for several decades. It was simple, modular, and damn near foolproof, which made it incredibly popular with pilots and quartermasters alike. In effect it was a smart airframe that could be configured to carry anything from a cluster of ten-pound bomblets to a single fifty-megaton warhead.

Each warhead could be configured to airburst or ground burst, or, in the case of an enemy gone to ground in a fortified position, for a ground-penetrating deep detonation.

The missile launched by Shiva One Zero hit the target ground straight on, going Mach Five. Designed to slam into and through armor-reinforced bunkers, the missile simply blew through the soft dirt like it wasn't there. It burst out into the mine tunnel below, then kept on going through to the next level.

Fifteen levels down, the bodies and limbs of Drasin drones strewn behind it like some kind of gory wake, the nuclear core detonated.

On the surface, everything was quiet for a moment, then a low rumble shook everything, and finally the dirt just blew straight up. Fifty megatons of power tore the mine to shreds, pulverizing everything inside it that it didn't incinerate, and finally leaving a single deep crater where once there had been nothing but flat scrubland.

▶▶▶

▶ "Shiva One Two, I need a flyover of the target site," Lyssa calmly asked. "Please ensure that your recon pack is fully activated."

"Roger, Control. Stand by for recon," Shiva One Two answered.

Lyssa watched as the imagery stabilized, sweeping back over the target zone. She flicked over to the infrared and began examining the scene.

"How does it look?" Marion asked softly.

"Imagery is still stabilizing," she answered. "Heat profile of the nuke is messing with things. Give it a minute."

They stared and waited, watching as the thermal spikes evened out. Finally Lyssa reached forward and opened the comm.

"Shiva One Two, target neutralized. Stand by for next target. Good job."

She closed the channel and looked over to where Marion was sitting. "Send a ground team with seismic gear into the region as soon as possible, just to confirm."

The colonel nodded curtly. "I'll arrange it."

"You do that," she sighed, turning back to her console. "I have more targets to service."

▶▶▶

▶ "By the gods, what *is* that?" Sun whispered, looking at the imagery they were capturing of the surface through the *Bellerophon*'s advanced instruments.

"Thousands of them, Captain," his instrumentation chief said. "Hundreds of thousands."

"I want all lasers prepared to fire. Nothing down there survives," Sun ordered, lips tightening. "*Nothing.*"

"Y . . . yes Captain."

The *Bellerophon* steadied over its target, weapons priming as they continued to record data from below them. After several long moments a low hum reverberated all around and the air began to shimmer under the bulk of the ship.

Over a dozen beams lanced out of the bottom of the carrier, boiling the sand and rock below directly from solid to gas. The beams sublimated the material above the mine, punching through into the first level, where they instantly did the same thing to thousands of Drasin in twenty milliseconds before continuing on to burn through the second level.

Level by level the beams of the *Bellerophon* did their job, burning through rock, dirt, and alien carapace with equal ease. A hundred feet, a thousand, *ten thousand* feet were burned through in just seconds, and then they kept on burning.

▶▶▶

▶ "Captain, thermal readings just spiked below us!"

Sun half turned. "We're turning the earth into gaseous metals. Of course the temperature is spiking."

"No, Captain, beyond that. I'm reading some very odd thermal profiles . . . something is coming up!"

Sun's eyes widened. "Cease fire! Pull us out of here, now!"

"Course?"

"Any course!" Sun yelled. "Move!"

The *Bellerophon* tilted in the air, moving away as the lasers ceased. Below her, however, the hole they'd burned into the ground rumbled and began to spit fire right back at them. Molten rock exploded into the air, the force of the blast actually shaking the kilometer-and-a-half starship as it tried hurriedly to pull away.

"All hands, brace for impact!" Sun called out, holding on to his seat as the Earth exploded beneath them.

Alarms screamed and the ship bucked under the shock wave from below, sending two crewmen on the bridge to the floor. For a moment the bridge actually *tilted,* something that should have been impossible with the artificial gravity systems in use, and everyone hung on for dear life.

And then it was over. They were clear and Sun was surging up from his seat again.

"Show me the site!" he ordered. "Show me the site!"

The wraparound screen flickered, and everyone stared in awe as they watched the huge lava plume erupting behind them. Smoke and ash was filling the sky as the molten rock already began to solidify into the base of what was, apparently, China's newest . . . and *largest* active volcano.

Sun stared for a long moment, then began to utter vile and profane words in both Mandarin and Cantonese.

▶▶▶

▶ The call went out, worldwide.

The enemy wasn't where they thought they were. New missions were scrambled, recon imagery was reexamined, and operational orders were adjusted. The five Heroes began to move across the continents, the big ships settling into place over rare earth mines and pausing just long enough to vaporize the ground below right to the mantle.

They tried to avoid the *Bellerophon*'s mistake of cutting too deep, but more than once they left a smoking hole behind with a rapidly growing cone of ash and rock forming around its circumference.

In each strike, hundreds of thousands of previously hidden drones vanished into their component atoms and molecules, and the carefully crafted plan of the Drasin ship minds went up in plasma right along with them.

CHAPTER TWENTY-NINE

▶ THE *ODYSSEUS* TORE through space at speeds that made a mockery of Newtonian math. Behind her, over seven hundred alien starships all but screaming in pursuit.

Captain Weston looked around the bridge, seeing some new faces, but many familiar ones as he savored the last few moments before the inevitable happened. A presence behind him caused him to half turn and nod as the admiral stepped up to the command console.

She waved him down as he made to get up. "As you were, Captain. I just wanted to be here for this."

Eric nodded. He could understand that.

"Best seat in the house," he told her. "Do you have any orders for me, Admiral?"

Gracen looked around, considering the situation, and finally just smiled.

"Make them regret having caught us, Captain."

Eric smiled back. "With pleasure, Admiral. Commander?"

"Yes sir."

"We're not going to have a wingman on this," Eric said, "so everything I told you about hotdogging . . ."

"Yes sir?"

"Forget it."

The man known as Stephanos chuckled evilly. "Forget what, sir?"

"Good man. Milla?" Eric half turned to look at the slim and slight Priminae woman.

"Yes Capitaine?" she asked softly.

"Steph is going to be pushing it. Try and keep up," Eric advised her. "Once we're in the thick of it, I won't have time to give you specific orders. When I give the order to fire at will, use your own judgment until I tell you to stop."

She nodded resolutely. "Aye aye, Capitaine."

"Alright then. Let's show these things what happens when you corner a dangerous animal," Eric said with a sinister smile. "Prepare to come about!"

"Aye sir! Standing by to come about!" Steph answered.

"Bring us about."

"Coming about," Steph said as he leaned into the controls and the stars rushed past them on the screens.

The *Odysseus* swung about hard, putting her weapons on target in just under a second as she began to warp space-time in the opposite direction as hard as she could. Bleeding velocity at incredible rates, the swarm of Drasin ships jumped at them from the black of space as Eric watched the screens light up with augmented data about their foes.

"Milla," he spoke. "Fire as she bears."

"Aye Capitaine," Milla Chans said, eyes gleaming as she looked out at the things that had killed her previous ship, her previous comrades. "All lasers . . . firing."

The lasers of the Heroics weren't quite as sophisticated as the ones on his *Odyssey*, Eric noted wryly, but they made up in power for what they lacked in sophistication. The beams lanced into the lead ships with the force of a hundred focused suns, and four Drasin drone ships vanished into oddly spherical bursts of plasma.

"Evade."

"Aye Captain," Steph said, twisting the controls and leaning into his NICS needles. The sharp twinge in his neck was an old friend and he couldn't help but smile as he shifted the warp field, slamming the ship hard to port.

The *Odysseus* responded impossibly, not even groaning under the sudden strain, and Eric noted in the back of his mind that it somehow felt wrong not to have *some* sort of acceleration effect. The Priminae gravity systems took care of that, however, leaving everything—even his filled-to-the-brim coffee—unfazed by the universe-bending actions they were taking.

"Laser bloom, Captain!" Winger announced. "I have the signature. Should I adapt?"

"No. Maintain best reflective settings," Eric ordered. "There's too many of them out here."

"Yes sir."

"Milla, fire at will," Eric said, leaning forward. "Steph . . . take us into the swarm."

"Aye aye, sir!" Both of them responded, and the *Odysseus* surged forward into the roiling storm that was threatening to sweep them all away.

▶▶▶

▶With the augmented systems fully online, Stephen Michaels had always felt a little like he was in a simulator more than the real thing, but on the *Odysseus* it was exacerbated by the artificial gravity systems. He missed the *feeling* of motion, the sensations that accompanied wrestling his fighting around a tight turn.

On the *Odysseus,* he may as well be sitting in front of a computer screen playing a game. Alright, it was a pretty friggin' *awesome* computer screen, he'd give that to the wrap-around system, but it was still just a screen. The augmented views supplied by the computer made that feeling even worse, of course.

As he guided the *Odysseus* into the swarm of enemy fighters, Steph watched the beams as they swept space, curling the big ship around, over, and under them as the enemy continued to try and get a bead on him.

No laser is perfectly focused. There are always stray photons to analyze, just as no vacuum is perfect either, and so the beams inevitably struck dust and particulates as they crossed space. The *Odysseus* computers took that data and used it to draw a vector map across his view, showing him where the lasers were and even where they were heading.

Granted, it was useless if the laser was actually aimed directly at him. They'd be hit before the information could reach them, but it did help to see the sweeping patterns the enemy used to try and box the *Odysseus* in.

He could also see the *Odysseus'* lasers as they flashed outward, guided by Milla's hand. Unlike the aliens, the *Odysseus* had no compunction about aiming for the kill and, as the attacker, the advantage of the initiative was also theirs.

Five more enemy ships vanished into near-perfect spherical explosions of plasma, but then they were within the swarm and it was the enemy's turn to retaliate.

▶▶▶

▶ "Laser strike! Deck five, section ninety three! Damage control groups are moving to contain the damage!"

Eric didn't bother turning around. He was more focused on the action behind the ship right then and he trusted the crew to do their jobs without his micromanagement. Right then, what he was really missing, was the antimatter weapons of the *Odyssey*. He understood why the Priminae might not like the technology. It made him grit his teeth sometimes as well, but with the power generation on the *Odysseus* and the short, close-range action they were now engaged in . . .

By *God,* they could ravage the enemy forces beyond all sanity.

"Second strike! We're losing air. Deck twelve, section one one three nine," Susan said. "They've got our range."

Eric nodded. "Do something about that, would you, Commander?"

"Aye aye, sir." Steph grinned a little too widely, suddenly through full acceleration to the space warp, dropping the ship toward the Sun like a stone.

They were headed right into a small squadron of the enemy, which would seem to be in flagrant violation of Eric's "request," but he didn't flinch. At the last moment, almost literally, Steph twisted the *Odysseus* out and around the group, then ducked in behind them and away from the lasers of their more ardent *admirers.*

"Don't shoot these guys, Milla," Steph called over his shoulder, a gesture highlighting half a dozen of the closest drone ships. "I have a use for them."

"As you say, Stephane," she uttered softly. "I have many others to choose from."

That much was an ironclad truth, Eric admitted. Despite the fact that the *Odysseus* was powerful and sophisticated enough to slaughter *dozens* of the enemy ships, they were dealing with *hundreds* of them. It was just a matter of time before the damage grew too severe for them to continue, and it was equally clear that the Drasin had no intention of letting them get out of the system and into any position to initiate a transition.

That made his job easier. It was the same job he'd had the last time, really.

Savage the enemy forces until they dragged him down, and hope against hope that he did enough damage to give everyone else a chance to survive.

Not really the ideal position to be in, but if you were there at least there was no complexity to your task.

"Watch your nine o'clock, Steph," Eric noted. "Incoming."

"I see them," Steph said, putting the *Odysseus* into a flat spin to bring the forward lasers to bear. "Nail 'em, Milla!"

The lasers pulsed, lashing across space as the enemy ships fired in return. The beams crossed space and one another with nearly unimaginable power. The *Odysseus'* beams struck true, three more enemy ships vanishing in the now-familiar zero gravity explosions, even as the Drasin beams burned into the armor and hull of the much larger *Odysseus.*

"Three strikes!" Winger called. "We're venting atmosphere all across the forward decks . . . casualty reports pending!"

"Get rescue teams up there," Eric ordered. "Milla, keep firing!"

The slim Priminae woman shook herself from the shock she'd felt, hand coming down on the command to unleash the weapons once more. The beams lanced out at new targets, boiling away the armor and hulls of the smaller Drasin ships instantly, lighting up the black of space with more death and destruction.

"They're coming around on us. We're about to get mobbed, Captain!"

"Steph . . . " Eric didn't even have to finish.

"Aye Captain, evading!"

A space-warp drive allowed a ship to do some incredible and, frankly, incredibly counterintuitive maneuvers. Without turning, or banking, or anything that might be familiar to a terrestrial pilot or observer, the *Odysseus* simply shifted hard to port at maximum acceleration.

Flying sideways was actually a bit of a confusing motion for Steph, however, so he pivoted the ship in the direction of flight. This wasn't because he had to. The *Odysseus* was quite capable of flying in any direction with equal power and efficiency, but it was slightly disorienting to plan maneuvers unless the ship was more or less aligned with his own perceptions.

He could *do* it, just not as well, so Steph did the best he could to keep the front more or less pointing in the direction they were traveling.

Their sudden shift in movement bought them a few seconds lead on their enemy, mostly due to the scant light-speed delays between the *Odysseus* and her foes, but it was enough to drag the fight out just a little longer.

The lasers of the big ship continued to lance out, bringing her kill total to just under twenty since the fight had begun, and everyone could hear the almost subaudible background whine of the laser systems causing sympathetic vibrations through the hull. It was a teeth-gritting sound, but under the circumstances Eric personally found it rather soothing.

"They're regrouping, sir," Winger told him. "Coming around, this time in greater numbers."

That was the true teeth-gritting element of the current situation, the fact that the enemy had unlimited reinforcements . . . effectively . . . and he, well, didn't.

"New signal! Captain, it's the *Big E!*"

Eric twisted, eyes falling on the gleaming light reflecting off the armor of the *Enterprise* now that the ship had dispensed with stealth mode. They were coming in fast and hard, and it was clear that Captain Carrow wasn't in any mood to play around.

"Watch for torpedoes!" Eric ordered Steph, as well as Winger. "The *E* is packing!"

Of course, just because he didn't have unlimited reinforcements . . . well, it didn't mean that he didn't have *some.*

▶▶▶

▶ "Stand by to launch fighters," Carrow ordered, coming to his feet. "Status on torpedoes?"

"Charged and ready, Captain."

"Targeting solution locked in, sir!"

"Fire!"

The *Enterprise* launched its little payload of the hellish weapons on a widespread scattershot. It was slightly risky, but Carrow trusted Weston to know what to watch for, and they needed to tear these bastards up as much as they could.

"Pulse torpedoes away!"

Carrow nodded. "Put Alpha into space."

"Alpha Flight launching, Captain."

The *Enterprise*'s first flight, loaded with ship killers, was indeed already streaming from the decks. He knew that if there were air to conduct the sound, their twin power plants would be screaming as they raced away.

"I want Bravo moving as soon as Alpha clears those decks," Carrow ordered. "I want *everything* we've got in this fight! Nothing held back!"

"Aye aye, sir. Bravo is already being taxied to launch positions."

Carrow would hope it was enough, but he knew deep down that it wasn't. Of course, the goal wasn't to win. The goal was to make the enemy quote Pyrrhus when it was all over.

We'll undo you lot yet, he thought savagely. *Just you wait and see.*

▶▶▶

▶It was clearly quality versus quantity, Commander William Briggs noted as he led from the vanguard position of his squadron.

It's too bad that quantity has a quality all its own, he thought wryly, completing the quote in his head as he focused on the job of picking out the targets his squadron was about to service.

"Alphas, stand by to fire," he ordered. "Remember, we're not going to saturation fire here. Make every shot."

His team acknowledged the orders as he finished assigning targets, picking ships from around the edges of the swarm where they weren't likely to double up with the ships the *Odysseus* or even the *Enterprise*'s own torpedoes would strike.

They didn't have enough weapons to saturate the enemy, so it was going to be a snipers' game.

"Alpha Lead . . . Fox Three."

▶▶▶

▶Carrow watched the tracks of Alpha Flight even as Bravo poured from the flight decks like water from a hose. He noted their choice of targets, as well as the restraint on Briggs' part, and approved.

They wouldn't be able to guarantee that there would be anyone around to reload the Vorpals in just a few minutes, so making every shot count was just good sense.

"Give me an attack run," he said. "Shannon, you pick the target."

"Yes sir," the helmsman said. "Got it. Tactical, do you have the data?"

"Roger that."

"Alright, we're going in."

Carrow nodded, sitting back. "Lead with the primary laser as soon as we're in range, but I want our own HVM banks firing as soon as possible. Fire them dry. We don't get bonus points for bringing ammo home."

▶▶▶

▶On the *Odysseus,* Eric was studying the instrument data so deeply that he looked completely disconnected from the events around him.

"Captain . . . "

He glanced to one side, nodding to the admiral. "Yes ma'am?"

"What are you looking for?"

He looked back, eyes on the enemy disposition, and his finger came up as he pointed.

"That."

Eric turned. "Steph, bring us hard to port! All flank to our new heading . . . One One Eight, Mark Three Negative to the system plane!"

"Coming about," Steph confirmed.

"Captain, that brings is into the center of the enemy ships!" Winger warned him.

"I know."

CHAPTER THIRTY

▶THE FIGHT WAS not turning out as calculated, though things were still progressing within the normal tolerances one might expect with a species of the red band. The ship minds had been momentarily surprised by the entry of the second ship into the fight, but in the end it wouldn't make a significant difference.

All it did was increase their room for error slightly, giving them a second ship to capture in case one was destroyed in the battle.

Still, they had to detach a section of their ships to deal with the newcomer, which was a distinctive annoyance at the moment. It would cause a slight derailment of the combat plans, but that was the way fighting happened sometimes.

A squadron of drone ships got their orders and turned to accelerate toward the new ship, breaking away from the current fight. The ship minds, satisfied, turned back to the main battle just in time to be shocked to the core as their quarry blasted right through the center of the fight and annihilated the detailed squadron even as it began to break away.

So sudden was the shift that for a moment the ship minds didn't quite know how to react.

▶▶▶

▶ "Bring us about," Eric ordered. "Milla, keep firing!"

The *Odysseus* twisted, lasers still beaming constantly into space as they swept about. Three more enemy shots had holed their armor. Eric knew that the big ship was bleeding air badly, yet he couldn't help but reflect on the fact that the *Odyssey* would have long since been destroyed.

Of course, if he'd been in the *Odyssey*, Eric knew that he would have played hide and seek with the alien armada instead of engaging them head on. The two powerful singularity cores that gave the *Odysseus* its incredible power also made it effectively impossible for the big ship to hide from any active searchers.

Always a tradeoff, he supposed.

The casualty list had begun to filter in. Some names he knew, most he didn't. Many were clearly of Priminae origin, but that didn't matter. They were standing with Earth, bleeding and dying in space to save her. They were his and he felt the loss of every name for that reason.

He couldn't turn away, however. There was too much at stake, too much to lose.

"Press the assault," he ordered. "No quarter."

"Aye sir," Steph growled, his focus entirely on the fight. "No quarter. No problem."

▶▶▶

▶ The brief distraction proved costly, but the ship minds adjusted quickly. They dispatched new vessels to deal with the newcomer, recognizing the configuration. It was a nuisance, but as it stood . . . alone, and in the open, they had its measure. Ten ships would serve to entangle it, limit its movements, and another ten would ensure the final disposition of it.

It was the larger ship, the new one, that was of the most interest. It *smelled* of the worlds they knew, but it did not fight like them. Nor was it equipped like them. The mysterious weapons matched those of the newcomer more than the old worlds. That spoke of a new race, with new capabilities, perhaps joining with the old worlds.

That was unacceptable.

The swarm had to locate this new enemy, the source of any possible alliance, and eliminate them entirely from the universe. This system would just be the first. The swarm would annihilate every world around every star in the entirety of the cosmos.

That was their purpose, their duty, and their obsession.

▶▶▶

▶ "Here they come, Captain!"

Carrow nodded, eyes on the incoming track. "Thin their ranks. HVMs fire as we bear!"

"Roger sir, high-velocity missiles firing!"

The big kinetic kill weapons launched, sending shivers even through the bulk of the *Enterprise*. Their CM fields kicked in shortly after, and they lanced away, having more in common with a laser than a missile. The volley struck true, two HVMs slamming into each of the lead ships in a shocking display of force.

It wasn't the clean kill of the *Odysseus'* lasers, but the debris that survived the impact ceased acceleration and flew on with no hand guiding the tiller.

"More ships are filling the gap, sir."

"I see them," Carrow said. "Have Bravo Flight come in from the port, flank them, and take them out."

"Aye sir."

The only time Carrow had seen anything like this was in the last dark days of drone warfare before the U.S., China, and other nations got together to outlaw the damned things.

He'd only been a kid at the time, just enlisted and assigned to a destroyer. Stationed off Taiwan, they'd been tasked with defending the island against the aggression of the mainland. The drones had started in the dark, barely showing up on radar, effectively invisible . . . loaded with enough explosives to take out a building.

And there had been hundreds of them.

Carrow shook the memory away, forcing his mind back to the present. These weren't Chinese drones, they weren't American, or Indian, or any other weapon of a sane world, or an insane one. They were abominations. They were things that should not exist, should never exist.

He'd never in his life known anything that absolutely had to be destroyed. Gray was where he lived his existence, no purity of good or evil had ever existed in Carrow's world.

He knew better.

Right until he came face-to-face with the Drasin.

"Go to rapid fire on all HVM banks," Carrow ordered. "Tear them apart!"

▶ ▶ ▶

▶ "Captain," Gracen spoke softly from behind him, "we should call in reinforcements."

"They'll never get here in time, Admiral," Eric whispered in return. "You know that."

"I know," she nodded. "But they can finish what we've started. These things can't be left to rebuild. You know what they can do."

Eric nodded, looking down for a moment.

She was right. He knew it, but calling out the other ships was effectively calling them to their own slaughter. They had to kill every last one of the alien things, or it was for nothing, yet he knew that even all of the remaining ships had no chance of that.

If they stayed on Earth, however, eventually they would face hundreds . . . thousands . . . more.

"Susan," Eric looked up.

"Yes sir?"

"Signal the other . . . Heroics," he said, tasting the word for a moment. "Tell them our status, inform them . . ."

He sighed, taking a breath. "Inform them that we are requesting reinforcements."

To finish what we've begun.

He didn't say it, but he knew Jason Roberts well enough. The man would understand.

"Aye sir. By FTL?"

"Yes."

Susan nodded and quickly entered the message. A moment later, however, she frowned and entered another command. She scowled, entered more commands, and then called for a technician.

"What is it, Susan?"

"FTL comm is offline," she said, shaking her head. "Never seen anything like it, but then again I'd never seen an FTL comm until a few weeks ago."

"No ideas?" he asked, one eye on the battle. Steph was handling the ship well. He and Milla were a good team.

"It reads like interference, but that's impossible," she said. "Not on a tachyon-based system."

Michelle Winger, across the bridge, scowled in turn and shifted her attention from the fighting for a moment. It only took a few seconds for her to let out a word that would have made Eric blush once, before he became a Marine. He turned in her direction. "Michelle?"

"We're being *jammed*," she said, her tone completely disbelieving. "The entire region is flooded with tachyons."

"That's not possible," Milla said, looking over, eyes wide. "I have never heard of something that could flood an area like that!"

"Every FTL scanner I've got is whited out," Michelle said, shaking her head. "We're not sending anything FTL anytime soon."

Eric scowled, but it didn't matter.

"Fine. Send the message via laser comm," he said, waving it off. He had a fight to conduct.

▶▶▶

▶The *Odysseus* twisted in space, lashing out with lasers in a near-constant flood. The region around her was a wasteland of plasma and debris, interrupted only by the constant influx of Drasin vessels.

As many as she destroyed, however, there were more to fill the empty spaces. And though *Odysseus* fired first and fastest, the enemy got in their blows in return. Atmosphere bled from the kilometer-and-a-half-long hull. Bodies of the dead hurtled alongside the carrier, caught in the space warp that powered her. Forty enemy ships fell to her lasers, another half dozen to the missiles of the *Enterprise,* and a double handful to the fighter craft that buzzed around the edge of the battle like lethal insects waiting for a target to sting.

The Drasin lasers were just as powerful, if not as sophisticated, and they cut deep into the *Odysseus'* hull with every passing moment. More air bled away, more systems were damaged and hastily patched by the crews within, working feverishly to do what they could.

For every hole they patched, three more would blow open, and for every system they saved, another ten would fail. It was a task worthy of Sisyphus, but the work crews of *Odysseus* threw themselves into it like the gods themselves.

In the end, it wouldn't be enough, of course . . . but then, it wasn't always about the end.

Sometimes it was the journey that counted and every one of them had signed on for an odyssey.

▶▶▶

▶ "The *Enterprise* is hit! They've lost their flight deck. They're losing air too fast!" Winger said. "The Vorpal fighters are coming about to help . . . they're going to be too late."

"Get us over there!"

"We've lost too much reactor mass, Captain. We can't make that kind of acceleration," the chief engineer said, shaking his head.

"Damn it!" Eric swore, slamming his hands down. "Put the *E* on screen."

"Captain . . ." Winger hesitated.

"Put her on screen."

The screen flickered and the crippled image of the *Enterprise* was front and center, everyone looking on as three Drasin ships circled around and came back in on her firing. Eric's eyes spotted pods launching from the ship, even as the *Enterprise* fired back and crippled one of the three with her main laser.

The beams intersected, slicing the gleaming hull of the Earth-built ship apart cleanly. The big ship separated, her engines floating one way while the habitats went another. The lasers stopped and Eric watched as the ships closed in on the pods and habitat modules.

"Don't look away," he said, his voice carrying. "This isn't something that should be forgotten."

The alien ships slowed as they got in range of the *Enterprise* habitat modules, their own bays opening as a mini swarm of drones launched across open space . . . and then everything vanished in a massive sphere of white light.

"W . . . what happened?"

Eric didn't know who spoke. He didn't care.

"Carrow blew his reactor, the Tokamak," he said. "Probably had a couple pulse torpedoes held in reserve just for that."

Even the Drasin seemed stunned by the action, and for a moment the attacks slacked off. Only for a moment, however, and it was clear that the aliens had no interest in giving them time to grieve for the fallen.

"The swarm has regrouped. They're turning entirely on us again," Winger said softly.

"Let them come," Eric announced. "They couldn't take the *Enterprise,* and they'll not take the *Odysseus.*"

The words were dark, but his tone was almost lighthearted, and for a brief moment those who heard him speak felt like they'd just watched a victory instead of a crippling loss.

"Miss Chans, continue firing, please," he said, breaking the moment.

"Y . . . yes Capitaine," she mumbled, returning to her task.

"Commander, bring us around to cover the Vorpals," Eric ordered. "Let's team up."

"You've got it, sir. Coming about."

With the *Odysseus* now covering for the Vorpal fighters that had survived this far into the battle, and they providing a fair amount of cover in return, the battle almost instantly raged back to that of a full-blown war. The Drasin were slowly cutting away at the *Odysseus*, however, leaving her crippled piece by piece.

Eric knew it was now just a matter of minutes, likely, before he was forced to do as Carrow had. He rather hoped he would be able to take more of the enemy with him when it came to that.

He couldn't go into the next life letting Carrow upstage him, after all.

Those morbidly amusing thoughts were thrown from his mind by a yell from Michelle Winger.

"What the . . ." She rose up from her seat, staring at her board like it had just bit her.

"What is it?" he twisted, looking over.

"Tachyon jamming is clear, Captain," she said.

That couldn't be what she was swearing about, could it? Eric shook his head. "Fine. Send the message FTL, Susan."

"Yes sir," Lamont answered.

Winger broke in quickly, however. "Sir, we have a tachyon event!"

"Bow shock?" he asked, cringing. More Drasin they did *not* need.

"Negative. Transition."

Eric blinked. *The only people who can do that are on Earth and . . .*

He smiled. "Well, good. Hopefully that'll be enough. Send a message. Inform any Priminae ships of what's happening and request . . ."

"Captain, it's not outside the system. They're coming *here!*"

"Impossible!" he uttered.

"On screen!" Winger countered simply.

Eric looked over, the tachyon disturbance clear on the screens. He saw something for the first time then—the appearance of ships from transition with his own eyes.

Two appeared, then four, and then eight, and finally sixteen.

Sixteen Heroic Class ships reformed from transition before his eyes, and Susan's board instantly chimed.

"Message from the *Atur,* Captain."

"On screen."

The screen flickered, and Eric found himself staring at the slight build of Admiral Rael Tanner. The Priminae officer grinned cheerfully at him. "Captain Weston. It is good, and somehow entirely unsurprising, to see you on the *Odysseus.* Please maintain course and speed. We will cover you."

"Y . . . you heard the admiral, Commander," Eric stammered a bit.

"Aye sir . . . maintaining course and speed."

"Get the Vorpals in tight, Susan," Eric ordered.

"Yes sir."

The Priminae Heroics turned in space, and they watched as the big long guns pivoted out and came to bear on the battle. The tachyon scanners surged as they fired, and space was lit up by dozens of balls of plasma erupting all around them. The Priminae ships continued to fire their transition cannons, not stopping until the very last of the drone ships was nothing more than dust on the solar winds.

Eric slumped a little, closing his eyes.

"Stand down from combat alert. Make sure all damage control teams have everything they need," he said. "Susan . . . get me the admiral again. I have to offer my thanks."

"Our thanks, Captain," Gracen said softly. "All of our thanks."

▼

EPILOGUE

▲

▶ THE DRASIN HAD come and gone from the Earth.

Rather, they had come and were destroyed to the last, but for the Earth it had been a long and painful war. One that seemed without much of a victory to cheer for. The world was ravaged, with millions dead at least, and the death tolls still to be tallied in most places. Cities had been razed, either by the aliens or by the defenders in an attempt to cleanse them, and infrastructure had been demolished beyond repair.

The governments were a shambles, aside from the Block and the Confederacy and a very few key allies.

President Mitchell Conner suspected that now was the time to unify, if ever there was such a time. He swore to suggest it to his successor, for after the orders he had given he felt no right to sit behind the desk he'd once claimed as his own. New elections would be held, soon, and he'd stay on until then . . . but only then.

He looked out over Washington, and was surprised as he had always been by how untouched the city was.

The defenses around Washington had topped anything almost anywhere else in the world, and they'd served the people there well.

I just wish we'd done the same for other places.

The President of the Confederacy looked up from the balcony of the White House, eyes on the massive bulk of the ship that was visible even in orbit. It was the *Atur,* the flagship of the Priminae colonies, and the savior of the Earth.

How the tables turn. We save them, they save us. I think . . . I hope, this is the start of a beautiful friendship.

He'd spoken with the admiral, an approachable man for a flag officer. He rather liked all the Priminae he'd met so far, though he was required by the nature of his office not to trust them entirely. He wasn't sure it mattered if he did, though. Whatever their intentions, they held all the cards.

They had the infrastructure to build more of the Heroics. They now had many . . . though not all, the key technical secrets of the Confederacy . . . and they had ten more warships in Earth orbit than the Earth had.

He just hoped to God that they were as friendly as they seemed, because it would be some time before the Confederacy . . . or the Earth . . . was ready to meet another foe.

Speaking of foes . . . I have a few duties left to deal with.

▶ ▶ ▶

▶ "Welcome, Mr. President."

Conner just nodded at the greeting, walking forward and making the man in the lab coat walk along with him. "Is it here?"

"Yes sir," the man said, gesturing. "Right this way."

He led them down a long hall, through three security doors and a pressure-sealed vault door until they reached a room with a large glass window that opened onto a freezer. Inside, Conner stared at the Drasin soldier drone that was standing there. It appeared dead for all he could tell, but he was assured that it was not.

"How do you know it's alive?"

"When our teams found this one in Antarctica, it was with a squad. They must have been trying to core through the ice, but it was too thick for them, I believe. We can detect some activity, and it still has a significant body temperature. It's alive, sir."

Conner nodded, his lips drawn tight. "What have you learned?"

"A great deal, though how much will be useful is another issue," the man admitted. "The reason I called you down, though, is this . . ."

He gestured to a screen that made no sense to the President.

"What is that?"

"Sir, are you familiar with the two methods humans have for storing memories?"

Conner nodded again. "Yes. Chemical and neural, right?"

"Precisely . . . watch this." The man hit a key and Conner found himself entranced as he watched what *had* to be the interior of an alien ship.

There were dozens . . . no, hundreds of drones just like the one in the next room, and they were all moving with military precision. He watched as the perspective moved as well, into some sort of pod, and then everything shook. When it steadied finally, the pod blew open and a roar of snow and wind obliterated the visibility.

He looked between the screen and the drone, frowning. "You can scan its memories?"

"Yes, Mr. President, but that's not the interesting thing."

No, Conner supposed it wouldn't be. It had been possible to do that for decades with humans, to varying degrees.

"What is interesting is that when we located the system for storing memories it was based on silicate atomic bonds, compared to our own chemically bonded memories," the man said. "But the . . . coding . . . that was identical to humans."

Conner snapped around. "Say that again."

The man in the lab coat sighed. "Whoever built these things, and yes we're sure now that they were built . . . this sort of parallel evolution is only marginally more likely than every star in the galaxy going supernova at once . . . but whoever built them was intimately familiar with human physiology, sir."

He scowled. "In fact, it's almost like they just cut and pasted part of our . . . part of *us* into the design of these things, just to save time."

"They don't *think* like us. . . ?"

"No, not at all. More like animals, if anything. No, this is just the memory system, Mr. President."

Conner rubbed his face, thinking about what he'd just learned. "Dig deeper. Learn *everything*. We *must* know where . . . who built these thing, how . . . and *why*."

"Yes Mr. President."

▶ *The entity who called herself Gaia found the rising of the Sun in the east to be . . . satisfying. It had felt that way ever since the last Drasin drone—save the ones in cold storage, of course—had finally been destroyed.*

She had almost resigned herself to not seeing another rising of the Sun, though technically she'd never not been witness to such a thing, since she existed in all parts of the world at once. It was a human thought, she supposed, one of many she was joyfully infected by.

Her captain had done it, mostly without her help even.

Okay, he had the help of others, but that was what he was good at. What she liked about him, really, that ability to inspire.

His journeys weren't done. His odyssey was far from complete, but for now she wished him a good and deserved rest. The universe would make his life hard enough before too long, she suspected. She looked out over all parts of herself and smiled down on everyone left.

"Rest. Be at peace . . . for tomorrow, we all have work to do."

▶▶▶

▶ Eric was standing on an observation deck, one of only three that hadn't been blown open to hard vacuum in the battle.

Repairs were going well, but they'd never get them all done without a shipyard. Tanner had offered the Forge, and Eric found himself looking forward to seeing it. He also looked forward to seeing one built here, to serve Earth.

There was a lot of work to do, but now at least they had a future to do it in.

The Drasin were, if not finished, then on the ropes. The Priminae were building more ships, and the Earth was still producing munitions. They'd not stop that anytime soon, not now. That was for sure.

Soon they'd be able to take on almost any number of the bastards and destroy them from a distance. He knew that they'd have to hunt the Drasin down. The invaders were too dangerous to leave at large in the galaxy, but it was doable now. It was a war that could be won.

Of course, somewhere out there, that still left the ones who had their finger on the trigger.

So much work left. Will it ever end?

Eric didn't know. He was just glad that it wasn't over yet. He wasn't ready for the next life.

▶▶▶

▶Deep in the singular mass of the *Odysseus* . . . a presence stirred, shifted, and then fell once more to sleep. Its time wasn't yet, but in its dreams a single word echoed.

Soon.

▶▶▶

ABOUT THE AUTHOR

Evan Currie is the bestselling author of the Odyssey One series, the Warrior's Wings series, and more. Although his postsecondary education was in computer sciences, and he has worked in the local lobster industry steadily over the last decade, writing has always been his true passion. Currie himself says it best: "It's what I do for fun and to relax. There's not much I can imagine better than being a storyteller."